GOTTA DIG Deep

FREED RIDERS MC
Book #1

MariaLisa deMora

Editing by Hot Tree Editing

Photography: Wander Aguiar, Photography

Model: Jose Luis Barreiro

First Published 2023

ISBN 13: 978-1-946738-77-6

DEDICATION

"In all the world, there is no heart for me like yours.
In all the world, there is no love for you like mine."
~Maya Angelou

To my muse: Thanks for sticking around.

You're my ride-or-die, truth.

Contents

ACKNOWLEDGMENTS

It's been a minute, huh? I cannot express my deep and profound gratitude to the readers who stuck around through the drought of No Words. And who were hugely excited on all our behalf when the flood of Fresh Words began. Through various life changes, surgeries, and a dearth of new releases, you plied me with kindness. Y'all are troopers, and I'm pleased to call you friends.

Huge thank you shout to Glenna Maynard, who let me model certain spicy aspects of the main female character after her quirky personality. She's an amazing human, and I'm proud to know her.

My Facebook crew also deserves thanks, because they had to listen to all the behind-the-scenes whining about how hard it all was now. Jamey, Kay, Kori, and Megan — y'all are the best, man. Gratitude to your continued friendship even through the epic freakouts.

Becky Johnson's Hot Tree Editing group did a fabulous job, as always. Wander Aguiar Photography had the perfect shot available at the exact moment I needed it.

Epic timing seems to be a theme with this book. Almost as if were meant to be. I certainly hope you enjoy reading it as much as I have getting these characters onto the page.

Woofully yours,
~ML

Gotta Dig Deep

Graeme "Horse" Nass is happy with where he stands in life. Enforcer for the Freed Riders, a position which demands respect from members of his club and outsiders, the role allows him to hold firm against all comers. It's rewarding, feeding his soul in its own way, and he gives it back to the club with everything inside him. Joining the club had been a watershed moment in his life, a point in time where his morality and beliefs swung freefall over a chasm of doubt, but he's come out the other side of the crucible stronger.

The only thing missing from his life is a woman willing to put up with the aggravation that comes with being in the center of all club business—good and bad. He's about given up on that desire, until he meets Glenna. She's a tiny, feisty whirlwind of a woman who blows into his life and turns everything upside down with her humor and biting wit. Pair her smarts with the stunning beauty of the woman, and what man alive would pass up on a piece of that?

Horse has taken the bait, hook, line, and sinker, but the joke's on her, because what they're about to go through will tie her to him just as tightly.

Abbreviation map:

- FRMC – Freed Riders MC
- RWMC – Rebel Wayfarers MC
- IRMC – Iron Riggers MC
- MDMC – Monster Devils MC

Chapter One

Shoulders propped against the wall opposite the door, Graeme Nass watched the antics of the other men in the bar with a cultivated tolerance. Most of them were just out for a good time, and as long as they kept it on the decent side of good, all would be well. Those were his expectations from years of doing this job night after night.

All was well, at least until the first glass bottle sailed over the pool table to slam against the boards not too far from his head. Way too close for comfort. Fortunately for the man who'd tossed the missile, the container didn't shatter, but the sound of the impact was loud enough to kill nearby conversations.

"Aww, shit." One of the offender's three companions offered an expression more snarl than smile. "Oops. Billy needs better aim." They were all dressed similarly in blue-collar shirts and jeans, and had gathered around the bottle-tosser like a pack. The rest of the men snickered at the comment, concreting their association in Graeme's mind.

Don't fuckin' matter much.

Scooping the bottle up from where it still spun on the floor, Graeme stalked across the room. As he angled around the pool table, the players vacated a path for him without requiring a single word, leaving a wide corridor through their midst. Ignoring the social aspects that separated the customers from himself, namely them a group and him alone, he slammed the bottom of the bottle against the high table surrounded by big men each with about two decades of age on him. He addressed the bottle-tosser identified as Billy. "Pretty sure you dropped something."

The man opposite where Graeme stood rose slowly to his feet, towering over the other men still on their stools. "Who do you think you are?"

Squaring up to the table, Graeme lifted his chin. "I expect I should introduce myself as the man who's gonna toss you out on your collective asses if you don't respect the other customers."

"He's Dorothy's boy." One of the seated men nudged the standing one with a firm elbow. "Drag your ego down a notch, dickwad."

"Dot's your momma?" Shoulders gradually relaxing, the posturing man slowly settled back onto his stool. "I didn't know she had any kids she claimed. Sure thing, boy. We'll keep it down."

Graeme didn't miss the fact these men were more afraid of his mother than of him standing right here in their faces. Still, he knew he could easily ignore their immature swipes at him personally, as long as they toed the line of no-violence in the bar.

Been doin' that same ignoring thing all my life.

"Sounds good." He glanced over his shoulder and caught the attention of one of the three waitresses working this busy Saturday night crowd. Lifting a finger, he called her over, turning back to the men when she gave him a nod. "Dorcas will take any replacement orders you need, but there ain't gonna be a damn thing on the house. You need to keep your own asses in check, yeah?"

"Yeah, no worries." The seated man who'd recognized Graeme offered a short-lived smile. "We'll keep it down."

Resuming his position against the back wall of the bar, Graeme scanned the crowd, gaze pausing longest on the end of the bar where his mother held court.

Dorothy Malcomb was beautiful, her smooth face appearing far younger than the decades she owned. Tall and olive-skinned, she looked nothing like Graeme, which made it easy for her to blatantly ignore their familial relationship. She'd always liked to play at being a worldly woman without baggage, and a kid—regardless of their age—was definitely considered baggage. The asshole at the table not knowing Dot had a boy old enough to work in the same bar she'd owned since before Graeme was born couldn't hurt him at all.

Their feeble attempts at cuts were small potatoes in the grand scheme of things.

He'd heard enough stories from his mother's lips to know few things she said was weighted down with the reality of fact. Lies and half-truths were his reality for a long time. The one thing she didn't pretend was having any kind of attachment to him. *Completely and totally reciprocated.* That lack of connection meant that regardless of what she had to say about whoever his sperm donor might be, he didn't take anything to heart.

"Tall, blond, and handsome, he swept me off my feet for a weekend."

That was a favorite of hers, and one he'd easily heard a hundred times.

But it wasn't the only tale she had to explain him away.

"Russian sailor, poor guy was stuck in port for a month. Man needed somewhere to stay. What was I supposed to do? It was only Christian, after all."

His least favorite was likely closest to reality. She only trotted out this particular story when she'd had entirely too much to drink.

"I never saw his face. Never knew who it was. Tore up his arms with my nails, trying to get away. Strong and brutal, he didn't say anything, just grunted his way through my body. I lay in a pool of my own blood for half a day before I could call for help."

The name Nass didn't even tie him to his mother. She'd pulled the moniker from her paternal grandmother's maiden name, slapping it on his birth certificate and using it to set him up in a way certain to be isolating. Every school function, Dot would float in, dripping with platitudes and sweetness, introducing herself with emphasis on her last name and then flipping her wrist to indicate Graeme with an "I'm with him," not even personally claiming the child she'd birthed.

He'd grown accustomed to her lack of maternal instincts, but that slow recognition had not been without wounds.

Her chin lifted as she swiped around the bar with a calculating gaze, eyes pausing when they encountered Graeme where he stood at the back wall. Coldly assessing him, she blinked slowly, then with a tiny eye roll, dismissed him to spin on her stool and laugh loudly at something one of the men said.

"Why am I still here?" A waitress pausing in front of Graeme was an indicator he'd spoken aloud. *Might as well go with it.* "No, seriously. Why am I still here? Not like she gives a shit, right?" That earned him a side-eye and quick retreat from the waitress. "But seriously, why?"

Rolling his shoulders against the wall, he pressed harder against the ungiving surface, forcing his muscles into stress-relieving stretches.

That night, the seed was planted.

***

Rolling out of bed the next morning, he settled his ass on the edge of the mattress. Both hands scrubbed his face as he worked the sleep sand out of the corners of his eyes before blinking blearily around the basement bedroom.

Nothing had changed. It was the same small space it had been since his bed had been moved here and out of the nursery at the ripe old age of two.

Not that he remembered those days, or anything about the second-floor office next to his mother's bedroom serving as an unwanted nursery, but pictures in his dead grandmother's photo book didn't lie.

I've truly got nothing to keep me here.

The fact *that* was his first cogent thought upon waking was probably important, but Graeme shook his head and pushed off the bed.

Dressing without urgency, he turned back, straightened the covers and glanced around the room a final time as he stamped into his boots. Nothing in the space even said it was inhabited, much less presenting anything of his personality. It could be a rent-by-the-hour bed. Sure, there'd been a time when he'd had posters and pictures on the walls, but age and indifference had stripped them away.

Padding up narrow, steep stairs to emerge in the shared kitchen, Graeme went directly to the coffeemaker, thumbing the switch to turn the already prepared device on. He perused the space with the same flat pique as he had his bedroom. Few things here said anyone lived in the house, much less a twenty-three-year-old man and his couldn't-give-a-shit mother. The sturdy coffee mugs were a matching set, not screaming male presence but also not effeminate in any way. A calendar hung on a space next to the cabinets, the picture a bucolic and serene scene, also gender neutral. And a month behind.

If I left today, there'd be nothing to say I was ever here.

For some reason that wasn't an alarming thought. Instead, the idea there'd be nothing of him left behind was comforting.

She doesn't wanna claim me while I live here? She shouldn't get to keep anything after I leave.

The certainty in his thoughts was a surprise.

Once his second cup of coffee was poured and doctored, he pushed through the back door and claimed a chair at the patio table. Half-baked ideas about what he could do floated through his head, but nothing as defined as a full-formed plan yet.

He had money saved, years of birthday and holiday presents from extended family amounting to a few thousand dollars tucked into a sock underneath his mattress. Half of his pay from the bar went to rent and household expenses, but he mostly banked the rest into a healthy savings account. The biggest barrier he could come up with was that he didn't have a vehicle. There'd been no reason to bear the purchase cost—never mind maintenance and upkeep—when the bar sat just a couple of blocks away, but he did have a license with motorcycle endorsement. He grinned at the idea, because he'd never been on a bike in his life but having a distant cousin who worked at the local motor vehicles registration had played in his favor.

Slowly sipping the coffee, Graeme decided his first purchase would be a phone, and the second should be some sort of transportation. He'd need to ensure he had enough accessible money to fund this escape, which meant a daytime trip to the bank for cash. That would be the one place he'd have to be careful to avoid recognition, because there was a cousin who worked there too. Hell, might as well clean out the account. It wasn't like he'd be coming back anytime soon.

And exactly why the hell do I need to hide what I'm planning?

His mother likely would give just as many shits about him leaving as him staying—which was to say none at all.

This was beginning to feel more like a fully baked plan than anything he'd had before.

***

"So much? You sure? It doesn't look like it's even road ready." Graeme leaned backwards and rested his shoulders against the side of the car parked just behind him. "It's got four different brands of tires, and there's oil dripping out the tailpipe." He grimaced and waggled his head side to side. "Doubt it should be that dear."

"Shows what you know about used cars, boy." The rotund gentleman standing next to Graeme laughed, fingers rubbing between gaping buttons across his belly. Gray and matted tufts of hair protruded through each, ruffled in turn by the edges of dirty nails. He looked like he worked on the cars himself. "Dear doesn't cover the half of it with this beaut." Mr. Embry, owner of Embry's Cars, slapped a palm against the roof and Graeme winced as the springs groaned in protest.

"You don't have anything for less?" Folding his arms across his chest, he scanned the small business for a final time before turning away. "That's too bad. Thanks for your time."

"I got a bike. About half the price of the cheapest car on the lot."

"What?" Graeme whirled and stared, waiting impatiently as the man coughed roughly and spat. "You do?" He hadn't noticed anything as they'd walked around the front rows of cars.

"Said I did, didn't I?" Lifting an arm, the man pointed towards the back fence. "Needs some work, but what doesn't these days?" He began walking, a stiff-legged shuffle as accommodating of his belly as any heavily pregnant woman's. "Come on, then," he tossed over his shoulder, the tease in his words dragging Graeme behind him. "I'll show you what I got."

Along the back fence, tucked in behind the rust-tortured remains of a van camper was a motorcycle. The bones of the bike rivaled any of the best rides the bikers who came to the bar had. At least, to Graeme's untrained eyes it looked like it, mostly hidden under the patchy paint and salt scum. He found he didn't hate the idea of a bike.

I could ride across the country on a bike, once I fixed it up. Follow the wind wherever.

It might mean his departure was delayed, but it wasn't like he had a timeline that was dependent on anything other than him closing a door. And how cool would he look on the bike? *Fucking cool, that's how I'd look. Fucking cool.* Graeme didn't say anything along those lines. It wouldn't do to tip his hand early during this round of negotiations. Instead, he pinned a scowl on his face worthy of his mother's worst day as he walked past the bike, pretending not to notice it at first.

"Whoa." He angled back, taking a couple of steps in reverse. "This thing? How much?" If the car had been the cheapest the man had at eight bills, then he'd be asking four for the bike. Well within Graeme's budget, even if he had to rebuild much of it.

I'm handy enough. Plus it's not like I don't have resources.

He had a suspicion that pretty much any of the bikers he'd become friendly with at the bar would be itching to get their hands on the bike too. The trick would be to ask for help without putting himself into debt with them.

"It's a classic." The man hawked and spat again, the phlegm splattering wetly against a nearby car tire. "Won't see one of these on the road in a thousand miles of riding."

"No shit. It's in such shape you wouldn't recognize it if you saw one." Graeme looked at the man from underneath his eyebrows. "Half of half still wouldn't be fair. Be a favor if I took it off your hands. Junk man would make you pay to haul it away."

"Now you're being just unkind." A tiny lilt at the end of the final word meant the man saw the gambit for what it was and had joined in the hunt from the other side of the fence. "Four bills *is* a steal, and you know it." Staring at Graeme, he let his lips twitch a tiny bit, pulling a relaxation of Graeme's expression from him. The man's eyes widened suddenly, and he stood straighter, then tipped his head down and glared down at the bike with a heavy sigh. The man's tone had changed when he said, "Jesus hell. You're Dot's boy, right?"

"Does it matter?" There went his hope of escaping without his mother finding out.

"Isn't right, what she did." Humor gone, his features were hard, lips pressed thin. No longer pretending to be the jovial businessman, it was a glimpse into his true nature. "What she's still doing. Tell you what, boy—" He shook his head. "Graeme, that is. Shit." He straightened, the gaps in his shirt front disappearing as he pulled in his belly, transforming himself even more. He no longer looked like a laconic snake oil salesman, but a man Graeme might have a beer with as they told tales. "Tell you what I'll do. Could be you're right about the junk value here. You take this off my hands, I'll pitch in a couple hundred for parts. I got a shed back of here you can use to work on the bike and connections for what it'll need to get the rot off it. Days you're here, if you answer the phone, I'll think about a little wage, maybe."

"What?" Coughing through a breath stuck in his chest, he stared at the older man. "You'll do what?"

"Don't look a gift horse in the mouth, Graeme." There was something ponderous about the man having transferred from calling him boy, to his given name. "I can't help you work on it, don't got the knees to do ground work anymore, but I'll do whatever else I can."

"I'll take it, Mr. Embry." Shoving aside any embarrassment at the generosity, Graeme held out his hand, not hiding a wince when the man's grip bore down on him. "With thanks."

"Medric, son. Call me Medric."

***

Four months later, with days-worth of elbow grease invested in the rebuild and a deepening friendship developed over late nights and copious amounts of beer with not only Medric but a half a dozen bikers—Graeme stood next to the bike as he pushed the ignition button. The rumble of the engine was loud and loping, the rattle of the exhaust stout enough to thud through his chest.

"Sounds good." Medric punched an elbow into Graeme's ribs. "Sounds real good."

He rocked the throttle just enough to hear the pipes ring a little louder. "Does sound good. Hard to believe we finally finished her."

"Her?" Shepherd Kelmer, also known as Junkyard, stepped up on Graeme's other side. He was one of the bikers who'd spent an abundance of spare time helping Graeme. "Give her a name yet?"

"Not yet." Graeme smoothed a hand across the tank, fingers trailing along the edges of hand-painted flames. "Figure she'll tell me what she wants to be called."

The shed—downplayed by the label Medric had given it, in truth it was more like a full-service shop—wasn't overflowing with bodies, but every man in here was someone Graeme had grown to know and trust. To the left of where he stood was Junkyard's bike, oil plug in a pan sitting underneath the engine, mid oil change. To the right was a small truck, hood up, waiting for Cage Knightly to finish fixing his wife's grocery getter. Cage claimed to have prospected for two different clubs, never making the jump to membership. According to him, it was the unfortunate first name that doomed him. Graeme was pretty sure it had more to do with his fuckery and less with his name. He might not be in a club, but Graeme had soaked up all the stories the men had been willing to share. Brotherhood wasn't backstabbing and being shifty; it was developing an understanding of needs and loyalty. Cage didn't have the last, for sure.

Right now, Cage was propped up along the back wall of the shed, elbow on the bench, lifting a bottle to his lips.

"Cage, you hear this sweet song?" Graeme grinned as he received a casual wave in response. "Seriously, man, you hear this?"

"What I hear—" Cage upended the bottle, draining it in a few swallows, "—is a pretty lady calling for her turn on the road." He struck a pose, empty bottle positioned as a microphone. "Give the lady what she wants," he sang, his high falsetto grating. "And she'll give it back to you." His eyes lit up. "Damn, that ain't half bad. I should write that down. Life advice from the experienced and walking wounded."

"Didn't suck." Graeme shot a glance at Medric as he fastened his helmet. "Open the doors for me? I'm going to take her around a block or two, make sure she likes me well enough."

A second benefit to having these men around him for the past months was that when Junkyard learned Graeme hadn't actually ridden a motorcycle, he'd arranged for a working bike to be dropped off. They'd spent part of a day in a nearby parking lot, and then had hit the road. The hours riding gave Graeme confidence that he wouldn't embarrass himself in front of his friends. *Hopefully.* He'd heard tons of stories of the most graceless moments each man had experienced. Fortunately, most of them involved a much larger audience than was present today.

Leg over the bike, he looked around the room again and over the rumble of the bike called, "You guys coming to the bar tonight?" Every head nodded and he grinned. "All right. Stick around, I'll be back in a minute."

Paddle-footing the bike through the opening, he steered towards the side entrance of the lot and then into the street. For the next several minutes, he played back and forth on the small roadway, working his way up and down the gears before he finally gave himself permission to round the corner and put the bike on an approach of the nearby main highway.

No cops in sight, Graeme pounded his way up the shifter to top gear and smoothly rolled the throttle, delighted when the bike leapt underneath him. Wind tears streaming from the corners of his eyes, he cursed his lack of foresight in leaving his shades behind. Speed slowing from the mid three-digits he'd reached, Graeme leaned the bike into the curve of the next offramp. Two left turns and he was back on the freeway, returning to the shop at a more moderate speed.

He'd just heeled the kickstand down when he blurted, "Freedom," to his friends clustered around him. "That's her name."

"And ain't a damn thing wrong with that name, brother." Junkyard's hand landed on Graeme's shoulder, fingers digging deep. "I take it your virgin ride went well?"

"She's a dream." He stood up off the bike and pocketed the keys. "Hurts my heart to leave her here, but I gotta get to work. Thank you." Shoving a hand towards Medric, he was surprised when the old man pulled him into a hug instead.

"You're a good man, Graeme Nass." Medric's fist thudded against his spine, driving the breath from Graeme's lungs so he couldn't respond, but the man didn't seem to need it as he stepped back and turned away. "It'll be the town's loss when you leave."

"Which isn't tonight." He chuckled, hoping to lighten the mood because the faces surrounding him were dark as thunderstorms. "What is tonight, is me working the bar because Freedom's gonna need regular feeding, so any extra money's good. But tomorrow? Tomorrow she earns that name."

"We'll be there," Cage answered for all of them. Graeme nodded and gave the bike a final pat on the tank.

That night at the bar, the back tables near Graeme's normal observation spot slowly filled. More than a dozen men had trickled in over the course of a couple of hours and greeted him before finding a seat and ordering a drink. The low buzz of conversation was constant, and they frequently pulled him in with questions and comments, laughter rattling around the room as tales were recounted. It occurred to Graeme that they were here to say goodbye. To him.

My friends.

At her place at the bar, Dorothy kept glancing at the full tables, then towards Graeme. She finally crooked a finger his direction even as she turned to face her drink. Graeme slapped Junkyard's shoulder on his way past and paused to shake another man's hand when it was thrust out at him. When he finally made it to where Dorothy sat, anger was evident in every line of her body.

"Who are those men? It's a weeknight, don't they have families and homes?" She lifted her drink and drained it, tapping the bottom of the glass against the bar top as if it were a shot glass. "Why are they here?"

"To drink?" Puzzled at her questions, he studied Dorothy's face in the mirror of the barback. "You're right, we've got good trade for a weeknight. I'm not going to look a gift horse in the mouth."

"Gift horse." Her shoulders moved restlessly, caught between a shrug and a shiver. "Not something you would have knowledge of."

"Kids *are* a gift, Dotty."

Graeme spun at the words spoken by a well-known voice. Medric stood at his shoulder, feet planted wide.

Head moving ponderously back and forth, the old man continued, "He is a gift horse, and you didn't do right by him. Wasn't Alek's fault he shipped out before he knew. Wasn't his fault he didn't come home, either. Wasn't your fault what happened to you. You got the shit end of a deal, and then you were lost inside your own grieving when you found out you had horror heaped on top. But that's not the worst of it, is it, Dot? Worst is that you had terrible things happen to *you*, and then have steadily taken it out on the boy. Pound after pound of flesh, drawn from your own child. Woman, you and I both know that isn't right." The edge of Medric's fist settled on top of Graeme's shoulder, pressing down. "Time to say your goodbyes, Graeme."

"What? Who's Alek?" The air was electric, sparking off the fine hairs of his arms. "What are you talking about?" Another hand touched his back, firm pressure spreading across his spine, and he whirled, shocked to see the men—his friends—crowded around. "What's going on?"

"Medric is speaking out of his ass, as usual." Dorothy rattled her dangling bracelets against the bar. "Refill, Donny. Chop chop." The bartender was at the other end of the bar and gave her a nod, but kept wiping and straightening bottles where he was instead of moving to answer her demand. "Well then, if the owner can't get a drink, I guess the bar is closed. Everyone has to leave."

"What the hell, Dorothy?" Graeme moved in a full circle, not surprised to find that outside of the wide ring of men surrounding them, every eye was on this encounter. "Bar's half full and last call isn't for another three hours. We're not closing."

"We are if I say we are." Hooking her heels over the rungs of the stool, she pushed up, arms braced against the edge of the bar so she was towering over the men gathered nearby. "Bar's closing. No last call, just tally up your tabs and go." Flopping back to the seat, she looked everywhere except at Graeme. "I don't control much, but I do have hold of this damn bar."

"Who is Alek?" He made the demand a second time, thinking back over what Medric had said, coming to his own conclusions. "He meant something to you, didn't he? Boyfriend? Lover? What happened to him?"

"Aleksandr Solkolov. Local boy who joined the Navy. Alek was killed in a turret explosion. He was my best friend." Medric tipped his head towards Dorothy, and Graeme saw how her shoulders had curled in, making her look small. "They were engaged."

"Is he my—" He couldn't finish the sentence, clamping his lips together.

Medric shook his head. "No. No, he was not."

He'd always known there'd been a thread of truth to all of Dorothy's stories, woven in between the lies.

Tall, blond, and handsome. A Russian boy. A sailor.

Never saw his face. Lay in a pool of my own blood.

He could pick his lineage out of that mix, and the realization chilled his blood. Knowing shouldn't matter, not in the grand scheme of things. He'd always accepted the start of him was something she had suffered through, just like she had his whole life. With that much hurt at her doorstep, of course she would reject him. Poison in her veins.

"I remind you of the worst possible things. I get it, Dorothy." Pain snaked up his arms and he lowered his head to look at fists clenched tight, knuckles white and bloodless, nails pressing pale moon crescents into the flesh of his palms. "I get it, and I won't do this to you anymore." He snorted. "Gift horse, right." When he looked up, he was surprised to see most of the bar vacated, the cluster of men surrounding him and his mother the last in the building. "I'm leaving. Medric has my phone number, if you decide you want to get in touch."

Donny hit a button on the register and the ding of the drawer opening was loud in the quiet room. He lifted the change tray and dug at the larger bills underneath, coming up with a handful. Dorothy took the offering, head down as she straightened the money, putting everything into order. Then she lifted her arm and without looking at him, thrust it towards Graeme. "Be safe."

Numb, he accepted the cash and shoved it into his front pocket. So many thoughts and words battered at his brain, shouts teetering on the tip of his tongue, a confusing tangle of demands and questions. In the end all he said was "You too."

The men murmured and shuffled so they stood between him and the door. It was like walking a gauntlet of affection instead of combatants, and by the time he'd been caught and released by each of them, he was fighting back tears. Then he was through the door and outside, only to be pulled up short by the sight of his motorcycle parked ten feet away. There were two bags already strapped to the rack over the back fender. Graeme turned and Medric was there, grin on his face, hands held out to the sides.

"You don't own very much, boy." Medric pointed to Junkyard, who had exited right behind him. "And this boy's got untapped skills at B and E."

Rolling his eyes, Graeme shoved a hand towards him, clasping tightly as he muttered, "Thank you."

"Got any ideas where you're headed?" Junkyard dropped his hand and ran it over the grip, fingers flicking the clutch lever a couple of times. "A direction?"

"Not here, that's the only sure thing. I'm just going to aim west, see where I wash up."

Junkyard pointed to the side and Graeme noticed another bike already kitted out, just like his. "Mind a little company along the way?"

"Sounds like a plan, man."

Shoulders shoved back, Graeme surveyed the front of the bar one last time, then dropped his gaze to the face of his unexpected champion. "Medric, what you said in there—"

"Nothing that shouldn't have been said long ago. I just hope you understand your own worth, Graeme, because what Dot's done isn't reflective of who you are. That's all on her." He cleared his throat. "I understand every biker worth his salt has a nickname. A road name. I think what was said inside that building tonight carried with it all kinds of truths. One of which is children are a gift, no matter how they come to being. But Gift Horse is a bit of a mouthful." Medric shrugged, then a bright grin took over his face. "Horse, however, suits you in a lot of ways. Junkyard and Horse, riding off into the sunset."

Graeme stifled a chuckle. "How did you come to that conclusion? Never mind, don't answer that." He wrapped his arms around the older man's shoulders, holding tightly as he whispered, "Saved my life, Medric. Thank you."

After that, their actual leave-taking was uneventful and once on the highway, Horse glanced over his shoulder to see a broad grin on Junkyard's face. Lifting his left hand, he pumped his fist twice, the movement echoed immediately by Junkyard as they both rolled their throttle just a little farther.

He might not have any idea where they were going.

But they'd get there fast.

Chapter Two

Horse

"This doesn't suck."

Horse laughed at Junkyard's summary of their morning. They'd been on the road nearly eight months, and the same couldn't be said for every day that had passed. Trekking through fifteen or sixteen states, they'd encountered a wide variety of weather, people, and prejudice. Graceful exits weren't always possible, and after one physically vigorous encounter, Horse had ridden several hundred miles with a broken bone in his hand as it healed, slowly.

Which meant he agreed with Junkyard's summary of their morning. "No, it sure doesn't. I'm likin' the piney woods and lakes, but without the massive mosquitos of Minnesota."

"Now"—he drawled out the word—"we were told we'd just come during the wrong season up there." Junkyard laughed and unwrapped a bandanna from around his handlebars and used it to wipe his face. "Only problem was the dude couldn't tell us a season they didn't have nasty tastin' bugs."

They'd fallen into an easy routine over the miles and months. They'd ease into a town and pick up on the local vibe. If it was welcoming, they'd find a hostel if available or a campground if not, then scope out the entertainment. It was amazing how many small towns had biker-friendly bars, and even more amazing that some of those locations were invisibly tagged as available to only a certain group. He and Junkyard had been tossed out of more than one bar when the local club decided they might be a threat. Their adventures made certain that both Junkyard and Horse had developed a sixth sense about *that* particular vibe.

Sitting on their bikes backed up to the front of a bar here in Northeast Texas was giving them both a good feeling. The campground owner had pointed out a spot that was perfect for bikes, with a flat pad for parking and trees to pitch their tents underneath. They'd done that, and then the man had aimed them at this bar situated on a small highway running next to a shallow river. In the time Horse and Junkyard had sat here, there had been four separate groups of bikers roll up, each with a different patch on the back. Even more important, each group had acknowledged him and Junkyard with a wave, a word, or chin lift.

"You ready to brave the masses?" Junkyard yawned. "I'm hungry for something to eat before we have to make our way back to the campground. The gates close at ten, so we'll need to be back on the road by nine or so and I'm starvling." He gave a piteous whine. "*Starvling*, I tell you. My stomach is poorly. So hungry."

"Okay...fine, we'll take care of your belly. I'm good to go, brother." They were close enough to be blood, at least in Horse's mind. Working side by side on various cash jobs, then sleeping within arm's reach of each other for so many nights meant they'd shared thousands of conversations. He knew Junkyard, inside and out, and believed Junkyard felt the same. Nothing sexual, even if he didn't give a shit if anyone swung that way, but a secure knowledge that no matter what went down, Junkyard had his back. "Beer and a burger sound pretty damn great right now."

Pushing through the door unleashed the full volume of music and conversation, and unlike many an inhospitable bar they'd been inside, neither level lowered. A few heads swung their way, but each of the ones who did turn to look wore welcoming expressions.

Two stools were open near the end of the bar and Horse took one, leaving the other for Junkyard.

Rubbing his palms together, Junkyard grinned. "I could get used to this shit."

"We'll see if the beers are cold and the burgers edible before we make any long-term plans, yeah?" Horse chuckled as he plucked a menu from behind a coaster holder. "The work mentioned by the campground guy sounded promising, though."

They'd done a variety of jobs as they moved through the eastern and middle states. Construction was the most frequent, and both had developed skills in that area, which made it easier to get a day gig. Nearly everyone needed someone to run the wheelbarrow or pitch bundles of shingles up onto a roof. All they had to be was courteous, responsive, dependable, and strong. *Mostly strong.*

"Can I get ya?" The bartender was a blonde woman with a ready smile, who never stopped moving. While waiting for their response, she was rinsing glasses, then gathering trash and used dishes from a position just down the bar, constantly in motion. "Beer or mixed?"

"Two beers of whatever's on tap. Just none of that light shit, yeah?" Horse gave her a grin she returned, nodding. "We'll order food too."

"Know what you want yet? I can put that in while I'm pullin' the beer." She restocked the coaster holder in front of him, then pulled a bottle from the cooler behind her and opened it, tossing the cap into the trash. "I'm a multitasker."

"I see that." He looked at the menu. "Burger and fries for me." Nudging Junkyard with an elbow, he broke the man's stare at the bartender. "Junkyard, what are you hungry for tonight?"

"Uh." Junkyard's mouth hung open for a moment, then closed with a snap. "Uh, yeah. Yeah. Same. Beer, burger, fries—can't go wrong."

Horse's glance traveled between the bartender and Junkyard, watching as she licked across her bottom lip and Junkyard's tongue followed the same pass across his own. Then she nodded and stepped back.

"Coming right up."

He elbowed Junkyard again, harder, aiming at his ribs this time. "Stop it."

"Ow. Shit, man, you stop it. What'd I do to deserve that?"

"Don't drool over the waitress. She's likely got a half a dozen protectors in this bar tonight, and the last thing I want is to pack up my tent in the dark to get back on the road because you offended the locals." He sighed. "Again." Shaking his head, he scrubbed a palm across his jaw. "Seriously, man. Reel it in, yeah? I just want a beer and food."

"She's pretty."

"Yeah, and so were the last dozen women who got you into trouble." He gestured around them. "I like this place, brother. Don't fuck it up for us just to see if you can get your dick wet."

"It ain't like that, man." Junkyard's protest fell flat between them as Horse glared at him. "Okay, maybe it is like that. But I didn't mean anything by it."

"That's too bad, because I did." Two coasters flicked to the bar in front of them, followed by a pair of beers, glasses already wet with condensation. "You're cute, and I don't have a ring." The bartender flicked her blonde hair over her shoulder. "But if you're not interested…"

"Oh, he's interested." Horse narrowed his eyes as he stared between the two. "But I for one don't want to get thrown out on my ass. At least not before I have my supper."

Laughing, she thrust out a hand towards Junkyard. "Laura. Laura McGonnell. Half-owner and bartender of this choice establishment." They shook, then she extended her hand to Horse. "And I get a say who gets thrown out, which means my vote is it's not gonna be you two."

"How the hell does he do this?" Rhetorical question aside, he gestured towards Junkyard. "His mouth seems sealed shut, so I'll do the introductions. Junkyard, meet Laura. Laura, this asshole is Shepherd Kelmer, aka Junkyard." He picked up his beer and took a long sip. "And by the silence surrounding us, I'm guessing this is going to be a long evening. I'm Graeme Nass. Not that anyone cares."

Emptying half his glass down his throat, Junkyard shook himself like his namesake. "Laura's a really pretty name."

"So is Shepherd." She winked. "I need to get to work, but if you stay right here, I'll come back, and we can chat."

Junkyard gave an exaggerated wiggle of his ass on the stool. "Not goin' anywhere, pretty Laura. I'll be riiiiight here."

"Jesus," Horse muttered, taking another sip of his beer as he looked around the bar. Predictably, there were dozens of eyes fixed on them. Not expected were the smiles and friendly nods sent his way by those same strangers. *Maybe Laura is like Dorothy, where what she says goes.* "I'm going to see if I can get a game of pool going. I'm guessing you're out?" Junkyard nodded without looking away from where Laura stood down the bar. "Okay. Keep my seat then, and I'll be back when the food shows up."

He slid off the stool and made his way past clumps of men and women clustered around the tall tables, excusing himself and getting mumbled acceptances as he went. There were two pool tables near the back of the bar, both in use and as he got closer, he realized the groups around each table wore vests and patches. The bikers who'd ridden in as he and Junkyard sat outside had taken up residence here, evidently.

"Hey." He offered one of the men a chin lift. "Can I buy into a game?" Normally all it would take was putting change along the rail to hold his spot for a game, but there wasn't a single coin in sight here, which told him the rules were different. *Now to see how I navigate things.* "Just a friendly game."

"Blackie." The man's call wasn't loud but carried well as he stepped backwards to give someone a clearer line of sight to where Horse stood.

Near the back wall was a stout man with sun-darkened skin, wrinkles at the corners of his eyes from staring into the sky, and more wrinkles at the sides of his mouth from laughing. His long beard covered his throat. Not tall but broad through the chest and shoulders, the man exuded a sense of power. Clearly the commander of this mixed group of clubs, he handed off his pool stick without a sideways glance, just expecting someone would be there to anticipate his need. They were.

Big dog.

Blackie stopped in front of Horse and made a slow show of looking him up and down. "Where you from, boy?"

The mannerisms were so like Medric's Horse couldn't kill his smile in response. "East coast—Jersey." He shrugged. "Came here by way of the Carolinas, Minnesota, and Colorado, and all points in between. Just rollin' through. Thought I'd see if I could play a friendly game of pool."

"You see something funny?" All humor had fled Blackie's features and Horse stilled. "Something worth laughing about?"

"No, man. You remind me of a good friend back in Jersey. Helped me rebuild my ride. Good man, good memories. Just stirred up pleasant associations for a minute." Shrugging one shoulder, he grimaced. "No offense meant."

"In that case, none taken. And as far as a game goes, we're starting a new one as of now. Teams." Blackie held out one hand and two pool sticks appeared out of nowhere. "You're on mine."

Grasping the length of wood thrust at him, Horse frowned. "Teams?"

"Yeah. I'm always lookin' to build my tribe. You feel me?" Blackie rubbed blue chalk on both tips, steadying Horse's stick as he did so. "So we'll play a game, see if you gel."

"See if I gel with what?"

Sweeping his arms wide, Blackie grinned, showing those deep creases in his skin were earned honestly. "With us, brother."

The next several hours became a blur, game after friendly game paired with glasses of beer. Laura had brought his food to him at some point, and he'd glanced at Junkyard to get a thumbs-up as if he were scoping out the ladies. He'd shaken his head, then eaten his burger and fries in between playing and cheering on Blackie's turn.

By the time the lights brightened in the bar, Horse realized he might not be three sheets to the wind, but he wasn't sober enough to ride off into the darkness.

"Dammit." He thrust a hand through his hair. "Shoulda stopped drinkin' hours ago." Pointing at Blackie, he faked an angry look. "It's all your fault."

"Yeah, yeah. I got broad shoulders. Dump it on me, I can take it. Why should you have passed on the beers, brother? Got a hot date in the morning you need to be fresh for?" Blackie scooped up what was left of Horse's beer and drained it, tipping his head to the ceiling to release a loud belch that earned laughter from the men to either side. Closing one eye, he squinted at Horse with the other. "Something this kind of fellowship is gonna keep you from?"

"No, man. Just my tent is already up at the campground, which means I need to ride my ass back outside of town." He looked around. "Anyone see Junkyard? He was just at the bar."

"Yeah, he was just at the bar a couple hours ago. When Laura's shift was over, he left with her. Came over to check on you." Grinning widely, Blackie made a hole with one hand and poked through it with a finger on the other. "Figure about now he's sleeping the sleep of the righteous, or at least the well laid."

"Oh yeah." He sighed, the foggy memory sliding through his mind and out again. "I still need to sober up and get to the campground."

"Nah." Blackie slung an arm around Horse's neck, the unevenness in their height pulling Horse down slightly. "Clubhouse is a block away. You can catch a few Z's on a cot there. Dale," he called over his shoulder and Horse saw a younger man look their way. He wore a vest labeled Prospect, but Horse had noticed Blackie treated him with grateful respect all night, even as he demanded the kid be the runner for their party. "Dale boy, you're gonna help Horse here walk his bike back to the lot behind the house. We'll keep 'er safe for the man tonight."

"I can—"

"Dale boy's happy to help." Blackie's tone left nothing to argue about. "Trust us, brother."

"Brother." Pursing his lips, Horse didn't try to hide how that word resonated. "Like the sound of that, man."

"No doubt. We'll see how things shake out in the morning, but that gelling I mentioned earlier is pretty much undeniable. You might as well have been a Rider all your life, the way you fit in with us." Steering Horse to the front door, Blackie called his men for their departure with a loud "Freed Riders—to me."

They burst through the door, men flooding out in front of Horse and Blackie, but there were men at their back too. All laughter died away instantly, and Horse tensed, the heaviness of the atmosphere immediately apparent.

Eight men stood in a line across the parking lot. They wore a mishmash of clothing, nothing to indicate they were together other than their shared stance. Hands on waists or hips, shoulders shoved back, they posed without moving. All of them stared at Blackie. The arm around Horse's neck tightened and Blackie whispered a soft, "Follow our lead, brother," just before the support was removed.

"Roscoe. The fuck you doin' back in little ole Longview?" Blackie strode between his men who'd exited the bar first, placing himself directly in front of their group. His attention was on a man standing at the center of the line facing them. "Thought you and me finally had ourselves an understanding."

"I'm thinkin' we need to rework that understanding." Roscoe gestured to the men on either side of him. "Boys 'n me decided we needed to expand our territory."

"There is so much wrong in that statement, I'm not sure where to start." Blackie's head swung side to side, but Horse noticed he didn't move it enough to break the stare he held with Roscoe. "You decide to follow a patch, I done told you we could have a chat about the FRMC absorbing most of your shitty-ass RC." He spat on the gravel, the action obviously calculated to rile the men, so Horse took note of which ones reacted. "Wouldn't be takin' your raggedy ass on, though. Ain't nothing changed from a month ago, when I beat your face in on the edge of town, or from six months ago when I beat your skanky ass in the front yard of my house. FRMC don't need ignorant shitslingers like you."

"Not sure you get to make that call anymore, old man." Roscoe took a step forwards, and another, and then the line of men began moving. They were like an arrow, with Roscoe on point. "Gonna have to go down here, find out who's standin' at the end of it all."

"Oh for fuck's sake." Blackie half turned back to his group. "You hear his brand of bullshit, boys? He's thinking we're gonna have to deal with them, and I guess any asshole can be right once in a while. As much as I'd rather go back to the clubhouse and let you all find a sweetbottom to make your dicks happy, we're gonna have to fuck them up. Shitfire."

Without a signal Horse could see or hear, Blackie had whirled and was running flat out within a single stride. He wasn't alone, every man on their side of the parking lot were moving with him. Within a few breaths, Horse stood alone, uncertainty keeping his feet planted.

This was not his fight, so he waited and watched as blows were exchanged, heavy cries and grunts breaking the sound of flesh hitting flesh. Most of the matches were unevenly paired, but even with the advantage, he could see no one on Blackie's side was actively looking to kill their opponent. This was clearly intended to be a painful lesson from the Freed Riders to the upstart idiots attempting a coup.

Until Roscoe pulled out a gun.

Up to that instant it had been a fair battle, fist-to-fist, no weapons.

Roscoe's hand came out from the small of his back with a pistol in his palm, and before he could plan or even decide what he was doing, Horse was sprinting across the yards to where the man fought against Blackie. Horse hit Roscoe full force, knocking him sideways and earning a misthrown fist against his jaw from Blackie. Didn't matter, because the asshole was underneath Horse, flat on his back, gun chucked to the ground only a couple of feet away.

Horse marked the moment Blackie saw it, his full body tensing. He stared at the man to watch as a mask of rage come over Blackie's features, mottled red and twisted.

"Planned this out, did ya?" Pulling back one foot, Blackie let fly, the kick landing solidly along Roscoe's flank. The man under Horse barked out a cry, short and shocked sounding. "Gonna go for a headshot, take out the leader, then you probably thought you'd step in." His booted foot connected with the meaty portion of Roscoe's thigh this time. "Fucking cuntmuffin. Can't stand spoiled asses like yours."

Horse realized the rest of the battle had ended abruptly, men encircling the two at the center of everything. Before Roscoe could seek out the gun, Horse rose and walked over to step on top of it, his weight holding it to the ground. No reason to lay a hand on it, especially not knowing what the weapon might have been used for before now.

"Let me up." Roscoe attempted to roll to his hands and knees as Blackie landed another hard kick, this against the man's hip, the heel of the boot catching and flinging the man sprawling to the side. "Fuck, man, stop it."

"You. Were going. To shoot. Me." Grunts punctuated the words, coinciding with each kick Blackie let fly. "I should fuckin' kill you, but I won't." More kicks. "Because I'm. Fucking better. Than you could. Ever be."

Panting heavily, Blackie stepped backwards, fists clenched at his sides. Roscoe writhed on the gravel, groaning out curse after curse. Surprised, Horse marked that the only blows to his face were from knuckles, marks made during the first part of the altercation. He appreciated that kind of control required, and how even in an extreme rage, Blackie seemed to keep his head about him.

Cool hand. Good man to have at your back.

"You're done here." Blunt features sharpened with a heavy scowl, Blackie scanned the men surrounding them. "And if the rest of you all retain any slim association with this dicktastic piece of humanity, you're done all around here too. I'll be certain you won't get a patch all through Texas. No fuckin' where. No fuckin' way," he shouted, leaning at the waist. "And if you think I don't have that kinda pull, then you need to think again, dillweeds. Motherfucker. God, I fuckin' hate shitheels like you. Cannot abide, man. Cannot abide." He pulled his foot back, but as Blackie's gaze snagged on Horse, he planted both feet and straightened, flinging his hair back and running a hand through the disheveled mane. "Now this man? That's a fuckin' keeper, standin' right here in front of me." His foot lifted again, and Horse fought against a wince, expecting the heavy thud of leather meeting flesh. "The difference between the two of you couldn't be clearer if I could shine a fuckin' spotlight on it. Son of a fucking bitch, you might just be better than handy to have around, Horse." Instead of kicking Roscoe, Blackie stepped onto his chest, then off the other side towards Horse, ignoring the pained cry from the man lying on the ground. "Brother." Hand outthrust, Horse didn't make him wait, clasping and matching Blackie's grip strength to strength. "Was thinkin' of keepin' you, and that shit's a done deal now. Owe you my life."

Horse pulled him in, shoulder to shoulder and pounded a fist against Blackie's back. "My honor, brother." He didn't know where the action or words came from, just that they seemed true. *Felt true.* Stepping back, he glanced at Blackie and then at the men around them. "Didn't seem right, him pulling a gun when the rules of engagement had already been settled. You aren't much of an asshole, so I thought I'd prevent him from putting a hole in you." He shrugged. "Good people are harder to find than most folks think."

"From the mouths of babes." Blackie laughed through the words, grinding down on the bones in Horse's hand for a moment. He released and Horse fought the urge to wring his fingers, then watched as Blackie crouched next to Roscoe. "You lived through this bullshit because I allowed it. Need to keep that a fuckin' sharp memory, Roscoe. Sharp as a fuckin' knife to the balls, man. Pull it out and polish that shit off every time you think about coming back to Gregg County. Or Upshur, or Smith. Rusk. Wood. Hell, boy, just stay the fuck out of East Texas. Draw a big circle and label it *not fucking yours*. You roll back in here, and I'll know. I'll know." He stood and pulled his foot back, chuckling darkly when Roscoe flinched, flinging his hands up in defense. "And you won't survive my wrath a second time." The square toe of Blackie's boot landed in the center of Roscoe's thigh with massive force, Roscoe's keening cry splitting the air a final time.

Blackie turned away from Roscoe again and pointed to Dale, then motioned to Horse's foot. The Freed Rider prospect stepped forwards and tapped Horse's lower leg. Horse retreated a stride, releasing the gun into the man's hands.

"Where's your ride?" Another man stood next to Horse and gestured with one outflung arm. "It one of that pair over there? That other one your brother's ride? Man who came in with you? We can roll it to the clubhouse, too."

"He'll have locked the forks. Bike'll go in a circle, but that's all." Horse moved so he stood next to his bike and rested a hand on the tank. "This one is mine. Freedom."

"Hey, Oaky." His shout carrying across the lot had another man turning to look to where they stood. "Oaky, tell Durango to get the van and the trailer, brother. Might as well load both as load one." A hand extended his direction and Horse gripped it, grimacing when the slap of their palms woke the ache left in the wake of Blackie's grip. With a light laugh, this guy barely pressed down. "Blackie's got a hell of a hello, for sure. I know man, I know. Hey, I'm Duane." He grinned. "And I'm a menace, at least according to our fearless leader." The men swirled around them, and Horse tried to keep track of the movement, finding it more difficult by the minute. "Buck up, brother. We'll have you in a bed before you can shake a stick."

A van pulled into the lot pulling a noisy trailer, looped connector chains spitting sparks as they dragged across the gravel. One of the FRMC members was driving, and he slowed to a stop in front of where Horse stood with Duane. The moment the van had parked, the area was swarmed by men, and Horse watched as a group of them crowded around Junkyard's bike. Gripping various sections of the frame, they counted down from three and lifted, then shuffled their way up and onto the trailer. They set it down and a couple of them immediately set to strapping the bike in place.

"You mind if Dale rides the bike up? Be easier than rolling or lifting it." Duane smiled his easy grin at Horse and held out a hand, palm up. "Come on, brother. Sooner we load it, sooner we get to the house."

Horse dug in his pocket for the keys and placed them in Duane's grip. "Be gentle." His plea pulled laughter from the men around them, as intended. "She's a good girl."

It was the work of moments to load his bike and strap it in place, then the van was pulling away. Horse followed the group of men who moved across the graded gravel, noting several who peeled off and went to various cars and trucks still on the lot. Somewhere in the midst of things, he'd lost track of Roscoe.

"Where'd the asshole go?" He leaned a little closer to Duane as he asked the question, hoping to keep his interest quiet.

"Roscoe? Probably home to our momma, cryin' about how bad I treat him." Blackie appeared next to Horse, matching him stride for stride. "Like he always does."

"Your mother?" That didn't make any sense, and Horse was willing to put his confusion down to the amount of beer he'd had along with the adrenaline dump from the earlier fight.

"Yeah, the rancid son of a bitch is my brother. And not in the 'I've got your back always' sense. Asshole." Blackie sighed heavily. "And I'm not nearly drunk enough for that story, man." He stopped in front of the porch steps and spread his arms wide, a broad grin reopening a split in his bottom lip. With blood smeared over his teeth and trickling down into his beard, he smiled at Horse. "Welcome to our humble abode, brother. This here's the house of the Freed Riders, and we're pleased you're accepting our hospitality."

The building was narrow and long, two stories tall along the back end. In the moonlight and scant streetlight illumination, it looked like a hole in the darkness. Then light bloomed in one window, followed by another, and another. Horse caught a glimpse of the inside. Furniture clustered close to foster conversations, walls painted a warm taupe. It gave him a sense of welcome.

Like the men it housed, the building might have looked rough on the outside, painted black as night, but the inside was good as gold.

Home.

***

"No, no. You didn't see it." Oaky lounged back in his chair, beer can balanced on the swell of his belly. "Cool as ice, this dude."

"Cool as ice and fast as fuck." Along with the other men in the room, Duane laughed easily, shoulder buried against the back of a loveseat, knee cocked up on the cushions near where Horse was perched. "I saw him still up by the building, and *bam*." He smacked his hands together, then leaned sideways to retrieve his beer from the floor. "He was in the middle of it and ridin' ole Roscoe to the ground. Prolly called Horse cuz he runs like a racehorse."

"Or is hung like a horse." Durango's laughter drifted across the room from where he was sprawled out across a chair. "Don't care to know that, by the way. But you should know if you fuck one of the sweetbottoms, we'll all hear about it anyhow. Swear those gals talk more than chickens cluck."

That was the second time he'd heard the phrase and Horse thought he understood the meaning, but he still quietly asked, "Sweetbottoms?"

Duane drained his beer and whistled loudly, holding the bottle up by the base. "Club whores, not to be rented out, but up for using. It's why they hang around. They like fuckin' bikers or some shit. No harm no foul if you go with any of them, cuz if a member wanted to slap a patch on one of them, he'd have already requested a PO. Means ain't any one of us got a claim on any one of them. They come, they make us come, they go." Dale appeared in the doorway to the kitchen area and nodded at Duane, vanishing for a moment before coming back into view with a handful of beers. "Want another one?" He pointed to Horse's still half-full bottle.

"Nah. I'm done, man. Hours of road under my wheels and then that shit at the bar? About to fall over where I am." He blinked and shook his head. "Blackie mentioned a cot?"

"We can do you one better. Dale? Hey, Dale."

The prospect paused in his circuit of the room and looked over his shoulder, "Yes, patch holder?"

That wasn't the first time Horse had heard him use the phrase tonight, but unlike sweetbottom, this one was easier to decipher. Honor paid to the members of the club the man was working his way into.

"Show Horse to the room Blackie mentioned, would ya? You know the one." He drained half of his new beer in one go. "About fuckin' time it was in use again."

"Whose room will I be taking?" *Depending on the response, it might be better to ask for a ride out to the campground after all.*

"Roscoe's room." Blackie walked from the kitchen area and stood with hands at the front of his waist, fingers wrapped around his belt. "Done holdin' out to see if he'll get his head pulled from his ass. Unfortunately for him, it seems a terminal condition with the little shit." Lifting his chin, he winked at Horse. "Come on, I'll show ya. I expect Dale's got more beer to get."

Shoving off the loveseat, Horse held his bottle out to Dale, who took it with a muttered, "Thanks."

Following Blackie up the stairs, Horse glanced out across the ground floor room one last time before the landing turned and was surprised to find Dale still staring at him, face twisted with what looked like anger. *Wonder what that's about?* Shaking off the unease the sight had caused, he entered the upstairs hallway and stopped when Blackie paused and fumbled with a cluster of keys attached to the chain of his wallet.

The lock opened with a click and Blackie stepped backwards as he shoved the door inwards. "Here you go." Horse eyed him cautiously and the man laughed. "No fear, brother." He yanked at the keys and Horse saw he was working one free of the ring. "Here's the key to the door. Oaky has one as my second, but long as you have this," he grabbed Horse's hand and slapped the metal against his palm, "the room is yours."

"Won't you need it for another member?"

"Hope not." Blackie lifted two fingers to his temple and flicked a mock salute. "Sleep well, brother. I'll cook us a spread in the morning. I'm all about that servant mentality in my officers, gotta model what I want them to emulate, ya know?" He turned and walked away, swinging out of sight through a door nearer the end of the hallway.

Horse studied the hallway for a moment, marking how the large window at the end opened sideways, noting it probably exited onto a landing for external stairs. That would be the rear of the building, hidden from his view as they approached the structure earlier.

Turning, he entered the room and closed the door. The room wasn't large by any means, the double bed inside took up nearly all available floor space. But it had been cleverly modified, with cabinets affixed to the walls up nearer the ceiling. Still in easy reach, but high enough he wouldn't need to worry about smacking his head on them. *No reason to open any of them.* Blackie had showed ample trust in allowing a stranger to stay in the clubhouse, and Horse wouldn't betray that confidence.

Footsteps up the stairs were loud, as was the knock at his door. It was swinging open before he got fully turned around and he had his hands up defensively before he recognized Oaky.

"Easy, brother. Easy. No, man. I'm not up for coppin' a fine for fightin' in the house. Fuck no." Chuckling softly, Oaky held up his hand, showing Horse's bag, retrieved from the back of his bike. "Thought you might like havin' your stuff close to hand. More secure than leaving it on the bike. Even if we keep a prospect on watch at night, it's always better safe than sorry." He gestured behind him. "I've got your brother's stuff here too. Want it inside?"

"Not a lot of room for it." Horse grabbed his bag and stepped out of the way as Junkyard's first bag soared through the door to land on the floor at the foot of the bed. "But I guess that'll work." The second, smaller bag thudded into place on top of the other one. "Thanks, man."

"No problem. And Horse?" Oaky stuck his head back through the door. Horse tilted his head slightly in question. "Well met, brother. Without you tonight, we'd be having a very different discussion downstairs."

He withdrew before Horse could respond, closing the door behind himself. Horse stared at the door and then glanced at the bags. He tossed his on the bed, used the key to lock the door then pulled out the ring holding his bike key and added it to that without thinking.

An hour later, he was still awake, lying on his back and staring at the ceiling when the doorknob rattled gently.

"The fuck?"

The soft mutter from the hallway underscored his unease, and he was glad he'd decided to just slip off his boots earlier. Moving carefully, he rose from the bed and stood next to the door, shoulders pressed tight to the wall.

The doorknob rattled again, more urgently.

"Fucker."

This time he recognized the speaker as Dale.

What the hell would the prospect want?

Just in case the man had been sent up by a member for some reason, Horse quietly unlocked the door and then abruptly flung it wide.

The movement yanked the doorknob from Dale's hand and the man's head jerked up, guilt painting his expression.

Not sent by a member, then.

"What do you need?" Horse didn't attempt to keep his voice quiet. Lying awake had allowed him to count footsteps up the stairs, and he knew that each bedroom had to be already occupied. "Can I help you, Dale?"

"No." Red color moved up the man's neck, embarrassment blazing its way into his cheeks. "Just checking to see if you needed anything."

The door opposite Horse's opened and Duane appeared. Naked except for a glistening condom covering his rigid cock, he looked annoyed. "The fuck you doin' on the second floor, prospect?"

Okay, that's new information. Horse hadn't been aware the man wasn't allowed up here. *But if it's off limits for a prospect, why did they invite me up here?*

"Just checkin' on Horse is all." Dale shook his head, already moving towards the stairs. "Didn't mean to cause a ruckus."

Duane didn't respond, just glared at the man until he was no longer visible before turning to look at Horse. His shoulders sagged. "Your lack of comfort is showing, brother." Duane gestured to Horse with one hand, shoulders to feet. "I know you don't got a sweetbottom in there, but you should at least strip to your skivvies to sleep. I get it, new place, new people and all that. Trust is earned, but you got nothin' to fear under this roof, brother." He glared at the stairs again. "Prospect won't bother you again." Then glanced over his shoulder, a grin splitting his face. "Can't say the same for me and the smart mouth in here." With a flip of his hand, Duane closed the door and Horse was left standing in the hallway alone.

He chuckled when a wave of feminine giggles passed through Duane's door, then stepped back through into what he was now calling his room. Key to the lock, he paused, then turned it, locking himself in again. *No harm in being cautious. Safe beats sorry, any day.* With Duane's words in his mind, he stripped down to his briefs, crawled under the covers and turned on his side facing the door.

Horse smiled, then laughed aloud as he relaxed against the mattress.

The rhythmic squeak and squeal of bedsprings lulled him to sleep.

Chapter Three
Glenna

Yawning loudly, Glenna Richeson bent at the waist and tipped as far upside down as she could manage and still retain her footing, adroitly gathering handfuls of her thick hair into one fist. She fished for the hair tie on her wrist with her other hand and snapped it into place, twisting the rope of hair into a messy bun. Righting herself, she looked at the coffeemaker just as it stopped spitting, indicating the pot was ready.

The back door opened and closed, bootsteps stopping nearly as quickly as they'd begun.

Glenna grinned over her shoulder.

Turned to face back towards the door he'd just come through, a tall man stood brushing scant raindrops off his shoulders. He slapped his hat against one lean thigh before angling to the side to hang the big, felt monstrosity on a hook above the tray that already held his boots. On socked feet, her husband came towards her, and she held the grin even when he bent and pressed a kiss to her lips, only losing it when she kissed him back.

"Mornin', darlin'." Pinning her to the kitchen counter with his hips, he reached around her for a mug and picked up the coffee carafe with his other hand. She let him fill the mug, then deftly stole it from his grip, ducking underneath his arm as she wormed away.

"Mornin'," she gave back, warmed by the smile he sent her direction. "Everything okay after that storm last night?"

Late in the darkness, there'd been a raucous storm rolling through the countryside with prolonged bouts of lightning and thunder. Loud enough to rattle the walls of their house.

"Yeah, most looks good." He had already filled the second mug she'd had waiting on the counter and brought it to his lips. Cutting a look at her while he cautiously sipped, the twist of his mouth was a warning. "Owl got into the chickens again."

"Son of a bitch." Squeezing the mug with both hands, she steadied it as she lifted it to her face. Hiding behind the mug, she asked, "How many are left?"

"Looks like three hens."

"He got Avril?" She let her head drop backwards, glaring at the ceiling. "Son of a bitch."

"Yeah. The netting got damaged, probably debris skimming across the top of the coop."

"Dammit, Avril was a good rooster." Blowing a rude raspberry, she shook her head. "At least two of the hens are broody. Maybe they've got good eggs and we'll have some chicks in a couple of weeks."

Hands settled on her shoulders and Glenna followed their lead, swaying back against the hard chest she knew so well. Pendleton Richeson had been it for her since she'd laid eyes on him ten years ago. It had hit her out of the blue, the feelings immediate, and strong.

He'd been in town visiting a friend and they'd literally run into each other in the grocery store. Him rounding a corner talking on the phone and her guiding her buggy whilst reading from the list her grandmother had written.

Their whirlwind romance lasting exactly six days had him turning in notice at his job in Kentucky and looking for work in Longview. Glenna's grandmother hadn't been in favor of their relationship at first, reciting lines of doom and gloom about marrying in haste leading to a leisurely repentance.

Four months into the relationship, Pendleton had proven himself and then some when a local rancher's bull had broken down a half mile of fencing. He'd not only separated their bull from the hostile visitor, he'd stayed on the fence line in a driving rain until every shattered post was replaced and every strand of barbed wire resecured. Penn might not have grown up on a ranch, but he took to the way of life as if born to it.

"Cattle good?" She stepped to the side and frowned, watching Penn massage the back of his neck. "Back still bothering you? I'm telling you, a visit to the doc would not go amiss. You've been hurting for a year."

"If it gets bad enough, I will. Until then, my routine of nightly massages from the talented fingers of my lovely wife is not a bad treatment." His smile lit up his face.

"Now I'm your lovely wife?" Moving to stand next to him, she leaned her shoulder against his sturdy body. "Pretty sure I was a harridan this morning when I was kickin' you out of bed."

"You can't hold anything I say against me if it happened before I had a shower and coffee. That's sleepin' Penn talkin', and he isn't the smartest peg in the house." Pressure against the side of her head was a kiss, lengthened and paused when he sniffed softly. "You smell good, pretty lady."

"Same shampoo I've used since before we met." Turning her head, she pressed a kiss to his arm. "You're such a sap."

"Your sap." He switched the coffee mug to his other hand and rubbed the back of his neck again. "Slept crooked or something. It's really buggin' me this morning."

Glenna ignored his actions and words, already having put in her plea. She knew from experience if she harped on the idea of a doctor, he'd sull up and then they'd argue. If he was still sore tonight, she'd get the jar of watered-down horse liniment and give him a good working over. But knowing still didn't stop her from worrying.

She tried to set it aside, focusing instead on their normal routine. "What's on tap for today?" Draining her mug, she reached for the carafe, but Penn beat her to it, twisting to bring it to fill her mug again. "Thanks, baby. I gotta go to town at some point. Do you need anything?"

"Going to the cemetery?"

She nodded, cheek rubbing up and down against the fabric covering his strong arm. "Yeah, need to say hello to Grammy."

Her grandmother had passed peacefully in her sleep nearly five years ago, and Glenna still missed her every day. The woman had taken her on as a sullen teen angry at a world that had stolen her parents away in a single moment, their lives snuffed out in a pile of twisted metal. After that bleak moment, it felt like every good thing in her life had come from the hands of the woman she'd eventually called Grammy. So Glenna made it a point to visit the gravesite as often as possible, just to sit and gossip, telling her grandmother everything that had happened since their last one-sided conversation. It helped keep her grounded and reminded her where she came from—her roots.

"I don't need anything from town, darlin'. Be safe when you go. I saw old man Snyder out runnin' fences this morning. He didn't say so, but you and I both know if he's out doin' his own work, probably means Jackson didn't come home last night. If that man's still in town, he'll be owly for sure."

"Mugh." Grunting her displeasure, she shook herself all over. "I hate them." She sighed and rephrased. "Not them, just Jackson."

The Three S Ranch to their south was owned by Chester Snyder, who had always been a good neighbor. Respectful of fence lines and understanding of how things went when there were thousand-pound animals in the mix of things. When his wife passed last year, Glenna and Penn took it upon themselves to continue with their neighbor's half-finished haying, putting up more than a thousand bales with the help of some of the other folks from town. That's just how it was done in the country. Everyone pulled together.

Except for Jackson Snyder, the third S in the ranch's brand.

Older than Glenna by ten years, Jackson had been an asshole as long as she'd known him. If he'd gotten drunk last night, it meant he'd probably gone home with the county-line bar's sole bartender. A sweet woman, Cynthia was older, which for some reason pissed Jackson off every time he woke up in her bed.

Glenna could tell the man one fix for his anger issues. *Well, two fixes. Don't get drunk, and don't go home with Cynthia.* She shrugged. "I'll watch for him. Avoiding Jackson is a fine art, and I'm proud to have mastered it from a young age." Out in the country, playmates and friends were usually drawn from the closest neighbors. Not so in this case.

"I know you have." Penn chuckled. "Now give me a kiss and go get dressed. I'll make some eggs and sausage for our breakfast."

"I knew there was a reason I loved you." She turned and stretched up, rolling to her toes to place her lips against his. With a whispered, "Man who cooks and gives up his coffee without a fight? That man's a keeper," she pursed her lips. He ducked his head and closed the fraction of space between their mouths, possessing hers with a surety and familiarity that spoke to the years they'd been together. "Love you, Penn," she said when the kiss broke finally.

"Love you more, darlin'."

***

Standing at the grocery store's meat counter, Glenna glared at the mounds of chicken breasts and thighs. "Owl got my rooster Avril last night. I don't know whether to let my broody girls set their eggs and hope for babies, or wring their necks and make stew." Her muttering had the man behind the glass-fronted case laughing. "You laugh now, Jeffrey, but my decision will determine if I have you wrap up some chicken for me or not."

"You won't kill your hens. You're not kidding anyone except your ownself, Glenna."

"I hate how you know me so well." She aimed a pretend scowl his direction. "Why are we friends again? I'll take four breasts and two thighs. It's barbeque night, and too dang hot to cook a stew in the house, so the girls live to cluck another day. But only because it's hot, not because I'm attached to them or anything."

"Glenna, you named your rooster. Chances are those hens have names too." He pulled the container from the case and turned to the back counter, ripping a length of waxed paper from a spool. "And yes, it's too dang hot to cook inside. Hope this weather breaks soon."

"Penn said the same thing this morning. The rains are good, but those storms are fierce. I worry about the electricity every evening, seems like."

"It goes out, you know what to do." Jeffrey turned and handed her the bundled package of meat, date and type written neatly along one long fold of white paper. "Take the blankets out and wrap that freezer up, first thing. I don't want to be selling you any beef when you raise the best meat in the county."

Grinning at him, she dropped the chicken into her cart. "You say the sweetest things."

"Don't tell your husband I was sweet talking you. He'd have my head."

"Penn's a lover not a fighter."

"More information than I need to know." Jeffery's laughter followed her to the front of the store.

Bags packed in the footwell of the passenger seat, she stretched her back as she glanced around the small community that had sprung up around the intersection. Over the past ten years, Belle, Texas had gone from a population of about ten people to more than a thousand, families lured from Longview and Tyler by the new gated communities built on what used to be prime grazing pasture. Slowly, one at a time, smaller ranching families without generational support had sold to a local developer, leaving their ten, twenty, or even fifty-acre plots of land changed forever.

I don't know what would be worse, having to sell the ranch to a Scrooge McJerk or Jackson Snyder.

Glenna shook off her thoughts and was climbing into the front seat of her truck when she noticed Penn's truck parked alongside the doctor's storefront clinic. *Good for him. About time he got checked out.* Sliding back out, she locked the truck behind her, crossed the highway with a quick look either direction, and jogged up the concrete steps in front of the clinic. A bell rang overhead, announcing her arrival and a blonde beehive peered around the edge of the receptionist window.

"Glenna, what brings you here today?" The nasally twang of the woman's voice grated on Glenna's nerves. Growing up in a small town had many benefits. It also had a few drawbacks, which was if her arch nemesis during high school didn't move away, and Glenna also hadn't moved away, the chances were high that she'd be running into this woman her whole life.

"Darcy Mae." Glenna gave her a brief nod. "Just here for Penn's appointment. What room's he in back there?" She grabbed the doorknob of the single internal exit from the receptionist area and jiggled it. *Why's it locked?* "Care to let me in so I can see my husband?"

"He's with the doc now." That teased and bleached head of hair shook back and forth. "Probably best not to disturb them. I'm sure Pendleton will be out soon if you'd care to take a seat?"

"At least tell him I'm here?" Glenna didn't like the tone of voice Darcy Mae had used. Something about it had her hackles up. Still, she gritted out, "Please?"

"If you'll just take a seat, he'll be out here soon."

Sensing there was no win for her in this confrontation, Glenna grumped audibly and chose the chair closest to the exit from the internal offices, grabbing a magazine from the nearby table. Two articles on deworming cattle later, the door opened outward, blocking her view of whoever was exiting. Darcy Mae's greeting left no question, though, and her cheery, "Pendleton. You paying cash like usual?" stopped Glenna in place, half risen from the chair.

"Sure thing, Darcy Mae." Penn's voice was subdued, and as the door slowly closed, it revealed her husband standing in front of the receptionist window with slumped shoulders. "Here you go."

Glenna straightened, gaze locked on the lines etched in what she could see of Penn's face. "Pendleton, you ready to get that lunch we talked about?" No way was she going to let Darcy Mae know the clueless and terrified state his expression had riled up in her.

Penn turned and froze when he saw her, then with two strides, he was pressed tight to her, hard chest against her softer one, face buried in the nook of her throat as his arms circled and bore down. It was almost like he needed her touch, so she skated a hand up the muscles of his back, cupping the back of his neck with her fingers in the ruff of hair there.

"Glenna, can we go home instead?"

"Whatever you need."

Their whispers were the barest of sounds, hardly any air moving against skin where lips touched and brushed, but every hair on her body lifted and stood at attention. His body heaved once and his arms clamped tighter. Then as her fingers threaded through his hair, he exhaled in a giant sigh and the bunched muscles under her touch relaxed.

"I want to go home."

Leaning back, she stared into his face. "Then home we'll go. I'll follow you." The unspoken question surrounded his capability to drive and when the corners of his lips curved up, she knew he understood her concern.

"I'm good, Glenna. See you there." His hand skated down her arm, fingers twining with hers. "Darcy Mae, I'll call when I'm ready to set another appointment." Penn pulled Glenna from the building before receiving a response, pausing when they were on the sidewalk at the bottom of the concrete steps. "Where are you parked?"

"Just across the street."

He must have seen her truck at the same time she spoke because he was already hauling her across the highway. She got a hand in the pocket of her jeans and found the key fob, pressing the button by feel so the truck booped once as it unlocked.

"You'll come straight home?" She pressed her cheek against his arm. "I had one more stop, but it can wait a day or two."

"Gimme two shakes and I'll be on the road. You can lead the way." Penn twirled her, steered her close using their joined hands, and rested his forehead against hers. "I'll be right behind you."

The kiss he gave her wasn't something meant for public, with people walking and driving past, but she gobbled up the intimacy of the moment. Teeth nipping at her bottom lip, he opened her mouth and plunged inside in a demanding movement. His hand gripped her ass and hauled her tight against his hips so the rigid pipe of his erection pressed into her flesh. Changing the angle of their heads, he dove deeper, tongue thrusting in a primal rhythm.

Eventually, he slowed them down, but only after she was ready to climb him like a tree, wanting to bounce her ass against his dick.

"God, Penn." Clutching his neck with both hands, she realized his arms held her, feet dangling inches from the pavement. "You gonna make good on that promise here or at home?"

"At home."

She slid down his front and when his arm left her waist, she was already arching into him in anticipation when his hand slapped her ass hard.

"Now get on up in that truck so we can take this private."

One tug of the handle and she was fumbling with the fob again, the length of the kiss having exceeded the previous unlocking's timeout. "You gotta let go of me so I can do that." His long arms had circled her from behind, and the way he was pressed against her was a promise all on its own. "Penn, you keep this up and we'll both be arrested for indecent behavior."

"I just…" His voice trailed off then his lips were beside her ear. "I love you, Glenna Richeson."

"I love you, too."

Chapter Four
Horse

Standing at one end of the long bar, Horse studied the crowd. He scanned each face as he watched for any signs of trouble and was pleased when he came up empty.

It had been six months since he and Junkyard had landed in Longview. After both taking a temporary gig as a day laborer on a job site, Junkyard had been hired on for a steadier position and Horse had reverted to his roots.

Freed Riders MC was the other owner Laura hadn't mentioned by name their first night in the bar. Once Blackie learned Horse had bouncer experience, he'd been placed on the payroll almost faster than he could sign the paperwork.

Two days after meeting Blackie, he'd ridden in a truck with the man to the campground to gather his and Junkyard's tents and other gear they'd left behind. That was still in storage in a locked shed out back of the clubhouse. Junkyard had taken up residence with Laura while Horse was still squatting in the bedroom at the clubhouse.

Tonight would change things, though.

Horse had plans and they hinged on one man's response to his request. A yes, and he'd be putting down roots, finding a house of his own. A no, and he'd be packing up his bike and moving on, solo.

"Yo." The loud shout could only be one person and Horse was already grinning as he turned to the door. Blackie and Durango stood just inside, Oaky and Duane fanning to either side. "Come play some pool."

"Can't." Horse shouted over the pounding music, shook his head, and pointed at the floor where he stood. "On the clock tonight."

"Dale boy." Blackie turned and reached behind him, pulling the man into view. "Stand where Horse is and if you see trouble, come get him."

Without a word, his gaze only turning to a glare once Blackie could no longer see his face, Dale stalked to where Horse typically planted himself and took up station beside him.

"Now you can," Blackie grinned.

Horse had learned to ignore Dale's simmering anger. He treated the man with respect, never gave anything that could be construed as an order or even a suggestion, and at bedtime ensured that his door was always locked. Things in that regard would change tonight, one way or the other.

"Thanks," he said now, as if the man had a choice in the matter. Then he followed the rest of Blackie's men back to the pool table area.

Through the months, he'd learned that the Longview chapter was the original, reverently called Mother by members. Blackie had two additional chapters, one in southern Oklahoma, and the other right on the Texas/Louisiana state lines. Members from those chapters had rotated in and out of the clubhouse, most of them staring at Horse as if he were an oddity when they found he had a room. That had continued to be a sore topic for Dale, and Horse had overheard Blackie refusing to explain to more than just Dale about why he had the outsider not just under their roof, but on the second floor as if he wore the FRMC patch.

And that line of thought brought him full circle back to the question he planned on asking Blackie.

On cue, his palms started to sweat.

It wasn't that he thought Blackie would outright turn down his request. It was the idea of being on a rung below Dale that bothered him. Or so he'd attempted to convince himself.

Mostly it was the idea that Blackie could shut him down and take away the sense of true brotherhood he was building with the members. With a word, it could be ripped away. It was a trust and faith unlike anything he'd experienced before, and Horse couldn't imagine his life without the FRMC at the center. He was willing to do anything for them, and believed down to his core that they'd do the same.

Well, except for Dale.

"Hey, Blackie," he began, but someone else called the man's name, pulling him to the other side of the bar. Rethinking his process on the fly, Horse turned to the men arguing over the pool sticks. "Hey, Duane." A smiling face swung his way. "Can I ask you a question?"

"Ya just did" came the grinning response and Horse groaned at the weak joke.

"Seriously." At his grumbling complaint, Duane made a show of wiping the smile from his face with one palm, flinging nothing to the ground as if it were a booger on his fingers. "God bless, do you ever stop joking around?"

"I'm just foolin' with ya. Whadda need, Horse?" Turned so his shoulders squared to where Horse stood, the man looked as if he were willing to jump any direction at Horse's request.

God bless, I'm humbled by these men.

Shoving his thoughts aside, he asked, "What's the process for a man joining the FRMC?"

"Any man, or a man like you?" All humor fled, with a serious expression on his face Duane cut straight to the heart of Horse's question.

Wiping damp palms against the outside of his thighs, Horse's silent nod was all the response he could muster. It didn't matter, because at the slight movement, Duane was again grinning.

"I'll be back in a minute. This is above my pay grade, so I'm gonna let Blackie answer you."

And with that unhelpful reply, Duane turned and said something quietly to Oaky who immediately cut a raised-eyebrow glance at Horse, then Duane left out the back door of the bar.

So much for getting answers tonight.

"What's this I hear about you finally takin' that leap of faith I've been waitin' on?" A few seconds later, Blackie's voice came from directly behind Horse, and he whirled to face his friend. Nothing in Blackie's expression gave any indication of the thoughts behind his question, and Horse's gut tightened, making it hard to take in a full breath.

Their encounter was pulling attention throughout the bar and Horse watched as various FRMC members began drifting in their direction. *Of course I had to pick tonight.* All chapters were represented in the crowd, along with members from a number of support clubs standing alongside the men. The mix of faces he knew and so many he didn't held Horse's voice captive. Sweat prickled along the back of his neck and across his shoulders.

The front door opened and shut and Horse saw Duane weaving through the patrons scattered in groups at tables and in standing clusters.

The few people who weren't already looking to where Blackie and Horse stood took note of Duane's passage, their heads turning to follow him.

Stopping directly behind Blackie, Duane offered Horse a serious smile over Blackie's shoulder, but didn't speak.

"Yeah. So, I was wondering what it took for the club to accept a new member." Gaze flicking between the two men facing him, Horse corrected himself. "Prospect, I mean. To take on a new prospect." Head turning side to side to take in the entirety of the crowd, Horse grimaced at being the center of attention. "Didn't mean it to be a spectacle."

"I did." Blackie's flat statement rang through the room. "My guys, FRMC, come and witness unless you've been assigned elsewhere." He turned and patted the air with one hand. "Actually, let's take this outside. Prospects stay in the bar." Gesturing to the counter, he nodded at Oaky. "Grab a couple of cases, bring them with. We'll hit the yard behind the clubhouse."

Blackie spun on his heel and Duane gestured towards the door with a sweep of his hand. Horse fell into line behind Blackie, the spot between his shoulder blades itching with the unfamiliar exposure. A hand landed on his shoulder and Horse lurched sideways, relaxing when he heard Duane's familiar laughter.

"It's all good, brother. Promise." Fingers gave a squeeze, then fell away.

Less than a minute later, they were single filing through the narrow gate alongside the long drive. The yard was cool in the early evening Texas heat, lush grass soft underfoot. He knew care of the property was something assigned to prospects and lower-ranking members of the club, and he realized they did an exemplary job of it. Not out of fear of reprisal, but because they held the club dear. More than an organization, it was a family, the connections between members stronger than anything else he'd ever seen. That was why the outcome of tonight's question and eventual answer mattered so much to him.

I want this for myself.

Chin high, he stopped when Blackie did. When the man turned to face him, Horse locked gazes and held Blackie's stare.

I need this.

"Ask me." Blackie's arms were relaxed at his sides, this conversation as casual and easy as any they'd had over the past months. "Go ahead, ask."

"Just ask?" Horse shook out his hands, then adopted the stance he took as a bouncer, feet spread to shoulder-width, arms crossed over his chest. *Maybe that's too aggressive.* He uncrossed his arms, letting his arms drop to his sides. *Maybe that's too casual. Shit.* Fingers balling into fists, he propped them on each hip. "Just like that?"

Blackie nodded, but his mouth twisted like he was holding back a smile and that gave Horse just a bit more courage.

"What's it take for a man to petition an MC for membership?" *There, not asking about patches or prospect periods. Just straight out.* "The FRMC, in case I need to be specific." *Shit.*

"Any man?" Blackie's torso inclined towards Horse slightly. "Or you?"

"Uh." The way Blackie echoed Duane's earlier words caught him off guard. "Me, I guess?"

"You guess or you know?" Shoulders lifting in a casual shrug, Blackie shifted his weight to one leg, hip canting slightly. "Matters, man."

"Me. What do I need to do to start the process?" *Okay, better. Hopefully.*

"You already did." One corner of Blackie's beard lifted, a flash of teeth showing it was a smile shifting his expression. "Hangaround is part of it."

"Oh. Okay." His head was nodding without his permission, rapid and desperate feeling. Horse stiffened his neck, stopping the movement. "That's good then."

"You want my patch, Graeme Nass?"

The usage of his name took Horse by surprise. It had been so long since he'd heard it spoken. Immediately recognizable, but his brain was rifling through memories trying to determine if he'd given it to any of the FRMC members.

"Yeah, I do." He choked the words through his blocked throat. Fear or another emotion, it didn't matter, the physical reaction to the possibility being dangled in front of him reinforced the rightness of this request. "I really do."

"Tell me why. The why matters more than the simple ask, brother." Blackie's stance remained casual and easy, but muscles in his shoulders and biceps tightened. This question was as important as anything, and that knowledge set Horse's nerves jangling again.

He looked around the yard, cataloging each face he knew and marking the ones he didn't. Not a single man looked angry. Instead, their expressions were attentive and interested. Oaky and Duane held a note of greater investment, and their postures were tense, anticipatory.

I know these men. I like them. That's what this is all about.

A sense of calmness swept over Horse, and he shook the tension out of his hands with a raspy chuckle. "The why. That's the crux of it, ain't it? I've ridden two wheels all over a bunch of the lower forty-eight states. Rolled into places and took a sample of what they had to offer. None of it was to my taste. Not until I shot pool with a bunch of rough-talking bikers in a bar that felt more comfortable than the one I grew up in. Now?" He swept his hands to the sides, indicating the entirety of the group of men. "Now I've found something I want to be part of. Want to find my place in the ranks, see where I can be of use to the club. Don't matter the how, long as you don't turn me away. I don't know where I'd be without this, Blackie. Don't want to find out either."

Pride rolled off Blackie and he stared at Horse in a way that reminded him of the looks Medric had frequently aimed his direction.

"Now that, my brothers, that's a hella answer, wouldn't you say?" Choruses of "Hear, hear" and "Fuck yeah" rose around them until Blackie patted the air, gesturing for silence. "The officers here in Longview have already discussed what we'd do if this man put words to the want we could see burning in him. We're in favor, in case it wasn't already clear." Laughter came from the strangers' mouths, and Horse twisted his neck, scanning the group again. "Now, Freed Riders is my fuckin' club and you all know it, but I try to run things so we all get along. By now the tale surrounding the night Horse had his trial by fire has probably made the rounds, and if you haven't heard the story yet, get with one of us and we'll educate you. What I'm going to do is skip right across something that's been in place for a decade, placed there by my insistence. I didn't want men dragging in and rolling up the ranks without a chance to test and try them. Like I said, if you've heard the story, you know this one has already grappled with and bested one of the greatest challenges we could have ever thrown his direction. I propose that for Mother, this man becomes a voting member today. We'll skip the prospect period entirely."

A few murmurs sounded along the fringes of the group and Blackie grinned, shaking his head in a slow side-to-side arc.

"I hear you. I do. Man's been a hangaround but already granted considerable member status, even assigning himself prospect grunt work. He sees something needs doing, he's all over it without even a request. Leading by example, and I tell you now that it's forced the official prospects to up their game to stay ahead of him and get noticed. About right, if you ask me. Prospects should work for that vote, and I might have been slacking on that education. Thing is, with how Horse has been, we haven't had any disciplinary incidents with a prospect. Not one." He laughed. "Uncommon crop, and none of my doing. Cultivated and tended by someone not even under my patch."

"I already told you, but he's got my vote." Duane stepped up beside Blackie. "You might not admit it, but you've been sponsoring him since day one. Dude didn't have a chance to do anything but excel."

"My vote too." Oaky spoke up from where he stood farther around the circle of men. "Respectful, trustworthy, quick on the uptake, and a hella fighter. Be good to have him officially on our side."

"In light of the vote we already had, we don't need to hear from anyone else here in Longview. Any other chapters, you got questions? Happy to entertain them for a short time."

Horse liked how Blackie had put parameters around the process and knowing it wouldn't run all night helped even more with his nerves. The high praise from the men he'd come to know and like made a difference too. He felt himself standing taller, shoulders shoved back just a fraction of an inch more.

"Nothing from Houston." A dark-haired man angled towards Blackie. "If I can't trust your instincts, then we've got different issues."

"Noted, JD. Appreciated." Blackie tipped his head in acknowledgment. "Good to see you, brother. How's Houston treatin' you?"

"Not bad. Not bad. Still, it's good to be back at Mother, my friend."

"Always better to be at Mother, brother." Blackie turned to look at another man close by. "Denver, what does Marshall chapter think?"

"I trust you. Same thing JD said, brother. I don't have a single problem with what you're proposing. Old school, man. Dig it." The man hooked a thumb in his belt as he nodded, looking casual and harmless. That façade was put to the lie by the number of weapons Horse could see scattered about his person.

"Done." Blackie clapped once and held a hand towards Duane. Horse watched as a black leather vest transferred hands. "Been plannin' on this for a while, brother. Mind droppin' your vest? Duane promises what he picked out will fit. Already had one of the girls do your sewin', this time around. We change up any plates at some point, that'll be on you."

Horse skinned out of his plain vest without hesitation, trading it for the one Blackie held. True to secondhand promise, it fit like a glove, settling into place as if he'd always worn it. Glancing up at the men around him, he immediately took it off again and turned it in his hands, tracing the edges of the sewn fabric patches. A feathery wheel in a center circle, the name of the club in an arc above the emblem, and below was a matching lower arc simply stating Mother. Lifting his chin, he locked gazes with Blackie as he again shoved shaking arms through the holes, letting the black leather fall down his back and sides.

Hand outstretched, Blackie took hold when Horse's palm met his and yanked him close. Meaty fingers grinding down on his had him wincing, as did the solid pounding against his ribs and backbone.

The "Brother" muttered in his ear made it all worth it. *Worth everything.*

Blackie stepped back and leveled a finger at his chest, bringing Horse's attention to the front of the vest. *Gift horse.* The not-unwelcome thought rolled through his head as he took in the white stitching spelling out his road name. *Horse.*

"Welcome, man." Duane gripped his arm and spun Horse in a half circle, pulling him into a one-armed clinch similar to Blackie's, if less painful. "About fucking time, brother." That was followed by a personal greeting from every man in the back yard. The genuine emotion was enough to take his knees out from under him. None of them had dissented, and each welcome was heartfelt.

The single thought that rolled through his head the rest of the night was comforting, each time it surfaced.

I'm home.

More compliments were directed his way when they returned to the bar. Members of the community were always supportive of the club, but it was a surprise that they kept track of things like prospects and hangarounds. He heard Blackie answer multiple questions about bypassing the standard process. For all the citizens, folks not in the life, Blackie did it graciously, his tone kind.

Then Dale spoke up, emboldened either with liquid courage or from hearing the bar's patrons as they questioned Blackie.

That little sortie went entirely differently.

"It ain't fair" was all Horse heard before Blackie swarmed the man, taking him backwards three strides until his back hit the wall with a thud, Blackie's hand around the man's throat. "The hell?"

"You questioning your president, *brother*?"

Stillness gripped those closest, spreading in leaps and fits to the crowd nearby, conversations falling away as all focus came to Blackie. He nearly covered the smaller man, shifting so his arm was pressed tight across his chest to hold Dale into place.

"No, but—"

"Ain't no butts gonna sit a motherfuckin' bike with my goddamned patch on it if they don't mind their mouths. Your mouth? Fuck, man. Mouth's writin' checks right here and now, Dale. You think you can cash that shit? Here? Against me?" Blackie stepped back and stood, watching Dale suck in heaving breaths. "It's shit like this that keeps extendin' the time I need to study you before I gift you with a patch. Shit like this makes me want to bounce you back to hangaround, pull that prospect vest off your back."

Dale's arms folded across his chest protectively, leather clutched tight in his fists. "Please, Blackie—"

"President. Goin' forwards, you call me by my station, my office, my role. Not my name. Maybe it'll remind you what I am before you mouth your 'ain't fair' shit my direction." Blackie swung half around, and Horse realized he wasn't giving Dale his back.

No trust there, not anymore.

"Anyone else want to say anything to me, just fuckin' don't. I ain't in the mood to entertain any kind of shit about any-fucking-thing now. Dale's mouth just cost you any petition-time you might have been workin' up to. Make sure everyone gets the message or I'll be bustin' more than a prospect down the ranks."

Inclining his head towards the back of the bar, Blackie's sudden grip on Horse's shoulder pulled him off balance so he had to double-time steps to keep his feet underneath him. The crowd faded away from the path Blackie set, attention turning slowly back to their own conversations.

"And that shit is why I value men like you so highly." Blackie pulled them both to a stop, his chest heaving. Lips pressed into a hard, bloodless line. The corners arched down, his grimace encompassing the whole of his features as his brows furrowed, the lines at the corners of his eyes bunching. "Because of shitheads like that who give lip service to the creed. Man shoulda been happy the club had gained a solid member today. Instead, he was caught up in his fuckin' me-me-me shit so he couldn't see the benefits."

"Think he'll give me trouble?" Horse remembered back to the first night he'd spent in the clubhouse. "Take his frustration out on my bike or something?"

"Naw." Duane replaced Blackie's hold on Horse with his own, leaning half his bodyweight against Horse's back. Mouth next to Horse's ear, he rested his chin on the broad width of shoulder covered in brand-new black leather. "I don't think Dale's got a death wish. He's like Blackie said, focused on what he wants and not seein' the whole picture yet. I'll talk to him and make sure he understands you did your hangaround time that first night playin' pool, and then did your prospect period in the parking lot that same night. You've been a fuckin' member since then, sleepin' on the second floor, workin' the bar, givin' service to the club every single day. He just didn't catch the same clue the rest of us had."

At a loss for words, Horse simply nodded.

"Blackie, we playin' pool or what?" JD called from the other side of the tables. Rolling a stick across the green felt, he made a satisfied sound as he picked it up. "Ready for an asswhuppin', old man?"

"You need a reminder of who I am too?" Blackie's grin transformed his face and genuine amusement radiated from him as he visibly put the altercation behind him. "Cuz I am not the one gettin' whupped, brother."

"What happens to Dale now?" Horse turned to Duane who'd stopped his imitation of a human blanket and had moved up beside Horse.

"Nothing if he sticks to the script. Prospects don't get a vote in anything for a reason. They keep that patch until their sponsor petitions the club to vote on membership. Unless he does something stupid, like epically stupid, Blackie won't take it from him."

"Who's his sponsor?" *That should be something I already know, shouldn't it?* The idea he'd been inattentive grated on him.

"You're lookin' at him." Duane sighed. "He's my brother's brother-in-law and the baby in his wife's family. Was bound and determined to hangaround the club before the motherfucker found out who I was. After? He was fuckin' relentless." Mouth slack, Duane tipped his head back to stare at the ceiling with a low groan. "Gawd, the hours of bullshit I've had to endure since then." Grinning, he angled his head back to the main entrance. "And there he stands. My prospect. Family sucks, brother."

Horse grimaced. "Sometimes they really do. Sorry for your luck." That earned Horse a chuckle as Duane walked over to where the chapter presidents were clustered, arguing about teams for pool.

Once the other chapter members had left the next morning to go home, the clubhouse had settled back into their normal routines.

As introductions to being a member of the FRMC, that night didn't suck. Three weeks past his patch day, life had returned to a new version of normal. Now, instead of vacating the clubhouse when the members needed to talk about business going on, Horse found himself drawn into the middle of those conversations, his opinion legitimate and valued in a way he'd never had before. That sense of belonging, of a found kind of family, had only grown stronger, and he could nearly see the ties he had to these men snapping into place.

Dale had been the picture-perfect prospect, referring to Horse only as patchholder, same as he'd kept to calling Blackie President, as demanded. And it didn't look like Blackie would be letting up on those instructions any time soon. It wasn't that Blackie went out of his way to remind the man of his infraction, but tapping a finger against his president officer plate when Dale was talking to him was an unsubtle reinforcement of his desires.

Tonight they were in the backyard with a blaze burning brightly in the firepit, coolers of beer near to hand. It was a members-only event, no hangarounds. Prospects were allowed in their service roles, so Dale and Seth, a newly minted prospect as of last weekend, were hustling between the grill and coolers, answering every member's request.

"How long you gonna hold his feet to the fire?" From Duane's question, Horse wasn't the only one paying attention.

"I'll admit, he's doin' real good lately." Blackie traced the lip of his beer bottle with the tip of one thumb. "Man's stayed pissed, though. Oh, I can see he's got it pushed down, tamping it back best he can, but he's pissed, my brother. Righteous in his mind, but pissed all to hell and back."

Exhaling a heavy sigh, Blackie said, "Don't think he's gonna cut it. Know that'll fuck with you because he's family, but that's my opinion."

"Not going to be a member?" Dale stood a few feet away from where Blackie sat, the look on his face incredulous. The flickering fire cast light and shadows across his features, giving him a sinister expression. "You're talkin' about me. Because Duane's brother's married to my sister, which means I'm the family that'll make his life harder. You're going to cut me."

"Yeap. Planning on it. Thought I'd do it quietly in my office this week, so you didn't have to face folks if you didn't want to." Blackie never dropped his head and he didn't try to backtrack anything he'd just said. His willingness to confront uncomfortable conversations head-on once more raised his estimation in Horse's thinking.

"Why?" Dale didn't sound angry, more stunned, but Horse still braced himself for potential violence. He knew if they were to try and take his patch, he'd fight for it, wouldn't hand it over willingly. It only stood to reason Dale would be the same.

"Because you're trying to fit this life into what you want." Blackie half turned in his chair, throwing one elbow around the back. "Means it'll be work for you. Every single day, this life will be work. Then, one day in the not-too-far future, a resentment will begin to build inside you. That could come out as you deciding to pack up stakes and leave. Or—" With a writhing twist, Blackie shoved to his feet. "—that could come out as resentment against the club, or me. I've seen it before, Dale. Plenty of times. Hell, you've seen the end result with how things fell out with Roscoe."

"And that's why you haven't patched me? You think I'm like your brother? You think I'd threaten you?"

"Not just yet. But man, a body can tell the life isn't in your heart. It's not what drives you forwards. Isn't the first thing you think about in the morning and the last thing you consider as you drift off to sleep. It's work and gets in the way of other things you want. I'd say I'm doing you a kindness, but I know that won't ever be how you see it." Arms lax at his sides, hands relaxed, Blackie faced Dale. "Come to me in the morning and we'll sort things out."

"I live here. I live for the club." The cracking pain Dale's voice was heart-wrenching and Horse had to force himself not to look away, a sense he needed to witness this rolling through his veins.

"I'll help you get set up. This is no fault of yours. You're just not made for the life."

"And he is?" Dale flung out a hand, finger pointed directly at Horse.

"Yeah. Hell yeah. Horse was born to it, just had to find his way home." Not turning his attention away from Dale, Blackie continued, "Some men fit the life better than others. Some are made for it. And some work at it, have to keep working at it the entire time they're breathing. There's no rest for those men. It's such a chore, a burden, it'll break their backs. Those men can take down clubs, kill the brotherhood for the rest of the members. I'll point you to Roscoe again, because he wanted the life but without the work, which means his attempts were filled with struggle and pain. I don't want that for you. Hell, if you give it a single thought, you'll realize you don't want that for you either. It's not all Easy Rider, Hollywood shit."

"I've seen things. Hell, I've *helped* with things you don't want anyone to know about."

Silence dropped into the backyard like a suffocating blanket. The only sound or movement was that of the flames, consuming the fuel that fed the fire.

It took a few seconds, but Dale finally realized what he'd just done.

"I didn't—that wasn't me threatening the club."

"Oh yeah, I think it was." Duane rose and joined the conversation for the first time. "That sounded like blackmail, and that shit's not happenin' on my watch."

"No, I swear." Dale took a step backwards just as a form materialized behind him. The next retreating step was brought up short as he ran into Oaky. "What's goin' on?"

"Man, you cannot be that stupid. Or maybe you fuckin' are." Duane looked to Blackie. "Shotcaller, call the shot."

"I vote we cut him. I'd like to believe he's got enough respect to mind his tongue." Blackie glanced at Horse, then Duane. "That's what I'd like to think, anyway."

Duane opened and closed his mouth, then his head dropped forwards, side of his hand scrubbing along the edge of his scruffy jaw. It had grown so quiet in the backyard, Horse could hear every raspy noise and the man's heavy intake of breath after breath.

Someone needed to break the silence, and Horse decided it should be him. "First night I spent in the clubhouse, he disrespected known rules to come to the second floor and attempt to intimidate me. Backed down immediately, and never gave another lick of trouble my way." Horse pushed to his feet and took a step forward. "I think he's noise and air, and no actions to back it up. I vote to cut the patch off his back."

His words seemed to tip the balance, and the rest of the members stepped up and voted the same. Duane turned to look at Horse and quietly mouthed, "Thank you," before he moved to Dale and held out a hand. The "give me your vest" was spoken with solid assurance his instructions would be followed. Unlike the actions Horse knew he'd have done if presented with the same demand, Dale complied. "Go to your room in the clubhouse and don't come back out until someone comes for you tomorrow. That means if you need to piss or take a shit, you do it on your way." He whistled and another prospect named Littleton trotted up. "Little, follow and stay next to his door until you're relieved, yeah?"

The two men exited the backyard and Horse sighed as the atmosphere lifted slightly. It didn't regain the ease and comfort from before, but at least there wasn't the level of tension that had existed moments before. He reclaimed his seat, watching as the other men slowly did the same.

"I fuckin' hate that shit." The words exploded from Blackie alongside a frustrated sigh. "Why can't people live up to their own expectations? Forget mine. It's their own shit that always trips 'em up."

"Question for the ages, brother." Duane settled on the ground on the other side of Blackie, not even dragging a chair over. "I shoulda seen it coming. I mean, I saw something, we all did. I just didn't know it'd come to this."

"Will he make trouble for the club?" Horse stared at the flames, going back over every interaction with Dale. "He's been pissed off at me just being here since that first night."

"He and Roscoe were friends."

Duane made a noise of surprise. "No fuckin' way?"

"Yeah. Back in early high school or late junior high. They hung together for a year or so." Blackie's words came slowly, not as if he were considering his speech, but like he was remembering. "I didn't remember it until Dale reminded me after I did the final ban."

Shocked, words burst from Horse, "You kicked Roscoe to the curb, and he took the opportunity to remind you that he might have ties to the man? Fuckin' read a room, dickhead."

Horse turned to look at the two men, both staring into the flames as he had been.

"Yeah." Blackie let a breath out as a loud raspberry. "I shoulda booted him then. I'd seen it comin', just was thinkin' we'd invested so much fuckin' time and effort into the man." He growled. "Ahh, fuckin' hell. He's not a bad guy, just not right for the club, or the life."

"It's done now." Duane pushed off the ground and dusted his ass and thighs free of dirt. "I'm gettin' a bottle. Beer ain't cuttin' it for me, not tonight. Anyone want anything specific?"

Horse shook his head, then Blackie did the same. They didn't offer any words as Duane stalked away, each thud of his boot heels echoing solidly against the packed earth around the firepit.

"He's going to carry this for a while." Horse thought his observation was obvious, proved true when Blackie nodded. "I'll help him as I can."

"Tomorrow." Blackie lifted a hand and gestured the direction Duane had disappeared. "Tonight he's going to sink into sweet, sweet pussy and lose his mind." Several women appeared from the darkness. "I'd already called the sweetbottoms before all this shit started. I know the timing is fortuitous, but it's entirely unintentional." Blackie's camp chair rocked on two legs as he leaned closer. "Don't tell a soul though. Let 'em believe I've got the sight or whatever." Leaning back the other direction, he settled his chair onto four legs. "They won't come over this way, so if you're lookin' for company, you'll have to go huntin'."

"Why won't they come over here? You're the president. I'd expect they'd be hot to bag that title between their legs." That fit the behavior he'd seen so far of the women who hung around the group of men. A club member was preferred over prospect or hangaround, and bagging an officer was something the women would occasionally fight over.

"I'm still in mourning." One corner of Blackie's mouth drew down. "They know better than to bother me."

"You had someone die?" It was the first Horse had heard of a significant other's death. "Your old lady?"

"Not dead, which means there's hope, however slim." Blackie went to take a drink from an obviously empty beer. "Goddammit." He crumpled the can with hard, angry gestures. "I don't want to talk about that tonight. Had enough bullshit happen on what was intended to just be a good night. Nothing to celebrate, nothin' to grieve over. Just a night to grow our brotherhood and Dale had to go and turn it to shit. Dillweed to the end." He pushed up from the chair. "I'm goin' to bed, brother."

Horse watched as his friend stalked away, his boot heels hitting harder than Duane's as he retreated into the darkness.

"Well shit."

"Want some company?" The lilting voice came from his right and he turned that direction to see a lithe young woman standing there. Wearing cutoff shorts that left little to the imagination, her crop top exposed the bottom curves of her breasts. "It's Horse, right? You looked lonely sittin' way over here by yourself." She stepped over his legs with exaggerated movements, the seam of the dissembled jeans riding tight against her crotch, pink flesh and dark curly hair on display. The hair on her head was blonde, tamed into a single-tail braid down the middle of her back. "Anyone sittin' here?" She gestured to the empty chair. "I'm Reena." Her extended hand turned into a tiny wave when he didn't reciprocate. Sitting delicately on the edge of the seat, she kept her body inclined towards him. "You're a quiet one."

"Not looking for company. You're wasting your time, Reena." He pointed across the flames to a grouping of chairs she'd evidently walked past to get to where he sat. "More receptive audience over that way."

"You've already got an old lady then? Story of my life." She tugged on the short hem of her top. "Sure you don't want a little tickle and a giggle? I won't tell."

"Not sure I owe you an explanation." He drained his beer and lifted it high, catching the eye of a prospect manning the cooler. "And I'd prefer it if you were to vacate that chair. Blackie went inside, but I'm going to hold it for him." She was up and out of the chair in an instant, eyes wide. "Thanks. Now go on. Sort yourself a lucky man for the night."

"I'm sorry. I didn't know." The words tripped over themselves as they fell from her lips. "I'll... Duane's always up for a good time. I'll see if I can find him. Thanks, Horse." Reena paused as the prospect approached. In a whisper, she asked, "Don't tell Blackie I was in his chair, please?"

"Sure thing." He swapped his empty for a full beer, leaned back in the chair, then stretched out his feet to the fire as he dismissed her. "Night."

He sat the rest of the evening like that, switching from beer to water after a couple more hours. As the fire died down, so did the party, members pairing off with girls or not, as suited them. Those who lived at the clubhouse disappeared earliest, leaving the married members who had homes to the drinks and music. He knew every face, every name, knew their families and kids and as he kept a vigil of sorts next to the slowly dying fire, he pulled the pleasure of that knowledge around him like a blanket.

It wasn't an epiphany because he'd already recognized this fact.

Still, knowing he'd found a family kept him warmer than the fire.

Realizing he was the final member still in the backyard, he directed one of the prospects to dump water from a cooler on the embers.

Then Horse went into the house, found his bed, and slept with a smile on his face.

***

"You don't understand." Blackie was fuming and all Horse could do was listen. "She's always been mine."

Today had been eye opening on many fronts.

First had been the eviction of Dale. The man must have expected a night's sleep to have mitigated his sentence, but Blackie had disabused him of that idea immediately when he'd found out the man hadn't even bothered to pack up his personal things.

The air had been blue with the anger of the club's founder and president. Horse had located an empty piece of wall next to Duane where they could both watch as Blackie removed the man with shirt by shirt thrown out the window. By the time Blackie had gotten to the drawer where the man kept his smalls, Dale's incredulity had turned to belief, and he was trying to stay ahead of Blackie's angry hands by tossing clothing into a hastily retrieved suitcase.

Last surprise had been that Dale left walking, using his two feet for locomotion rather than two wheels. Duane's mutter was quiet, but enlightening. "Bike was supposed to be a lease-to-own, but shoulda realized he wasn't a keeper when he didn't maintain his payments." Blackie had counted it in default and remanded the bike into Oaky's possession for now.

Then just as things had settled down, they'd heard the unmistakable rumble of a bike's exhaust out in front of the clubhouse.

Exiting the building Horse had expected to find Dale and whatever friends he could scrounge up on short notice, surprised when instead it had been a lone couple, man and woman riding double on a stately old Indian motorcycle.

Blackie had taken front of their group as he confronted them, and something—a thing he now knew was the woman's pregnant condition—had unraveled every bit of the big man's control. His diving strike to the rider's jaw had knocked him clean off the bike and half across the broad driveway. Then scarcely even two minutes later, Blackie had been inviting them both inside.

Peaches was the woman, Andy the man, and although their positions on the bike might have indicated otherwise, they weren't a couple at all. Peaches was the name no one had been willing to speak when Horse had asked about Blackie's single status. Given the advanced state of her pregnancy, Horse knew Blackie wasn't the father, unless he'd been sneaking out without making it clear to the club.

Horse wasn't the only one who'd listened at the doorway to the kitchen, only catching every other word but still enough to put the puzzle together. He'd have put money on Reena being the reason this Peaches had run off, the club whore either not knowing or not caring that Blackie had hooked his future to this woman who looked like sunlight made flesh.

After a quick glance around at the men also snooping, their expressions filled with unmistakable elation, Horse whispered to Duane, "This Peaches, she's important to Blackie?" Clear as the truth in the man's voice when he spoke to her, but Horse wanted to know more. "Think this is a chance for him to reel her back in?"

"Man better. He doesn't, that one in there will take care of her for himself. I'm thinking this little trip was to test Blackie's mettle, and not a small bit a chance to see if the smolder she had would leap back to flame. Blackie's proven himself in how he is with Peaches."

"And you'd have to be deaf to not hear how she feels." Horse stepped backwards. "Gonna give them the illusion of privacy, at least. Think it's too soon to have a prospect clean Dale's room?"

"Definitely not too soon." Duane turned with Horse and walked beside him back through the house. "All the current prospects got housing elsewhere, but would make a good guest lodging."

"On the main floor, too. That'll keep what happened with me from happening anywhere else."

Duane laughed so hard he bent double, hands propped on his knees as he tried to catch his breath. "You really—" Breath wheezed out of him and he shook his head. "Fucking hell. You really think you coppin' that room on the second floor was anything other than purpose-led from Blackie? You'd kept his blood brother from killing his ass while that fuckin' prospect stood around with a thumb up his ass. The room he'd been holding just in case his brother wised-up about what path was best." Swiping at his face with the backs of his hands, Duane cut himself off midgale of laughter. "Horse, I thought you were smart."

"Sometimes." He shook his head. "It's just hard to believe that things were ordained by Blackie back that far ago."

"You really think—know what, doesn't matter. You know now, and I suspect you've really known for a while. Regardless, you're patched and locked in now. Time to get your dominance in on things." Duane arched backwards, face to the ceiling as he yelled, "Prospect."

Running feet from two different directions preceded the men who converged on Duane's position. Horse shook his head again.

"This patchholder has a job for you. Do it to his specifications, and not a whit less. He won't have to tell me how it was done, because you'll do it yourselves, hear me?" Duane tracked the movement of the two men's heads. "Now git, and get busy."

Horse sauntered away with complete confidence he'd be followed. Not because Duane told the men to do his bidding, but because they knew him and trusted him.

Leadin's better and easier when it's from a place of belief than fear.

***

Horse

Hammering against his door woke Horse with a start.

Blackie bellowed, "Get a fuckin' car ready."

He looked at his phone, then stared at the still closed door in confusion. What could Blackie be waking the house up at three in the morning for— *Oh!*

Less than five minutes later, he had the van backed up to the front door and was opposite Blackie as they helped a laboring Peaches down the stairs. Duane followed with a bag in hand, slipping into the driver seat as Horse and Blackie settled Peaches in the back. They took off as soon as all the doors were closed, Duane making good time on the nearly empty city streets.

"Want me to make any calls, pretty lady?" Duane's question was soft and timed between contractions. "Your daddy?"

"We'll call him after it's all done and dusted," Peaches responded, pulling in a hard breath as the van's suspension bounced them into the hospital's driveway. "I'm just ready to get this little one into the world."

"Good enough, good enough." Duane was grinning as he parked in front of the emergency entrance doors. "Let's get you inside so you can do that thing."

From the ER up to the obstetrics unit, Blackie kept quiet, determinedly attached to Peaches by their clasped hands. When the nurse was ready to start an intravenous needle, she gave the big man one look and moved to Peaches' other arm without complaint.

"Did you do classes for the birth?" Horse knew from shows on television that those things existed. "What happens next?"

"I'm not really sure. I didn't think I'd need any help. Was planning on doing all of this by myself." Peaches didn't glance at him as she answered, her gaze turned inward. "Another one is coming, Blackie."

"You've got this, baby girl. Tough and strong don't even begin to describe what you are. You've got this." Blackie shifted so he could look at her face. "You do whatever you need to do. I'll be right here with you. Ain't leavin' for nothing."

The door opened and a man wearing a white coat walked in. With a nod at the nurse, he took a look at Peaches and smiled. "In the thick of it, I see." Approaching the bed, he introduced himself. "I'm Dr. Abraham. I'm just going to check things out down here. When that contraction eases off, why don't you tell me about the pregnancy? Has it been tough or easy? Do you have a regular OB?" He flipped the sheet up from the bottom of the bed, exposing Peaches' feet. "Gentlemen, if you could step outside, please?"

"I ain't goin' nowhere, asshole."

Horse and Duane had moved immediately but stopped in uncertainty at Blackie's words.

"Not you, sir. Not unless Charlotte doesn't want you in the room for these exams. My hope is you can remain and support her like you already are."

"Good thing, because I ain't leavin'." Blackie gestured towards the door with the top of his head. "You guys get the fuck out of Dodge, though. No way you're seein' my woman's coochie." As the door closed behind them, Horse heard, "And her name might be Charlotte, but she's Lottie or Peaches."

Horse looked at Duane and they both broke up laughing. "Coochie," Horse got out between guffaws. "Prez called it a coochie."

"Peaches is a coochie momma now." Duane swiped a hand down his face. "Ahh, man. I needed that. I've never been around a birthing woman before. Made me nervous as shit, brother."

Still laughing, Horse looked up and down the hallway. He walked to where a few chairs were stacked near what looked like a waiting room and grabbed two, bringing them back so he and Duane could sit on either side of Peaches' door.

"I understand these things can take time. I figure we should get comfy as we can." He settled into the chair, leaning back and stretching his legs out. "You should probably go move the van before it gets towed."

Duane jumped up from the seat he'd taken. "Aw, fuck, you would think I'd remember something like that. I'll be right back."

The two men bantered quietly as the hours slipped by, the nurses and doctor not paying them any mind. At odd intervals Horse would catch a word or two from Blackie, the changing tone of his voice indicative if he were speaking to Peaches or questioning one of the medical personnel.

Slouched sideways in the chair, Duane had dozed off before the traffic to Peaches' room picked up to a steady stream. Horse stood and held the door for a nurse wheeling a tiny bed. He chanced a glance inside.

Blackie stood beside Peaches, much as he had before, only now he wore a backwards hospital gown, the fabric gaping wide to highlight the club's patch riding on his back. He was leaned down, mouth near Peaches' ear, talking softly while her eyes stayed closed in concentration.

A nurse laughed brightly. "Nearly time, little mother. Don't push yet."

Horse let the door settle into its frame and turned, reclaiming his seat. He grinned at a still-snoring Duane, but allowed the man to sleep a while yet.

Just under an hour later, he kicked Duane's chair leg, startling him awake. Behind them, the robust cry of a newborn sounded strongly through the closed door.

"They okay?" Duane's voice was rusty, crackling with sleep.

"I'm taking the lack of frantic activity as a good sign." He indicated the door with a head tilt. "There's like ten of 'em in there, but nobody's been runnin'." He stretched out his legs, shifting weight to the other hip. "Everything's gonna be okay. Blackie needs this."

"That he does. Never seen a man as gone on his woman as he is." Duane tipped his head back, aiming a wide yawn at the ceiling. "Gotta say, I don't hate it. It's good to see."

They both swung to their feet when the door opened abruptly. Horse took in the proud, relieved expression on Blackie's face before turning his attention to the pink-wrapped bundle in his arms.

"Miranda … Randi wanted to say howdy before I have to run her down to the nursery." Blackie's eyes never lifted from where they were focused on the little girl's face. "She's good. Peaches is good. They're both perfect."

"Hey, Randi." Horse knew his voice was gruff, filled with emotion. From the look on Blackie's face, he wouldn't be catching any ribbing for being soft in this moment. "Little precious girl. Look at you. I'm Uncle Horse."

"Honorary Uncle Duane over here, sweetheart. You're gorgeous, aren't you." Duane stood shoulder to shoulder with Horse. "She's so teeny, Blackie. Everyone okay?"

"Yeah, they're both absolutely perfect." Blackie never looked up, eyes locked on the newborn. "Peaches did great. She's a real trooper. Randi was a little stubborn but listened to her momma in the end."

"Mr. Langdon, we need to get the little one down to the nursery." A nurse appeared at Blackie's elbow. "We've got the bassinette ready."

"You said I could carry her." Blackie didn't turn. "I'm carrying her. It's just down the hall. One of you boys come with me. One of you stay here."

Horse glanced at Duane who pointed towards his own chair. They nodded in unison and Horse fell into step with Blackie as they moved along the wide corridor. Blackie's steps were sure and certain, but Horse felt a need to steer him since the man simply wasn't willing to look away from his daughter's face. Made Horse grin to see how he'd fallen already.

"She's got your number. Only minutes old and has you wrapped around her tiny, little finger."

"Hell yeah." Blackie's easy acceptance came with a widening of his smile. "Turn the world on end for this girl."

"Peaches did good?"

"My woman's a fuckin' rock. She took care of business, didn't let anything get in her way. Doc's doing his thing right now, then she'll go to a regular room. By then, they should be done measuring Randi and we'll all be together."

"When that happens, I'll head back to the clubhouse, finish putting the crib together and shit. Gonna be different, having a nursery there. But everyone will adapt."

"Yeah, do the crib thing, but you should know that me and Peaches looked at a house over the weekend. East of town, just off Highway 80. It's a good size place, got some land to it. Already decided that while the club is family, kids need to grow up with some dirt under their feet. Older rancher nearby might sell me another plot, would add enough to it for pretty much anything we want." Blackie angled through a door a nurse held open and gently placed the infant on a wide table she indicated. He kept both hands on the baby, bracketing her tiny body. "Right now, though, I'm going to stay here with my eye on my girl. I appreciate you takin' care of things at the clubhouse, Horse. Always looking out for your brothers. Wouldn't expect anything less."

"Whatever's needed, you know how I feel, brother." Horse backed through the door, into the hallway. "We'll see you when you get home. I'm gonna go tell Peaches I'm proud of her."

"You do that, brother." Blackie's muttered response came while he watched the nurse like a hawk. "I'm gonna stay riiiiight here."

Congratulations delivered, Horse and Duane waited in the hallway until they saw Blackie striding along, carefully pushing a baby bed on wheels in front of him. When he caught sight of them his brow furrowed, and with his voice pitched low, he called, "What's wrong?"

"Nothing, brother. Your woman was exhausted but trying to stay awake to talk, so we stepped out here to let her sleep if she could. Nothing's wrong."

"Jesus. I've been so wound up the whole time." Blackie shook his head. "Not just today, but since she came back to me. Worried something would drop out of the sky and splat me like a coyote. This good shit? Not my normal kind of luck."

"Looks like your luck's changed." Horse gripped Blackie's shoulder and pulled him in to pound one fist against his back. "Lucky, lucky man. We're going back to the clubhouse, which leaves you without a ride. Call one of us when you need, and we'll come get you." He stepped back. "Lucky, lucky man."

Horse and Duane were quiet on the short drive back to the clubhouse. It was only as they were pulling into the back driveway that Horse roused himself enough to speak.

"Blackie's buyin' a place out east of town a bit, not Hallsville, but close. Said it's got some acreage with it, give him and the family a chance to spread out."

"Not a bad idea." Duane parked the van, setting the brake. "Kids and clubhouses don't work long term. Can you imagine the grousing if the baby's still squalling for a two o'clock feeding a month down the road? Blackie's a smart man to look into the future like that."

"Yeah. I get it. I get it's a good idea." Horse laughed as he swung out of the van. "I just don't like change much."

Chapter Five
Glenna

Seated at the kitchen table, Glenna kept an ear open for anything coming from the front room. That's where Reggie, a neighbor and frequent visitor, was waiting while the traveling home nurse evaluated Pendleton's condition. Something Glenna didn't need a degree to know was in a steep decline. Since the last health care visit a week ago, Penn had gone from eating at the table with her for meals to not being able to get himself out of bed to go to the washroom. She'd managed things so far, but only just.

"Glenna?" The man's voice was pitched soft and low, which told Glenna that Penn was sleeping, something he seemed to do more and more. "I'd like to talk to you for a few minutes."

Waving him into the room as she pushed away from the table, Glenna gave him her back as she busied herself at the coffeemaker, not bothering to keep her activities quiet. She knew from experience that it took more than a little rattling dishes and cabinet slamming to wake Penn these days. Lord knew she'd tried, feeling guilty about it the whole time but still hoping and praying for a few extra minutes with Penn.

"Talk. I can listen and do this." She didn't look over her shoulder, concentrating instead on the next step of the process, making her movements precise and controlled. That's how she did everything these days. Didn't matter if it was out working the cattle, folding laundry, or helping her husband onto the bedpan. Precise and controlled allowed her to keep a muzzle on the anger raging inside her head, the pain that swallowed each breath and strangled her deaf and dumb.

"According to the nurse, we're past time to bring hospice in." Wood sliding across the floor told her he'd taken a seat at the table. "They've been able to keep him mostly comfortable, but hospice has different rules that she said we can work to Penn's advantage."

"Hospice?" The whispered word itched like poison ivy as it passed her lips, a horrid vibration that left painful tingles behind. Hospice would be acknowledging this was the end, admitting that there wasn't anything left to fight with or for. *I don't want them taking him out of here.*

"Yes, ma'am."

At that, she shot a glare over her shoulder to see he'd used that word to get a rise out of her. "Stop it, Cooter. Don't ma'am me."

"Nobody calls me Cooter anymore." Reggie "Cooter" Arnold chuckled dryly and gave her a tiny uptick at the corners of his mouth. "But I needed to make sure you were listening."

"All I've done now for a year is listen." With the coffeemaker gurgling happily, she couldn't pretend she was still working on anything. Turning to face him fully, Glenna let him see the anguish that rode her hard every day. "Caught late. No symptoms until the pain hit him. No treatment. Hell, they opened him up six months ago and didn't do anything except close the incision. 'Nothing to do, Mrs. Richeson.' That's what they told me, still in their paper slippers. A five-hour surgery over in twenty minutes. All I can do is listen to Penn, to the doctors, to the lawyers." Even though she was his wife, the lawyer had urged them to set up various power of attorney documents, and had Penn sell her his half of their place for a couple of hundred dollars so the medical debt wouldn't steal everything away. They'd recommended a divorce, but Glenna had put her foot down on that one. "They want to call hospice in. What will they do for him that the nurses can't?"

"They can be here round the clock. A large part of what they do is focused on the patient, but they also are here for the caregiver, because nothing about this whole shitty thing is easy." He shifted in the seat and pulled a folded sheaf of papers from his back pocket. *Had them prepared even before they got here today.* "I've got some information, and I had the nurse make a preliminary call to the local coordinator. They've got standby staff ready to start today and can guarantee you we won't get any pushback from insurance on this. Also, hospice at home is a damn sight cheaper than in-facility, and I know being away from the ranch is not what you or Penn want."

"He can stay here?" Locking her elbows with hands flat on the countertop behind her, Glenna covered the sudden weakness wobbling through her knees. "In our home?"

"You've made a more than passable nursing room in there. Plenty of room for what's needed. A lot of the machines can go back to the pharmacy, when you're ready. The folks from hospice will be able to help with all of that." Reggie paused and blew out a breath. "I can help with the outside work. Me and family. My pa and brothers would be happy to do whatever they can. Pa already called me twice today to see if I'd talked you into letting him help. Since selling his place, he's been angry as a rank bull penned for no good reason. You'd be doing Ma a service, promise. And me, if it'll keep him off my ranch for even a handful of days."

"I don't have anywhere for them to stay." Glenna fought to keep her chin from bumping as her voice quavered. *I will not cry. Not now. Not for this.* "It's always just been me and Penn out here, so I don't have a bunkhouse or anything. Not like the big outfits."

"Like I said, Pa's ready. Ma told me he's already got the travel trailer hooked to the pickup, ready to roll. You'd just need to tell them what to do. The boys—my brothers and their oldests—they'll all take turns with him, so it doesn't hit any of them too hard."

For some reason, admitting she needed help with the ranch was harder than saying yes to hospice.

Reality hurt, but in the end, Glenna approved both proposals. Before the sun had set, a camper was parked up next to the big barn and already had a summer kitchen set up next to it. Inside the house, the local coordinator had shown up with the two care providers who'd be working with Penn, ensuring Glenna had a chance to at least meet both of them. The generous gesture had helped because hearing the two nurses echo Cooter's words and watching them nod as the organizer informed about the process worked to settle something in Glenna's gut.

Penn had woken twice, confused at first, but once he'd laid eyes on Glenna, he'd been uncaring about anything else around him. It soothed both of them, so she'd sat with him for hours. Talking quietly about nothing in particular as she traced his fingers with her own, she hadn't paid attention to the daylight seeping away outside, not until it was gone and past dark.

Without asking permission, she stretched out next to Penn in the narrow hospital bed and wrapped his arm around her as she watched his face. Close like that, when the pain had pulled him awake the next time there'd been no confusion or fear, just the expression she'd always taken for granted—love. Nothing but love in his eyes as they lay together.

Midnight came with the clock in the hallway chiming the hour and Glenna stirred, easing off the bed and stretching until her back popped. She dragged a chair close and stared down at Penn as the gloomy lighting striped his face with shadows, making him look far older than he was. Even knowing that much was an illusion, Glenna couldn't ignore the toll the disease had already taken on him. Skin slack from weight loss, the hair at his widow's peaks had receded another half an inch, and the flesh of his hands and arms were mottled with bruises from injections, blood tests, and IVs. He slept quietly and Glenna didn't move, keeping her quiet watch for hours.

Noise behind her wasn't important enough to take her eyes off Penn, so she waited for whoever it was to speak.

"Mrs. Richeson." The voice was deep and rough, and Glenna nodded in recognition of Cooter's father.

"Mr. Arnold, I appreciate what you're doing for me and Penn." The sheets rustled as Penn's legs moved restlessly and Glenna stretched out her hand and smoothed the fabric down his chest. "We appreciate it."

"It's nothing more than neighbors should do in times of need."

Glenna glanced over her shoulder, seeing the older man still paused in the doorway to the kitchen. "Not a lot of folks would do it, though." Penn's heart thudded reassuringly underneath her palm, and she turned to stare back down at him. "'In times of need.' That says so much, doesn't it, Mr. Arnold? Thank you."

"Me and my boys will be up and at it daily, get the herd worked into the paddocks. Notes have them needing vaccinations and drenching, so we'll handle it all, Mrs. Richeson." Tension in his voice made Glenna wonder if he expected her to argue. *He'll wait forever for that right now.* "Already got the vet lined up."

"I know we're behind in the normal upkeep." If she weren't standing next to the hospital bed holding her dying husband, Glenna might have dug up some remorse for the cattle that had been left to languish in the pastures. She'd even found a home for the few remaining chickens. Anything not Penn felt like just too much. "I kept up with feeding and watched the calving close this year, but there just hasn't been time for much else."

"Ain't a single thing to apologize for, Mrs. Richeson."

"Please, call me Glenna. I've known you and your wife since Cooter and I were kids, and I've eaten dinner at your kitchen table more than once. Call me Glenna."

Leather scuffed across the floor and a hand settled on her shoulder, fingers digging in just right to soothe. Solid and reassuring, Mr. Arnold said more in that single touch than she'd heard from anyone over the past year.

"Death comes for all of us sooner or later, Glenna. Anything I can do to help ease this for you, my boys and I are ready. Give you the time you need with Penn. Give you as much time as he's got left. We'll take care of it all. Nothing to worry about, and nothing to thank me for." He gave her shoulder a squeeze, then patted the center of her back. "You do what's needed in here, and we'll do the same out there."

A minute later, she heard him speak to the hospice nurse, then the kitchen door closed behind him, leaving Glenna with Penn.

Palm flattened on his chest, Glenna gazed at Penn's face as he rested, mapping every change in his expression. No fear or pain, but he seemed filled with a profound exhaustion, something that drew his brows together and caused his shoulders to hunch.

Glenna crawled back into the bed alongside Pen, arranging their limbs so they tangled comfortably.

"Do you remember the day of the twister?" Her whisper wouldn't carry past his ears, and she kept it soft as she started another story. "Sky dark and rolling black clouds, and you were determined to finish that last section of fence. Do you remember? I rolled up on the four-wheeler and you wanted to cuss me out so bad, I could see it on your face. 'Glenna, why aren't you in the storm cellar?' And my answer was enough to take the wind out of your sails. 'Because if you're out here, this is where I belong too.' We finished the fence, and you followed me in your truck, honking and waving all the way back as if I didn't see that rope dangling from the clouds just like you did. We got into the cellar just in time, because that twister got close enough to toss the well shed around, breaking it up into kindling. You kept asking me why. Holding me close, us listening to the storm overhead, and you asking 'why, Glenna, why?' And I never changed my answer. I won't now either. Where you are is where I'm supposed to be, Penn. So you stay here with me, you hear me? Stay with me."

Chapter Six

Horse

"Hey, boss." Horse answered the phone, holding up a single finger to Devil, the Houston member he'd been talking to. Didn't matter what he was doing, if Blackie called, Horse would always pick up. In the months since becoming a member, he'd been kicked up the food chain and become the home chapter's fixer, so it wouldn't do to miss news on a potential problem. "What's up?"

"Andy... Slate, needs our help." Anger was held on a taut leash in Blackie's voice, the emotion so fraught with need it snapped Horse's spine straight. "Rebel Wayfarers have a few folks there in Houston at the show, and they've found themselves in possession of a package needing delivery."

"Anywhere, anytime. Tell me where to go. RWMC are good allies." Angling his head, he focused on the words in his ear. The ones spoken, and the silent message, arguably more important. *A package is a person.*

"I'll let JD know what's up." *Good.* That took the responsibility off Horse trying to give orders to a chapter president when he was a lower officer, albeit from Mother. "Houston has a van. Take Turk and Angry Mike with you." Blackie rattled off directions that had Horse gesturing at Devil for a pen and paper. "Meet up with Slate, make nice with the visitors, and pick up what they've got boxed and ready to go. Boys down there in Houston should know the kind of receiving area that's needed."

Horse repeated the instructions back to Blackie, the single grunted response confirmation he'd remembered everything. Pushing down any misgivings he had, Horse shoved a pair of sunglasses onto his face and gritted, "You got it, boss. We're on it."

Hours later, he was poised on the edge of a bench in the back of a van looking down at a man marked for death. They'd left the highway behind a while ago, and then abandoned the county roads for private ones bisecting pastureland. After crossing yet another cattleguard, the vehicle bumping and jolting, he told Turk, "Looks as good a place as any."

Three of them, him, Turk, and a big man called Angry Mike, had picked up the bull rider outside Houston, and after their last similar run, it should have been Angry Mike's turn to ride with Turk. The two of them had a conversation while Horse was in the bathroom at a truck stop, and before he knew what had changed, they were dropping Angry Mike off at a well-known whorehouse. Turk's laughing promise to pick him up on the way back had pissed Horse off. He wasn't at all pleased with the arrangement leaving just the two of them to deal with the matter at hand, but it wasn't his chapter, so it wasn't his call. His presence at the charter's launch had been chance when Blackie got the call from Slate, or he'd have been hearing about everything second- and thirdhand.

Bending over now, he loosened the rope holding the small bull rider into a hogtie position. With three they could have lifted and carried, but just him and Turk would require more handholds to wrestle the guy out of the van.

"How you wanna do this?" Turk's question was barely audible over the sounds in the van. "We need to send them something afterwards."

"You know how hard it is to get something out of your head?" Once he'd regained consciousness, the bull rider had been mumbling throughout the entire ride, and Horse had gotten good at ignoring him.

He opened the side door, slamming it behind him and then opened the back of the van just as Turk rounded the corner from his side. Each of them grabbed a boot and walked away, dragging the man onto the ground, still muttering about riding bulls. Then his words turned to the woman he'd tried to kill earlier tonight, someone the Rebel Wayfarers counted club royalty. Seems this Ray Nelms had been hunting and hurting her for years, and the bad karma he'd built up had finally caught up with him in a big way.

"Shut him up," Turk complained loudly, and Horse yanked off his shades to glare at him, then down at the man on the ground.

He's going to be dead in a couple of minutes. Maybe he's got something important to say.

Pulling back and tucking an arm of the glasses into the neck of his shirt, Horse told Turk, "His jawin' don't bother me none. We'll have to take the vest off him for this. It's got that shit bull riders wear. Not Kevlar but close."

Nelms seemed to finally realize he was about to die. As Horse leaned down and pulled at the tabs holding the vest closed around his chest, the man arched off the ground and shrieked, "The families. They'll never know." Arching his neck, with red-rimmed eyes, he glared up into Horse's face. "They gotta know."

A chill went through him at the words, but he brought out his gun as Turk started a countdown. "On three." The metallic sound of a round sliding into the barrel of a gun was loud in the open air. "One."

"Gotta know what, asshole?" Leveling the weapon, Horse kept his expression impassive, not wanting to reveal the sudden urge to know his words had woken.

"Two."

Nelms looked into Horse's face, past the gun aimed at his head and breathed out a long, slow rush of air. "Where they're buried."

"Three."

The report from Turk's pistol sounded just before Horse's finger tightened on the trigger, both their bullets finding the mark. Turk pulled another round and then fired a third time, Nelms' body jolting with the impact. The man's eyes had already started to glaze over, lids sagging half-mast as muscle tension fled with the end of his life.

Horse stared down at the man lying in the dirt, lethal bullet holes in his head and body, blood and fluids already leaking out into the sand of the desert. "Did you hear what he said?"

Turk bent over, grabbing one of the dead man's arms. "Help me get him over to the ditch. Wind'll cover him with shit pretty fast if he's down in that little gully." When Horse didn't move, Turk angled his head to stare up at him. "Jesus, Horse, fuckin' pull your weight here. I ain't doing this shit by myself."

"*When the hell you live in is inside you, what do you do?*" The bull rider's voice echoed through his head, but he shoved that down, not wanting the words to take up space inside his mind. Stooping, he gripped a limp wrist and tugged, surprised as always at how heavy the dead could be. Together, he and Turk wrangled the body to the nearby dip, rolled it down the slope, and let it lay as it had landed, elbow angled up towards the sky, a wing that would never take flight.

A sand-filled gust of wind deposited a first wave of debris along the side of the corpse and Horse took a minute to kick more on top of it, suddenly not wanting to see the man's slack face anymore. The corpse's eyes were still open, and he felt as if everything they did was on display.

"Hold on, lemme get a pic. You said Blackie mentioned they'd want one." Turk bent at the waist to angle his phone as he took several pictures, consulting the screen with each one, ensuring they met whatever documentation standard was in his head.

"Did you hear him?" Horse couldn't let it rest. The man hadn't just been hunting the Rebel's princess but was apparently a serial killer. "He said some of his kills were still out there."

"So?" Turk slammed the back doors of the van, then he and Horse climbed into the vehicle. Twisting the key in the ignition, he asked, "You care?"

"If it were your sister, wouldn't you?"

Sand crunched loudly underneath their wheels and Horse aimed his gaze to the side out the window, watching the angular form of the body until it disappeared into the distance.

This wasn't the first cleanup and disposal he'd done since joining the Freed Riders. Blackie, their president, kept to most of the old school rules, and that was just fine with Horse. He liked how things were predictable in the club. Had always liked when events in life followed a path he could track. Liked it better when men did the same.

And that was his problem with how things had shaken out today.

"You don't want to know what he meant? It doesn't pique your interest at all?" Horse changed position, lifted a foot to the dash and wedged himself into the seat.

"Nope." Turk twisted a dial on the radio and the local DJ's voice swelled in volume, this a clear tactic to get Horse to shut up about the dead guy.

Pulling out his phone, he texted Slate.

You guys still at the rodeo?

It took a minute, but Slate responded with typically cryptic language.

Could be, you need me there.

Think we should look for some parked storage also used as transport.

Another minute went by and his phone rang instead of buzzing with a text.

"Son of a fucking bitch."

"Hello to you, too, Slate." That would let Turk know who Horse was talking to, and by the way he turned down the music, it seemed he still cared about club business overall, just not when pushed by a low-level officer from Mother. "Just want to make sure we don't leave any arrows out there that could be construed as pointing towards anyone."

"Fuck me. We knew he was taking her somewhere when he dragged her off but hadn't made that mental jump yet. Thanks for the push, brother." Slate sighed heavily. "I'll start walking and looking. We got a look at his rig a week or so back, but he could have been in a livestock truck too. I'll text you if we find anything."

"Gonna be a little while for me, but I'll be there. I'll hit the clubhouse first, pick up my own ride and then meet you back at the grounds. When we do find it, I want to take a look at it. Man said a few things that make me itchy, and I want to see if I can figure anything out about it."

"Don't give that fuckin' asshole any space in your head, man. He was sick."

Horse snorted softly. "Yes, he was. I just want to satisfy my curiosity. We'll be back in town in a couple hours. I'll be in touch."

The call disconnected and he shoved the phone into his pocket before leaning over and turning up the music again. This time it was him who didn't want to spend time talking to Turk. He passed the rest of the ride turning Nelms' words over in his mind.

Families. Plural. Families out there not knowing where their daughter or sister is buried, or even if she's dead.

That wasn't gonna be acceptable.

***

When they found and entered the trailer—the locating portion of the quest made simple with a click of a key fob and a car alarm chirp from the big diesel truck— and discovered Nelms' hidden room inside, with knowing what they knew, the intended use was unmistakable. The truck itself wasn't anything to call home about, just a muted color cowboy-special seen in any of a dozen configurations in most towns across the southwest.

The trailer, though, that was something else.

A six-horse rig modified to accommodate only two horses, the rest of the space walled off and taken up by what had been Nelms' living and killing fields. The very front portion of the trailer had a tiny house feel with a fold-down bed, two-burner stove with narrow oven, an armchair to watch TV in, and a slim table hosting a single seat pushed underneath. Cabinetry along the walls all sported thumb latch doors, ensuring they'd stay closed even through rough driving. Closer to the table and stove were plates and cups, a couple of pots and pans, a tiny section of shelf with spices. Nearer the murphy-style bed were drawers and a closet with clothing.

But it was about ten feet shy of using all the space not taken up by the animal quarters.

Horse stood in the middle of the apartment-area and studied everything they'd uncovered so far. Everything was neat and organized. He got the sense that Nelms would have known where to put his hand on anything he wanted. Still, it was ordinary in an obsessive-compulsive way. There'd have been nothing to spook a woman Nelms decided to bring back to his base.

He swiveled in place, looking through what had been a hidden opening, and into the rest of the trailer with unease.

A metal divider swung open into the living space, even though there was more open room in the back half of the section. There were additional cabinets mounted on these walls, leaving a wide section of floor open and empty.

Horse glanced over his shoulder to where Slate sat cross-legged on top of the small table. He had a pile of papers in hand, studying each of them in turn. Neither had spoken much since they'd opened the door, unlocking the trailer with the keys the Rebels had taken from the bull rider before Horse and the FRMC members had finished the job.

"I think part of the ceiling comes down. Anything you see so far indicate if he had remote controls or anything?" Horse turned back to the space and looked up. "That's gotta be it. There's about a two-by-eight section I think suspends from the ceiling."

"No, this bullshit is just all his sick spewing and crowing after the fact. Page after page of what he did to the women. Limited location information. Some tactical notes about what not to do in the future. Nothing about how he did what he did, or the trailer modifications." Slate's bootheels clicked on the floor, indicating he'd climbed off the table. "Sick fuck."

"He'd have to do everything himself. Probably had it all sorted so he could get them into restraints with one hand if needed." Horse stretched tall and placed a palm flat on the ceiling. "Motherfucker was short, so it can't be him reaching up to it." He looked at the cabinets lining both walls. One side resembled the inside of an ambulance, with variously sized stainless-steel doors covering every inch, floor to ceiling. The other had a long workbench over more typical cabinets, and additional mounted storage above. "I bet there's a button or a latch or something over here."

He bent at the waist and studied the underside of the upper cabinets, grimacing when he saw a toggle switch. He flipped it with no movement. "Think we'll need power for this."

Slate backed up and opened the door to shout to the Rebels left outside. "Pop the genny." They'd restricted access to the interior of the trailer to just the two of them so far, agreeing on the decision without having to speak about it.

A moment later, there was a machinery hum and the lights in the room brightened considerably.

Horse flipped the toggle again and wasn't shocked when the center of the ceiling began descending.

"Fuck I hate when I'm right about shit like this."

Two different kinds of restraints were affixed to each corner of the suspended table, wide straps and handcuffs. The table itself had a deep groove around the outside lip and Horse could see a rubber gromet plugging a hole on the far end. *Drainage. Shit.*

"So he brings them to his little apartment and what? Drugs them? Took us a while to find the latch to open this shit up, so it's unlikely he'd let just anyone see his dungeon."

"I thought dungeons were supposed to be underground?" Horse faced away from the table, studying the wall lined with shiny doors. He opened one at random. "Ax and a hedge pruner in here. Maybe you're right about the dungeon." Another door revealed an electric saw. "Jesus. He's got power tools too."

"Fuckin' lair, then. Whatever we call it, he'd only open up this backend if he were certain of himself. Woman sees this and gets away, his gig is over." A cabinet opened behind Horse and Slate grunted. "Five different kinds of pliers. Fuck me. This is gonna haunt my goddamned sleep."

Horse moved around the table to stand next to Slate. He tugged on a drawer handle, surprised when it didn't move. "This one is locked." It went unsaid that if Nelms had seen fit to lock something inside his inner sanctum, it was important.

The latch was inside a cabinet below the drawer.

The drawer held one thing. A folded map of the United States.

Horse spread the map on the table, still descended from the ceiling. It turned his stomach that it was a perfect size, perfect height for Nelms—a little low for Horse, so he had to bend slightly.

They stared down at the map. In addition to the printed lines and colors, names of cities, counties, and rivers there were also little circles, crosses, and boxes, all drawn in different colored ink. A quick count of the icons hand drawn on the paper left Horse with forty-six potential areas of investigation.

"You think those mark where he picked them up, killed them, or left them behind?"

The memory of something Nelms had said during their drive, the ramblings that might not be as mad as Horse had assumed. "I think the boxes are the ones he found that fulfilled his need the most. He said your gal Mica was a box that let him put all the sickness inside and be normal for a while."

"Shit." Slate blew out a heavy breath. "Fuck, man. And the others?"

"I don't know. A circle could mean almost as good as a box, and the Xs might be failures. It's hard to know for sure, since the man didn't leave us with a key to decipher things. If each one indicates an individual, then that's a lot of death laid at his doorstep, man." Standing straight, he rested a fist on each hip and stared down at the map. "I've got an idea. If we can get this rig back to Longview, I can tear it apart, see what else I can find. Then I can set a prospect to researching this shit. Find missing person reports, that kind of stuff. If we can follow the information Nelms has left for us, we'll see if we can bring any closure to the families. He said as much, just before we popped a cap in his ass. That the families would never know. I want to prove that motherfucker wrong."

"Rebels have a guy who can help with the research side of things, as needed. Myron's a whiz at finding what's unfindable and leaving no trace behind when he does. Most security-minded dude I've ever known. Funny as hell to boot." Slate leaned against the cabinet behind them. "Between you and me, I'm not sure I want Duck to know shit about this, though."

"Still hard to wrap my head around them being brothers."

"Blood don't leave you no chance of declining, you know what I mean? Duck's solid, and the most stand-up guy you'll ever meet. He takes it personal, though, what Ray's done. Be better to keep him out of it if we can."

Horse gave a decisive nod. "I don't see a problem with that."

"Okay, let's get the fuck outta here then. Place gives me the creeps in the worst way. Evil lived here, and all that bullshit the asshole did feels like it left a mark."

"Not arguing with you on that." Horse refolded the map and placed it in the drawer, then flipped the toggle to retract the table to the ceiling. It moved smoothly and efficiently in near silence. "This shit is enough to make my skin crawl just knowing what he must have done back here."

"Remember…" Slate swung the divider closed and they pushed the chair back into the divots next to what now looked like a wall. "You volunteered for the extra credit work, brother. If it gives you bad dreams, that shit's on you."

"Yeah, yeah. I'm a big boy. I can handle a few nightmares."

Stepping out into the humid heat of a Houston evening was a relief. Slate locked the trailer and handed the keys to one of the Rebels standing nearby. Horse called Blackie and told him what was happening. With approval from his club president, he gave the Rebel member directions to a garage the FRMC owned near Longview.

"I'll get on that when I get home. I have one more support club visit planned, and then I can head up that way. Might as well finish business before I dive deep into whatever this will turn out to be." He lifted a hand to Slate and got a warrior's grip in response, pulled close for a back-pounding half hug. "You're good, brother. FRMC is proud you tagged us for help. You know Blackie'd do anything for ya."

"How's Lottie and the little one doin'?"

"Well. She and Blackie found a place and moved into it a couple months ago. Now she's talkin' more kiddos." Horse laughed softly. "Blackie's been talkin' more kids since before Randi was born, so it's good to see them both workin' the same program."

"That's awesome to hear." Slate chuckled. "They're good people."

"That they are. Don't be a stranger, hear me?" Horse slung a leg over his bike and settled into place, key inserted and turned in preparation. "We do like to see your face."

"Heard and noted, brother. We're headed to the Longview-Tyler area after this, I think, up where Mica's aunt and uncle are."

"Then make time to visit the clubhouse. You're one of the few that doesn't need an advance call. Just fuckin' show up, brother." He gripped the clutch lever and pushed the start button with one thumb. Over the roar of his pipes, he shouted, "See you soon," and got a hand lifted in response.

He rolled carefully over the uneven turf and gravel between him and the road, and once out on the highway, kept his speed to legal limits as he aimed his front wheel towards the support club's hometown. He'd been supposed to have been there earlier today, but the RWMC business had taken priority.

Once well on his way, out of Houston proper and on state roads as opposed to interstates, he let the information he had on the support club roll through his head.

Iron Riggers MC, the president was Skyd, the SAA named Critter. Their clubhouse was a dilapidated old house near Fairfield, the county seat of Freestone. They wanted part of the bigger club's clout as a support club, but so far hadn't been interested in leaving behind their main patch. Where he was going was their mother chapter, but they didn't have a cohesive network. As men had left Fairfield through the years, they'd taken the IRMC patch with them, setting up a new charter wherever they landed. No mind had been paid to fitness of being officer material or if they were leaders. It was more a riding club than anything.

With delusions of grandeur.

Horse scoffed and rolled the throttle a little more, wanting this day to be over.

His phone buzzed against his thigh, shoved deep into his pocket for the ride.

Probably yet another thing for the fixer.

The smile stretching his lips gave lie to the disgruntled theme of his thoughts.

He was happiest when he had a problem to solve.

Chapter Seven
Horse

"No." Horse answered the question aimed his way from Duane. "Nothing since the last text. You think the Rebels guy is really going to be able to figure anything out about it just from an anonymous number?"

It had been a busy day since leaving Houston.

He'd arrived at the Iron Riggers MC clubhouse, hearing shouts as he killed the bike's engine. Inside he'd been presented with a fight between the president and a patched member. By the time Skyd and Dynamite had run out of steam, they'd been battered and bloody, and hanging off each other just to stand upright.

Sorting out those goings on had taken longer than expected, and the presence of the unread text on his phone had slipped Horse's mind until much later. It was only when Blackie called near midnight that he pulled the device from his pocket, and after answering the questions his own president had for him, Horse had flipped over to the text message app and then stared at the phone.

Do what we say and she doesn't get hurt

The cryptic message was accompanied by a photo. Face disfigured with swelling, bruises darkening the skin around her eyes and jaw, he still recognized his mother's emotionless features staring at him out of the phone.

He'd called Blackie back immediately, forwarded him the picture and info about the number, and then got in the wind headed back through the dark of night to the clubhouse in Longview, something in his gut screaming at him to get himself home and safe.

Now it was the next day, and he'd heard from the anonymous phone number a few more times. The first had been a taunt, filled with confidence.

You know we'll deal with her if we have to. Don't make us.

The next had been a list of instructions, none of which made any sense. They'd ranged from driving directions mentioning landmarks he remembered from living in and roaming New Jersey, to a rising count of numbers he presumed were a monetary demand, and then a final one which had sounded very much like a lunch order.

The Rebels tech guy was doing his thing in the background, but so far hadn't delivered much other than it was an unregistered number.

Blackie had been behind closed doors all morning, leaving Horse to pace and stew, and Duane to take the brunt of Horse's frustration.

"Yeah. Everyone I've talked to that's dealt with Myron praises the guy. Highly. He developed a secure call and text app for their club that a couple other MCs have bought into. One inside track at the FBI said they'd tried and failed to hack it. If the dude can do shit like that, locating the phone texting you this bullshit should be cake." Duane gently shoulder checked him on Horse's next pass by where he was standing. "You need to settle, brother. Wound up as you are, you're gonna be wore out before we have a direction to head."

"You saw the picture. I might not get along with my mother as well as you do yours, but seeing her like that?" He swallowed hard, forcing the anguish back down his throat to where it burned in his chest. "Killin' me, brother."

"I get it. I do. But you gotta trust Blackie to have your back just like you've always had his." Duane slung an arm over Horse's shoulders. "Come on and sit your ass down, brother."

Head thrown back against the top of the couch, Horse fisted his hands and blew out a heavy breath. "I've called folks I know back in Jersey. Bar's been closed for a week. Unexpected. She'd fired the manager a month ago, so she was the only one with keys. When she didn't show up to open the door, people waited a few minutes and then just melted away. Three of the waitresses have already found new jobs, like her being missing isn't worth their time." He huffed out a humorous laugh. "I haven't spoken to her in years, don't know why I'm holdin' hate for them for making sure they can pay their bills."

"Because it's your ma. Doesn't matter how far from home we roam, family like that still matters."

"She's a real bitch, though. That's why I've been out of her orbit for so long. Decided I didn't need to have her bullshit raining down on me all the time. Shouldn't matter to me what happens to her."

"She's your ma." Duane semi-repeated as he thudded a fist against the side of Horse's thigh.

The door creaked open, and Horse was on his feet instantly. The look on Blackie's face was dark but held a hint of satisfaction, and when they met in the middle of the room, he clapped a hard hand on Horse's shoulder. "Found 'em."

"Who is it?" Horse's back teeth clenched as he gritted, "And my mother? Is she...?"

"She's okay. Nothing more than you've already seen on those fuckin' proof of life pictures, brother. Got her into a hospital and they're takin' real good care of her." Blackie's fingers dug in deep, and for an instant, Horse thought that might be the only thing keeping his feet underneath him. "Brother, she's good. Wouldn't lie to anyone about that shit, man."

"Oh God. I wasn't… shit, man. Shit."

"Breathe, brother." Duane's voice came from beside them and Horse turned his neck to see the man. The relief on Duane's face matched the feeling inside Horse and they exchanged a solemn nod as Horse filled his lungs with a hard breath, tension easing in tiny increments. He looked back at Blackie.

"Who was it? Who'd do that shit to my family?" Horse straightened as the expression on Blackie's face morphed to barely contained rage. "Give me a name, Blackie. Aim me, before I go fuckin' insane, brother. Give me a direction."

"Taken care of, Horse. That shit's all dealt with. You can stand down." Blackie's fingers tightened on Horse's shoulder. "It was a bullshit group out on the east coast. They're mostly limited to the northern Florida area, but still total bullshit. Supposed to have ties to some Mexican cartel families. That might be a burned route, cuz this was such an amateur move, seems the cartel won't even claim the assholes. The guy behind this supposed MC—and I hesitate to call them a club because they bear only the slightest resemblance to a true brotherhood—has assured me that he's dealt with the cancer in his organization. Offers his deepest apologies."

Horse felt his lips twist to the side as bile filled his mouth. "And you believe him?"

"Everything I hear about the dude makes me lean that way, yeah." Blackie lifted a shoulder in a questioning movement. "Fury sounds like a stand-up man. Tied into a bullshit club right now. Man might be one to watch, see if he's lookin' for a better home down the road."

"Fury." The name wasn't familiar to Horse. "Tell me what you know about him. Who was the crew that snatched my mother? If Fury's down Florida way, what happened to push a big enough group up the coast to Jersey?" Now that the immediate danger to his mother was past, Horse's shoulders dropped an inch and he arched backwards. "When you say he's dealt with them, what does that mean?"

Blackie's head tipped towards the office door. "Come inside. Let's chat."

Horse paused in the doorway, surprised to see the conference phone still lit up as if a call was active. He lifted an eyebrow at Duane, who shrugged as they both took seats. Blackie closed the door and rounded the table, dragging a chair out on the opposite side.

"Myron, I'm back, brother. I've got Horse and D-Man here with me now. What assurances do we have that fucktard Fury actually did as advertised and dealt with the bullshit those fuckin' Diamante visited on Horse's mother?"

"Horse, Duane, hello. I can confirm that after they extracted the location out of one of the men, they immediately worked to secure the release of Dorothy Malcomb. She was transported via private vehicle to a local hospital, where I already had a doctor waiting to take over her care. Mostly it was the bruising evident in the photographs sent over, but there was also an untreated gash on the back of her head requiring a couple of stitches. They're keeping her overnight just for observation, but my understanding is that's already under disagreement by Ms. Malcomb. Seems she doesn't want to be away from her own house any longer than required." Myron hadn't even waited for them to exchange greetings, just diving directly into everything Horse wanted to know from the outset.

"I can see why everyone likes you, Myron. Thanks for helping take care of my mother."

"Horse, trust me, it's my pleasure. Family shouldn't ever come under fire like this. Now, if I were in your shoes, I'd want to know what happened next, so I'll cover that now. The men Fury called and set on this group were diligent in their application of every statement Fury had directed their way. He asked for a wipe, a scorched field, and from the official emergency phone traffic I've been monitoring, he got what he wanted. There's a small storefront that's been burned to the ground, and the first responders have pulled several bodies from the rubble so far. Those were stacked near the front door, and I have every expectation that once the wreckage cools enough for a deeper dig, they'll find the other ones. He picked a few names to pull out for questioning, and my sources say they are secured."

"Multiple men against one old lady?" Horse shook his head. "That doesn't make any sense."

Blackie shifted in his seat and shook his head. "Naw, brother. More like all those men against an asset that could turn a leverage member of a well-respected MC poised to take off in whatever direction they want. If they'd gotten to you, if you'd responded directly to their demands, they thought you would either sway the FRMC to their side, or at least grant free passage." Blackie's knuckles rapped against the table twice. "She wasn't the target. You were."

"But why? Did they think I was that weak?"

"Jesus, you're thick." Duane grinned and slapped a palm against the side of Horse's head.

"The fuck?" Glaring at him, Horse refused to lift a hand and show the blow had stung. "The hell you do that shit for?"

"Because you're being dense, brother. They picked you not because they thought you'd cave, but because if they could get you to bend even a little, they'd have the ear of one of the most influential FRMC members. You've ins with not just FRMC, man, but Rebels, and another dozen different clubs and RCs. Making your way across the country as you did, treatin' every club with respect and leaving them better than you found them? That's a hella lotta sway." One corner of Duane's mouth ticked up higher. "Dumb as a box of rocks, apparently, but a box with a fuckton of sway."

Horse held his tongue, turning his gaze from Duane to Blackie, where he found a matching maniacal grin. "You believe this too?"

"It's not a fairy tale, Horse." Myron's amusement came through clearly, his chuckle loud enough to rattle the speakers on the phone. "I could name probably ten clubs that if you picked up the phone and made a call, on behalf of the FRMC or just yourself, they'd answer in a heartbeat."

"So then, what did the Diamante want? Their messages were not the easiest to understand."

"Not the Diamante, this was a splinter group. Not one Fury was in charge of, either, so I don't think he's blowin' smoke on this. Calling themselves the Monster Devils MC. Seems they were looking for a money base, thought they'd strongarm your mother. When that failed and she refused to pony up their protection 'fees'"—Blackie made air quote marks around the last word, showing his disdain for the tactic—"they turned their focus on you. Without good intel, either, because while they knew you were FRMC, they somehow simultaneously also thought you were in Jersey."

"That doesn't make any sense." He shook his head slowly. "I don't have anything to do with the bar anymore, haven't for years at this point. Why would someone commit to something with such potential to go sideways without at least doublechecking their information?"

"Pending interrogation, we'll hopefully understand more soon."

He straightened, glaring at Blackie. "I want in on that."

"Not happening." One corner of Blackie's mouth curled down. "Much as it pains me to say it, the process will go faster without your involvement."

"They beat on my mother." Horse shoved his chair back several inches, pushing away from the table. "Bloodied her fuckin' face, brother."

"Hold on." Myron broke in before Horse could continue. "I just got notification that the interview is concluded. Unfortunately for your desire for retribution, I can confirm that the ones involved won't be answering any additional questions. I'll debrief folks better in a bit, and then can have a final report in your hands before end of day, Blackie. This wasn't expected, but things happen in the heat of the moment."

"They're dead?" Horse couldn't decide if he were disappointed or glad the men who'd mistreated his mother might be beyond reach.

"Very. They're sending me images now and there's no way someone's still breathing with that kind of damage." Myron made a tsk sound. "I'm convinced this was an unsanctioned action and the ones responsible have been dealt with." In the brief pause, Horse could hear the clacking of a keyboard. "And your mother just left the hospital. She called a cab and signed out AMA. Strong-willed woman."

"Yeah, she's always liked being the captain of her own ship. She wouldn't stand for someone telling her what to do, even if they wore white coats and had M.D. after their name. Doesn't surprise me." Horse propped a knee against the edge of the table. "What's next, Myron? Is there anything left for me to do, or did you organize everything?"

"Wouldn't say I covered it all, but hopefully I got damn close." Myron chuckled and Horse felt a wry grin lifting one corner of his mouth.

"My gratitude, brother." Horse lifted his eyes from the conference phone to find Blackie's approving gaze on him. "Rebels need anything from me personally and it's mine to give, you've got it."

"Love accepting those markers." Myron's voice held a note of amusement. "Blackie, Mason said to tell you this one was free."

"Fuck that," Blackie barked, brows lowering. "FRMC pays their own way."

"Take it up with the big man next time you see him, then." The clacking keyboard sounded again. "He also recommends we pitch you the app, just to make things easier going forwards."

"Done. Send me the info." Blackie slapped the top of the table, the crack of his palm meeting the surface loud in the closed room. "Been wanting to test drive that puppy for a while."

"I'll send you a few devices. How many you want to start with? The three of you?"

Blackie flicked his gaze from Horse to Duane and nodded. "Yeah, sounds good, Myron. I'll echo Horse's gratitude, brother."

"Always a pleasure to come out on top." The sound on the call muffled and got quiet. Horse strained and could just make out two voices talking in the background before the quality returned. "I gotta go, Blackie. Be well, old man. You're a good'un."

"Back atcha, boy." Blackie tapped a button on the phone to disconnect the call. "Questions from you two?"

"Not Diamante?" Horse chewed on the inside of his cheek as he waited for confirmation.

"Nope. Fury's Diamante, which is why he reacted with extreme displeasure at their antics. They didn't claim the name but still threw it around enough that—splintered group or not—it was in his best interest to nip it in the bud."

"Scorched earth?" Shaking his head at the phrase Myron had used, Horse leaned back in the chair, hooking an elbow over the top rung. His heart still pounded, but the adrenaline in his body was ebbing away. "I'd say he was displeased."

"Like I said, he's a decent dude, just hung up with some bullshit clubs so far. You can tell a man who hasn't yet found his home, and Fury strikes me as exactly that. We'll need to keep our ear to the wire for anything else with the MDMC, but for now, it's done and dusted." Blackie gave a jaw-cracking yawn. "I'm headed home. Time to take over from Momma for a bit, give her a rest." The smile on his face said it wasn't the hardship his words might have made a person think. "Call me if you need me, brothers."

"Will do." Horse lifted half out of the seat and reached across the table, grabbing Blackie's extended hand. Holding tight, he pushed as much earnestness into his voice as he could. "Thank you, sincerely. Thank you."

"As Myron said, it's my pleasure." Blackie squeezed and released, then yawned again. "Headed out now. See you later."

Horse settled back into the chair and twisted to look at Duane as Blackie closed the door. "What do you think about all that?"

Duane's mouth twisted. "That's some bullshit. That's what I think about it. Motherfuckers took your ma, beat her to hell, and you don't even get to skin a knuckle on their janky asses. That's some bullshit, brother."

"Yeah, no argument there. But the reaction? Sounded like Rebels burned some intel or info to get to the right dude. Who is this Fury, anyway?" Horse shook out his hands. Muscles tense for hours hadn't quite gotten the message that all was well. "And my mother." He tipped his head back with a groan. "Just like her to leave the hospital. I bet some good-intentioned doctor got an earful on her way out too."

"Tough." Duane thudded a fist against the table. "Apple didn't fall far from that tree with you."

Horse chuckled and rolled his eyes. "I need a drink."

"Let's walk to the bar. See what kind of trouble we can find."

"I'd be down for trouble tonight." Horse stood and stretched. "Long as it can be solved with fists or fuckin', I'd be down." He hesitated. "I'll follow you in a minute, yeah?"

Duane slapped his shoulder as he walked past. "You bet."

The door closed behind him, and Horse stared down at his phone for a moment, then dialed from memory.

"Dotty? It's Graeme. You doin' okay?"

Chapter Eight
Glenna

"Haw there, cow." Glenna turned the four-wheeler in a tight circle, blocking the exit a reluctant cow thought she'd spotted. "Get into the damn paddock." With a shake of her head, the cow stood for a moment and bawled loudly, then trotted up along the fence and through the open gate. Glenna shook her own head as she roared up and stopped, bailing off the vehicle and grabbing the wide metal divider. Swinging it closed, she looped the chain through the slot and clipped the links together. "About damn time."

Leaning on the top rung of the gate, she surveyed the cattle milling in the three paddocks closest to the barn. Today's work was done, bringing all the animals in so they could be sorted, doctored, and then either released or loaded on trailers and headed for the sales.

"Done all I can do on my own." Glenna slapped her worn ballcap against her thigh, knocking a layer of dust off both. "Better go make my calls."

She turned and stared at the house, noting again the slight sag in the porch roofline, tiny peeling strips of paint around the windows, and the porch steps that angled up on one end, loose nails giving a warning squeal every time a foot dared tread on them. Penn's truck was parked next to the house, dust covered and unmoving.

In the years since Penn had died, she had thrown herself into taking care of what she could with the least amount of outside help possible.

A glance over her shoulder showed a reminder that the reason she could corral the cattle on her own was because she ran about a quarter of the number they'd had before. Small enough she could deal with virtually everything by herself, but still make enough money to live on when the yearlings went to the auction.

"I'm gettin' by just fine," she muttered to empty air before climbing back on the four-wheeler. With a twist of the key, the vehicle roared to life, and she settled into the seat, riding the quarter mile to the house without thought, her mind forced into silence by the pain that lurked just under the surface.

She kicked her boots off just inside the kitchen door, setting them in the low box reserved for that purpose. It looked empty, holding just her sneakers, boots, and flipflops for when she needed to plod around outside. Glenna blinked and overlaid was a picture of the box overflowing, two pairs of Penn's boots stacked near the back, his running shoes and knockabout sneakers lined up beside her own, his plastic slides resting on top of her flip-flops so when she wanted them, she always had to move his shoes. Another blink and it was back to the new normal, which was just her footwear.

"I'm doin' okay."

Whirling, she reached for the phone just as it rang, and a quick glance at the answering machine showed her Cooter's number incoming. She answered with a smile.

"Cooter, I was just about to call you." He'd remained the go-between for her and his father, because the older man seemed to think it was okay for her to ask and pay for favors from Cooter, but balked at taking money directly from her. "I got the cattle moved close today, so we're good to go for tomorrow. Vet'll be here early enough, so we can start at seven or so. Sound okay?"

"Right to business, just like always." Glenna closed her eyes and imagined Cooter's grin taking over his face, pleasant and known. "I wasn't calling about tomorrow, though. I never doubted you'd have everything penned and probably sorted before we get there."

"What's up then?" Snagging a finger through the loop on the sole upside-down mug in the drainer, she poured cold coffee nearly to the brim before placing it in the microwave. It was chugging away before she realized Cooter hadn't answered her. "Cooter? What's up?"

"I wondered if you wanted to get dinner?" His familiar voice had turned strange, strained and thin. "Tonight?" He cleared his throat roughly. "With me?"

Glenna stared at the mug turning in useless circles inside the microwave, the spinning wheel underneath it driving the movement. The light went off and the device started its annoying beeping. One beep. Two beeps. There wasn't enough air in the kitchen to breathe, but her feet were stuck to the floor. Ten beeps, then a long shrill tone before silence fell around her.

"Glenna? You there?" Cooter's voice was still strange, tight and filled with tension. He was waiting for an answer.

"I gotta go." She didn't wait to hear his response to her broken whisper, blindly thudding the receiver against the wall a half a dozen times before it caught on the hook.

She turned and walked through the entry to the front room. The room where Penn had danced with her so often, dipping and twirling around as lights flashed brightly in her eyes.

The room where Penn had died.

Glenna had been with him when he passed. Curled up in the bed at his side, so much more room than even two weeks prior, she'd had ample space to bring her knees to her chest and still curl next to his withered body. Fingers twined together like a childhood prayer, wet cheek pressed to his shoulder, she'd watched his face as he'd breathed in and out. In and out. In, so slowly, then a softer exhale that went on forever. His chest hadn't risen again.

Thirty minutes later, the nurse had come in to check on him—on them, and she'd given Glenna a look filled with such sorrow, it had weight, driving Glenna against the mattress. When she'd opened her mouth, Glenna had held up a hand and shook her head. "I know." Acknowledging the last thing she'd wanted to happen.

Cooter's words ran back through her mind, loud and jarring. He had to have known what her answer would be, but still he'd asked. And regardless of her refusal, he'd be here tomorrow with his father and brothers to help her work the cattle. If she asked, he'd climb a ladder to scrape and paint the window frames. Without complaint. Because that's the kind of man he was.

"I'm not ready." She slid down the wall just inside the room, staring at the carelessly arranged furniture.

After the rented hospital bed and machines were all returned to the pharmacy, the room had stood bare for weeks. A span of open flooring declaring to anyone the tragedy it had witnessed.

One night Glenna had been prowling the house in the dark and she'd stumbled over the loveseat where it was shoved into a corner of the dining room. Sailor-worthy curses fled her tongue, spilling over her lips like a creek in flood.

Filled with fevered purpose, she'd spent the next couple of hours traversing the house to retrieve every piece of furniture that had been displaced to make room for the things Penn had needed. Gathered into the space, the seating and tables took up too much room, so she'd moved them around, and around, and around, never quite landing on an arrangement that felt right.

This room was where her heart had been carved from her chest. It seemed fitting that even the furniture reflected the hole left behind.

Five years wasn't long enough.

"I might never be ready."

***

Glenna removed her ball cap and swept the back of one wrist across her forehead. *Need to grab a bandana at lunch.* Tying the fabric around her head would keep the sweat from running into her eyes for the afternoon.

With a knee propped on the seat of the four-wheeler, she rested a moment, watching Cooter and his brother working together to move the culls through a narrow alley and into the last holding pen. The truck would be here within the hour, at least that was the promise, but nothing had run according to plan so far today.

"Haw cow," she shouted, rolling the throttle of the vehicle as she braced herself against the sudden movement. She picked up speed and swung wide around the tail end of the group she was moving to a handling pen. These were the keepers, her choice cows, either bred or with calves at their side, the open heifers, and the herd bull.

Just as the last cow fled through the open gate, the bull rounded on Glenna, head down, white slobber slung to the ground on either side and over his shoulders as he pawed the earth, threatening her. A couple of the younger cows stopped too, crowding closer to him, eyeing the opening. Glenna stared at the bull, reading annoyance in his posture. No fear, which could have made him genuinely dangerous. She bailed off the vehicle and raced for the gate, swinging it hard at the locking post, following with her hands extended to catch the gate as it rebounded.

"Jesus, Glenna." Cooter's voice sounded right behind her, and she glanced over her shoulder as she secured the bolt, slamming it home just before the bull made an abbreviated run at the gate. The drawn expression on Cooter's features surprised her.

"What?" Holding her cap by the brim, she waved it at the bull who snorted as he wheeled away. "He's a lotta hot air."

"He's a thousand pounds of pissed off." Cooter double-checked the locking bolt. "He coulda run over the gate and taken you with it."

"Nah, he's a sweetheart. Just annoyed about being put in the pen, which he knows meant a vet visit. Horatio hates those. Plus all the commotion." She shrugged and slogged back to the four-wheeler. "You guys get the sales stock sorted out?"

"Glenna, you gotta have a care." Cooter's hand landed low on her back and Glenna clumsily wrenched herself out of his hold. "Did you think more on what I asked you yesterday?"

Fighting not to let the sick in her stomach show on her face, Glenna turned away, ready to remount the four-wheeler. "I already said. I can't."

"Honey." Cooter's voice was soft, but the intent drilled painfully into her head as she fought not to retch. "It's just dinner."

She took a long breath in and held it before turning to look him in the face, because as a friend, he deserved to see the determination on her face. "Not to me, Cooter." He reached a hand towards her, but Glenna sliced her palm through the air, stopping him in his tracks. "It's expectations and tacit agreements. It's an unspoken assumption that the door might open for more. It's not just dinner, and I'm not ready."

"I know you loved Penn."

She slashed her hand through the air again, this time with anger fueling her movements. "I love Penn. Love. As in today. My heart still beats for him. It might always be that way for me. I can't imagine any man would be okay with dinner knowing how I feel, not even one as sweet and caring as you are." She sucked in another hard breath and lifted her chin. "You're my best friend, Cooter. That's where I stand."

He nodded slowly, shoulders still just as straight and proud as before. In part of her brain, Glenna was glad her rejection hadn't settled on him like a weight, that maybe it wouldn't change things between them.

"I understand." His soft words broke the bubble of silence that had settled around them. "I'm proud of our friendship, and I'm glad to share that with you."

Her nod of response was jerky, and Glenna knew her smile trembled slightly, but she firmed her lips as she swept her cap off, slapping it sharply against her thigh. "I think that was the last of the keepers."

"We got everything else sorted out. I believe we're ready for the truck." Cooter accepted the topic change gracefully. "Might even have some time for a cold drink."

"I put a jug of sweet tea in the shed fridge this morning." Picking her way to the four-wheeler, she swung aboard and twisted back to look at him. "Want a ride or hoofin' it?"

With a rueful grin, Cooter shook his head. "I'll meet you there. Give myself a minute to gather my thoughts."

"You're a good man, Cooter." The machine came to life underneath her and Glenna swung it in a tight circle, noting movement on the road. Shouting over the engine noise, she gave him a wide smile. "I'd bet ya, but it's not a fair race." He lifted a hand and waved her off, giving Glenna the chance to escape. Wind ruffled through the tendrils of hair and threatened to lift the cap from her head. For a few moments, the only things she had to think about were rough ground and securing her headgear.

Before she was ready, the shed and stables loomed large in front of her and Glenna swept the machine in a wide circuit, visually verifying everything was ready for the transport she'd glimpsed turning off the highway onto the ranch's drive. *All is well*, she thought as she backed the four-wheeler up to the shed and turned off the motor. Cooter was making good time, having covered about half the distance to the shed so Glenna ducked inside and filled several plastic cups with cold tea, emerging from the dimness of the barn into the brilliant sunshine with two of them just as he strode up.

He lifted a hand to his mouth as he reached for a cup of tea, giving a shrill two-fingered whistle to call the other men in. Glenna smiled and did the same, aiming for higher pitched and louder. As always, her competitiveness made Cooter laugh, which was her intention.

"Always got to get the last word in, doncha?" He drank deeply of the cold liquid, letting out a satisfied "Ahhh" as he smacked his lips. "it's good, Glenna. Thanks."

"You hear anything on what Jackson Snyder's gonna do?" Glenna sipped her own cup, pointing the other men into the shed as they neared. "I've not caught wind of anything, but you and I both know he's not suited for ranching."

"Nothing. I figured he'd slap it up for sale the day after Chester passed, but not a thing so far."

"I don't know if I'd rather he keep it and run it in his half-assed way, or sell it. Depends on who he sells it to, I guess." She huffed air at her sweat-plastered bangs. "My luck he'd sell it to a Dallas developer who'd carve it up into half-acre plots."

"Your luck he'll keep it and quit tending fence, lookin' to get free servicing from that pissed-off bull of yours." Cooter tipped his hat back. "If I hear anything, I'll let you know."

"Appreciate it." She half turned to look at the other men. "Everything, and every one of you. Appreciate you all." The rumble of a truck pulled their attention to the drive and Glenna gave a little whine as she sighed. "Well, the truck's here. Time to get back to work."

An hour later and the truck was loaded and ready, which meant by the time Cooter and the others left, the remaining cattle had been turned out into the pasture, leaving Glenna to head back to the house.

Alone.

Tonight she found the thought wasn't as unwelcome as it had been, with the reality of Cooter's unsolicited invitation hanging over her head. She kicked off her boots and surveyed the empty kitchen.

I should get a dog.

Chapter Nine

Horse

"No reason to expect anything other than advertised." Blackie's confidence projected through the phone, soothing emotions in a way Horse envied. "This is just another chapter in the FRMC saga. Ain't no thang, boys. Ain't no thang."

Hundreds of miles away, nearly fifteen men were seated in a circle around a bonfire in the backwoods of the Florida panhandle, including Skyd from the Iron Riggers. Around the clearing, similar meetings were happening with the Rebel Wayfarers, Incoherent, Bama Bastards, and the Caddo Hobos. All the heavy hitters along the Gulf Coast were represented, with national and international presidents among the attendees.

Blackie had left out early this morning, riding for a long ten hours with Peaches on the queen seat, timing their arrival for mealtime. Randi was with Peaches' dad, who wasn't against getting some baby time.

According to Blackie's report, Mason and Slate from the RWMC had been the first to greet them, since the meetings were taking place on property owned by one of their nomad members, Truck. He'd moved here to live with his woman, Vanna, someone who held a place of respect in the FRMC. She meant a very special something to every long-time member of the Mother chapter. *Tangled threads.*

"My proposal, depending on what Bane feels is right for him, is to spin up a FRMC chapter here." Blackie's statement was met with quiet murmurs.

"I thought you wanted to plant IRMC colors?" Skyd's voice was known to Horse, and his comment was both a question and statement of fact, because it was what Blackie had been talking about most recently. "I'm cool either way, I just want to know my place in this mix."

"More I gave thought to the issues of a charter so far away from the arms of Mother, more I realized it was likely easier to do a direct chapter. IRMC is a good club, and well balances the tightrope of support for FRMC while being its own entity. This way that particular challenge is mitigated. I won't say we shouldn't look at IRMC for a future expansion, but it seems to be smarter to pave the way with the patch that holds more sway."

"Makes sense," Horse offered, watching on the screen as sparks shot from the fire. "You think the other players will be open to the idea?"

"Bane is FRMC. I'm not letting that man go. He fought too hard to carry our patch, brothers. He belongs with us." Blackie's tone left no room for argument.

"True story." Horse rubbed his knuckles. "Gotta respect a man who falls down ten times but gets up eleven." He'd been the barrier to Bane's membership. Blackie had heard rumblings of the man's connections with a bad news family, and had wanted to ensure Bane was joining for the right reasons. Ten beatdowns in a row and still coming back to ask again had proven his dedication, and nothing in his membership since had said they'd been wrong to trust him. Even if that problematic family was the founding member of the MDMC, who'd escaped the arms of Fury's retribution. *More tangled threads.*

Right now, Bane was on a run up to Kentucky with Gunny, a high-ranking RWMC officer, and the general consensus was Bane would be staying in the Florida panhandle for the foreseeable future. Thus the need for figuring out a way for him to keep his patch.

"Would mean he'd move up in the ranks." Horse offered something he knew Blackie would have already thought about. "If any man's earned it, it's Bane."

"Truth. But I'd like to hear from his own mouth what's comin' down. Expectation is he'll stay here, but the man could surprise us all." Blackie stood, planting fists against his low back as he stretched muscles apparently sore from the long ride.

Whoever was holding the phone on their end tracked his movements in a way that made Horse grin. *Probably the prospect he took with him. Dedication right there.*

Blackie continued, "I need to find my woman and get us somewhere private. Don't stay up too late, kids. Dawn will be here before you know it."

"Night, boss." Horse offered a wave and disconnected the call. He looked around the faces gathered in the office. "Tomorrow morning early, let's put our heads together and figure out the first things Bane's gonna need. All of it in Baker. So we'll scope out available property, housing, members—we'll get it all sorted and have a list ready for Blackie when he calls with the done deal."

Back in his room, Horse stretched in a way similar to Blackie's movements, then sighed deeply. As enforcer, this club move would have him on the road more than he liked. Not that he was against visiting outlier chapters and support clubs, but he also liked the comfort of his own bed.

"Gettin' soft in your old age." His complaint hung in the air, reenforcing an idea that had started poking its unwelcome head up frequently. Not the getting older part. He wasn't worried about losing his edge due to age. It was the idea that the only person he had to talk to in the privacy of his down time was himself.

"Club is family." The thought of his mother flashed to mind, and he scoffed softly. Their relationship hadn't improved much over the last few years. "I've got a better found family than the one she threw away."

With that settled, he sat on the edge of the mattress and started a list on his phone, identifying elements and potential players in the new chapter in way-the-fuck-out-in-Florida Baker.

When he finished with that, he'd pull up the latest research the prospects for FRMC and RWMC had done on the information taken from the bull rider's trailer. It was taking much longer than he'd anticipated, and while the outcomes were satisfying, the buzz of the knowledge there were always more dead woman ate at him. There was no lack of work.

Just a lack of companionship.

"Jesus. Shut the fuck up, asshole."

***

Glenna

"Did you hear who Jackson Snyder sold to?" Glenna twirled the old phone's cord around her finger as she waited for Cooter to respond. "All I heard was he'd gotten top dollar."

"It's a group from out east. Investors, I'd bet. You called it. They'll probably hook in with a developer either local or from back where they're from and carve that land up into half-acre plots. We're close enough to Tyler for an easy commute. Hate the idea that it'll go that way." Cooter sighed heavily. "I don't know anything other than the buyers are from away, though. Not really."

"Speculation with intuition is kinda like fortune telling." She smiled. "I hope you're wrong, but you've got a pretty good track record with this kind of thing."

"Wish I didn't. Hope I'm wrong." There was an awkward pause, something that wouldn't have registered as such a year ago, but Cooter's persistence in asking Glenna out had driven a wedge of tired and offended rejection between them. "You need anything else, Glenna? I've got paperwork to tend to."

"No, nothing else. Tell Pa I said hi." The frown on her face drew the skin of her brow tight. "Appreciate you takin' my call."

"Anytime. You dial my number, I'm always gonna pick up, Glenna. I'll convey your greetings to Pa. Bye."

"Talk to you soon." Her last two words were to the dead air on the disconnected line and Glenna stifled a groan as she clicked the receiver back into the wall-mounted phone. "Well, that went about as well as expected."

Nails clicking on the floor pulled her attention to the doorway and a real smile relaxed the rest of the frown from her face as she watched her dog enter the room. Wiry hair on top of Shamu's head was raised in a faux-mohawk and the expression on his face was almost comical. A Peruvian Inca Orchid, the nearly hairless black-and-white dog had become Glenna's best friend and companion.

"Hey, puppy," she crooned, slipping a hand across Shamu's head and down his warm neck. "Whatcha doin', fella?"

Head cocked to the side, Shamu stared up at her, concern wrinkling his brow in an echo of her own frown from earlier.

"Oh, it's okay. It's just Cooter bein' Cooter. Man doesn't know how to take no for an answer once he's got his mind set on an idea. He'll get over himself sooner or later." She gathered the loose skin of his cheek into one hand and shook his head gently. "He always does. Nothing for you to worry your pretty little head over. You're a good boy, sure enough."

He pressed tight to her leg as she moved towards the kitchen table, keeping that position while she picked up her coffee cup and drained it. "We've got work to do, you terrible thing. You can't be plastered to me the whole day." He shifted so more of his weight pinned against her leg. "Seriously, Shammy. Everything's okay." The huff of air he delivered said volumes about his belief in her read of the situation. "Ready to go for a ride?"

Finally he left her side, dancing from foot to foot in front of the door, gaze fixed on the window just over his head. When she went back to the coffeemaker to fill her thermos, he huffed again, this followed by a demanding, rumbling bark entirely at odds with his seeming frailness.

She wasn't sure how the breed of dog had come to her attention. Probably one of the thousand nights of little sleep spent browsing the internet for articles on ranching, cancer, astrology, quad-runner maintenance, and the most unique everything. But once she'd seen a picture, she hadn't been able to get the dogs out of her mind. Excessively loyal and head-strong didn't scream good companion, but she'd joined a forum of owners and found out the breed was so much more than the surface description.

A short time later, she'd been tapped by a rescue group for fostering the black-and-white dog and had proudly become what the folks called a "foster fail" because Shamu had found his forever home with her.

Thermos in hand, she patted her back pocket to ensure the gloves that lived there hadn't been misplaced, then paused to laugh at Shamu who was still dancing from foot to foot. "Okay, we're going. We're going." The instant the door opened, he was gone like a shot, angling to the left so he could loop the house and check for intruders. By the time she'd made it to the quad runner, he'd finished his initial search and was fast approaching from the right. Barely giving her time to throw a leg over the seat, Shamu bounded up behind her, slapping his front feet into place on her shoulders.

Pushing the ignition button, she settled her thermos into a bag between her legs as the motor warmed up. A quick bark beside her head told her the process was taking too long and she reached up to playfully hold Shamu's muzzle closed. "Patience, grasshopper. Patience." He wrestled out of her hold and barked again, quieting as she rocked the throttle. "Here we go."

Four hours later, his enthusiasm for their work of the day hadn't waned. He'd faced off upset momma cows as Glenna inoculated their babies, nuzzled encouragingly at the few calves that didn't immediately regain their feet when she was done, and plastered himself to her back every time they moved to a different pasture or paddock.

"You're like that battery bunny, Shammy. Where do you get your energy from?" Easing the quad runner to a stop in front of the shed, she gave him a moment to dismount before she parked the vehicle. After restocking the bags with everything she'd used that day, Glenna walked next door and stood for a minute staring down the aisle running the length of the stables.

Empty horse stalls stood on either side, reminding her she needed to finish her business plan for boarding animals so she could advertise the opportunity. Every little bit of income helped, and as Cooter had noted, they were near sprawling urban areas in a state where residents longed for olden times—but without the hardship, of course. After reviewing the offerings for stabling in and around Longview and Tyler, Glenna knew she was onto a good idea. "Now, I just have to make it happen." Glancing around, then gazing out at the pastures dotted with the specialty breed of cattle she'd settled on, she shook her head. "Along with the other million things I've gotta do."

A bark brought her back to the present and she felt the familiar weight of Shamu as he leaned against her leg.

"The things *we've* got to do. I know, I know. I shouldn't dismiss your contribution, Shammy. But for now, let's load up and go home."

He beat her to the quad runner and danced beside it on nimble feet.

***

Horse

Horse saw a familiar head peeking around a tree and smiled. That'd be Marian, sister of Bane's woman, Myrt, someone he'd become quite familiar with over the past couple of years. She was beautiful and sweet, and he'd come to realize that she could maybe be more than his friend.

The question was if he wanted to push it.

Marian had come to the Baker, Florida, group after being rescued from her own family. She'd been broken emotionally, and it had taken her months to lose the fear and expectation of pain that had followed her down from Kentucky. She'd slowly come out of her shell, and Horse had been glad for a multitude of reasons to visit the new chapter because each also granted him the chance to see her.

"Fishing tomorrow?" Her question as quiet and sweet, a soft request instead of a demand, and he smiled at her.

"You bet, little sister." Her face lit up with pleasure, lips parting on a soundless laugh, and Horse reined in his imagination. *Time for that later, when I'm alone in the guest bedroom.* "I'm always down for fishin', and have just the lure for that honeyhole Gunny's always talking about." He winced internally, hoping she didn't see the innuendo that seemed so clear to him. *Not what I meant, but I'd be ready for her in an instant if she'd only see me.* "You had supper yet? I rolled in about fifteen minutes ago, stopped to say hello to Vanna and Truck first."

"Not yet. Gunny and Sharon took the kids to the movies, my brothers included. I've got a roast in the oven, and it should be ready soon. Myrt and Bane were in their room, so I escaped the house for a bit." She lived

125

with her sister and Bane, and Gunny had bought a nearby house, so the three households made a little triangle compound of FRMC members. Her cheeks pinked up prettily and Horse had a good idea why she'd gone running. "I mean, I decided to take a walk."

"Their noises ran you out, little sister."

Face blazing red now, she shook a finger at him. "I know what you're doing, friend, but you won't get a rise out of me."

Another innuendo rolled through his mind about things rising, but Horse managed to clamp his lips shut. "Who me?" He aimed at innocence, stifling a laugh at the way she rolled her eyes. "I'm glad we're friends, Marian. I look forward to seeing you every time I come visit."

All humor left her face as she studied him quietly for a moment. A smile finally parted her lips, the tip of her tongue touching along the bottom with a tiny side-to-side swipe. The gleam drew his gaze and blood started to run south, his cock chubbing up in his jeans.

Before things could become obvious, Marian slipped closer and slid her hand into his. "Remember that panic attack I had when we first met?"

"Yeah."

Like he'd forget something like that. Battered black and blue from the fists of her father, she'd gotten startled and froze like a bunny, hoping nearby unseen enemies would miss noticing her. Horse had protected her, drawing her close until he could get her to a place she saw as safe. That had been the start of a continuing feud between him and Gunny, because the other man had seen him as a threat to the tenuous hold Marian had on any sense of security. He'd proven Gunny wrong time and again, but the man's go-to attitude was to assume the worst of Horse.

Bane had put the kabosh on it multiple times, and Horse had bent over backwards to reassure Gunny, but the fact remained that his interest in Marian drew it from the man. Gunny saw her as a sister, his wife, Sharon, the same, and anything that had the potential to threaten her wellbeing, health or mentally, wasn't something Gunny would tolerate.

"You make me feel safe, Horse. I like you visiting as much as you do. Keeps that safe feeling going, you know?" He gave her fingers a gentle squeeze when she leaned her head trustingly against his shoulder. "I'm glad you're here, even if you tease me."

"I only tease people I like. The more I like someone, the more I pick on 'em." Angling his head, he watched a tiny smile play across those plump lips.

"You must like me a lot, then, because you always have a comment for me."

If you only knew, darlin'.

The next morning saw them out along the creek in the deeper of the fishing holes, and he watched with a mix of pride and expectation as she pulled in fish after fish. Even Gunny showing up to spar verbally with him couldn't dim his enjoyment of the time spent with Marian.

They'd walked back, Gunny on one side and him on the other, the conversation between the three of them free flowing and easy, and for a change, Gunny wasn't jumping on everything Horse said, looking for a sideways barb at Marian's expense.

That mood had been broken when Marian called out another man's name, "Einstein," and had taken off running, everything in her hands abandoned to the ground as she raced to throw her arms around the Bama Bastards nomad.

A hand settled on his shoulder and Horse glanced over at Gunny. The expression on the man's face was solemn understanding, and Horse suddenly realized he'd likely been out of the running for months and simply hadn't known.

"He's a good one." Horse banked his pain to offer the words quietly and Gunny nodded.

"He is. Motherfucker doesn't realize what he's got in his hands yet, but I can see where he'll come around. He's good for her, like you are, but different. She loves you like a brother and enjoys any chance she has to see you." Gunny's fingers squeezed tighter as he doled out the unwelcome news. "But when Einstein's here, it's a different level."

"She's something special, Gunny. A once-in-a-lifetime find for a man like me." The twisting in his gut echoed the words. "Gonna suck to see him sweep in and take it all away."

"Gotta remember she wasn't yours to start with. Hell, she's not his either. The thing is he's hers, and you can see it plain as day, just like I do. She's not a wallflower to be picked up and swept off her feet. She's a strong woman who's coming into her own more every day, and it's her choice."

"I hope Einstein realizes all that."

Gunny's hand slapped Horse's back hard, pushing him towards the man and woman now engaged in a lively conversation. "Like I'd let him get by without knowing what she's worth."

"True story." Horse chuckled as he bent to pick up the things Marian had dropped. "Hope you ride his ass hard as you've ridden mine."

"Wouldn't do things any other way, motherfucker. Now, tell me about that one-eyed winker cock and balls bait. Where'd you buy such a thing?"

With that to ease the way, he and Gunny chatted while Marian guided Einstein inside. He'd have to find a way to be okay with only ever having her friendship. He'd need to help her understand her own worth, and knew that his grudging friendship with Gunny was about to become something different.

It'd be a hard road, but Marian was worth cherishing what he could. Gunny was right that she'd made her choice, even if she didn't realize it yet.

Still sucks.

Chapter Ten
Glenna

Penn's old truck rattled roughly as she crossed the railroad tracks on the edge of town, making Shamu bark irritably.

"I know, but you're the one who had to come along." Normally he'd stay home, but he'd been insistent this morning as Glenna got ready for a visit to the feed store. "You can't go in the store either, because you pick fights with their cats."

Giving her a brief but clearly annoyed side-eye, Shamu turned his attention back out the windshield.

"Cats aren't demon spawn. Just sayin'."

The front of the store was filled with other ranch trucks, forcing Glenna to park around the side. She shoved the gearshift into neutral and pulled the handbrake, killing the engine as she winced, waiting for the typical backfire racket. When it failed to come, she patted the dash with a murmured, "Good boy." Her truck had died a couple of years ago, so this was her only mode of transportation into town.

Shamu turned his elegant head to glare at her and Glenna had to laugh at the expression of betrayal on his face. "You're a good boy, too, Shammy. Very good boy."

Reaching across in front of him, she rolled the manual window down a couple of inches, then did the same to the one on her side of the truck. If not contained somehow, the dog would abandon his post at the first sight of something to pursue. There'd be no guilt involved, either, even if he failed to bring back the squirrel or bunny. *Or cat, small dog, maybe a child.* Glenna sighed silently at those memories. Sight hounds were built different, she'd found, but still wouldn't trade anything for Shamu.

"I'll be back quick as I can." With a final rub of his soft skin, she slipped from the truck, ignoring the expression of shock when she closed the door in his face. "Told you that you couldn't get out, dorkimus."

"Talking to yourself?"

Glenna whirled at the derisive words, knowing a frown already bunched her brows. "Jackson." She acknowledged him with a chin lift. She'd learned early on to adopt more forceful behaviors around people like Jackson Snyder.

"Not going to answer me? Not surprised, that seems to be a bitch's go-to when it comes to dealing with a man." His top lip lifted to show his gleaming front teeth in a move probably supposed to mimic a smile, but came off as more of a sneer. "You didn't return my last couple of calls, Glenna."

"I felt my silence was enough of an answer and took less of my time." The only way to deal with him was head-on.

"Shoulda sold to me when I was offering top dollar." He shook his head, pretending sadness. "Now you've lost your chance."

"I heard you sold your granddaddy's place." She'd never call it his, no matter he'd inherited it. "I bet your daddy'd be real proud of you."

"I didn't sell it."

There was real anger in his voice as Jackson took a long step toward her. To keep from his chest crashing into hers, Glenna backed up until she crowded against the side of the truck. Faintly, she heard Shamu's frantic barking but ignored it in favor of keeping her full attention on the looming threat in front of her.

"Nope, still my name on the deed. Just have some investors now."

"Good for you, Jackson. Long as your mouth hasn't written checks your ass can't cash, sounds like a deal." *Why are you prodding him?* Glenna firmed her lips and lifted her chin again. It never worked to show weakness to bullies like Jackson, but she could be smarter about antagonizing him.

"I got plenty of anything you'd be interested in." His hand snapped forward and Glenna caught his wrist in one hand, holding him at bay with effort. "And probably some you wouldn't."

"Stop it." Her voice was slightly breathless, but she wasn't wooed, more alarmed. He'd never resorted to physical violence before.

Without warning his other hand was on her breast, groping roughly, the sharp pain levering her to her toes. "Or maybe you would."

"Ow! Jackson, stop it. Let me go." She spoke over his words, pushing back as hard as she could.

"You're the one keepin' me here." He leaned in closer, mouth opened in a slash, his intentions clear as Glenna shifted on her feet, trying to slide to one side and avoid the kiss. She was straining to hold him off her, Jackson not even appearing to recognize the effort he had to be applying to hold her in place. "I know I've got a powerful interest."

"I'm not interested in anything you've got to offer." Finally getting her balance again, Glenna lifted a knee sharply, catching him on the inside of his thigh. "Now"—she shoved hard, wedged as she was against the side of the truck—"get the fuck off me, asshole."

"Everything okay over here?"

Jackson's head whipped to the side and Glenna saw the doctor had stopped on the stoop of his office across the street, one hand on the doorknob.

"Right as rain." Jackson's call came as he backed away, one hand drifting towards the wrist she'd held in an aborted movement. "Me and Glenna are just having a friendly conversation between neighbors."

"Get away from me, Jackson Snyder. Get away and don't you ever put your hands on me again." Glenna raised her voice to ensure their audience of one caught every word. "Get the fuck away from me and keep my damned name out of your mouth. You touch me again and I'll make one call." She'd leave it up to him to wonder who that call would be to. "You sicken me."

"Glenna, you okay?" Doc Martin had left his stoop and was halfway across the street. "You need anything?"

"She's fine. Like I said, we were just talking."

Jackson couldn't seem to know when to walk away. Glenna glimpsed a couple of ranchers towards the front of the building who'd paused in the act of getting into their vehicles, giving them a larger audience.

She raised her voice again, nearing a shout. "I said get away from me, Jackson Snyder. Don't touch me again. I don't want anything to do with a man like you. Scum." She spat to the side and watched the anger flare in his eyes again.

"Bitch." His single word response wasn't as quiet as he'd thought, because the ranchers and Doc Martin all moved quickly towards where they stood. "I want you. I'll take you. No way you can fight me off forever,

Glenna. Remember, you live way out there in the boonies, with a lot of miles of shared fence with my land."

"Snyder, you should shut up and get gone."

Glenna didn't know who'd given the instructions, but Jackson reacted immediately, taking two long steps away from her truck. He didn't say anything else, just spun on a well-polished boot heel and stalked out of sight around the feed store.

"You okay, ma'am?" One of the men lifted a hand as if to support her elbow and Glenna nodded as she moved away.

Shamu was still barking furiously and when she turned her head, Glenna was shocked to find he'd forced the window down another few inches, almost enough to allow him to come through. His head snaked towards the man who'd offered the assistance, teeth snapping together threateningly.

"Stop, Shammy." Pulling in a breath that was shakier than she wanted to let on, she tried to smile at Doc Martin. "He's protective. And yes—" She took another breath that came in much smoother. "I'm okay. Jackson's all talk and hot air."

His manhandling of me didn't seem like empty talk.

Another breath filled her lungs. She gave them another smile, and like the air in her throat this expression came much easier. "I'm good, gentlemen. Thank you for the rescue, though. I'd never turn down chivalry like that."

"If you're sure." The frown on Doc Martin's face reminded her of the last days of Penn's life. As his time had gotten shorter, the lines on the doc's brow had deepened. "Might not hurt to stop and talk to the county sheriff. That was a clear threat he laid down. We all heard it."

"All talk. I'll give the sheriff a call if he does anything else, though. Don't worry. My grandma taught me not to suffer fools." Glenna patted the hand Doc had laid on her arm. "Now I should get into the store and place my order before Shammy tears his way out of the truck."

"Maybe have him on a leash next time. Bring him out with you." One of the ranchers suggested as he tugged the front of his hat down in respect. "He'd make any man think twice about layin' a hand on a pretty lady like you."

"Good point." She laughed as lightly as she could manage, given her insides were still quivering in fear. "He's a good companion for me."

"If you say so, miss." The other rancher nodded his goodbye and the two men returned to their trucks, chatting as they went.

"I'd never thought about you being all alone out there. I'm gonna worry about you now, Glenna." Doc Martin turned his hand over and clasped her fingers. "Don't be a stranger, sweetheart. Keep me in the loop if that Snyder boy doesn't mind his manners going forwards."

"I'll do that, Doc. I'll do that," she lied as she gave him a squeeze and turned to the truck, using one hand to push Shamu's head back through the window as she opened the door. Two cranks later, the window was set at the previous level and Glenna was on her way into the store, digging in her pocket for the list she'd made this morning.

A glance showed Jackson nowhere in sight, and when she cautiously looked around inside, he wasn't there either.

Already left to run home, tail between his legs.

A shiver danced up her spine, goose bumps raising on her arms as she thought about what could have happened.

Nothing but hot air.

Somehow the reminder wasn't as reassuring as she'd hoped it'd be.

***

Horse

"No, brother. I'm happy for him." Horse shook his head as Blackie continued to stare at him as darkness fell. A small fire started by prospects cast a glow around the area. "How can I be unhappy when Marian is the happiest I've ever seen her? I might not want to trek out to Baker again for a bit, and by that, I mean I will if needed, just won't be raising my hand for volunteer trips. At least for a bit. Let them get settled into themselves."

"That's a real healthy attitude, my friend." Blackie's fist rattled Horse's bones as he pummeled his bicep. "Better than I'd have expected, knowing how gone on her you were."

"Ow, Jesus. Fucking hell, man, why are you punishing me?" Horse moved closer and wrapped Blackie in a one-armed clinch, disarming his attempts at continued playful—but powerful—punches. "Gonna leave a mark, asshole."

"That's president asshole to you." Blackie's arms tightened as he made to lift Horse from the ground.

"Put me down. Jesus, what's gotten into you, brother?" Horse kept his feet underneath him when he landed, barely.

"Peaches is preggers again and she greenlighted me telling you." The smile that split Blackie's beard was brilliant, transforming his normally glowering visage into a beaming, proud father-to-be.

"Congrats, man. Sincerely." Horse pulled Blackie close again, fists thudding the middle of their backs as they embraced. "Happy for you. That's awesome, brother."

"It really is." Blackie stepped away, never losing the smile that had brightened his face. "She's over the moon, and I'm right there with her. Randi's gonna be the best big sister too. Three years is a good split between siblings, so says Peaches. So happy, brother. So fuckin' happy, man."

"Nobody deserves happy more, Blackie." Horse reached into a cooler and pulled out two bottles, opening both and handing one to Blackie. "To babies making a house full of love even fuller."

"Amen." Blackie lifted his bottle and took a healthy swig. "I told Peaches we had three more rooms to fill with babies and she nearly decked me." Laughing, he rubbed his jaw playfully. "She was sick a bit in the beginning, and I see now I should have waited for the glow to share my plans."

"Pick your battles where it comes down to timing, for sure." Horse tipped his bottle up as more men filtered into the backyard of the clubhouse. "You doing a general announcement?"

"Yeah, thought I'd throw it in at the end of our meeting tonight. Something good after all the regular shit." The delight on Blackie's face dimmed. "Skyd let me know there's been pressure on a couple of their chapters to change affiliation. We're going to have to snip that back, aiming for castration if needed."

"You target any one of us that direction and we'll fly true."

"I know and am proud of what we've all built here. Sometimes, we just gotta fight for what's ours. Put people in their fuckin' place. I don't want word to get back to Bane right away, because rumor mill is churning names, one of which is MDMC." Blackie's lips twisted. "Motherfuckers are a long way from Jersey, if they think to come here and stir the pot."

"That's bullshit, and they know it. If it is them, they'll be expecting us to hit them back. The biggest challenge with them is they don't seem smart enough to back down. We'll have to pick the men we use carefully, because that shit leaves a stain." Horse grimaced. "I'll hope that the news settles out so it's someone else."

"Hope all you want, still won't change the outcome if it is."

"Oh, I know, Prez. I know." Horse drained his beer and motioned to a prospect, holding it out. He gave a headshake when the prospect indicated a cooler, turning down another beer for now. "It's about time to call shit to order. You doin' general out here first, then officers inside?"

"Yeah, keep it normal as possible for now." Blackie smiled again. "Love you, asshole. You're family, I hope you know that."

"Awww." He pretended to wipe a tear from one eye. "I'm touched, brother."

"In the head," Blackie taunted, reaching out to smack Horse's bicep one final time. "Brothers," he shouted, angling his head back to get more volume. "It's time to pull everyone with a patch, including prospects, into the circle. Hangarounds, you're dismissed." Standing upright, Blackie indicated the back gate of the fence. "Off you go, we'll see you next party. Don't let me catch you dawdling either. Scoot on outta here, assholes." Four men made their way towards the gate, hands lifted in farewell. "Prospect, make sure that's locked up tight like, yeah?" Two prospects beat feet towards the opening, scuffling to be the one to close and lock the gate. "Yeah, buddy, put some hustle on it. That's what I like to see."

The general meeting went as expected, with congratulations all around and cries for shots to celebrate Blackie's news at the end. They gave the process a few minutes, then Horse gathered up the officers and they all headed inside, Blackie at the head of the line.

As soon as the door was closed on the room, Blackie leaned back in his chair, his gaze latching onto each man at the table in turn. "All righty. Hard shit now. We've got some interesting developments with the IRMC chapter north of Longview. They've had three—count'em, three—visits by an unpatched rider who's offered them various renditions of doom and gloom if they don't drop their support patches."

"As in plural? They're wanting them to pull RWMC as well as ours?" This was news and Horse wondered why Blackie hadn't been clearer earlier.

"Yeah, got a text from Skyd while we were outside. He's up at that chapter and they had to run off a new guy this evening, after he'd handed a letter over. He's going to send a copy of it to everyone standin' here." Blackie's features tightened. "Hear me now, I want to keep this close. Nothing to any other chapters, especially Baker. Whispers are running that this is coming down from the Monster Devils, and every man jack of you know how Bane'll react to that. After the shit that's happened, we protect our own. Yeah? We want to make sure of the intel before we distribute it." He looked around the table again, getting nods from everyone. "This is need to know, and I've told everyone who needs to know. Zip yer lips."

"How do you want us to handle this?" Duane rocked his chair back on two legs, the casual movement at odds with the angry expression on his face. "We go up in force, Prez?"

"Nope, not until we know for sure. I'm sending Horse to suss things out. He's got connections back east not tainted by the MDMC, and between that and him knowing Skyd real well, I think he's the right choice."

"Agreed," Duane said, thumping his chair back to four legs. "Wanna thump anyone for intel, though? Since it's now involving RWMC, should we loop them in?"

"Let's get a handle on how much of a threat it is first," Horse offered. "Yeah, there've been multiple contacts, and yeah, it appears to be escalating. But I'd hate to call them in before time. They'll only muck shit up with the posturing that's sure to be included."

"Horse is right. We keep them in our back pocket, knowing they're a force we can call to arms if needed." Blackie blew a raspberry on a sigh.

"I hate shit like this. Motherfuckers should just stay out of our territory and leave shit alone."

"Not the way of the world, boss. Sorry." Duane laughed at Horse's fake resignation, and Oaky shook his head. Grinning, Horse continued, "I'll head out first thing in the morning. Wait for Skyd-boy to get the rest of the info over, and maybe even catch a good night's sleep. I don't mind going alone, Prez, but you let me know if you change your mind on that."

"Will do. Duane, help put a folder together, yeah?" Blackie pushed away from the table, reaching for the gavel. He knocked it against the metal plate insert in the table, delivering three sound hits. "Meeting adjourned, motherfuckers. Let's head back to the fire and bask in the knowledge that your president is workin' on populatin' the next generation of FRMC."

Laughter followed them out of the room and Horse gave Blackie a wave as he detoured towards the stairs. He'd spend the evening reading everything that would be on the secure server, because as casual as Blackie tried to appear, he knew Duane would jump on the instructions to log everything, all so Horse had what he needed. Between the three of them, they'd have a clear view of the potential threat by morning.

***

Yawning, Horse slid a mug out of the cabinet and poured a cup of coffee. He leaned a hip against the countertop and took a cautious sip as he surveyed the room. Half a dozen other members were arrayed in chairs and on stools, head down over their own mugs.

"Musta been a good party," he observed, pitching his voice louder than necessary.

"Shut up, asshole," Oaky muttered, shooting a dark look at Horse. "You failed to celebrate, and don't think it wasn't noticed. Where were you?"

"Studying for midterms." He chuckled. "While you frat boys were getting prepared to conduct the porcelain throne conga line, I was studying."

"Fuck you." Duane rested his head on one arm. "I'm too old for this shit."

"You got that one right." Horse grabbed the carafe and made the rounds, topping off everyone's mug. "Need you two alert and cogitatin'. Think you can do that, brothers?"

"Stop using thousand-dollar words, asshole." Oaky took a healthy swig of the fresh coffee. "Whatcha need from us?"

"If you're up to it, a quick session in the office to talk about my chores for the day." Prospects were drifting in and out of the kitchen, forcing Horse to resort to nonspecific phrases. "I'd like your input."

"If someone will make another pot of coffee so it's ready when we're done." Duane pushed back from the table and lifted his mug, downing the coffee quickly. "I'll need more joe, prospect. Get to movin'."

"Yes, patchholder."

Horse waited for the two men to enter the office before closing the door. He sketched a salute to Blackie's empty chair and pulled out one to the right, leaving Duane and Oaky to pick their own seats.

"Word is the rumors are true and it's the Monster Devils playin' havoc out here in our space. Info says several key members have *not* been seen around the east coast for a couple of weeks, and text messages indicate significant others are talking amongst themselves about a mass move to Texas. Stands to reason their ole ladies will have the right of it, if they're lookin' to uproot families." Horse let his gaze drift between the men opposite him. "Physical descriptions don't match the MDMC big dogs, so it's likely not Dom or his main boys, but he's definitely sent a squad of members to try and carve out a place to set up." Dominick was Bane's blood, and the source of all MDMC woes.

"Well, shit." Duane cracked his knuckles. "Want me to ride up there with you today?"

"Nah, I'm just going to hit the IRMC clubhouse. Skyd's expecting me, so all should be fine."

"Shoulda, coulda, woulda—if it's not fine, it'll be hella too late to do anything about it." Oaky raked a hand through his hair, flipping it over his shoulder. "I think you should have company."

"Nope, I think you need to be here to catch my call when I find out the who and why. That way Blackie has you two at his back when he calls the Rebels. If needed, after we do those chats, I can ride out to Baker, let Bane know in person."

"Respect, brother. This won't be easy on him." Duane shook his head, slinging an elbow over the back of the chair next to his. "Good idea thinkin' of that."

"I might as well have sponsored him, the way things shook out. Regardless, I don't want him to get a text. That's shitty."

"Shitty kitty kind of bullshit the MDMC would pull. Pussies, all of 'em. Fuckin' assholes." Duane cracked his knuckles again. "When you leavin'?"

"Soon as we get done. You got the various data sorted last night, and I put it together into a story early this mornin'. I'm confident in my read, but another respect piece is me going to Skyd and getting his tale direct from his mouth." Horse yawned and lifted his coffee to take another drink. "Won't be a long ride, but I don't know how much time I'll spend talking. I figure we don't have to call out and wake Blackie just yet. Give him and Peaches a chance to sleep in as much as Randi will let 'em." He smiled. "You see his face last night? Never seen a man as proud about knocking up his ole lady."

"He told me Peaches gave him a long lecture about loving Randi the same. Poor Blackie didn't understand any of it, I think because he's always viewed that little girl as his. Honestly confused, but he said he kept reassuring Peaches it will all be okay."

"Sounds like him." Oaky laughed and slapped a hand on Duane's shoulder. "We're lucky sumbitches, you know that?"

"Yeah, we are." Horse didn't hesitate to agree. "My lucky day when me and Junkyard rode into Longview looking for something good."

Duane stood, a smirk curling one corner of his lips. "Lucky day for all of us." He indicated the door with a tip of his head. "Better get that coffee in you so you can hit the road."

"Agreed."

As Horse made his way around the table, Oaky stood and pulled him into a one-armed clinch. "Shiny side, brother."

"Shiny side." Horse repeated the words, the familiar warmth of the brotherhood shared filling him.

"Prospect," Duane yelled, yanking the door open. "That coffee ready yet?"

"Yes, patchholder."

By the time Horse made it to the kitchen, another mug of coffee was waiting for him.

Two hours later, he was less pleased with life in general. He'd slipped out of Longview along Highway 80, headed west, and then peeled north and west after Hawkins. The Iron Riggers clubhouse in question was near a rural town named Belle, but damned if he could locate the road the instructions said should be right here.

Idling into town, he parked along one side street and walked to a pharmacy half a block away. The temperature inside the business seemed to fall by a dozen degrees once the cashier caught sight of him. Horse hadn't expected that, because bikers in general weren't a rare sight in this part of Texas, and the Freed Riders patch was reasonably well known and respected. Not by this man, however, given the deep scowl directed his way.

Snagging a bottle of water and a candy bar, he stood in the short line waiting for the cash register, out of courtesy giving the little old woman in front of him a respectful nod. Once at the front of the line, Horse endured the glare, waiting until the man spat out the total before he risked a question.

"I'm looking for a farm-to-market road, one that's supposed to head south out of town, but I didn't see it as I rode through. Can you help me?" He pulled his wallet out and plucked a couple of dollars to slide across the counter. "I'd appreciate it."

"FM2942 runs parallel to town before bending south." The helpful voice came from behind him and Horse turned to find a man about his age, cowboy hat perched on top of his head. "Take this street down two blocks and turn right. Two more blocks and take a left. That'll put you on the F&M, no problem."

"Thanks much." Horse inclined his head, reaching for the change from his purchase. The cashier deliberately missed his hand, dropping the coins over the edge of the counter, leaving silver and copper discs to bounce against the tile flooring.

"Oops." The snideness of the non-apology ruffled Horse's feathers, but he tamped down the anger. Nothing good would come of making a big deal over a few cents, especially in a small town like this.

"That's okay," Horse responded as evenly as he could. "Just a few pennies." Nodding at the man behind him, Horse thanked him again as he walked away.

"Jacob, that's a shitty way to treat your customers. Mayhap I should let your uncle Cooter know how you acted." Seemed Horse didn't need to take the man to task over his behavior since the man who'd given him directions was ready to step into that role. He left the business with a broad smile on his face.

The road was exactly where the directions said it would be, and Horse hummed along to the song playing from his speakers as he rode out of town.

Chapter Eleven
Glenna

Staring at the phone on the kitchen wall, Glenna shook her head, fighting off the unease that had settled over her in the past weeks. She'd called in her last feed order changes instead of going to store in town, but this morning had decided she would be damned if she'd let Jackson have that much control over her.

"He's just an asshole." A tiny huff of agreement came from the dog pressed tight to her leg. "Nothin' to be afraid of." Shamu whined lightly, his head seeking her hand. She gave in and caressed his soft-as-silk ears. "I'll have you with me."

Turning, she plucked an intertwining handful of leather and fabric strips from the counter.

"Which means we need to get the harness on." At the dreaded word, Shamu's ears laid flat back to his head. "Otherwise, you stay stuck in the truck." His lip lifted slightly, showing a few teeth. "I mean, it's your decision." She made to put the harness down and he snorted, dropping his head to make it easier for her to slip it over his streamlined body. "There's my good boy."

Leash snapped to the harness, she followed him to the truck where he vaulted through the open window, not waiting for her to reach the door.

"Brat," she scolded with a grin, letting the lead snake through her fingers. "Here we go."

Their trip to town was quick, wind streaming in the open windows, Shamu's happy face pushed hard against the current of air. Glenna backed the truck up to the loading dock before going inside, Shamu at her side. The usual crew of old-time ranchers greeted her, gathered on their feed barrels and five-gallon buckets around the cold potbellied stove in the corner of the store. Shamu remained quiet as Glenna conducted her business, ordering her normal lot of feed.

Chewing on the side of her lip, she hesitantly stopped the old store owner from turning away. "Bob, I'm thinking of leasing out the horse barn to boarders. When I'm ready to order in all the stuff it'll take to convert things, how much lead time do you think you'll need? I'm talking about hay nets, corner feeders, rubber mats for the stalls themselves, you know, fancy stuff like that."

"Oh, let me give it a think." His gaze dropped to the counter, flicking from catalog to catalog, looking like he was deciding which company would receive each part of the order. "Most it'd take would be a month, I reckon. We might find some things are easier shipped and some should be picked up in Dallas or Shreveport, but we could outfit you quick enough."

"You going into the boarding business, Mrs. Richeson?" One of the old timers had overheard part of their conversation and was looking to pick up some prime gossip.

"Might do so, Mr. Pearson. Right now it's still in the thinkin' stage. We'll see if it advances past that." Glenna turned and smiled at him.

Shamu growled softly and Glenna looked down at him in surprise. He'd been quietly well-behaved up until now. Glancing up at Bob, she gave him a nod, saying, "Thanks so much."

"Boys'll be loadin' your truck now, Glenna. We'll bring the bulk out on the flatbed later today." Bob stuck his hand out and she gripped it firmly, giving it a shake. "Let me know when you're ready to order the things for the boarding business. I'll work to get you the best deals I can."

"Boarding business?" The words were spoken in the unfortunately familiar grating voice of Jackson Snyder. "You're opening a stables now, Glenna? This is the first I've heard of this."

Shamu growled louder, shifting his body to crowd Glenna away from the man.

"Well, Jackson"—she placed a hand between Shamu's ears, feeling the way his skull vibrated from the deep growl—"seein' as I don't talk to you, that isn't surprising." Inclining her head at the store owner, she offered a quiet and respectful, "Bob," and turned, finding Jackson had neatly boxed her in. Shamu stood proudly between them, showing more of his teeth as the guttural growl grew louder. "Back off, Jackson." She stepped to the side, Jackson taking a similar pace. Shortening her hold on the leash, Glenna shook her head. "Back off."

"Tell me about this business. Maybe it'll up the price I'm willing to pay for your place." Jackson made as if he'd step closer, then glanced down at Shamu and made the right decision not to. "First thing I'll do is get rid of that mutant mutt." Cocking a finger and thumb, he pretended to shoot her dog. "Stables sounds like a good idea. Maybe I'll do that over on my spread. Diversify."

"Snyder, did you have business in my store?" Bob came around the end of the counter and pressed forwards, pushing Jackson back a pace. "If you don't, then take your ugly mug and hit the road. We all heard about your harassment of Glenna, and none of us think it's anything more than pure venom and bullying. Now, get gone."

"I need to order some rat traps." Jackson sent a glare around the room. "Big ones. Seems there's some huge rats in this town."

"Only rat I see is standin' there in shiny boots and dust free jeans." Mr. Pearson stood, gnarled hand resting on top of his cane. "Man behind the counter said you should leave, and I tend to agree with him. I'm surprised at you, Snyder. I know for sure your daddy taught you better than this. Shame on you, spitting on your daddy's memory by actin' like an a-hole."

Jackson stared at Glenna. "Maybe, if you come with the land, I'll let you have the stables as a hobby." He straightened, rolling his shoulders back. "Maybe, if you come with the land, you'll learn your place."

Glenna loosened her hold on the leash, giving Shamu a few inches of freedom and the dog immediately lunged towards Jackson, who stumbled awkwardly backwards just in time. The rancher's glare intensified, and Glenna caught the first flare of real hatred in his eyes.

Ignoring her sudden shot of terror, she worked to clearly enunciate each word. "I will never sell to you. Never. And there's nothing that would ever entice me to entertain the idea of there being a me and you. Never and nothing." Shamu was still pressed tight to her leg, the vibrations of his growl rolling through her bones. "And you better not ever touch my dog. Never, nothing, and not ever. If you take away anything from today, remember those words in your little pea-sized brain, Jackson. Remember them."

She watched as he turned and walked away, his stride purposeful and arrogant, knowing every eye in the place was on him. Once the door clicked shut behind him, Shamu stopped growling and his muscles relaxed slightly. His gaze was still fixed on the door, however, watchful for the threat to return.

"Glenna—Mrs. Richeson—I'm sorry that happened to you. I heard he's been an irritant, but I don't think I realized just how serious a threat he was." Bob placed a hand on her shoulder. "I hope you know you can call on nearly anybody in town. I worry about you all the way out there by yourself." He squeezed her reassuringly, then moved back behind the counter. "I can promise you nothing like that will happen in my store again."

"It's okay, Bob. He's nothing but hot air." Glenna trotted out the words she'd been telling herself since the first frightening encounter with Jackson. "He don't bother me none."

"I think you should call the sheriff, Mrs. Richeson." Mr. Pearson had moved up beside Glenna and was now fondling Shamu's ears. "Good pup, takin' care of your momma like that. Good pup."

"If he does anything else, I'll give them a call." It wasn't lost on her that she'd promised him the same thing she'd given the doctor after the last time. "And Shamu is a good boy. Helps keep me safe from rogue bulls or men full of bullshit." She gave him a smile she didn't feel. "I don't worry about too much with him by my side."

"Man threatened your dog, ma'am." Thumping his cane on the wooden floor, Mr. Pearson scowled at the empty door. "Threatened you."

"I'll stop by the sheriff's office next time I'm out that way, let him know what's happened." It didn't cost her anything to make the promise. "Meanwhile, I need to run by the diner and pick up lunch, then head home. Always a load of work to do. You know how it is."

"That I do, young lady." She'd moved from Mrs. Richeson, to ma'am, and now to young lady. That earned him a real smile he returned. "Drive safely."

"Will do."

Giving Bob a wave, she walked outside and got herself and Shamu into the truck. He was still sticking to her side so there wasn't a flashy window-entrance this time, just his grumble when she took too long to climb in beside him. That was when the shakes hit, her fingers trembling so strongly she missed her grab at the key dangling from the keyhole three times. Cupping one hand under the other, she made contact and twisted the key finally, the truck engine roaring to life.

"So much for an uneventful trip, huh, Shammy?" Aiming the truck at the nearby highway, she debated the wisdom in picking up a meal she wouldn't have to cook—an attractive idea—with the thought of a potential meeting with Jackson again. "He's not gonna run me out of town." Decided, she turned left to go further into town, giving a friendly wave at the rider of a lone motorcycle going the other direction.

"Want some fries with that, Shammy?" At one of his favorite words, the dog's ears perked tall. "I'm thinkin' a burger for me. I'll get a double order of fries, so we can share. Wanna share some fries with Mom?" His bark was bright and happy, and the sound put a smile on her face as they drove to the diner.

***

Horse

Wind blowing against his face, Horse downshifted the instant he noticed the quickly looming change in pavement. The road he was on went from a soft oiled surface to gravel, which pulled a grimace and sigh from him. It looked well-packed at least, so hopefully wouldn't slow his travel too much.

Approaching the fifth or sixth sharp curve, he'd just angled the bike to sweep from outside to inside when he felt the rear wheel lose its grip on the unstable surface. Gentle braking only made the movement worse, then the quickly approaching raised berm along the outside edge of the curve launched him towards the ditch and fence beyond.

"Goddammit."

The bike wasn't moving terribly fast, but the momentum was more than enough to push him past the dry ditch and through the fence, strands of wire parting noisily when the frame of the bike hit them. Then he was on his ass, literally, in a field of endless green grass. A few cows in the distance lifted their heads to look at him for a moment, then went back to grazing while Horse sat stunned, one leg underneath the now ominously quiet bike.

"Sonuvabitch."

Wire was wrapped around the forks and when he tried to pick the bike up the metal-on-metal grind was loud in his ears. That sound seemed to bring back a soundtrack of ambient noise, bird song mixing with the ticking of the cooling engine.

A second attempt at extricating himself from the wrecked bike was successful, and he stared down at the twisted metal of the forks and front wheel, tire flat. Pain in his thigh was just more background noise, with his gaze fixed on the bike sitting damaged in front of him.

A vehicle pulled to a stop in the curve and Horse looked up in time to watch a tiny spitfire of a woman jump put, all dark brown hair and deep blue eyes, and judging mouth.

"You okay?"

Her voice was soft, pitched to carry to where he stood.

Horse nodded, then looked down at the bike again.

"I'm gonna need a ride somewhere." Digging in his pocket for his phone, he was surprised to come up emptyhanded. "Not sure where my phone went to."

"Well, drag that bike back through the fence. We'll get you somewhere you can make a call. Town's only a few miles back." Turning to her truck, she rose on her toes to open a toolbox attached to the bed. Pulling on a pair of gloves, she shoved a tool in her back pocket and angled back towards him, making her way through the ditch. "Come on, we don't have all day. Do you need help getting it back outside the pasture?"

"No, I got it." The bike wouldn't balance on the wheels, not with the front one angled to the side. He realized the frame was likely warped too. Horse wound up doing an awkward slide-flip-slide to get it to move, and by the time he'd made it to the ditch, he was winded and exhausted, head buzzing and dizzy. "There." He turned too quickly and found himself back on his ass, watching the woman deftly weave the strands of fencing back together, threading in extra pieces as needed until she'd created a barrier. She twisted them together with the tool in one hand. "Wow, you're good at that."

"It'll hold for now. It's a poor patch job and needs two new posts, but it'll hold." She tipped her head to one side, studying him. "You okay, mister? Not hurt, are you?"

"No, just shaken up. Was a wild couple of seconds." Horse managed to get to one knee before tumbling awkwardly back to the ground. He rested his elbows on knees and hung his head, trying to let the swimming feeling fade away. "Give me a minute."

A hand appeared in front of him. "Come on, up you get."

Grasping the gloved hand, he was surprised at how delicate her bones felt under his grip. Then was surprised again at the strength behind the tug to get him upright. "There we are," he muttered, reaching out a hand to steady himself against the side of her truck. "Thanks."

"You are hurt." She was kneeling in front of him, face dangerously close to his crotch, giving him a momentary fantasy of her doing something wicked with that gorgeous mouth. Then those strong hands pulled at a rip in his jeans, widening the tear and he saw the hole in his leg, blood pumping out and down his thigh. "Boot's got blood in it. This is a bad cut." She stood and opened the passenger door, shoving something out of the way. "In you get." He followed her directions and found himself angled into the seat, leg straight in front of him as she stood in the door. Something loomed over him, and Horse looked up at the strangest animal he'd ever seen. The giant hairless rat opened its mouth and growled at him.

He blinked twice, but the mirage didn't go away before his eyes closed for a final time.

***

Glenna

"Stop it." Her admonition to Shamu went unnoticed. Shifting with the bumps, he managed to stay in the same position, menacingly arched over the unconscious man, lips lifted and his growl still rolling through the cab of the truck. She pulled into the ranch driveway and sped up the lane to the house. It would have taken much longer to get back to town, and even then, the closest ambulance was twenty miles farther. This way she could evaluate the wound and decide if calling an air evac was warranted.

"Now we just have to get him inside." She had a push-sled in the stables for the heavy bales of alfalfa they once fed to Penn's horses. It should work. *Maybe.* Locking the brakes, she let the truck drift sideways towards the house, then slammed it into neutral, killing the engine as she pulled the handbrake. "With me," she ordered Shamu, and he bailed out of the truck right behind her. Racing to the stables and back seemed to take a thousand years, but the man still hadn't moved when she returned. She positioned the sled under the door and opened it, pushing her shoulder against his shifting body to hold him into place.

As gently as she could, she let him slowly drop to the sled, arranging his limbs and checking the temporary tourniquet she'd placed on him when he'd passed out. Satisfied that he was as okay as could be, she started the process of getting him into the house. One beach towel slide into the living room later, she gave up the idea of him being on the couch for the next part and went to the kitchen for the extensive emergency kit she and Penn had put together over the years.

Probing the wound with her finger, she was pleased to find the artery wasn't punctured as she'd feared. The bleeding had come from other veins, and they were all clotting satisfactorily now that the tourniquet had temporarily held the worst of the bleeding at bay. She'd doctored Penn many times, and the process came back easily to her now.

The pre-threaded suture needle helped things move forwards smoothly, and with a mattress stitch she'd learned from her grandmother, she sewed up the three-inch gash in the man's leg.

Releasing the tight belt from around his leg, she watched his appendage regain color, the repair not even seeping blood. She pulled off his boot, startled at the amount of blood that spilled out. His sock was saturated all the way up his leg, so she removed that too. The pulse in the top of his foot was strong and steady, if a little slow. Convinced she'd done all she could for now, Glenna let herself relax back against the side of the nearby couch, taking in a deep breath and pushing it out slowly.

"Jesus, Shammy. That was too close for comfort." The dog stood beside her, staring down at the man lying in the floor. "I'll get him on the couch in a bit, after I've recovered a little. Maybe the food would help."

Struggling to her feet, she used an old blanket to cover him, removing and balling up her sweatshirt as a pillow for his head.

He's good-looking. She shook her head at the idle thought. It was something she'd noticed right away, the moment she'd seen him standing next to the pile of twisted metal she suspected was the bike she'd waved to earlier in the day. He hadn't argued with her directions, and now she guessed it was the shock that had already been setting in from his wound. Either way, it had been kinda nice to have someone respect her knowledge and expertise. *Course, it'd have been better if he hadn't been bleeding to death.*

Shamu looked up at her as Glenna snorted a laugh. "Man tried to bleed out in the front seat of my truck. I fixed him. I guess I can feel a little good about today's work." Skin on top of his head wrinkling, Shamu glared at her. "Ready for your fries? They'll be cold, but we can nuke them if you want."

The dog followed her out of the room, sending a final threatening growl over his shoulder.

"Oh, stop it. He's no threat right now, that's for sure."

Grabbing the phone from the wall, she dialed a number from memory. She plated the burger and fries while she waited for the call to connect.

"Glenna, how are you today, pretty lady?"

Multitasking while ignoring his opening, she shoved the plate in the microwave and got straight to business. "I need a favor, Cooter. There's a motorcycle in the ditch right on the corner of my land, there in that bad curve. Can you take one of the boys and load it up, then bring it to my house?"

"You bought a motorcycle?" His voice rose in volume, echoing through the speaker. "And wrecked it?" His voice rose again, this time in at least an octave. "Are you okay, Glenna? My God. How in the hell did you do this?"

Now choosing to ignore his demanding tone, she continued with how she'd seen the conversation playing out in her head. The numbers on the front of the microwave counted down. "Bring your bag of goodies too." That's what Penn had called Cooter's all-inclusive first aid kit, and the memory drew a pang of hurt from her throat. "I'm in the house, so just come in when you get here. Dump the bike up by the shed, if you would. Thanks, Cooter. I appreciate it."

Hanging up on his sputtering questions, Glenna rested one hand on the receiver, waiting to see if he'd call straight back. When he didn't, she patted the phone and opened the refrigerator, surveying the contents. Plenty of supplies for a couple of days. Snagging the warmed-up food from the microwave, Glenna leaned against the counter as she scarfed down her burger, tossing Shamu more than his share of the fries.

Done eating, Glenna glanced at the phone, giving thought for a moment of calling the sheriff, but discarded the idea nearly immediately. Neither Jackson nor the stranger warranted that complication right now.

After a quick look in on the patient, still resting comfortably—sort of— on her living room floor, she whistled for Shamu and they went outside, moving the truck up to the shed. Glenna was still unloading the items she'd purchased at the feed store when Cooter roared up the drive. Sparing him a glance, she waved and then picked up the final box of cattle medicine, lugging it into the office in the shed and dropping it on the cabinet there.

"Glenna, what's going on?" Over his shoulder, she saw two of his nephews wrestling the wrecked bike out of the truck bed.

"Thanks, Cooter. Appreciate it. I didn't think I'd have enough oomph to lift it."

The boys half-lifted, half-dragged the bike close to where they stood, letting it come to rest on its side there.

"Whose bike is this?" Cooter's expression was puzzled and a little wild.

Glenna made a split-second decision. She'd called Cooter with the intention of having him look over the man in the house, but then had wavered in that resolve, the reason she'd still been stalling here in the shed. The raw instinct to protect the unconscious man was visceral and overwhelming, but Cooter was her oldest friend. *If I can't trust him, then who?*

"I can haul you home in a bit, if you don't mind having the boys take your truck." Staring at Cooter, she waited for him to catch up with her silent communication, and after a few heart-straining seconds, he nodded.

Raising his voice, he called, "Keys are in her, boys. Just leave her at your granddad's house. I'll be by to pick it up later." He grabbed the big first aid kit out of the bed, then turned to the boys who were still staring down at the twisted motorcycle. "Thanks much. Appreciate you helpin' out."

After a silent and uncomfortable wait for the truck to rattle back down the gravel drive, Cooter gave her a cool look.

"Tell me why I'm here, Glenna."

"There's a man in my house. He wrecked his bike, and I already had him in my truck before I realized how badly he was hurt. Only thing I could think of was getting here and fixing his leg."

Laid out in such stark detail, she realized it sounded slightly crazy.

Only slightly?

Before Cooter could do more than open his mouth, she continued, "If he'd needed to get to the hospital in Tyler, I'd have called the air ambulance. He was bleeding bad, but I got it taken care of. Now, I need help getting him on the couch, and wanted you to double-check my work."

"There's a man." Cooter took a heavy breath, one hand scraping across his brow. "In your house."

"Yeah, he had just wrecked when I happened by. Wasn't yet on his feet."

"And instead of calling for an ambulance, you loaded him up and brought him here." Cooter's arm swept out behind him, indicating her house. "To your home."

"Is there a question in there?" Glenna was feeling itchy. Being away from the unconscious man for so long was unsettling her. "Let me show you." She pushed past Cooter, noting that Shamu was already waiting by the back door. "It'll make more sense that way."

"Not sure that's a true statement, but lead on, Glenna." His footfalls came from behind her, the tread steady and comforting. "Let's see this stranger. This biker type you've apparently decided to adopt."

"I'm not adopting him. He's just. I don't know, Cooter. It felt right to bring him here."

"It felt right." He repeated her words, and she glanced back at him. Brows furrowed, he reached around her for the edge of the door, pulling it wide. "It just felt right."

"Still no questions in there." Glenna preceded him into the living room and dropped to her knees next to the man, her fingers automatically seeking out the important pulse points that would tell her the repair was still holding. "He's doing good."

"He's a big'un." Cooter walked around the corner of the couch but held his distance, coming to a stop a few feet away. "How the hell'd you get him in here?"

"I managed." She'd never admit how exhausted she still was from the efforts it had taken. "Come down here, let me show you what I did."

"I can see well enough from here, thanks." Cooter made a scoffing sound, and she glanced up at him, surprised to find him still wary. "If he wakes up and you're right there, man this size could put a hurtin' on you."

No he won't. Not like Jackson Snyder would.

Licking her lips, Glenna tried again. "He's not going to hurt you, Cooter. And if he does wake, there's plenty of room to ease back."

"How long did you have the belt on his leg?"

"Just from the corner to here. Eight or nine minutes total, I think." *Finally, questions I can answer.* "When I saw how he was bleeding, I wasn't sure if it was arterial or not. It wasn't."

"What gouged the hole in him?"

"The brake handle, I think. When I looked it over quick, it had a tiny swatch of jean material on it. Probably when he went through the fence."

"You fixed the break in the fencing? I saw it had been patched up."

"Yeah, while he pulled the bike out of the pasture. That was before I realized he was really hurt. It's a temporary job. I'll deal with it better later."

"This man should be in an ER, Glenna. Probably needs a tetanus shot, and some stout antibiotics. The kind of stuff I can't do for him." Cooter finally edged closer, squatting down next to where Glenna knelt. "Toes are nice and pink, so I think you fixed his circulation issue without making things worse." He ran a hand under the man's untucked shirt, lifting it to look at his belly. "No bruising on his torso, so probably no issues with internal bruising. Did you check his back?"

"Yeah." She nodded and stretched out a hand, restoring the man's shirt so it covered him. "No bruising there either. He didn't have any grass in his hair, so I'm guessing he didn't hit that on his way down."

"Well, all told, he fared better than I'd have expected after seeing the condition of the bike. Did he call anyone, or tell you anything? His name?"

"Nope, but he'll wake up soon, right?"

"Should, unless he was runnin' on empty before the wreck. His body will take its time, I'm sure." Cooter pulled the man's other boot off, setting it beside the blood-soaked one on the floor. "Let's get him on the couch."

"I'll put a sheet down first. Give me a second." Glenna hurried to the hallway closet, returning with an armful of covers. Cooter helped her spread the sheet over the couch, awkwardly following her lead to tuck his half of the fabric under the cushions. "Thanks."

Cooter positioned himself at the man's shoulders, and Glenna hooked a leg under each arm. Between them they lifted him smoothly, setting him gently on the couch. The man groaned lowly and shifted to one side, farther from the drop to the floor, then lapsed into silence again.

"You call the sheriff?" When Glenna shook her head, Cooter gave her the exasperated look she'd become so familiar with over the past year or so. "Why ever not, Glenna? The man's probably got family who'll be worried about him."

"No ring." She shrugged quickly. "It's a no-fault accident, so it's not like I'm helpin' him break any laws."

"That you know of." Cooter opened his kit, pulling out bandages and gauze, ointment, and other things he would know she didn't have. "He's a biker type. They're all outlaws."

"That's a sweeping statement." Gathering up the items as Cooter laid them out, Glenna dropped them into a nearby basket. "I don't know what I'm—there's just something about him. Once he can tell me what he needs, I'll be sure to help him with whatever it is. But right now, knowing he's here—" She lifted a shoulder, nodding towards the couch. "—it feels right. Don't ask me to explain it, because I can't."

With a heavy sigh, he finished handing her gauze and closed the latches on his box. "You can't explain it, but you've got a pressing need to have him here where you can look after him." He looked at her from under his bunched brows. "I don't understand it, but I'll respect whatever this is."

A spiral of tension in her chest unspooled slowly. "Thanks, Cooter. Thanks much."

"He'll sleep for a bit yet. Want to run me back to Daddy's now?"

"Sure. Sure." She stood and offered Cooter a hand, which he ignored, pushing to his feet with a laugh. Glenna felt her lips twist and concentrated on smoothing out her smile. "I'll leave Shammy here."

"He won't kill the guy, will he?" Cooter hadn't liked the dog when Glenna had gotten him, but he and the animal had come to an agreement a while ago. They simply ignored each other when possible.

"No, he'll be fine." Glenna led Cooter outside to where the truck was parked.

He walked to the driver door and paused, then laughed. "Habit."

"Yeah." She angled around him and climbed into the truck, jamming the key home on the first try and gritting her teeth as the engine rattled to life. "No worries."

***

Horse

Head pounding, Horse eased his eyes open and looked around the room. It hadn't changed since he'd last surfaced from unconsciousness. Bright with sunshine, the room was filled with ample light through the tall windows that spanned a long wall that looked out over a bunch of cows.

He felt more alert this time and hoped that would translate to a longer period of wakefulness. He still didn't know where he was or what had happened after the bike had gone through the fence. There were flashes of memories that didn't make sense, just a mess of sensations more than anything else.

Undisputable was that this was someone's home, not a hospital room. It wasn't a house he could identify, either, which had him wondering about what had really happened to him.

What do I know for sure?

The sutured wound in his leg looked to be healing well, which meant he'd been out for at least a day. The couch he was lying on was good quality, and his leg was propped on a pile of pillows that smelled of sunshine and flowers. He was in just his skivvies and a shirt he didn't recognize, which meant his clothes were damaged or removed for treatment maybe. They didn't matter, and he could see the only thing he'd really worry about lying folded on the arm of the couch, the nearby black leather of his vest a comfort.

So, not very damn much.

A growl from across the room pulled his attention to the doorway where a large black-and-white animal stood. Was it a dog? Lean lines spoke of tuned musculature, but the only hair he could see was on top of the dog's head, where the thin, black fur standing on end like a mohawk. *I think it's a dog.*

"Hey, dog." His voice was rough, cracking and broken. "You a good boy?"

The dog's lip lifted as if in answer, the growl growing more guttural.

"Well, I'm not goin' anywhere anytime soon, boy. Sorry to disappoint."

With a sharp bark, the dog turned and disappeared.

"Shush, Shamu. You'll wake our guest."

The woman's voice rattled his memories a bit, and he thought she might have been in his dreams earlier.

"Oh, you're awake." Horse turned his head and focused on the figure standing in the doorway. Hair a mass of curls framing her pixie face, the diminutive woman stood firmly on both feet as if to weather a storm. "How you feelin' today?"

"Okay, I think. Where am I?"

"My house just outside of Belle. You were in a motorcycle wreck."

"I remember the wreck. Sucked. The loose gravel got me."

He cleared his throat roughly and she startled into movement, disappearing for an instant before coming back into the room at a fast pace. In her hand was a glass with a straw, and when she leaned over to offer it, Horse didn't try to take it, simply opening his mouth in mute acceptance.

With a tiny smile, she bent farther, bringing the straw to his lips.

The first sip was heaven, and Horse found himself gulping huge swallows, making a discontented sound when she removed the glass from his reach.

"Slower is better, trust me."

"I'm sore all over."

"It looked like you had quite the ride." She placed the glass on a nearby table and moved the blanket, unsticking the bandage over the hole in his leg with a deft movement. "You're healing well and haven't had a temperature. I think you avoided the worst of it." She patted the blanket as she recovered him and Horse shot his hand out, capturing hers.

The dog was there in an instant, lips lifted, that ever-present growl rolling out of him.

Horse released his hold and she smiled, shifting so her hand covered his. "Shush, Shamu. I keep telling you, this man isn't a danger to me." Arching an eyebrow at him, she asked, "Are you?"

"No, ma'am, I am not."

Shaking his head ratcheted up his headache and he must have winced because her hand appeared on his brow, cool and gentle as she dragged her palm and fingers across his forehead.

"Headache? I've got some over-the-counter stuff that'll help." She sat on the table next to the glass, reaching into a basket he hadn't noticed. She came out with a container and shook a couple of tablets into her hand, then offered them to him along with the water.

Two more sweetly satisfying gulps of the water to wash down the pills had her pulling the glass back out of reach.

"I'm Glenna Richeson, and this is Shamu, my noisy protector."

"Graeme Nass, ma'am." He gestured to the vest. "My friends call me Horse."

"My friends just call me Glenna, or pain in the ass, depending on the day." Her smile was bright, as if a ray of sunshine had speared through the windows and landed on her face. "I'm overly glad you're awake and coherent, I gotta tell you. It's been a worrisome bit of time. Not sure if I'd made the right decision to keep you here."

"So a hospital wasn't an option?" He'd have expected to wake in an ER, with the blinding overhead lights and constant noise. "It's a much nicer place to be, that's for sure, but I hate you went out of your way."

"It just seemed right." Glenna rolled her eyes. "I know that sounds crazy, but I can't explain it better than that." In an aside, as if to herself, she whispered, "And Lord knows I've had to try to tell Cooter multiple times."

"I appreciate it." He looked around. "Do you know where my phone is?"

"Oh." She jumped to her feet and moved out of his view for a moment, then came back and dropped his phone in his lap. "Your jeans were ruined, so I took everything out of your pockets. It's all just over there."

She pointed and the dog shoved his head under her hand. "Shammy, stop it" was her idle complaint, then she rewarded the dog with ear rubs. "Your shirt wasn't in much better shape, so that's why you're in one of Penn's."

"Pen?" The phone was dead, of course. "Do you have a charger?"

"Oh, gosh, yes. I should have thought of that." She was gone again, the dog pinning him with a glare before he followed her. Another instant later and she leaned over the back of the couch, plucking the phone from his hands. "I'll need that, sorry." From not too far away, she called, "And Penn's my husband."

Horse smiled and relaxed deeper into the couch. She was a hoot and a conundrum all at once. From what he remembered, she'd ordered him around on the side of the road, supremely confident in her ability to take control of the situation. But now she was flustered at the idea of not charging his phone.

I bet she's a handful for that husband.

Chapter Twelve

Glenna

Shamu stopped growling, which told Glenna that Graeme had gone back to sleep.

"I don't know why you don't like him." She thumped the dog lovingly on top of his head. "He's not a threat. I promise you."

She worked at the counter for a couple of minutes, assembling two sandwiches. One went onto a plate and was covered with clingwrap, and the other she ate standing over the sink, crumbs dropping harmlessly next to the drain.

Before she went outside for chores, the plate and a fresh glass of water were deposited on the coffee table within easy reach of Graeme. She considered leaving him a note about where she was, then stifled a groan. He wouldn't care that she wasn't here when he woke up again.

Since she'd gotten a late start, things seemed to take longer than normal as everything that could go wrong, did. Of course. Then she took the time to walk through the stables again, adding to her mental list of what would be needed. Next time she went to town, she'd stop at the bank and talk to them about a loan to cover the startup costs.

"I guess we're doing this, Shammy. Are you going to be okay with more people around?" Rubbing between his ears as they walked into the kitchen, she shifted and grabbed his collar when Glenna realized Graeme was standing by the sink. "Oh, you're up."

"Thanks for the sandwich. I was hungry." He'd taken the shirt off and knotted it around his waist in a rough kilt, the black leather vest covering his shoulders and back. Graeme gestured at himself. "I wasn't sure what to do about clothing and didn't want your husband to be upset at me runnin' around in just my tighty whities."

"Oh." Pain socked her in the chest, knocking all the air from her body. "Penn can't—I mean he wouldn't have." She struggled to breathe. "He's not going to—"

"Hey." An arm rounded her shoulders, guiding her to sit in one of the chairs around the table. "Are you okay? Did something happen?"

Shaking her head, Glenna dipped her chin to her throat, trying to find the words. "Penn died a few years ago."

"Oh, Jesus. Glenna, I'm sorry." Graeme tried to squat next to her and groaned with pain, finally dropping to one knee. "I didn't know." His hands covered both of hers, holding tight. "I'm so sorry."

"You couldn't have known." Glenna shook her head again, blinking tears away. "Let me get you a pair of sweats or something. I didn't think about that. I'm the one who should be sorry."

She pushed to her feet and looked down into Graeme's face, his clear anguish at hurting her salving her emotions somewhat. Glenna extended a hand, and he grasped it, letting her guide him to a standing position. "You go back to the couch. I'll be in there in a minute." She realized Shamu was silent and looked around for him. "Where'd Shammy go? I wanted to introduce you two properly, so he'd stop growling at you."

"Not sure, but he and I get along well enough. I'll be out of your hair soon as I can call one of my brothers."

"The phone should be charged enough now." Opening the drawer Penn had rigged up for their devices, she pulled Graeme's out and handed it to him. He went through the process of booting it up and smiled when it gave the welcome screen. "Make your calls. I'll go get you some clothes." She dipped her head. "I do appreciate your efforts to not make things awkward. It's a nice gesture."

"Respect for the woman who saved me." Turning that smile in her direction, she was stunned silent at the way his features transformed from handsome to striking. "Not hard to do."

"Back in a minute." Walking faster than normal, she fled the kitchen.

What's wrong with you, woman?

Nothing was wrong with her. She'd just lost her composure for a moment. He didn't have any way to know Penn was gone, because she hadn't mentioned that earlier. And the way he tried to comfort her was beautiful. Her mind drew unwelcome comparisons between his attitude towards her and Cooter's, and she shoved that discontent aside.

"Sweats, and maybe a pair of jeans with a belt. Another shirt, if there's one smaller. Socks." Muttering her list as a reminder, Glenna opened the closet and slowly turned to the side she'd been ignoring for years. Penn had been slightly broader in the shoulders than Graeme, but they looked of a height. His clothes should fit well enough. She pulled the string to turn on the light and stood there, shadow cast at her feet.

Jeans at the front of the rack, folded over hangers. Those were easy enough, and she grabbed the first pair in the row. A belt hung helpfully over the hanger hook, so it was a twofer. Button-down shirts were next, and those were a slower review. Glenna's fingers ticked across each hanger in turn, memories flooding her of events where each had been worn. She could see Penn standing at the podium of a conference hall in a nearby town, giving a talk on the minutia that made up a small rancher's life. He'd been proud of that invitation, one of the first. She hadn't worried about his ability to talk to a large group, but the way he'd held attendees spellbound was something she'd treasured—still treasured.

There was a dark green shirt near the back and Glenna pulled it out. The pattern didn't evoke any memories, and she nearly laughed aloud when she saw the tag was still attached.

"Perfect."

Penn's dresser was pushed against the wall underneath his hanging clothes. The top drawer offered her bundled pairs of socks. She took two of the newest-looking pairs. At one end of the drawer was a never-opened package of underwear, and it joined the other items in her hands. Tees were in the next drawer down, nearly all of them in solid colors, no graphics to be found. Something they'd always disagreed on, because Glenna thought it was a bonus if the saying on a shirt could add to a conversation, while Penn decided his mouth got him into enough trouble.

"Liar," she said fondly. Penn didn't have any enemies, not a one. "Hadn't had any."

A pair of sweatpants from the next drawer rounded out the pile in her arms and she bumped the drawer closed with one hip, catching the light string in her teeth and pulling sharply, plunging the closet back into darkness.

Depositing the clothing options on the end of the couch, Glenna was surprised Graeme wasn't in the living room, but then heard his voice from the kitchen.

He must have called his people.

"Naw, Blackie, it's all good. This gal doctored me up real fine. I'm going to need a ride out of here, but it's late. You go snuggle with Peaches and talk to that little one. You and Randi can take turns singing to Peaches' belly."

There was silence for a minute, followed by a deep, attractive chuckle.

"Yeah, brother. I'll call you tomorrow. Let everybody know I'm good. Wasn't no foul play involved. Just careless ridin'. See ya."

Graeme paused as he walked through the doorway, his gaze catching on hers. "Phone charged, enough anyway. I've let my friends know to call off the search parties."

"If I'd been thinking and had your phone charged, I could have answered it." She fussed with the hem on the T-shirt, patting it flat. "Sorry to cause them so much worry."

"Glenna, don't do that."

He stopped at the end of the couch, and should have looked ridiculous in bare feet, a shirt knotted around his waist, and the ends of his leather vest swinging against his hips, but he didn't.

He looks hot.

"You've helped me out considerably. No apologies needed, honest." He reached for the clothing. "These the things you're lending me?"

"Oh, I don't need them back. Consider them a gift. The shirt and drawers are brand new." She flipped the fabric over to show the tag. "Everything else is gently used. It's all clean, though."

"I appreciate it. Is it okay if I get a shower? I'm all-over sticky. Combination of sweat and blood, I think."

"Sure." She pointed down the hall. "Bathroom is just there. Towels are in the cabinet over the toilet. Feel free to use any razors or anything." She glanced at his face, taking in the heavy beard lining his jaw. "Or maybe not. Either way, help yourself."

171

Flustered, she kept her seat on the coffee table while he gathered up various items and disappeared up the hallway.

"Get your shit together, Glenna." Shamu pushed his head against her elbow, levering her arm up so he was tight against her side. "He's handsome, and respectful, and has friends. He's just a man. Stop being a ninny."

She bent to smack a kiss against Shamu's nose.

But he is handsome, and right now is about to be naked in my shower.

"Shammy, your momma's a ninny."

***

Horse

Horse peeled the bandage off and studied the neat line of tiny stitches holding his skin together. Glenna had indicated she'd been the one to treat his wound, and he had no memory of anything different.

The question was why?

Why hadn't she called an ambulance to cart his ass off to the hospital?

Why had she kept him in her home, a man she didn't know from Adam, and had nothing but her intuition to tell her he wasn't a threat?

Why hadn't she insisted he leave as soon as he was awake and mobile?

And what was it about her that he found so intriguing?

She was gorgeous, but he'd met plenty of good-looking women through the years.

She was kind, but that wasn't something he typically based an attraction on.

And he couldn't deny there was a deep, simmering attraction. Every interaction with her piqued his interest even further, until he'd been half a second away from bending her over his arm and kissing the hell out of her.

Even with Marian, the fondness had grown through the years. It hadn't been an immediate sizzle, like he'd grabbed hold of a live wire, the desire arcing through his body. And when her preference had become clear, he'd missed the possibility more than ached for them as a couple.

The fuck's wrong with my head?

He looked down at his dick, swiping a hand up the hard length.

"You don't have a say in a damn thing, so don't get any ideas, asshole."

Trying to ignore his erection, he turned on the water in the shower, retrieving a towel from where she'd said they would be. Flipping through the clothing, he wondered again why she had it. From what she'd said, her husband had been dead for a while. It didn't track that she'd have held on to worn jeans and sweatpants. The socks looked new, and the briefs were still in the package, but other than the shirt, everything else had been worn by her husband. Her dead husband.

Hope it won't jack with her seeing me in his clothing.

Pushing that thought away, he stepped into the shower, groaning as the hot water sluiced over sore muscles. He had a muddled memory of the bike as a mess, forks and handlebars bearing the brunt of the ride through the ditch and the fence.

"Rebuilt it once. I can rebuild it again." He hoped there would be enough left to rebuild. "I'll call the old man back east, see what Medric thinks the options are."

Tipping his head back, he ran rough fingers over his head, scrubbing at his hair and beard. With his eyes closed, the scene running through his head wasn't the wreck. No, what he saw on a loop in his mind was the way Glenna had gotten adorably flustered, unable to keep her eyes away from the bare sections of flesh exposed by his makeshift wardrobe. Horse had felt the weight of her gaze like a touch, grazing across his chest, arms, and everything else bared to view.

She didn't hate the view, that's for sure.

Horse chuckled at himself, still trying to ignore the insistence of his throbbing cock.

"She saved your ass, son. Better keep the respect on display so she don't throw you out middle of the night."

The shampoo he picked up from the shower shelf did the job but had the side effect of filling the shower with the scent of the woman.

"Leave her alone, man."

Ignoring his own advice, Horse gave up and slipped one hand down his abs, cuffing his cock in a grip that was unyielding. Muscles tensed, he leaned a forearm against the side of the shower, letting his fingers wander while his mind did the same. He imagined Glenna, hair tousled from bed, leaning over him so the scent of her engulfed him. The heated water became the touch of her mouth on his neck. A nail flicking across his nipple where her naughty fingers tweaked gently. His hand shuttling back and forth on his cock was her body slipping and sliding across him. The first burst of his climax a ghost of the heat her body would hold.

Breathing heavily, Horse opened his eyes in time to watch the last of his spunk swirl down the drain and disappear. His cock hung heavily along his thigh, and his balls throbbed demandingly, as if he hadn't just come his brains out merely thinking about fucking her.

"You're in trouble now, son."

He tended to agree with his own assessment of things.

***

Glenna

Standing at the sink, Glenna was straining her ears for the sound of the shower, wanting to hear the instant it turned off so she could prepare herself to see Graeme again.

The man turned her sense around backwards, making everything all mixed up in her mind. There was no reason to think about him intimately, no reason at all.

Yet, she couldn't stop her mind from taking her down that path. Again.

Gonna cream my panties if I don't quit.

Listening hard to things inside the house as she was, the grinding of wheels on gravel didn't register until the vehicles were nearly all the way up to the house. Glancing outside, Glenna saw three vehicles pulling to a stop even with the fence for the first paddock. She didn't recognize two of them, but the one bringing up the rear belonged to Jackson Snyder, not someone she'd wanted to see on her place, ever.

Drying her hands quickly, Glenna shushed a growling Shamu as she shoved her feet into the boots next to the door. "Stay here, Shammy," she instructed as she slipped out the door, closing it in his snarling face.

"Hello," a man called from behind the passenger door of the truck in the front. The driver didn't exit the vehicle, but two additional men were milling around the back of the car parked behind. Jackson rounded out the unwelcome group as he strolled towards the man nearest Glenna. The one who had greeted her raised a hand and she noted the clear-polish manicure of his nails. His face was drawn into severe lines, almost a brother to the angry farmer in the classic painting with the pitchfork. "Mrs. Richeson? Good to meet you. I'm Sean Moorcock."

"What can I do for you?" She didn't approach them or hold out her hand. Manners notwithstanding, she hadn't invited them here and had a feeling she wasn't going to enjoy the upcoming interaction.

"Glenna, Mr. Moorcock has a proposition for you." Jackson had stopped near the man, hands shoved into his pockets. "Would do you good to listen to him."

"Mr. Snyder, I'm certain I can speak for myself." Moorcock's disdain for Jackson wasn't reassuring. If they were associates of some kind, maybe the investor in the Snyder place, then wouldn't they have a better relationship? "Mrs. Richeson, Glenna, if I may? This is a very nice spread you've got. I understand you and your husband worked it until his untimely passing, yes? It's nice, good pasturage with a predictable water source. But it's showing its age, just a little. It's a lot of work for one person, isn't it?"

"What can I do for you?" She angled her head back, staring down her nose at the man. Better to appear to be slightly aggressive than a pushover, and his oily patter told her this was a set of statements he'd practiced for a long time. "Mr. Moorcock, as you've noted, there's always work to do in ranching."

"I won't take up much of your time today." Slight emphasis on the last word expressed his expectation there would be other conversations. "The offer I've made Mr. Snyder wouldn't work for this place, I'm afraid. It's too small for an infusion of cash to be helpful. But because it's adjacent to the Snyder place, those connecting miles of fence help to increase the value of the land, so—"

"Not for sale." She didn't hesitate to interrupt him, sweeping one hand through the air in a decisive arc. "You've made a trip for nothing. Sorry for your luck." Feet planted wide, she landed a fist on each hip. "Jackson led you a merry chase."

"Oh, it wasn't Mr. Snyder who brought me here." Moorcock gave her a thin smile and she had a moment to think how odd it looked on his face. "It's just good business."

"Like I said, my place isn't for sale." She didn't move an inch, standing firm. "You can see yourself out."

"Glenna," Jackson blurted, stepping forward in a rush. "Listen to him at least."

"The fact you're vouching for him and had the brass balls to bring him onto my place after the way you've acted towards me is one of the biggest reasons I'm unwilling to do that, Jackson. You've proven your level is low, and I've no intention in allowing myself to stoop at all." Hoping her hands wouldn't betray the trembling in her body, Glenna pointed a finger at him. "Get off my land."

"Bitch, you either listen to him and take the deal, or I'll fuck you, ruin you, and then you'll still take the deal. You sell and I could even be talked into letting you continue to live here." He leered at her, eyes glittering as they locked on her. "As long as you understood there'd be a price to pay that wasn't rent."

"Pretty sure the lady told you to leave. Might wanna get your collective asses back in your rides and get the hell out of here."

Glenna didn't turn as Graeme approached from the house. An instant later, Shamu pressed himself to her leg on one side, the big man holding his leash lining up with them.

"And you, asshole, you talk to her like that again, it'll be the last time you open your piehole without pain, feel me?" The rumble of Graeme's voice vibrated through the air and Glenna was pleased to see Jackson's face go pale. "Threats like that'll get you a one-way ticket to a place you don't wanna visit."

"You should think about it long and hard, Mrs. Richeson. As Mr. Snyder indicated, it's in your best interest to give it your fullest attention." Moorcock dipped his chin. "Goodbye for now."

Once Moorcock was seated in the truck, the other men retreated to their vehicles, Jackson taking longer because he spent half the time with his head rotated to keep an eye on where Glenna stood with Graeme.

A minute or two later and they were gone, a light haze of dust the only evidence of their quick turnaround and exit.

"You're trembling," Graeme said as he wrapped an arm around her shoulders and pivoted them towards the house. He bent slightly and unclipped the leash from Shamu's harness, but even released, the dog didn't move from his place at her side. "Let's get back inside and you can tell me what the hell that was all about."

Her teeth were clattering lightly by the time he got her maneuvered into the living room and had her ensconced on the couch. A blanket settled around her back and she grasped the edges tightly, pulling it across her chest. Shamu was lying on her feet, crowded as close as he could get to her.

Glenna stared out the front window and ignored clattering from the kitchen punctuated with expletives. She was mentally redrawing the encounter, picking apart the things that had been said and what had been inferred. Nothing she could take to the sheriff, but enough so every rancher in the area would be up in arms if they heard about it.

Still think he's just hot air?

Glenna's muscles shook with a rigor and hands landed on either side of her neck, holding her shoulders tightly.

"I got you, lady." Once the spasm of trembling had passed, Graeme moved in front of her and sat on the coffee table. Glenna took an instant to reflect on the juxtaposition of their positions, changing from yesterday to today, where he was the one comforting her. "Now, drink this." He picked up a mug from the table, bringing the lip of the vessel to her lips. "Sip, slowly. You're okay."

She didn't even attempt to fight free of the blanket, pursing her lips to take a tentative drink. It was strong coffee, cut with sugar and milk until it was a muddy approximation of its original flavor. The temperature was perfect for gulping, which she attempted. He pulled the mug away quickly.

"Slowly. You had a shock. I don't understand it, but I recognize the symptoms. We need to get you back to level ground."

The mug made its way back to her mouth and Glenna obeyed him this time, sipping in measured pulls until the level was about half what it had been. Then she wrestled one hand out of the blanket's folds and cupped it around the mug, her fingers overlapping his. Together, they lifted it to her lips for another slow drink.

"I'm better." Her voice came out in a whisper, weak as a kitten, and Glenna grimaced. Clearing her throat, she tried again. "I'm fine, Graeme. Thank you."

"You were right the first time, but not the second." He reached through and found her other hand, bringing it to wrap around the mug as a replacement for his hold. "When you feel steady, let's talk about what that asshat wanted so much he was all up in your face."

"He wasn't in my face. Trust me, I've been there, seen that. This wasn't anything." She shook her head. "That's not right. I don't know what the other men were doing here, but I assume Moorcock is the investor Jackson Snyder found to help fund his ranch. So it's not that it wasn't anything, but he was relatively civil. At least he didn't get close enough to try and grope me again."

Heavy gusts of breath were the only indication Graeme was still alive. He'd frozen in place, his gaze boring into her.

Lips tight, his voice was filled with gravel when he asked, "Man laid hands on you?"

Glenna nodded slowly. "Just the once."

"Once is still one too many times." Veins popped in his forearms, exposed below the rolled-up sleeves of the shirt he'd slipped on over the tee, which she just noticed was clinging appealingly to every inch of his chest. His hands clenched into rigid fists, slowly relaxed, then clenched tight again. "His place is the next one over? Cock and balls man said you had fences adjoining?"

"Yeah, the ranch was his great-granddaddy's place, handed down to him as the last living relative. Kind of like this was my grandparents', then mine after Grammy passed. His is a lot bigger, which makes the offer even odder. Not that the man ever got to a real-dollars-on-the-table talk, but there's no way they'd need this place. The Snyder acreage far exceeds mine, so adding these few hundred wouldn't be a drop in a bucket against the thousands they're already in possession of." She tipped the mug up only to realize it was empty. Graeme took the cup from her and held it, twirling it round and round in his hands. "Everything—hell, that whole thing was weird."

"You didn't know any faces except the dickwad who was runnin' his mouth like a turd toad?"

Glenna giggled, slapping a palm over her mouth. "Turd toad?"

He shrugged, glancing at her from under his brows. "I'm tryin' to tone it down, but he got on every single, last nerve I own. Your dog was havin' a fit at the door, so I slipped over to see what was going down. When I realized it was five against one, the naked rat and I thought we'd even the score." His lips curled at the corners. "Turd toad is in place of a dozen highly vulgar things I've already called him in my head."

"Well, it's an apt description. His daddy was salt of the earth, and Penn and I got along with him real well. Jackson—" Shaking her head, she blew out a stream of air. "Not so much. He never bothered me while Penn was here, but in the past months he's made himself a pest. Only in town, though. I thought—" Hesitating, because now her assumptions seemed naïve, Glenna bit her lip. "I thought he wasn't anything but hot air."

"Some men start that way, but if they get a little success, they can change. Might be you were right about him when your husband was living. If he suddenly saw you as available, he could take that as his first round of success." Graeme planted his feet and pushed upright. Glenna stared down, doing her best to avoid the expanse of physical real estate directly in front of her. "Turd toad fits him. Maybe he'll come to the understanding you aren't on your own anymore and stay on his side of the road."

"You certainly gave the impression I wasn't alone." She lifted her gaze to his face.

Graeme looked vulnerable for a moment, then his expression hardened. "If it keeps you safe, I'd do it again."

"You're a good man, Graeme Nass." Glenna offered him a smile she hoped wasn't trembling. This moment felt much bigger than it should have, as if their interactions were setting the foundation for something.

"I'd like it if you'd call me Horse, Glenna. I haven't answered to Graeme for a lotta years." He swept the cup up and walked around the end of the couch, heading back to the kitchen. "Want another cup of joe? I'm going to make myself one."

"You aren't even limping anymore." Glenna marveled at the man's resilience. "And I'd be honored to call you Horse, sir. Honored."

"So that's a yes on the coffee?" Laughter rolled through the house and Glenna caught her breath at the welcome sound. "I'm stiff more than anything." Clattering accompanied his words, and she twisted on the couch to look through the door into the kitchen. Horse moved around as if he'd lived there for years. "I think the healing took place while I slept my life away. I'm glad I was able to give them the idea I was whole and hearty, though. I wouldn't have wanted their gunmen to have the idea I'd be an easy mark if push came to shove."

"Gunmen?" She was staring and knew it but couldn't bring herself to turn away. The hem of the untucked shirt swung at the top of his thighs, giving her glimpses of his jeans-clad ass that were as mesmerizing as his bare thighs had been earlier in the day. "What gunmen?"

"The two at the middle car. They were packin'. So was Cock Blocker, for that matter. I hoped they'd assume I was too." He returned to the living room, taking a seat at the other end of the couch from Glenna. "Do you know what happened to my bike? I was going to ask after my shower but got distracted by asshattery. My stuff's in the bags."

"It's up by the barn. Everything from where you wrecked. I had a friend pick it up and bring it here."

"Righteous. I'll check it out later. This friend in the know about me being here?" He sipped his coffee, blowing air across the top.

"Yeah, Cooter helped me evaluate the wound and what I'd done to stop the bleeding. He's been my best friend forever."

"Would he have talked to anyone about me being a stranger helped by the grace of your hands?"

"Well, he'd have no reason *not* to mention it, especially to his family. He brought two of his nephews for the heavy lifting, and Cooter has a close relationship with his father. It would likely have come up over the course of dinner or something." She angled her head to the window. "In fact, now that I'm thinking about it, I'm surprised I haven't seen him since you started waking up. As cautious as he acted, I don't know why he wouldn't want to meet you."

"So he was here while I was dead to the world?" The grimace on his face said loud and clear what he thought about people he didn't know being around when he was vulnerable.

"I wouldn't have let him hurt you." Glenna laid her hand on his and the cup stopped twirling. "Promise, Horse."

Giving him the nickname lightened his expression and he offered her a tiny smile, more a twitch of the lips behind the deliciously attractive salt and pepper beard. "I believe you, Glenna." Staring at her, the air between them was briefly filled with tension, then he dipped his chin, breaking their locked gazes. "Tell me more about this Snyder character. Why did he need cash badly enough to take on someone like Moorcock? I don't know much about ranching, but I expect it goes in cycles of bad years followed by good as weather and markets change. Why'd he need the money?"

"I don't know exactly. There was speculation in town that he'd taken out loans that came due once his daddy died, but no facts to back up the whispers. To my knowledge, they weren't expanding or anything else that would need a sudden infusion of cash. In fact"—she raked a hand through her hair, containing a mass of curls above one ear—"we all thought he had sold it to a property development company. It made the most sense, since Jackson never acted like holding onto his family property was important to him. We're close enough to a few cities to make development here a real probability. It's happened all around us." Releasing her grip, Glenna shook her head, the unrestrained hair bouncing back into place alongside her face. "My place alone could be broken into around eight hundred or more half-acre plots, and the rolling nature of the land itself would make a picturesque setting."

"Got it." Horse's lips pursed as he thought. "But instead of a buyer, he's turned up with an investor. So it's not the land itself but maybe the location? Off the beaten path, but like you said, not far from town. What would they need so much land for?"

"Nothing makes sense."

"Including why they'd need to be packin' heat when they come to talk to what they suppose is a widow woman, isolated and alone. That makes the least amount of sense out of all of it." Horse pulled free from her and stood abruptly. "I'm going to check out my bike and take a little walk around."

"You shouldn't be exerting yourself much." She pointed to his jeans-clad thigh. "It was pretty bad."

"Yeah, but you fixed me." He took a step away, then stopped. "Why? Why did you treat me with something a run-of-the-mill good Samaritan wouldn't even know how to do? Stitches are a pretty specialized thing, and that's been bugging me. Why?"

"I told you. I don't know. It just seemed right."

"Seemed right," he mused. "I don't disagree, especially after today, but I don't like things I can't hold up to the light." Horse shook himself all over and huffed out a laugh. "I guess I'll chalk it up to one of life's great mysteries. You said the bike's up past the house?"

"Yeah, you can't miss the shed. The bike is in front. You can't miss that either." Glenna swallowed, her dry throat clicking. "I could walk up with you?"

Horse immediately held out a hand. She studied and then slowly placed her palm against his. When his fingers curled around her hand, it was warm and strong, the grip firm. As if they'd done this a thousand times and he knew just how to do it.

"Okay then. We'll—" Her muttered response was stifled, and she cut herself off, staring down at Shamu who had forced himself between them, nose pressed tightly to Horse's fingers. "It's okay, Shammy."

"Yeah, Shamu, it's gonna be okay."

Apparently reassured, the dog preceded them to the door and waited, panting as he stared outside.

Once the door was opened, he was out like a shot, disappearing around to the right of the house.

"You don't worry about him takin' off like that? He's a pretty dog, striking looking. I bet he'd bring a pretty price in Dallas or Houston."

"He's good about staying close to the house. This is just him making his rounds. He always checks for coyotes or raccoons, then he'll come back to wherever I am." She grinned at how their hands swung slightly. "Likes to ride around on the ATV, so if he hears that start up, there's no getting away from him."

"Really? Huh. I wouldn't have taken him for a speed demon." They crested the sloped hill and Horse caught sight of what was left of his motorcycle. "Awww, dammit. It's worse than I remembered."

"You remember the accident?" When he dropped her hand to kneel next to the mangled bike, Glenna's breath caught in her throat at the unexpected sense of loss. "I'm surprised. You were pretty out of it when I stopped. Couldn't have been more than a couple minutes after, because you were not quite on your feet."

"I remember parts of it. The sinking feeling when the gravel took the wheels and the knowledge I was going through the fence." Horse opened a bag hung on one side of the bike, rustling through the contents. "Good deal, all my stuff's here." He looked up at her, corners of his mouth lifted in a grin. "I remember you bein' all bossy, bossy, makin' me drag the bike back to the road so you could fix the fence. Nothing after that. Not really."

"I was kinda bossy, wasn't I." The tips of her ears went hot. "Sorry."

"Don't be." He stood, a bag in one hand. She supposed he'd gathered up what he'd wanted and put it inside. "It was hot."

"Hot?"

When had he stepped so close to her? She felt the hair on her arms raise as he reached his other hand out and wrapped his fingers around the back of her neck.

"Oh, hell yeah. Hot as fuck." The last word was a whisper, heard only because he'd bent towards her. "Bossy bossy."

The sound of tires on gravel came from the driveway just as Shamu started barking. Horse moved faster than Glenna could think, placing himself between her and the approaching vehicle. She laid a palm against his spine to steady herself as she peered around his shoulders. The truck was familiar, and she let out a breath she hadn't realized holding.

"That's Cooter." Shamu had planted himself in the driveway, blocking the truck from advancing. "I told you I was surprised he hadn't come over sooner." Raising her voice, Glenna yelled at the dog, "Shammy, it's just Cooter. Knock it off."

"I suspect I'm gonna like Cooter about as much as you do, Shamu." Horse's back flexed under her hand. "Introduce me?"

"Sure." She moved around him, pulled up short when he recaptured her hand, threading their fingers together.

"Cooter, this is Graeme." Glenna caught Shamu's collar as he leaned against her leg. She was sandwiched between the dog and man, and the idea of that had her smiling. "You come by to check on us?"

"Something like that." His easy drawl had sharp edges to it, and he stalked closer, one hand outstretched. "You look a far sight better than the last time I was around, Graeme."

"I'm feelin' a lot better." Their hands lifted and dropped twice, then Horse disconnected and moved back a step, which had the effect of moving Glenna away from Cooter, since they were still connected by joined hands. "Appreciate your part in makin' sure I'm good. And thanks for movin' the bike here. I'd hate to lose her."

"Glenna," Cooter ignored Horse's gratitude, "did Jackson come see you?"

Horse's fingers tightened around hers. He responded to Cooter before she could speak. "We haven't seen anyone all day. Why would you ask?"

Glenna found herself staring up at him, puzzled at the lie.

Cooter ignored him again. "Jackson's been making the rounds, Glenna. Half a dozen ranchers in town said he'd made them deals it'd be hard to turn down. I wondered if he'd hit you up yet."

Horse's grip pulsed twice, and Glenna turned to look at Cooter. "Want to come in for a cup of coffee?" Maybe if she ignored both of them, they'd start actually talking. She stepped back like Horse had done earlier and he came with her easily. "Let's all go inside and have a civilized conversation."

Chapter Thirteen
Horse

From the moment he'd looked through the kitchen window, listening as Shamu's sounds of distress became louder and louder until now, walking back through the door hand-in-hand with Glenna, Horse had been through the gamut of emotions. Anger and exhilaration tied for highest on the list.

He'd recognized the men exiting the vehicles for what they were, primarily muscle for the leader, but the unfortunately named Moorcock wouldn't have been afraid of performing his own dirty work. Horse recognized the type.

Hell, I am the type.

Standing up to them hadn't taken more than starch and bluster, but it had helped when Glenna had gone along with his ruse. Hell, it not only had helped with the ruse, but had raised a need in him he hadn't felt—ever.

Shamu hadn't even argued when Horse had insisted on the leash. He didn't want the dog getting shot for being protective, and the vibes he'd felt from the men had been enough to raise his hackles, never mind the dog's.

Headed back into the house now, Cooter being escorted by Shamu who hadn't stopped growling yet, Horse waited for Glenna's response, wondering which direction she'd take things.

"Yes, Jackson was by here today." Glenna turned to face them both, dropping his hand as she did so. "Shamu, come here and be quiet."

The dog sank to his haunches as he stayed halfway between Cooter and Glenna, and when he shot Horse a dark glance he had to laugh.

"Why does your dog hate your best friend more than he hates me, a relative stranger?" Cooter made a sound at Horse's question, shuffling his feet. Angling his head, Horse stared at Cooter consideringly. "Yeah, Jackson came and made some threats. But why does it matter to you?"

"Because we've known each other basically all our lives." Glenna pulled a chair out and flopped into it, resting her head in her hands. Dark ribbons of hair covered her face. "Jackson said some ugly things, Cooter. Graeme and I were just talking about it."

"Horse." The correction came without thinking and he settled into a chair next to her. His hand found her thigh and he gave it a gentle squeeze. "From you." Glancing at Cooter, he added, "Graeme to you."

"Well, Graeme, I don't know why you thought you needed to answer for Glenna earlier, or why you decided to lie, but I'm really only interested in what Jackson wanted." Cooter yanked a chair out on the other side of the table, the movement caused Shamu to increase the volume of the growl that hadn't stopped. "He's a canker sore, and I'm looking for ways to get him out of our lives."

"I agree on the canker sore aspect. Some of the shit he brought with him today fit that description too." He leaned to the side and settled the bag on the floor. He ignored the metallic clunk and turned to face Cooter who was staring at him with head cocked to one side. "That's my equalizer."

"Oh." Cooter shook his head. "Never mind that. Glenna, what do you want to do?"

"Do?" She sounded genuinely confused.

"Yeah, about his threats. When his daddy was alive, he kept his boy in check, but now that he's on his own, I don't trust him." Cooter's hands spread on the top of the table, and Horse was surprised to see they were trembling. "I don't know what we can do, but I want to do something."

"You can press your contacts and find out what kinda deal Moorcock dealt with Snyder. That'll tell us if his partner is liable to put a hold on the asshole, like his daddy did, keepin' him under control. I'll do the same, and seein' as how we run in very different circles, we'll pull a better picture together." Squeezing Glenna's leg until she swung her head to face him, he smiled at the confusion on her face. "Between you and me, we'll keep the homestead covered." Cocking his head at Cooter, he let his pride in Glenna show through. "She's a force, man. Didn't really need my help facin' them down, but I was glad to put myself at her back."

"She's always been fierce. Her husband used to say he had to trot double time just to stay in step with her." Cooter's face softened and Horse realized the man held feelings for the woman at his side. Heart pounding in his ears, he clenched his jaw as he stared at the man. His fingers tightened again, then relaxed as her hand settled on top of his, fingers wrapping around.

She doesn't return those feelings. He didn't know where the certainty came from, but it made his racing heartbeat return to near normal. *Not for Cooter, anyway.*

If he was very, very lucky, she might find her way to something for him, though.

That flash of "this is it" had never happened to him before, and no matter how much his friends talked about it, he hadn't really believed in love at first sight.

Until now.

He'd do anything for Glenna, anything at all. Legal or not, if it meant she'd sleep easy, he'd be all over it.

I'm so fucked.

***

Glenna

The two men seated at her table held a silent conversation with just their stares. Glenna knew the instant it was concluded because Cooter tipped his head to the side while Horse sat a little straighter in his chair. Shamu glided to stand between her and Horse, and she was amused to find the dog leaning on the man next to her, instead of his normal position against her.

Guess Shammy approves.

"I'm assuming Glenna has your number, yeah?" Horse's fingers twitched and she squeezed tighter for a moment, reassuring him about something she didn't quite understand. "I'll kick off my side of the inquiries soon as you leave, and we'll call you once we know anything."

Glenna looked inside herself for the annoyance she normally felt when someone made decisions on her behalf and couldn't find it. Somehow Horse taking charge of this situation felt right.

Cooter nodded and pushed back from the table. "I'll hit up the feedstore and talk to the attorney in town."

"Sounds like a plan." Horse turned to her and fixed her in place with a smoldering look. "Thoughts on anything else for here in Belle?"

"Hit up Doc Martin's office and talk to the receptionist. Darcy Mae is a shameless gossip and hates me, so if there's anything that would cause me distress, she'll gleefully pass it along." Glenna gave his hand a final squeeze and released him, rising from her chair and moving around the table. "Thanks, Cooter." Arms wide, he met her with a hug, his strength wrapping around her gently.

"Anything for you, Glenna." His whisper next to her ear was quiet and sad, and she pulled back, studying his face. He shook off her concern, chuckling brokenly. "I'll call with what I find out."

"Do that." Horse appeared behind her, his hand on her waist, and Glenna stepped back so she was pressed tight to his chest. "Much appreciated."

Once Cooter was out the door and gone, Glenna turned to Horse and watched as he took off Shamu's harness then pulled his phone out, not looking her way as he hit a couple of buttons. "Back in a minute," he muttered, putting the device to his ear before pulling the door open. Then he went outside, Shamu slipping through the closing door with ease.

"And then there was one." Glenna shook her head as she tried to make sense out of the last hour. Jackson showing with a strongarm entourage was weird enough, but Cooter running to her defense and then backing down was another heaping helping of strange.

She wasn't sure she was ready to look closely at her reaction to Horse standing firm at her side, or his comments about potential violence. And she sure wasn't ready to study the way he'd had a wordless conversation with Cooter that had given her butterflies in her chest.

She sure wasn't ready to examine the almost-kiss. Nope, not at all.

"I'll make more coffee."

Direction decided, she busied herself in the kitchen, then moved to the living room to tidy things there. Gathering the sheets and blankets left from Horse's recuperation, she started a load of laundry, then returned to the living room to see if anything else needed attention. She found Horse seated in a chair near the windows, Shamu at his feet.

"Oh, I didn't hear you come back in." She hooked a thumb over her shoulder. "There's coffee in the kitchen, if you want a cup."

"I'll get one in a minute." Jaw tense, Horse leaned forward and propped his elbows against his knees. "We need to talk, darlin'."

The sweetness of the endearment flowed over her, and Glenna tried to hold the evoked emotion tightly, needing to understand how it made her feel. Cherished was the first word that popped into her mind, and Glenna shook her head, because that didn't make any sense.

Neither did your willingness to kiss a stranger, woman.

"About what? Did you already get some information?" She pushed her thoughts aside and settled on the edge of the couch, holding her muscles tight.

"I did. It only took my guy a minute to find out who Moorcock works for, and it seems your trouble might be tied into some problems my club's been battling."

"Do I need coffee for this?" She held up her empty mug and was rewarded with a brilliant smile.

Horse scooped her cup into one hand and strode towards the kitchen. "Probably wouldn't hurt" was tossed over his shoulder just before he passed out of view. He was back in a minute with two cups, placing one on the coffee table in front of her. Glenna was surprised to see it was the exact shade of milky she preferred for everything except the first cup of the day.

"You put creamer in for me?" Picking it up, she blew a stream of air across the top, then took a sip. "It's perfect, Horse. Thank you."

"Okay, for an intro, there's some info I can't give you. If it's club business, it doesn't belong in this discussion. Except"—he held up one finger—"where it intersects your trouble."

"And they cross paths?" Given his intro, she was pretty certain of this, but wanted to verify.

"Yeah, in a big way. We're still trying to sort out what the deal is with the land up here, why these dillweeds would be hell-bent on gaining control of so much of it, but I can confirm that we believe at the seat of it is someone we—the club—knows well. If we're right, he's an asshole, and dangerous."

"How dangerous? I know you said Moorcock was armed, as were the people with him, but are they the shoot-first-and-lie-about-it-later type?" She sat her cup on the coffee table, proud that it didn't tremble. "Or are they the talkie type?"

"Trust me, if I say he's dangerous, it's to my level of knowledge, not yours."

"Okay." Glenna pulled in a huge breath, holding it for a count of four before blowing it out slowly. "This is out of the realm of my normal. What do we do?"

"'We' don't do anything." He plugged those air quotes into the sentence again. "I'll start—"

"Baannnnt." She made a buzzer sound, startling Shamu into looking her direction for a moment. "It's my place, not yours. This isn't something you're going to ride off into the sunset to fix on my behalf. Just because he's someone you know doesn't make this your problem solo. It's not a 'you' thing, it's a 'me' thing." She threw in the air quotes to mock him and from the strained expression on his face, he caught the sarcasm. "So you might want to rethink that statement."

"Glenna, you don't know these people—"

"I'm gonna keep cutting you off until you listen to me." Glenna was proud of herself for not shouting, but it was a near thing. "I'm not some dainty damsel in distress waiting for the handsome, hot-as-fuck, hero man to sweep in and take care of the dirty work."

The muscles along the side of his jaw bunched and she could swear she heard his teeth grind together. He took a breath, not as deep as the fortifying one she'd inhaled earlier, but it was an attempt to keep his anger under control, where hers had been to drive back the fear. Not that she'd admit to the feeling, but it was probably a healthy reaction to hearing someone a hardened biker thought was dangerous was tangled up in her world somehow.

"You think I'm hot as fuck?"

The segue caught her off guard, and her head was bobbing up and down before she could stop herself. "I do." Her mouth had gone rogue too.

Fuck.

"I think you're one sexy woman. So we're clear on this important bit of news, you need to understand the interest isn't one-sided. Not at all." He leaned closer. "Doesn't change the fact that I'm going to do everything I can to keep you out of the line of fire."

Dammit.

Her mind wanted to stay on track, but her body was clearly in control because the warmth in her middle was in direct response to the satin heat in his voice. Shamu lifted his head again and stared between the two of them, his gaze transferring from one to the other until he got bored and collapsed again.

Focus.

"I'm not going to stand back and let you put yourself in danger on my behalf."

There, better. Stay focused on the danger.

"Glenna—"

"No, Horse. If there's going to be a fight over my land, I'm going to be in the middle of it. I don't mind slinging insults if needed, and I'm a fair hand with a gun. I can't think it'll come to that. We're not back in the wild west. But if it does, then I'll be ready."

"Sexy." The timber of his voice dropped an octave, and she felt the vibration land directly between her thighs.

She realized she wasn't appalled at herself for being aroused or for being interested in a man. Every day she wished life had dealt her and Penn a different hand, because she'd planned on growing old at his side. But that didn't happen, and Penn would be pissed as hell at her for not striking out before now.

In the short time she'd known Horse, the feelings had gone from noticing he was attractive, to being attracted, and now it was out-and-out lust. Like they had with Penn, her emotions were moving fast, and she didn't know if Horse really felt anything beyond reacting to her surface looks, but Glenna didn't think it mattered. Not right now. The thing was, he made her feel seen. She liked feeling noticed and sought out, and so emboldened with the knowledge that she had his full attention. From her side, the connection wouldn't matter if it was a one-night stand or a weekend fling. She'd try to take what was offered, gladly, and let him walk away at the end. Their worlds were very different, after all. It wasn't reasonable to think he'd want such a drastic difference in styles to be his permanent reality.

"I didn't overstep, did I?" Horse's chin dipped as his eyes traveled across her body. "I hope not."

"No, not at all. Just sorting some things in my head." She fixed her gaze on him. "I'm serious about whatever's coming, though. If you want to help, we can stand together."

"Woman, nothing would please me more."

Chapter Fourteen
Horse

Horse frowned down at the incoming video call on his phone. He connected and reached for a chair, dragging it over so he could perch comfortably. When the static dissolved, he was treated to a close-up of Gunny's nostrils and one eye. Startled, he choked on a swallow of coffee, narrowly missing spewing it all over the phone.

"Jesus, man. Give a brother warning he's about to be checking your sinuses."

Gunny pulled back, a heavy frown on his face. "There was something on the lens. You know what, shut your piehole. I called for a reason."

"Yeah, your calls are always for a reason. Lay it on me, brother." He rested his elbow on the counter, propping his head in one hand, the other still holding the phone. With everything swirling around, Blackie had tasked Gunny with letting Bane know the score. It had meant Horse could stay here, with Glenna—just in case.

Right. Just in case. Keep tellin' yourself that, man.

"You talk to Blackie in the last six hours?" Gunny's question was clipped, terse.

Horse straightened, all humor fading away. "No. Last contact I had was yesterday."

"Well, you should call him. He's got news. Myron dug a little deeper. Bane's beyond, man. It's something big, I think."

Myron had become a resource the FRMC was glad to have access to on occasion. Horse wasn't surprised that Blackie had activated that contact, but he was surprised to hear about it from Gunny.

"I'm guessing Bane took what's going on badly. Sonuvabitch. I hate he had to find out at all, much less before things were settled. Why don't you tell me the news, save me the trouble of buggin' the old man." Horse's stomach roiled, apprehension twisting through his guts.

"Well, that's the thing. I get the sense it's not something he's gonna pass on your direction, but I disagree. Sincerely disagree with that assessment." Gunny drew the phone closer to his face again. "However, as a patch holder and officer, I don't want to go directly against the national president, but this call seemed a way to edge around the sides of things."

"So you're calling me to tell me you can't tell me anything, but that you think Blackie knows something. Is that about right?"

"Ayeap. So you should call him." Gunny sighed. "Or I could just patch him into this call. He's dialin' my ass right now."

"Bring him in, brother."

The screen grayed out for a few moments, then came back with a split view, one half showing Gunny and the other framing Blackie's face.

"Prez," Horse greeted him. "I can hang up if you don't want me on the call."

"No." Blackie sighed heavily, the weariness in his voice warning Horse that whatever was coming, it held weight. "Stay. Easier this way since this motherfucker decided to stick his big schnoz into things."

"My nose is average size." Gunny's eyebrows wiggled. "My dick, on the other hand, is way above."

"Not the topic of the day, brother." Blackie's scold was slight, hardly there, unlike his usual comebacks. "Horse, I tagged Mason for an assist, and he had Myron spin up his miracle gadgets. In all of that, he found the Monster Devils are involved, but it hits a little closer to home too."

"MDMC is close to home for me. I know you remember my mother and the treatment she suffered at their hands. I won't ever let that shit drop, and you know it a hundred percent." Horse struggled to keep his tone level. "What's going on?"

"First, the why. We already knew they were lookin' to expand their base of operations. Rumor says they were going to turn the Snyder place into a whorehouse, and you and I know that's code for trafficking. They'd be lookin' for leverage clients they could threaten to dox, so they'd add shakedown to their unpublished schedule of services offered. Once they had the money rollin' in, they'd bankroll a clubhouse in town and tie it to a legitimate business. What they didn't count on was you bein' smackdab in the middle of their where and when." The tension in his face didn't change, didn't relax, so Horse knew there was more to it than just chance.

"And what you aren't sayin' is…" He waited.

Blackie's lips thinned and his gaze bored into Horse for a long minute of silence. Then he ground out, "Roscoe is tied in."

"Roscoe?" The disbelief in his voice brought a quick snarl of teeth from Blackie. Gunny was frowning, and it was likely he didn't know the whole of the story, since he'd come into the club so long after it all went down. "Seriously? That fuckin' weasel hasn't raised his head in years, man. Years."

"It goes still deeper, brother." Blackie snorted humorlessly. "Dale patched into the MDMC about three months ago. A couple weeks after Roscoe did."

"Fucking hell. Dale too?"

"Someone wanna clue me in on this shit?" Gunny's ire was reflected in his hot gaze. "I'd like to buy a vowel, please."

"Roscoe is my blood. I'd say he was my brother, but he tried to kill me too many times for me to count that as truth. Horse's first act as an unofficial Freed Rider was takin' Roscoe down in a parking lot as he tried to shoot me. And Dale is an FRMC cut." Blackie laid it out there for Gunny.

"And Dale's also Duane's in-law family. That made things string out longer than they should have, I think. He was cut the same night I got my patch, so he's always had a hard-on for me." Horse shook his head. "It doesn't seem right to think about them patched, even into a shitty outfit like the MDMC."

"Seconded. It's bullshit is what it is. But it does make more sense, why they'd pick you to target now. Ya know, since you were handy and right there. Both of 'em hate your guts."

"Lotta people hate my guts, but they don't try to jack with me." Gunny's expression was puzzled. "Wonder why that is."

"It's because you're special, Gunny. You let your crazy just hang out there and they understand pretty quickly it's not worth it." Horse tapped a finger against the counter. "With me, I'm quiet, and they don't get how dangerous I can be."

"Fuck, man, just because it comes outta my mouth don't automatically make it wrong," Gunny groused.

"Roscoe should understand," Blackie put in. "You fucked him up."

"It's been a long time since then. I hold the view that lessons like that need to be reapplied for them to really stick. The more painful the application, the better the retention. Hold on a minute." Gunny laid the phone down, the view shifting to the ceiling. "Sharon, can you go outside and see what that fuckin' donkey is killing now? Sounds like Randy's in the chicken pen again."

Horse chuckled as his comments broke the tension, and Blackie grinned back at him.

"Regret savin' that ass yet?" Horse laughed again at the spew of profanity that met his question. The view shifted again and Gunny was scowling darkly.

"Every fuckin' goddamned day. Swear to God, if those boys didn't love him, he'd have already been ground-up for sausage. Or maybe not. I do love to eat ass, but not that kind." A shout came from offscreen and Gunny looked away. "Sharon, everyone already knows I'm nasty, the fact you enjoy it is just between us."

"Not anymore," Blackie muttered, then cleared his throat. "Gettin' us back on track. Horse, now that you understand the depth of the threat, how do you want to handle it?"

"Handle it?" He lifted his gaze to the window and watched as Glenna rode past on the ATV, Shamu sitting behind her, feet on her shoulders. "I think they'd only have picked this place if they knew I was here. There's still no info sayin' that shit is true. So maybe my being here is just the universe at work. Hell, all I know for sure is I want to do whatever's needed to keep this woman safe. That's how I want to handle it." She passed out of view and he returned his gaze to the phone screen. "If that means creating terminal options for those motherfuckers, then I'll be all over it. I don't fuckin' care about relations with a shitty club like the MDMC, no matter where they think they're gonna expand. We'll shut down their asses. Like Gunny said, we turn them into sausage. Those motherfuckers don't belong in our territory, period. Full fuckin' stop. I vote we wipe the ones who're here, including Roscoe and Dale, wipe them fuckin' out. However that shakes out."

"I do not disagree, brother. You think your woman'll have a problem with that solution, though? I don't want to fuck things up for you at the beginning of whatever this is."

"She's—" Horse sighed and dropped his eyes. Fiddling with the clean mugs sitting on the counter waiting to be put away, he adjusted the order, smaller to larger. "I don't know what this is, if it is anything. You know the saying about want in one hand and shit in the other. Right now, I don't have anything to hold onto. Do I want that? Yeah, pretty sure I'd be all in if she was interested. She's a widow woman, though, and hasn't even so much as dated since her husband passed." He gestured towards his body. "Every stitch of clothing I've got on was his, though, so I don't know what that says."

"It says she sees you as something to hold onto. Shit, man, she didn't call a bus to pick up your ass on the side of the road, but loaded you into her truck, where you then bled all over her shit. There's something. It's up to you to figure it out, brother." Blackie stared into the camera and Horse was pinned by the intensity of emotion on his face. "If she's important to you, don't let a day go by without telling her. If you want her, then work for it, man. And that includes protecting what's precious to her."

"Like this ranch." Horse was nodding, because what Blackie said resonated with him. "Yeah, I think she'll be good with whatever resolution we have with the MDMC. It'll be worth it. To both of us."

"That's decided then. I'll circle the wagons here and we'll sort out next steps. Just needed to know you were on board."

"Yeah."

"Don't forget us out here in Baker," Gunny cut in. "We've got a history with the MDMC, and not a single man would turn down the opportunity to balance the scales."

"I'll let you know." Blackie shut down the call, the image of Gunny filling the screen.

"Does he always do th—"

Horse disconnected with a grin, knowing he'd be leaving Gunny fuming.

He turned to head outside just as the door opened and Glenna came in, Shamu at her heels.

On impulse, he held out his arms, wrapping them around her as she walked into them. Holding her close settled something inside him, and he drew in a long breath.

"Thanks," he murmured against the side of her head.

"I'll never turn down a hug," she responded, her cheek tucked in beside his neck. "They're the best."

"Truth," he returned, swaying them slowly side to side.

A hard nose pushed at his hip, then a whipcord-thin dog's body wedged between them. Horse and Glenna both laughed and backed up a step, his hands still on her shoulders as they looked down at the disgruntled dog staring up at them.

"Guess Shammy loves hugs too." Her voice held more laughter and Horse grinned. "Or he doesn't like his momma gettin' some without him involved."

"I'd vote on the latter." Horse leaned against the counter, his arms falling away. "He's kind of a jerk."

"Yeah," she crooned as she rubbed the dog's head, the wiry mohawk standing back up after every stroke. "He's a good boy, though."

"Sure." Horse chuckled. "Bless his heart."

"Hey." She looked up at him, lips spread wide in a smile. "He's Texan too, so he knows what that means."

"Just how I meant it, then."

He stared at her, cheeks rosy from the sunshine and wind outside, eyes shining with laughter, mouth pouting adorably.

Blackie's right. I think she's it for me. I should tell her.

Instead, he cleared his throat, not surprised when she straightened immediately, face adopting a serious expression. "I've got some additional news." He patted the air. "Not good news either."

Instead of looking alarmed, Glenna folded her arms beneath her breasts and took in a deep breath.

"Tell me." Her demand was strong and steady, and he noticed Shamu had sat next to her, his shoulder pressed against her leg in a posture nearly identical to Glenna's. Head up, eyes attentively fixed on him.

They're a formidable pair. Put us all together, we're gonna be unstoppable.

***

Glenna

"I should call Cooter and loop him in." She was standing shoulder to shoulder with Horse. They were washing dinner dishes and discussing everything he'd learned for the third or fourth time. She didn't think he'd held back anything, even though he'd warned that strictly club business would not be shared, but it was impossible to know for sure. That was typical of what she knew about motorcycle clubs, and she found she trusted him, even after only knowing him for days.

I trust him, and I like him. A lot.

The honesty was freeing, because while she hadn't imagined herself being with anyone other than Penn, ever, she could picture having something with Horse. Here was a man who had wakened her body and mind, easily pulling her from where she'd been sleepwalking through life to full awareness.

"I'd like to be careful what we pass along." He wasn't telling her not to call Cooter, which was a big point in his favor. "He doesn't need the backstory, and we can't tell him how we learned things, because the methods aren't exactly legal."

"I like that you're open with me." She decided to let him know how it made her feel. "I like it a lot. Makes me believe I'm special."

"You are special, Glenna." He hip-checked her and she laughed. "Seriously, it's more than just you rescuing me. I don't understand where my head's at, not logically, but my gut still says I should trust you to not do anything to hurt me."

"Isn't that the woman's line? 'Don't hurt me.'" Smiling up at him, she watched as his gaze flicked from her eyes to her mouth, enjoying the way his eyes darkened. Their almost-kiss danced through her thoughts. The only thing she regretted right now was being interrupted.

"I'd never hurt you. Hand to God. Even if this is all we ever have, this kind of friendship. Hell, just you takin' care of me like you did deserves loyalty." He leaned closer, every word emphasized. "I'd. Never. Hurt. You."

"I believe you." His mouth was so close, she rose to her toes on impulse and landed her lips on his in a brief, chaste press. Not lingering, she dropped back to her heels with a breathless "I believe you, Horse." Everything about the movement felt so natural, so right.

His hand wrapped around her hip, fingers squeezing gently. "The things you do, Glenna. You don't even know." He hovered there, mouth a breath away, holding her in place. "Ah, God. The things I wanna do to you." His voice was rough and deep, trembling with control.

With a groan, he dipped closer, taking her mouth in a long, slow kiss. His tongue danced along the seam of her lips, asking for permission and she opened, tasting him for the first time. The mix of chocolate from the pie they'd eaten with dinner and a dark flavor she supposed was all Horse filled her with desire.

She relaxed into his hold, wrapping her arms around his neck to pull herself up, taking as much as she gave. It went on for a long time, renewing over and over, long enough she felt the beginning of whisker burn on her chin and cheeks. His hands roamed her body, up her back and sides. He cupped one breast with a sigh, thumb delicately stroking the edge of her nipple.

She molded herself to him, the hot steel of his erection pressing against her belly through their jeans. Fire raged in her veins, a need like she'd never felt trying to push her over the edge of no return. She didn't recognize the mewling sounds coming from her throat. Glenna was shaking all over when he broke off the kiss and rested his cheek on top of her head, holding her tight.

"Don't think I don't want you, woman. Do not read any of that bullshit into this. I promise you that this isn't me sayin' never, but right now is the wrong time to take a step like this. For both of us." He pulled in a shaky breath. "And fucking hell, you can kiss. Coulda gone on all night like that."

"You're no slouch either." She shifted back, lifting her head to look into his face. "Thank you." Understanding flooded his face and she nodded. "I'm willing to go there, but you're right. I'd like it to be a considered decision. Not simply lust." Her throat tightened and she squeaked out the final words. "I want it. Want you like that."

"I know, darlin'. I know." Cupping his hands around her face, he stared down into her eyes. "I believe you. And I get that you might need space sometimes. If I don't see it in the moment, all you have to do is tell me. Communication isn't my specialty, but I'll work on it for you."

"I think you communicate just fine." She turned her head to press a kiss against one of his palms. "I appreciate you."

He leaned in and softly pressed his mouth to hers, eyes open and staring as she gazed back. "I know." He kissed her forehead in a gentle caress. "And you need to make a phone call. I trust you to protect me and my friends. Tell me what you need from me, and I'll do anything I can to make it happen."

"I'm a big believer in following my gut."

"And what does your gut tell you about me?" Horse's head cocked to one side as he smiled down at her.

"That you're important. I'm not going to mess that up." She smiled and rose on her toes to steal a final kiss. The feel of his erection rubbing against her was erotic to the extreme, and she shivered lightly as hot want curled low in her belly. "And one day soon, we'll make a deliberate excursion to the bedroom."

"Gonna hold you to that," he whispered, following her down to capture another sweet kiss.

"Hope you do more than hold me," she returned, grinning up at him. "But like you said, we got a little bit of something going on right now. Let me make this call and see if Cooter learned anything of importance, then we can regroup and decide what to do next."

"Sounds like a plan." He stepped away, leaning back against the counter. Glenna hated the sudden loss of his heat against her body.

This man could twist me up. He could twist me up and I'd like it.

She gently touched her lips with her fingertips, noting how his muscles tightened as she ran her thumb over her bottom lip.

I bet I could twist him up just as much.

She shook herself mentally and went to the phone, lifting the receiver and dialing Cooter's number from memory. Turning around, she hooked a leg of a chair with one foot and dragged it close, then plopped down into the seat.

"Glenna, is everything okay?" Cooter sounded out of breath when he answered the phone, as if he'd rushed to pick up the call.

"Just checking in to find out what you've learned." She sorted her statement to give a little and hold back a lot. "Tell me what you know, and I'll do the same."

"Not a lot." He sounded funny and Glenna tried to pinpoint what was different about his voice. "Just that the investor is from out east. I found out they've really only approached a few of the other owners, so they're not interested in a big spread. Bob at the feed store said no one was raising a red flag yet, anyway."

"Nothing specific? Just that general knowledge stuff? No names, no company information?" She closed her eyes to concentrate on Cooter. "You sure?"

"Yeah, I'm sure. I just said it, didn't I?" Anger filled his voice at her tiny challenge, which was entirely out of character. "What did you learn? Oh, I mean, what did Nass learn, since he's the one with the contacts?" More anger and an edge of something else. *Pain.*

"We." She paused and started again, emphasizing the plural designator. "*We* found out the threat starts in New Jersey, and that these aren't savory characters. Nothing we want in our county, much less as neighbors. It doesn't surprise me that they're not going whole hog to acquire dozens of places, but I think adding mine to Snyder's makes sense, in a twisted kind of way. They'd have right-of-way access from three different highways then, with the easement already established along a couple of fence lines. If they wanted discrete entrances, they'd have 'em in spades."

Silence greeted her and she pressed the receiver harder against the side of her head, trying to hear anything from Cooter's end. Finally, she caught the sound of quick breathing, shallow, and distressed.

"You fuck him yet?" Cooter's question caught her unawares and she jerked the handset from her ear, staring at it for a moment while it buzzed with more words. She returned it to her ear to catch a fragment of a sentence, "—do so much better, Glenna."

"Not a single bit of that is your business, Cooter." She fought to keep her voice even. "And I'd expect that kind of crudeness from Jackson, not you."

"You want him though, don't you? I could see it in the way you looked at him. And how he looked at you. If you haven't done it yet, you will. I just don't understand. Why him? Why not me?" That pain she'd caught earlier bled through his tone now, a broad river of anguish that made it hard to be mad at him. "Why?"

"It was never going to be you, Cooter. We've been friends forever, and I trust you to the horizon and back, but I can't feel for you that way. We work best as friends."

"Friends." He scoffed. "Right. First there was Penn, and it was fast for you. He was from away, and exciting, and you couldn't see me through the spotlight you had on him."

Glenna pulled in an unsteady breath.

Back that far?

"I had no idea, Cooter. I'm sorry."

"No idea, right. Who's always there for you? Look at that instead of some exotic outsider, would ya? Remember when you were twelve and got bucked off down by the river? Who let you ride his horse home? Who wrapped your bleeding leg? Who's been there for you through the years?" His words came in a rush. "Well, that shit stops now. You don't pick me? Okay, I'm done being your leanin' post, then. Hope this new guy Nass can hold you up, because otherwise you'll be the one picking your own ass outta the dirt this time." His voice quavered. "And stop calling me Cooter. I'm Reggie from here on out."

The line buzzed as the call disconnected and Glenna stared down at the top of the table.

Heat at her back was all the warning she had before the receiver was plucked from her suddenly nerveless fingers. A hand wrapped around the back of her neck, thumb and fingers rubbing firmly as she sagged in her chair.

"He hates me." The concept pained her, because she'd had no idea he'd carried a torch for her. "I never meant to hurt him." Eyes closed, she could see various interactions with Cooter—Reggie—play out on the backs of her eyelids. His expression when she turned down dinner, the way he'd stand close when he saw her in the feed store, how his face would lighten when they'd joke around. "I never knew what he felt for me."

"His attraction to you was not something he tried to hide, but if you've been friends forever, it would be easy to not recognize it for what it was."

Her chair slid on the floor, turning, then Horse's arms wrapped around her, lifting her to her feet. She flung her arms around his waist and pressed her cheek against his chest.

"He's been a good friend. I thought I could count on him." She mumbled this against Horse's shirt, tears dampening the fabric. "Not in this, though. He's cut me out. Like a cance—like a disease, lop off the offending limb." She straightened and shook her hair back, staring up at Horse through watery eyes. "It's stupid that it hurts so much."

"Not stupid." His lips pressed firmly against her forehead, and the bristle of his beard helped ground her. "He lashed out. Man's in pain because he's lost an imagined chance, and he wanted to spread the pain around. He tried to hurt you and hit the target because you're a damn good woman, Glenna."

"Oh, and he didn't have any news other than we're one of the few ranches the scumbags have approached since they took over the Snyder place. That's it, sum total of his contribution." She leaned back in, resting her forehead at the center of his chest. "Way to help out, Cooter." She winced. "Reggie."

"Nothing more or less than I expected, really. And knowing they aren't doing a wholesale sweep of the area does help." One of his hands slid up and down her spine, the other again cupping the back of her neck. "Glenna, doll, it's okay to be angry."

"I'm not mad." She shrugged. "Except at myself, maybe. I just feel like the worst of friends." She relaxed into his touch. "He already had ideas about me and you."

"Well, I've got ideas of my own on that front." Horse's voice was pitched lower, quieter. A folded knuckle lifted her chin until she was staring up into his eyes. "And if we weren't in the middle of a mess, I'd have already acted on them."

"Maybe I want you to act?" Glenna's tongue slipped out to wet her lips and she watched as his eyes followed the movement, darkening. Feeling bold, she rested a hand on top of his shoulder and lifted to her toes. "Maybe that's what I want?"

With a groan, he captured her mouth, lips sliding across hers. His head angled and she opened, touching her tongue to his lips, remembering what he'd liked. Another groan rumbled from his chest as he took control of the kiss, tangling their tongues together, thrusting and gliding across the other. Her breaths came in gasps, sounds he took in, giving back that pleased rumble as she renewed the kiss. His arms were around her, rigid bands at her back and waist, while her hands traveled. Up his neck and into his hair, they explored down the front of his chest to his waistband, untucking the shirt hem to find his flesh.

Horse made a desperate sound as he broke off the kiss, holding her to him firmly, yet gently, as if she were a fragile prize.

"Woman, you make it hard to be good." He was pressing tiny kisses to the side of her head, mouthing the lobe of her ear. "Gonna wreck me. I already know."

"Why do you have to be good?" Her core was throbbing insistently, and she pushed her hips forward, hissing when she gained pressure from his erection. "We're both adults here."

"Yeah, but there's also an end-of-the-world group of assholes out there ready to do bad things. The last thing I want is to have you in bed and then be interrupted by havin' to kick someone's ass."

"I see your point." Glenna's lips curved up. "But I find I don't like how sensible you can be after a kiss like that."

"Darlin', if things were any other way, we'd already be doing dirty, filthy, naked things together."

Horse urged her head towards his chest. She went easily, standing and swaying in the quiet with his arms around her and the soft, steady thud of his heart underneath her ear.

The rest of the day and the entirety of the next were just as frustrating. Nothing seemed to be happening, and while her days were filled with the normal chores around the ranch, it felt as if the whole world was holding its breath, waiting. For what, she didn't know, and wasn't sure she wanted the knowledge.

While Horse was attentive and sweet, feeding her attraction with gentle kisses and tender touches, he determinedly went to his own bed in the guest room every night. Her mug of coffee would be waiting for her the next morning, and Shamu would be standing by the door, ready to get to work, but Glenna wasn't sure she'd felt this lonely after Penn died.

Knowing he was right down the hallway wore on her nerves, and she'd conjured a dozen scenarios where she'd *need* to wake him in the night. None of them were reasonable, or something she'd ever do, but the idea of walking in on him sleeping and simply crawling into his bed pressed in on her, turning her into a rambling grump.

The third time she'd snapped at Shamu for being underfoot Glenna knew something had to give.

Another thing she didn't know was what.

Chapter Fifteen
Horse

"Nothing, seriously?" He tried to tone down the bark in his voice, knowing that the man on the other end of the line didn't deserve it. "Sorry, Retro. Shit, man. This is just fuckin' hard, you know?"

"I get you, brother. But there's nothin' twangin' the web of info out there. We've cast our net far and wide, and it's pissin' me off just like you that we got nothin' to show for it. Can't say we've never had some shit go dark like this before, which means we don't quite know where to go next. You gotta trust me that we're all pullin' on contacts and pokin' into holes to find out something." Retro's accent was thick, his voice dark with anger, and Horse knew the man was giving him the unvarnished truth. "Way I heard it, you've got a dog in the fight now, so I completely understan' wantin' to keep your woman safe. Always said you were a good man, Horse. You've proved it time and again."

"She's more of a want than a certainty," he hedged, then grimaced when he heard the lie in his own voice. "Shit, okay, it's more than a want. I believe she's it for me, man. I know it in my bones. I just gotta get her through this and then see where things stand with her." Taking in a hard breath, he told Retro one of his greatest fears, "Make sure even without the threat that things go both ways. Know what I mean?"

215

"Fuck yeah, I lived that, brother. My ole lady was in a fuckin' mess when I met her, and I stole her away, then I held myself back until she could get her feet underneath her." Retro's voice turned musing. "Once we got to that place, though, lovin' her was sweet as pie and twice as delicious. I'm tellin' you, it's worth the wait."

"I believe you. The little tastes I've taken have only whetted my appetite for the full meal. When that happens, though, I don't want shit swirling the drain, you know?"

"Fuckin' know it, man. I'll keep pokin' and pullin' best I can, see if we can get you to the other side. I'll give Myron another call, keep him in the loop and vice versa. One of us will reach out if we hear the least thing."

"Thanks, brother. Means a lot."

"Oh, ho. Don't think this shit is rent-free, man. I'm keepin' a tab runnin' for you."

"I'm good for it, Retro. I'm good for it."

"I know you are, asshole. Plus, Blackie wouldn't have it any other way. I guarantee he don't want you in debt to me, so if you can't settle things, he for fuckin' sure will."

Before Horse could respond the line disconnected, the secure app they used for communication offering a summary of the call.

He killed the app and stared down at the phone for a minute, then locked the screen and shoved it into a pocket. Glenna was outside and he wanted to be with her. He didn't try to lie to himself now. The want was a need, and not just so he'd be on the front lines if Moorcock or his muscle showed, but also because he liked working shoulder to shoulder with the woman.

"She's it for me." He repeated his words and liked how they settled into his gut, warming him from the inside out. "One way or another, once things are sorted, her and me'll have something."

Bolstered by his own encouragement, he walked outside to see her playing with Shamu. The dog had something in his mouth, and he was doing a good job of keeping out of her reach. Glenna was laughing, and when she looked at Horse, she smiled wider.

"Help me. He's being a jerk." She lunged at the dog and Shamu twisted neatly away. "Asshole. Give it to me, Shammy."

Horse walked up to where Shamu stood and patted the dog on the head, then held his hand under Shamu's mouth. "Drop it." At his calm urging, the dog deposited a gnawed-on bristle brush in his palm.

"How'd you do that? He wouldn't give it to me, even when I said the same command." She was next to Horse, staring down at the dog. "Traitor dog."

"He's not a traitor. He just knew you needed to laugh a little bit." Horse patted the dog on the head again. "Worked, didn't it?" He handed it over. "What is it?"

"Horse brush. I was in the stables, and he decided he needed in the tack room." She snapped the bristles against her thigh. "Nothing in there's been used for a long, long time."

"Show me." He took her hand, curling his fingers around, loose enough she could have easily broken his hold. When she didn't, he tightened his grip slightly and tugged her closer to his side. "I've only been inside the once."

"Not much to see," she muttered as her feet started moving. "It's been empty for years now."

"Why? You had horses before, right?" At his question, she lagged a bit, then leaned against him as she caught up. "If it's too hard to talk about, just tell me, Glenna."

"No." She huffed a broken laugh. "It shouldn't be, anyway. The horses were something Penn wanted. Once they were affordable, I'd always used ATVs to work the cattle, but he had a picture in his head. It didn't hurt anything to make it happen, so we had a few working horses. He got good enough to ride in competitions and did pretty well."

They entered the shadow cast by the long barn and Glenna shivered. Horse pulled her tight against his side. It wasn't cold, per se, so it had to be memories making her react.

"How many horses did you have?"

She steered them, drifting to one side of the main aisle where a large stall stood empty. "Just five here at this end. We'd gotten up to seven at one point, but it didn't make any sense at all to have so many. Even five was a lot, but he had his three favorites. I had two so I could alternate days with them whenever I wanted to ride." Resting a hand on top of the stall door, she rattled it in the frame. "This was his side of the barn. And yes, we had sides. He liked the more aggressive horses that liked to battle, and I kept the easy ones who'd do what was asked without arguing."

"According to your different personalities, then?"

"Yeah, Penn always did like a challenge."

Horse held back what he wanted to say, about Glenna probably being Penn's favorite challenge. Now wasn't the time to interrupt her memories.

She sighed. "When we knew he had a short time, we sold them. Placed them with people who'd treat them well and use them the way they needed. Horses are like dogs, happiest when they have a job. We held onto Penn's favorite longest, and the day the rancher showed up to pick up the horse, Penn was in the hospital bed. He hadn't been upright in days, but he made it to the door to watch the truck and trailer drive away. That was a hard day."

Horse urged her to cuddle closer and she went easily, resting her cheek against his chest.

"Would you have done anything different, knowing what you know now?"

"Yes." Her response was immediate. "I've have kept Penn's three. Not mine, because given a choice, I'd ride the ATV any day, but if I still had his horses, it'd be like I had a little bit more of him around."

"And the idea about making this a boarding facility? What's the barrier to that happening? The barn looks in good shape, no needed repairs jumping out at me." He looked around. "It's dusty, and has a musty smell, but that's just old hay. It doesn't smell wet or like anything's rotten."

"No, the stables itself is in good shape. I'd need to build some more turnouts, eventually. The only stalls that have them now are the five we used the most. Maybe expand the tack room, depending on the actual demand. Put in a round pen large enough for folks to ride in, for warm-ups or if they had a green horse." She shook her head. "It's the smaller things, which are still hella expensive. Plumbing routed to each stall for automatic waterers. New corner feeders and hay bags. We just had eyebolts in the wall to hold up buckets, and wooden hay mangers. They'd need to be removed too. So it's time and money. Those are the barriers."

"Show me," he said, reaching for the latch on the stall door. She stopped his hand and pointed across the aisle.

"Let's... look at those instead, okay?"

"Whatever you need, darlin'." He leaned in and pressed a kiss against the side of her head.

A few minutes later, he had a good handle on what was needed, and a few things she hadn't thought about, like a sprinkler system in case of fire, which could also be used to dampen dust from the center aisle during the heat of summer. The manual labor for the projects wouldn't be an issue. Anything that was beyond his skills, he knew there was a brother around who could pick up the slack. The money for the upgrades wasn't a problem either, because he had a healthy bank account. Living at the clubhouse meant his expenses had been limited to his bike and dues, and like most officers, he had a weekly payout from the club coffers.

Glenna still had a faraway expression on her face, so Horse knew better than to bring up any of that right now.

But it was in his head. All of it. Including her genuine regret at selling Penn's horses.

Chores were next on the list, but all the while they threw hay squares and checked on cattle, an idea was brewing in Horse's mind.

Glenna had phone numbers written on a piece of paper thumbtacked next to the phone in the kitchen. While she showered before dinner, it was the work of moments to find what he needed and enter it into his phone.

Water was boiling for noodles when she got out of the bathroom. He also had sausage frying in a pan, ready to be drained and have the heated spaghetti sauce added. She stood next to him, slicing a loaf of bread nearly through, then tucking squares of butter inside. He already had the foil out, and she quickly had the bread wrapped and into the warm oven. With them working in unison, the meal came together with impeccable timing. Horse grinned as he made a plate for Glenna and handed it over, her reaching across the table to put a piece of the toasted bread on his plate.

"We're a pretty good team," she remarked as he sat. Feeling the weight of her gaze on him, Horse looked up in time to catch a fleeting smile on her face.

"I like that," he told her honestly. "I like a lotta things about you, Glenna."

"Backatcha, mister." She picked up her fork and spoon, skillfully twirling a mouthful of noodles. "I like you too."

He watched her for a minute, then shook his head with a smile. Silence descended on them as they ate, but it wasn't uncomfortable. It was as if they'd done this a thousand times already, reading each other's needs without words.

This is what a relationship feels like.

He decided he was definitely a fan.

The next day, it was easy to find a few minutes alone to make the needed call. Horse didn't want to, but when there was only one source of information a man had to suck up his ego and reach out, no matter if he disliked the other person or not.

"Hello," the voice on the other end of the call answered, an uptick of question at the end of the word.

"Cooter, this is Graeme Nass." Silence fell, this a crawling uncomfortable one, and he sighed audibly. "Don't hang up. I've got a few questions for you about Glenna and Penn."

"Reggie." Finally, the man said something, and Horse understood that as he'd withheld his club name out of the man's mouth, he wasn't going to be given the green light to use the nickname. That single word was cold as a New Jersey winter, but Horse hadn't expected anything less.

"Reggie, got it."

"What do you need from me?"

"You've known Glenna for a long time. Was her anchor all through the pain of Penn's diagnosis and death. She's talked fondly of you and how you helped her deal with everything."

"Fondly. Sure." Sarcasm sat thick on Reggie's voice. "She's fond of me."

"She is, and while I know that stings, you're the only one who knows her well enough to help me out."

"Why would I help you with anything?" Pain dredged along each rough sound. "Why?"

"Because you care about her, and this won't cost you anything. Not even your pride. I'm looking to find out who bought the horses they had to sell. Penn's horses, specifically. She said they picked the people with particular ideas about why they'd be a good fit for each horse. If they're local at all, I hoped you'd know who those buyers were." Horse paused, giving Reggie time to interrupt. When he didn't, Horse continued, "She's talked about opening boarding stables. I want to give her that if I can. But part of what I want to give her is a little bit of her husband back. She said she regrets selling his horses. Didn't say this flat out, but I got the sense she'd do nearly anything to take that one act back. This is me trying to see if it's doable."

Reggie cleared his throat once, then a second time. When he spoke again, his voice was low, quiet, and holding a little less pain than before. "Yeah, I know who bought their horses. All of them. It was me. I asked other ranchers to conduct the transactions, picking up the horses and all that, but all five of them are living the life of Riley on my little ranch."

"You did that for her." Horse shook his head in disbelief. "Without knowing if she'd ever thank you, you did that for her."

"I'd do pretty much anything for her." Reggie's voice was stronger, certain. "And if that means me stepping back for a good man she feels for, then I'll do that. Not gladly or willingly, but I'll do it."

"You're a good man, Reggie." Horse nearly called him brother, surprised at his own eagerness to believe in this man. "Let's see if we can come to an understanding about the horses. She said she doesn't care about the two that were hers, but if you've got all five, then we'll deal all five."

"It feels halfway wrong to take any money for them." There was a pause, then Reggie laughed. "But if it's all the same to you, I'd be happier knowing you paid for them. That way there's no question in my own mind about what's happening here."

"Sounds like a plan. I'm all about setting boundaries so there aren't any misunderstandings later."

Ten minutes later, they'd come to an agreement, set a date for the horses to be returned, and ended the call.

"Horse," Glenna spoke from the kitchen doorway. "Want more coffee, or are you good?"

He thumbed the phone to silent, shoving it deep into his pocket as he turned. "I'm real good, darlin'. I'm real good."

***

Glenna

She twisted the sheets, shoving one leg out from underneath and into the cool air. Staring up at the dimly lit ceiling, she tried to calm her mind. Without success.

It had been like this for the last week. The less information was available, the more anxious it made her. Somehow it felt like the calm before the storm, and she hated being in a position of weakness.

The situation with Horse hadn't changed either. He was free with his affection all day long with Glenna, earning kisses every time they were close. His tender touches to her face or arm, the back of her neck, or just the warmth of his hand settling in the small of her back—each electrified her, and the lack of forwards movement was frustrating to the extreme.

Maybe I should have pushed him harder.

She knew what she wanted. Horse in her bed would do for a start. Horse with her anywhere, actually. That would solve a good bit of the emptiness inside her, this aching longing for closeness with him. Something more than the make-out sessions they'd had so far, each of them cut short by Horse's sense of valor.

She pushed the covers to her waist, spreading arms and legs like a starfish. Hot, she was too hot, and not just from the temperature. Her fingers dipped to the angle of her hip, then slid to the center between her legs. A slow stroke of fingertips against her core over fabric wasn't enough, so she pulled the gusset of her panties out of the way, thudding against her clit with the pad of her thumb. She gasped quietly, legs stirring restlessly. Another dip of her fingers into the space created rewarded her with the slippery feel of her own excitement.

I want Horse to be touching me like this.

Pairing her ring and middle finger together, she thrust inside, gasping again.

Shamu got up from his pile of blankets at the foot of her bed and slipped out where she'd left the door cracked slightly.

He's probably on his way to Horse's room.

She thrust again, scissoring her fingers as she slowly withdrew them. Wiping them on the outside of her panties, she rose from the bed and walked to the door. Horse's door was across the hallway, and closed, no light showing at the bottom. Shamu wasn't in sight anywhere and Glenna shook her head.

She turned and climbed back into her bed, angry at how lonely it felt tonight.

Who am I fooling here? It's been lonelier than ever since Horse came.

She ruffled the covers, cooling off the sheets as she flipped her pillow. Dragging them up to her waist, she stretched out again, cocking one leg to the side so it was uncovered.

Closing her eyes, Glenna concentrated on the tension in her muscles, working her way from toes to head in an effort to lure sleep closer. Half an hour later, she was still twisting from side to side.

She left the bed a second time and made it all the way across the hallway, fingertips a breath away from scratching on Horse's door. Shamu was still nowhere in sight, but she knew where Horse was. Locked away from her by half an inch of wood, sleeping peacefully. They'd both worked hard today, like always.

He deserves his sleep. Go back to bed and take care of yourself.

Self-scolded and embarrassed by this deep longing for something she'd never had, she plopped back onto her mattress, not even bothering to straighten the covers this time. She leaned backwards, then pulled her knees up and turned to the side, curling into a ball in the middle of the bed.

Her door clicked shut and Glenna turned to see Horse standing there. The dim moonlight from outside highlighted his face, muscles taut with some strong emotion.

"Horse." Her whisper hung on the air between them. "Please." Not even certain what she was pleading for, she repeated the words, "Please, Horse. Please."

"I got you, darlin'." His voice was gruff and quiet but spread a blanket of rightness over her nerves.

He stepped closer, lifting the edge of the covers in his hands.

"Get under," he urged, drawing the sheet up to her waist as she rolled to her back and complied. He joined her, his arms bands of strength that circled her and pulled her body closer to his hard chest. "Need to lose these clothes."

She made a sound of assent and smiled as he went to work. His fingers were deft and gentle as he undressed her, rolling her side to side at will. Glenna went willingly, lifting her hips to help.

His hands slipped along her sides, body moving down the mattress while his questing fingers grazed across her belly and hips as he zeroed in on her center. She wanted to memorize the sound that came out of his throat when he discovered how wet she was. Learn by heart the feel of his hands touching her, rough fingers spreading her wide as he lowered his head between her thighs.

The first touch of his tongue against her core drew her back taut, neck arching as she called out to the ceiling. "God, Horse. Yes." He responded with eagerness, mouth caressing every intimate fold of her pussy. His tongue pierced her, finger and thumb strumming her clit like an instrument. "I'm going to, oh God, Horse." He continued stroking her as she quaked and shivered, legs tightening around his head when her orgasm peaked, tossing her like whitewater. Breathing hard, she gripped his hair, lifting his head to see his pleased expression, his tongue darting out to lap against her a final time.

She always wanted to remember the reverent way he touched her breasts, her throat, the curve of her jaw when he angled her head for another kiss, his lips tasting strongly of her. The kiss was deep and long, stealing her breath again as he rolled his hips against her belly. His hot erection prodded insistently, and she moaned into his mouth. "Please."

Her plea shifted something inside him, and Glenna was instantly bereft when he left her for a moment. That was followed by a belly-shaking thrill as she got to watch him roll a condom down his thick, veined cock.

Our first time.

Everything about this moment was precious and special. This was Glenna taking back her life, after a years-long hiatus. Not forgetting Penn, God no. He'd always be part of her. No, accepting Horse into her bed—

demanding his presence there—was a moment of healing as much as it was shared passion.

He seemed to understand this without words, because the only sounds in the house were ones from them. His hard and strong body moving above her, while every stroke pulled a cry from deep inside her. Gravely tones rolled from his chest as he curled himself around her when she climaxed a second time, keeping her safe while she flew high and slowly settled back to earth. Then came the welcome slapping sounds as he railed into her, chasing his own orgasm, her heels pushed hard against the mattress as she met him stroke for stroke.

She cherished his choked groan when he came, the sound of her name repeated over and over as he gathered her against him. Glenna couldn't stop the tiny whimper when he slipped out of her and he shushed her, lips against the side of her head. He dealt with the condom, then held her as if she were the most precious thing as he drifted off to sleep with his mouth touching hers, and she wasn't far behind him.

A scratching at the door woke them early the next morning, Horse rolling away from her and stalking towards the noise, ass in the wind. Not that she was going to complain, because it gave her a very nice view.

Shamu burst through the door, head down, a growl for Horse as he circled the end of the bed, first one way then the other. He barked at Glenna, then bared his teeth at Horse.

"I don't think he liked being locked out." She held her hand towards the dog, and he came closer on stilted legs, every muscle tense.

"Well, I didn't want him watchin' me lovin' on his momma." Horse picked a shirt off the floor and shoved it over his head, stepping into his boxers next. "He'll get over himself."

Glenna's hand swept over the dog's head to his back, but he remained focused on the man still in the room. "Will he have a chance to get used to it?" Maybe it was needy, asking like that, but she wanted to know where they were.

"Fuck yeah, he's gonna *have* to get used to it. I plan on doing that again. Soon, and often. I'm done denying us this, Glenna. So fuckin' done." Horse planted one fist next to her hip, the other hand cradling the back of her neck as he swooped in for a hard and fast kiss.

Shamu's growl kicked up in volume, not trailing off until Horse had moved to the doorway.

"Then he'll get used to it," Glenna promised Horse, her gaze fixed on his face. "We'll have to give him ample opportunity, though. So keep that in mind."

"Like the way you think, woman." Horse grinned broadly at her. "I'm gonna get the coffee makin', and see what's shakin' in info land. You hang out here long as you want. We're in no rush this mornin'."

"No rush," she agreed with him and watched him walk out of the room. Shamu went to the door and nosed it closed, hitting it with his shoulder so it latched. She laughed at the dog, then flopped back to the bed, fingers trailing along her kiss-swollen lips. "Shammy, I think he really likes me."

***

Horse

Taking his phone from his pocket, he shot off a quick text to Retro and Blackie, then worked on getting a pot of coffee brewing.

He hadn't intended to sleep with Glenna. Not yet at least. Not until after their business was settled. But the second time she'd cried out softly into the dark and then stood in front of his door without knocking, there was no turning back for him. Even if the timing didn't match what he'd had in his head, being with her had met every dream and fantasy he'd had about her. And he'd had a lot. He'd jerked off more in the past week than in previous years.

Having her under him was exquisite. She was responsive and generous with her reactions, something he loved. Seeing her engrossed in passion had been a huge turn-on, knowing he was the one taking her there. Then she'd reacted exactly as he'd dreamed, accepting him into her body willingly, eagerly.

Horse shoved at his persistent semi with the heel of one hand, silently groaning at the contact. "Down boy," he muttered, just as his phone buzzed on the countertop.

"Nothing new. Just catching at smoke." He read Retro's return text aloud, then flipped to Blackie's to find a similar message. "Shit. I doubt the assholes have just gone away, but if there's nothing, then there's nothing." He responded to them quickly, then reminded both to let him know if anything changed. Needlessly, he knew, but it made him feel at least a little more proactive.

The coffeemaker finished burbling and he made two mugs, doctoring one of them the way Glenna preferred.

He was surprised by the closed door, but a quick knock got a laughing permission to enter.

Shamu met him with another growl and lifted lip and Horse squatted down, fearlessly putting his face near the dog. "Gonna have to get over it, big boy." Shamu looked over his shoulder at Glenna who was still laughing softly, then back to Horse. He growled, then darted forward and licked a stripe up Horse's jaw. "Okay, I get it. We're still friends, but you're upset at me. I can work with that." He stood and offered Glenna her mug. "As dogs go, he's a good one."

"He'll come around again. Hopefully sooner than he did the first time." She accepted the mug and sipped at it. "You always get it exactly right."

"I pay attention," he said, and shrugged. "I want to make you happy."

"You do," she said shyly. "I don't understand why you'd pick me, but I'll take it."

"Oh, let me see." Coffee balanced in one hand, he climbed into bed gingerly, placing his back against the headboard while she shifted around to snuggle close to his side. "You're gorgeous, funny, kind, intelligent, loyal—"

"Oh, hush you." She placed one hand over his mouth. "I get it. You see things in me that I don't. I'll just believe and be happy."

"See, you're also super smart." He kissed her fingertips. "So, what's on the agenda for the day?"

"Workwise, we've got some fencing to check. Just a precaution, but it's heading into the time of year for storms, and I want to make sure we don't have any deadfalls ready to come down. It's a pain in the ass to get cattle back in normally, but in the middle of a storm, it's nigh-on impossible."

"Gonna let me drive my own ATV, or want me behind you?"

"As enticing as it is to have you ride with me, motorcycle man, we'll need both of the vehicles along with the little wagons for supplies." She paused to take a drink. "You should look at your bike, and we can see about ordering whatever parts are needed to get it running. I'd like to see you upright and riding again."

"Again?" He didn't bother trying to hide his surprise. "When did you see me before?"

"I was on my way through town as you were headed out. I waved at you. You know how small-town girls always lift a hand at every vehicle, but you didn't see me."

"I was blind, then. How could I have missed you?" He leaned over and kissed the top of her head. "And then, you rode to my rescue like a princess on a white horse."

"Turnabout's fair play, right?" She was giggling.

"Absolutely," he agreed, draining his mug. "I'm going to get a shower." Without giving it too much thought, he offered, "Want to join me?"

"Love to," she said quickly and set her mug aside. "That'll wake me up faster than caffeine any day."

Horse did his level best to ensure she was wide awake by the time he entered her, water beating down on them both. With both her forearms wedged against the tile wall, he covered her back, thrusting up hard and fast. It didn't take long to make her come the first time. Horse worked leisurely to bring her to the edge a second time, heads turned to the side so he could muffle her cries with his mouth. She nearly melted as he pulled out, stripping the condom off in a single motion. It only took a couple of pulls for his orgasm to hit hard, and he'd striped her back and ass with white streaks.

Seeing his release on her skin like that set off a sense of powerful possessiveness in him, and Horse reached down and rubbed it into her skin before shifting them to let the water clean everything off. The water ran to cool by the time they climbed out of the shower and fell back into her bed.

The chores waited until mid-afternoon, and he wasn't upset by that delay at all.

This was his woman, his perfect match. Gunny and Blackie could talk about soul mates, and from this day forward, he'd agree with them. No argument.

Glenna was it for him. He'd known it before, but this had morphed into a soul-deep understanding, unlocking something inside him.

Chapter Sixteen
Horse

"We got movement." Retro's voice was as clipped and cold as his Southern drawl could be and Horse closed his eyes as he listened intently. "There are a fuckin' big bunch of small groups headed your way. They've been sighted in Alabama, Tennessee, and Mississippi, and I've got confirmed intel they're *all* talking about East Texas as a destination. I'm gonna inform Blackie, Mason, Twisted, Wrench, and Po'Boy next, and Jesus but that's a fuckin' mouthful—but wanted to get the news to you first. Way these assholes are working their way across country, and with what they're sayin', I'm less confident than I'd like to be that this is the only wave of members on their way. Could be we missed a few groups. These ones are followin' backroads, and it was only chance that I had tipped off people who were in the right place to see 'em."

"And you've confirmed Longview is the target?" Horse made his shoulders relax down, lifting his head and breathing deeply. "That's for sure?"

"East Texas. That's the word, but knowin' they're invested in that spread near you, I have no doubts of their destination. Not the FRMC mother clubhouse, because even the Devil Monsters wouldn't be stupid enough to do that." Retro sighed and Horse wished this was a video call, so he could see the man's expression. "However, we both need to remember that as shocked and disappointed we are that they're stupid enough to try and set up a charter in that territory, so could be we're all underestimating the level of idiocy they hold in their fuzz-brained heads. I doubt it, but it could happen that we got something wrong. That's why I'm leveling with every club president with a presence and interest in the region."

"Roger that." He blew a soft raspberry. "Just when I'd been hopin' they'd seen the fault and error of their ways."

"Naw, brother. They ain't smart enough for that. Like I heard repeated the other day, takes a hella lesson to learn some people." Retro's voice adopted a brisk diction. "Gonna let you go, man. Got a lot of fuckin' calls to make and fast."

"Respect, Retro. And gratitude."

"Yeah, yeah. I'll hit Blackie up for payment."

They were both laughing as the call disconnected.

"News?" Glenna asked from the doorway behind him.

Horse had stepped out onto the stoop off the kitchen door to take the call, and he hadn't heard the door latch behind him. Which meant Glenna had overheard at least some of his side of the call.

He turned to look at her, his position on the steps putting him eye level with her. His woman was stunning standing there in an unbuttoned shirt with the tails trailing just at the top of her thighs. She had on panties, but nothing else, so her body was framed by white material. With dark tousled hair tumbling around her shoulders, arms bare to the elbow, and a defiant fist planted on each hip, she looked like a warrior princess ready to jump into battle.

Or jump into bed.

He moved closer, running an appreciative hand up her belly to cup one breast. The dark nipple was roughly peaked in an instant, pressing against the palm of his hand. Her breath caught as her throat worked, and the eyes she lifted to look into his face were dark, pupils wide with desire, and muscles in her face strained with want.

"Yeah, there's some news. Sounds like we've got a few hours at most before things might get busy around here. My friend in Alabama is going to alert key folks, and I'd like to take a run into town to see if there's anything to report from our end yet."

He tweaked her nipple between thumb and fingertip, lifting his other hand to her waist to pull her a little nearer, then tugged to bring her closer yet. She came willingly, her hips pressed against him with a heat he could feel through his jeans.

He'd had her again this morning, lying behind her in the bed and rocking into her slowly. Building her pleasure until it bubbled over in a series of long, low moans accompanied by rippling movements of her body. Then he'd lifted her leg over his hip and thrust harder, finding his orgasm in moments. She'd strained to reach the back of his head, turning her face to watch him and urging him on until he'd filled the condom with cum.

"I'm not ever goin' to get tired of you, Glenna. Got me wrapped around your little finger. Hell, all your fingers." He bent to kiss her deep and slow, tongues working in a lazy dance. "Hope you know that."

"I do now," she offered, lifting her chin in silent demand.

He descended on her mouth again, lapping at her tongue, nipping her lips until she groaned softly.

"Horse, I know it's fast—"

"But it's right." Her smile at him finishing her sentence warmed him from the inside out. She was confident of her place in his arms, and he loved seeing that look on her face. He kissed her again, dipping his mouth to trail more kisses along her jaw to her ear. Whispering, he told her, "I think I love you."

She turned her head to place her mouth next to his ear, fingers tightening on his neck to hold him in place. "I don't think. I know."

Horse crushed her to him, wrapping himself around her protectively and possessively, holding her close as emotions rushed through him. Relief, followed by a joy so ecstatic he had to catch his breath.

"Can't. Breathe." She was laughing through her put-on wheeze, and he shook his head as he laughed along with her.

"Get used to it." He leaned back at the waist, keeping his arms tight around her. "I don't know what I did to deserve an angel like you." Shamu's hard nose pressed at his hip, and he glanced down at the dog. "Or what I did to earn a spot with your dog." His words were answered by a silent snarl, the dog lifting one lip to show teeth to him. "He'll get over it eventually."

"Eventually," she agreed, then laughed lightly. "Probably."

"Much as I'd like to take this to the next logical step, we should shake off the dust and head out." He wrapped her hair around his fist, angling her head backwards with a gentle tug, not surprised to see deep lust instantly appear in her expression. His woman liked things rough and rowdy, and it thrilled him each time he uncovered another facet of her personality. "We can save this for later." He pressed a kiss to the corner of her mouth, chuckling when she made a greedy sound and turned her head to line up their lips, tugging against his hold to lift her mouth to his. "Promise you everything you want, Glenna mine. We'll break the bed tonight." He took her mouth in another long kiss. "Promise."

"Gonna hold you to that, Horse." Thrusting her hips forward, she left no question about how she felt with the delayed gratification he was demanding. "Because it's not gentlemanly to leave a woman wanting."

"Never said I was a gentleman." He nuzzled her neck and pulled away, carding his fingers through her hair. "I'm a good man, but that's as far as I'll go."

"Coffee, dressed, then a truck ride." She whirled to lead the way back into the kitchen and lifted the mug already waiting for her. "I'll take this into the bedroom with me. Coffee never disappoints." Casting a coy smile over her shoulder, she caught him looking at her ass. Exaggerating her walk, she swayed down the hall and out of sight.

Shamu barked once, bumped into Horse as he reentered the house, then followed his mistress with clicking nails that somehow shouted disapproval.

"Yeah, yeah. I get it. But you'll get to ride in the truck with us." He was laughing as he called after the dog. "I hear you like french fries. That should earn me some points."

Twenty minutes later, they were driving into the little town of Belle, and Glenna angle parked the truck just up the street from the feed store.

Horse clipped Shamu's leash onto his harness and exited the passenger door, meeting Glenna at the front of the truck. It was the first time they'd been into town since starting to sleep together, and he planned to leave any demonstration of affection up to her.

Glenna didn't disappoint. She stood on the curb and looped a hand through his arm, then lifted her head. He was happy to meet her halfway with a soft kiss, chaste as could be. Shamu pushed between them, shoving Horse backwards a step. Glenna laughed and took the leash, scolding the dog as she grabbed Horse's hand with her other one. She threaded their fingers together and led the way up the sidewalk and into the store.

Their entrance was met with a bubble of silence, followed by a round of applause begun by the older man behind the counter. Horse looked on with amusement as Glenna was folded into his arms, the man holding her tenderly before releasing her to Horse's arms again.

"'Bout time, kiddo," the older man said as he pulled himself up to sit on the countertop. "We were runnin' out of gossip about town doin's. Tell us everything."

Several older ranchers gathered in a semi-circle nearby laughed from their seats on overturned buckets and folding chairs. A couple of them chimed in with versions of "Hear, hear," and Glenna giggled, turning her face against Horse's shoulder.

"Everyone, this is Graeme. He's with me, as you can see." She made an expansive sweeping motion with her arm. "Graeme, this is everyone. I won't give you names, because they're being nosey parkers. They can introduce themselves when the time comes."

As one, the men smiled at Glenna, and Horse saw the caring in every face. They knew her, had known her husband, and had watched her go through a terrible experience. None of them would fault her for finding happiness again, no matter how much they'd respected Penn. Acceptance like that was a gem to be polished and kept safe.

"Hi, everyone. I hope to have a chance to meet all of you again." He nodded to each in turn, feeling like he was in church with his brothers. "We've had some trouble out at Glenna's place and wondered if any of you knew anything about what's going on. If you'd seen anyone new in town." When the store owner cleared his throat, Horse tossed a grin his direction. "In addition to me, I realize I'm from away too."

"Snyder's place seems to be a beehive of worthless pot stirrers." That came from one of the group of men, and Horse turned to face him. "Seen any number of new faces when I delivered a trailer of roll hay to them. Weren't any of them hands either. Didn't have a clue how to run a tractor." He hooked a can towards him with one foot and spit a stream of brown liquid into it. "Hopeless. Made an old man like me get out and do it myself. Useless as tits on a boar hog." His lips shifted into a wry grimace.

"Heard them talkin', though. Thought themselves big men. Shakin' each other down with threats and promises. I'm thinkin' it's more a big man, little pond thing."

"How many did you see, Mr. Pearson?" Glenna jumped in with a good question and Horse waited for the response.

"Saw the same thing," another man answered. "Probably two dozen when I was out there a couple days ago."

The first man nodded, then shrugged. "At least a couple dozen that I saw. Doubt they were all outside, though. There were bikes there. A lot of them." He pointed at Horse, who was wearing his Freed Riders MC cut. "Different patch from you, and they don't look reputable, if you know what I mean." He cleared his throat. "No disrespect to a brotherhood, but not every club's good to have around. Not like your men."

"No disrespect taken. If they're who I think they are, then they're as different from my brothers as night is to day." Horse reached out a hand and the man took it, shaking solemnly. "That's what we were looking to know." He grimaced. "Well, we were hoping for no news, but I'm glad to have things validated."

"They gonna bring trouble to town?" This was the store owner again, and he looked angry and alert. Horse didn't blame him. Lord knew there'd been ample publicized about club wars over the years.

"If myself and my brothers can stop it before it starts, it shouldn't spill over. Now that you folks have confirmed things, I'll get my folks rolling this way. This group isn't one we want in our territory, because they're known for having short fuses and very bad ideas. We'd rather they limit themselves to their own place, way back on the East Coast." He gave Glenna's fingers a squeeze. "Hand to God, I'll do my level best to not let Belle take their shit."

"This one is one of Blackie's boys, so in my opinion, you can take it to the bank." A thin, older man stood up off his overturned bucket and rubbed his hindquarters. "Ass is hurtin'. I'm headed to the diner. Not gonna waste any of my brain power worryin' over somethin' I know Blackie's gonna take care of. He's a good'un."

"He is," Horse agreed. "I'm proud he's my brother."

Four or five of the men shuffled to their feet and followed the old man out the door.

"Easy as that?" Horse asked, turning to the storeowner.

"Easy as it needs to be," the man answered, jumping off the counter. "My name's Bob, by the way. Glenna, did you need anything delivered? I got most of the order in the other day, was just waitin' for the last items to come in to give you a call."

Looking up at Horse, she shook her head, puzzlement in her face. "Order?"

"That's mine," Horse told the owner. "It can wait for everything. You got my cell, so you can let me know when things are ready."

"No problem. Y'all take care now."

Horse led Glenna and Shamu out of the store. Partway down the sidewalk, she pulled him to a stop and asked, "Order?"

"Yeah, some things I needed. He was the easiest way to order them. Since I used your ranch's address, he must have gotten confused." Pressing his lips to hers in an echo of the kiss she'd initiated earlier, he muttered, "Want to grab food while we're in town? I might have promised fries to someone who's been grumbly."

At her nod, he took the leash for Shamu and made his way to the passenger door.

"Horse? Do you want to drive?" She was standing at the front of the truck, fingers twisting together nervously. "Instead of riding shotgun?"

"Nah, you're a good driver. Don't bother me none to ride on this side with you." He shrugged and opened the door for Shamu to jump in. "I've got some calls to make too. Easier to do that if I'm not worried about chuckin' us in the ditch."

"You're an interesting man, Graeme Nass." Her smile was worth everything, especially over something as easy as not pitching a fuss about riding with her.

He grinned back.

***

Glenna

She stripped off her work gloves as she made her way up the couple of steps to the kitchen stoop, dusting them against her thighs before tucking them into her back pocket. Shamu was beside her, head down, just as tired as she was. It had been a busy day, caring for the cattle with a plan for not doing it again for a couple of days. Not that they were taking a vacation, but if things came to a head somehow, she didn't want to be distracted by chores she could put off.

Horse was in the living room, one arm spread across the back of the couch, the other holding a phone to his ear. He gave her a distracted wave when she came in, clearly focused on whatever was happening on the call.

She shucked her boots at the door, then hung up her hat while Shamu pushed past her. Glenna threw a frozen casserole in the oven and set the timer, then went up the hall, already anticipating how good the shower would feel.

Having been halfway hopeful Horse would join her, she parked her disappointment in a back corner of her mind. They both had their roles, and his was ensuring backup that would be needed if the other club came in force.

After their visit to town, it sounded more and more like things would come down to physical violence, something Glenna wasn't looking forward to. She knew Horse would do his best to keep her out of it, not because he believed she couldn't cope, but because he cared. That was another thing she parked in that dark corner of her mind. If there was a war, Horse would be on the front lines, and if things heated up before his friends arrived, it would be just him and her, and they wouldn't be able to protect each other.

Parking that, too. Gonna get real crowded back there. Might not have room for self-control.

She grinned weakly at the idea.

The casserole still had forty-five minutes on the timer, so Glenna poured herself a glass of sweet tea and chucked Shamu under the chin. He was stretched out in his favorite bed near the back door and didn't offer to move when she walked past him to the living room.

Horse had shifted around on the couch, legs sprawled wide with both feet firmly on the floor. His arms hung over the cushions, phone still gripped idly in one hand. Head back, he was stretching his neck when she walked in. She made her way to the back of the couch and settled her hands on his shoulders. Bending over, she kissed him upside down, laughing softly when he tried to deepen the caress.

"Hey, you," he said when she pulled back, then dug her thumbs into the muscles at the top of his shoulders. "Holy shit, that feels good."

"Hey backatcha." She deepened the intensity of the impromptu massage, finding hard knots with fingers and thumbs and working them loose. "You get your calls all made?"

"I did. We've got folks coming in starting early tomorrow." His head lolled forward, wagging back and forth with her rubbing. "That's really good."

"Dinner's in the oven." Glenna's concentration was on the stress in his muscles, focused on relaxing him. "I got things taken care of outside. Moved most of the cattle into a pasture farther from the house, so if something happens here, they won't be disturbed."

"Sounds like you had a long day." His breathing slowed as knots and tension let go. "I should be the one doing this to you."

"I won't turn it down later." She bent and pressed a kiss to the bared nape of his neck. "But let me take care of you right now."

"Yes, ma'am." Horse angled his neck and joints popped, making him groan. "Fuckin' shit, I didn't realize how much shit hurt."

"Easy to get tense when you're waiting for something bad to happen." She made her touch lighter as she moved down his shoulders to his pectoral muscles. "When one thing tightens up, another follows until, before you know what's going on, you're taut as a bowstring."

"Truth," he muttered, laying his head back on the couch and staring up at her. "Prettiest woman I've ever seen, right there."

"Oh, shaw." She kissed him quickly, then moved her massage down his arms. "Eeep," she squeaked when he gripped her shirt and pulled her over the back of the couch, ending in his lap. "Horse," she laughingly complained. "I was working on you."

"Yeah, you were working on me all right." He thrust his hips up and she felt the stiffness behind the zipper of his jeans. "I don't think I'll ever get enough of you, woman."

"Well, I'll have to keep up being awesome, then, won't I?" She twisted in his arms to press her breasts against his chest, liking how his breath hitched at the contact. "With a kiss—" She put the words into action, placing a chaste kiss against his mouth. "—and a few other things."

Glenna slithered out of his arms, folding to her knees between his feet. "Maybe even some things I really like doing." Keeping her gaze locked with his, she pulled the tail of his belt free from the loops, working the buckle loose. "Things like this." Bending forward, she mouthed his cock through the fabric, dragging her teeth along the seam. "Which I enjoy so much. I can't believe I haven't shown you before." She thumbed the button loose and the zipper made a ticking sound as it traveled several teeth down without her touching it. "So much fun to play," she whispered, blowing hot air through the fabric, her fingers tugging the zipper the rest of the way down.

"Darlin'." His breathing was heavier already, lips wet from where his tongue had darted out to lick a swipe across the bottom. "You sure?"

He lifted his hips to let her pull his pants and boxers down. His cock popped out, a pearl of precum already beading at the tip. Tugging his clothing down to frame his cock and balls, she reached for a cushion and placed it underneath her knees.

"I'm real sure." She batted her lashes and he smiled quickly, the expression morphing into eagerness as she wrapped her fingers around his cock. "Graeme Nass, may I suck your cock?"

"Doubt there's a man alive who's ever answered no to that question." His hips rocked and he thrust through her fingers holding him loosely.

"Not asking every man." She dipped her face closer, blowing a stream of air across the head. "I'm asking you if I can blow your mind?"

"Yes. Fuckin' yes, Glenna. Whatever you want, darlin'." His eyes were dark, pupils blown at just her handling his cock and she smiled.

"Here we go, then." She licked a stripe up the length of his cock, tonguing the thick veins twisting up the shaft. Moving one hand to his balls, she tested how sensitive he was by plucking at the tender skin, then rolling them in her hand while she gave the head of his cock long, slow kisses. The way his sac drew up said he liked it, and she smiled as she pressed her mouth against his cock, working her tongue down the length to where her fingers were wrapped around the base. Nuzzling into the thatch of hair there, she pulled his balls into her mouth, lapping at them wetly with her tongue.

"Jesus fuck, Glenna." He shoved his shoulders back against the cushions, eyes fixed on where her head moved in his crotch.

"Oh shoot," she said in between long licks of the base of his cock. "He can still speak. We can't be havin' that."

She traveled up his cock to the head, teasing the slit with the tip of her tongue. His flavor was mixed musk and salt, and she used her grip on the shaft to milk another drop of precum onto her tongue. Making a show of curling it into her mouth, she moved to teasing the edge of the glans, softly sucking at the sensitive area just under the ridge.

He shouted then and she looked back up to see he was gripping the back of the couch with bloodless fingers, holding himself back. Glenna reached way up and tugged one of his arms free, drawing his palm to the back of her head. She took his cock into her mouth for the first time, then, relaxing her jaw to help make it a smooth transition. Fluttering her tongue against the base of his cock, she swallowed and then lifted slowly, working every inch of flesh. His fingers clutched her hair as she paused on the upswing, then pushed gently when she took him deep again, working hard to get him farther into her throat.

This was one of her favorite things to do, and while it had been a long time and he was larger in every way than Penn had been, she was determined to take him down as far as was physically possible.

Fingers alternately teasing his sac and pumping his shaft, she swallowed him down again and again, head bobbing up and down. The weight of his hand would increase on every up movement, as if he couldn't bear losing her mouth around him.

Focused on her self-appointed task, she tried to ignore the heat in her own body, not wanting any distractions. With long slow strokes, she took in more and more, until her nose was nestled at the base, her hand now free to slide up inside his shirt. Fingers tweaking at his nipples, she swallowed around him, taking tiny breaths through her nose until that was no longer an option. Holding out as long as she could, Glenna pulled off fast and gasped hard, sucking in as much oxygen as she could, then took him to the base again in a single slide.

"Glenna, I'm there," he warned her, hand gripping a hank of her hair as he tried to tug her up. She fought his hold, forcing herself back down and sucking hard.

He came down her throat with a shout that got Shamu barking. Glenna pulled off just enough to get some of his spunk on her tongue, rolling the flavor around in her mouth as she swallowed the rest of his load.

When he was finished, soft cock still filling her mouth as she tongued it gently, she slowly let it slip free as she pushed away to look up at him.

Horse looked wrecked, hair in disarray, shirt pushed up to his armpits as he'd cleared the way for her wandering hands. With his soft cock curled in his lap, mouth still panting air, and an expression of adoration on his face, she decided she was keeping him forever.

Pushing up on her knees, she stretched herself to place her mouth on his. Horse didn't balk at deepening the kiss, lapping into her mouth as if searching for his own taste.

"You really enjoy your work." He smiled against her lips, and she laughed.

"I do. There are few things I like more. When it can be all about you, that cranks my engine."

"Well, I'm here to serve. I'll be your sacrifice any day, Glenna. Fuckin' hell, woman. That was spectacular."

He shoved his hands under her arms and pulled her up, dropping her in his lap. She wiggled until she could feel his cock against her ass, then collapsed against his chest, as ready for a nap as he seemed to be.

They stayed like that until the timer went off in the kitchen, signaling the casserole was done.

Glenna didn't know if she'd ever had a more peaceful handful of minutes.

***

Horse

It was well past midnight when Horse stepped outside to make his calls. After getting Blackie's voice mail, not knowing why but especially with Peaches expecting, Horse decided to move to texting. Waffling for a moment on which group to text first, he pulled up the secure app most of the major Northern American clubs utilized and flagged a dozen FRMC officers to receive. After a few moments' consideration, he added a couple more, grimacing as he clicked on Gunny's name.

"Not that I don't like the asshole. It's just he's an asshole," he muttered, head down and focused on the screen in his hands. "All hands: Heat is applied in Belle, Texas. Need volunteers ASAP." He shifted and took a couple of steps down, planting his boots on the beaten grass of the back yard. "Might as well add a voice mail to it."

Lifting the phone, he started the voice recording function. "Local intel says MDMC assholes have been seen in numbers. I'm guessing it'll be soon when they try to kick things off." He paused, a noise from the front of the house catching his attention. It wasn't repeated, so he bent his head back to the phone. "Asking for any volunteers. This is just going to FRMC, but feel free to spread the mess—"

Something whizzed past his cheek, close enough there was a fleeting sensation of heat, then he heard the cracking report of the gunshot.

Running back to the door, he thumbed the Send button which stopped the recording and sent it along with the text message to the group he'd selected. Another gunshot sounded, followed by the wasp whine of a ricochet.

Horse threw open the door and shouted for Glenna. She called out, "Here," from the living room. He slid around the corner to see her crouched on the floor against the front wall. Shamu was standing next to her, his head lifted, and ears pinned back against his skull. She pointed to the window. "They're still out front, between the house and the road."

"Are they on the driveway?" He hadn't taken the time to look for anything, wanting to get back to Glenna fast as he could.

"No, they're parked along the road. The cab lights flashing when they got out pulled my attention. I only saw two people. I think." She sounded winded, each word exiting on a tiny gasp.

"Are you okay?" He crawled closer and pulled her into his arms. Shamu was pressed tight to her, his growls vibrating against Horse's hand.

"Yeah, sure. It's just... I've never had a gun fired in my general direction before." She pulled in a shaky breath. "Did you talk to your friends?"

"I sent a message just as the excitement started." Horse reached behind him and adjusted his gun, securing it against his low back. "Glenna, we need to round up some power like we talked about."

"Yeah." She lifted to her knees, head masked from the window by the blinds. "I can't see them, but that doesn't mean anything. We need the moon tonight. Why does it have to be cloudy?"

"Let me at the window. I've got an IR camera on my phone." Another one of the widgets they'd acquired from the Rebel Wayfarers' tech guru. "Let's see what thermal says."

He lifted the phone and tapped to launch the app. Once he held it above the windowsill, it showed deep blues and greens directly in front of the house, with blobs of orange off to the side. From the shape and way they moved, those had to be the few the cattle that hadn't moved to farther pastures. Sweeping the device left to right, Horse studied the screen and gritted his teeth when he landed on what looked like a vehicle about a quarter mile down by the road. "I see one vehicle." He adjusted the settings on the app to account for the distance and was rewarded by seeing three moving red blobs. "And three bad guys."

"Are they still on the other side of the fence?" She gave his hand a squeeze as she moved backwards, still staying down. Once away from the window, she shifted to a stooped crouch and went towards the hallway leading to the bedrooms. "If they are, then that means they didn't cut the fence. There are enough strands of barbed wire between us and them it'll be harder for them to make their way on foot without cutting them."

Horse kept his attention on the phone's screen. "Maybe they're too dumb to have cutters with them. Looks like they are down by the road, so I don't think they're through the fencing." His phone dinged and an alert flashed across the screen. "Just got a confirmation from one of the guys, so my text went through."

"How long will it take them to get here?" Glenna called, sounding distracted. "You want long guns as well as pistols?"

"I'll take whatever you've got."

"Honey, this is Texas. I've got quite a lot." Horse smiled at her quip, not surprised she was holding it together well enough to joke. "I'll just bring out everything I'm familiar with and we can divvy them up. I'm going to leave two rifles in here, though. I'll prop them next to the window."

"They're moving away." There was a bright yellow splash on the screen, and he looked out the window to see a truck's interior lit up. Two silhouettes climbed into the cab and a single red blob slipped into the truck bed. He heard another gunshot, and the muzzle flash showed it was pointed it up to the sky. "That's a parting salvo."

Once he was convinced the men were gone, he flipped to the secure app to see a half dozen responses. Most would be able to make it to the ranch within a couple hours. He sighed in relief. No matter the assholes had already bailed on their initial attack, he suspected strongly that wasn't the last they'd hear from the MDMC.

Another message came in and he groaned when he saw it was from Gunny.

Be there in a flash. Already on my way, so I'm about a hundred miles out.

He thumbed a thanks and sent it in response.

"What's wrong?" Glenna walked into the living room with three rifles tucked under one arm, and a small bag held in her other hand.

"One of the men coming isn't my biggest fan. That's all. I'll be glad for his help, but Gunny seems to always be in a place to bust my balls. I like him, and he's one loyal son of a bitch, but—well, you'll see when you meet him." He met her in the middle of the room. "Show me what you've brought."

Chapter Seventeen
Glenna

It felt a bit surreal to be staging loaded guns around her house while waiting for an outside force to come back. More like a movie than real life. But the fact they'd fired at the house was enough to make her a believer, especially when Horse mentioned how close one of the rounds had come to him.

Surely God won't do something like that to me twice, will he?

She knew even thinking that was akin to tempting fate. So instead of following the thought to any kind of conclusion, she focused on making sure each gun had ammunition placed nearby.

Horse was on the phone again, as he'd been intermittently since the first volley of gunfire subsided. Someone in Alabama was organizing everything, and apparently there were men coming in from as far away as Florida and as near as Longview. The first of them should be arriving any minute.

She finished with the guns and looked around the room. Everything was done as Horse had requested, with blankets fastened halfway up the windows, rolls of duct tape close to each of the guns, and battery powered lanterns positioned on strategic tables.

251

"I'm going to make coffee." Glenna was proud that her hands didn't shake as she measured the grounds and poured the water before flicking the switch to start the brewing cycle. She opened the refrigerator and surveyed the interior. "What does one cook when defending one's home?"

"Darlin', it's going to be okay." Arms swept around her middle, pulling her back against Horse's muscular chest. "Coffee's good, though. Thanks for thinking of it."

"I hate this waiting. It's been a long time since they left. Why would they start something and then just sail off in the middle?" She pounded the back of her skull against his shoulder. "Failure to launch? Maybe they were out past curfew? I don't understand."

"They probably got a recall back to the Snyder place. Leaders over there are likely going through open options, knowing that I'm not going to be standing on my own. If they're even sure I'm here. But I'm not alone." She smiled when he squeezed her tightly. "And neither are you. You're not alone in this."

"Well, the trouble landed in both our breakfast bowls, so I think it's only right we stand together." Resting her hands on his forearms, she relaxed into his hold. "And I'm banking on you. In fact, I'm betting on you. I think it's going to be a one-and-done meeting at some point and they're going to hightail it out of town."

"We can wish, but we'll also prepare. I think we've done all we can except wait." His lips laid claim to her ear, teeth nibbling delicately as he pressed his mouth against the sensitive point behind her ear. "I don't think I thanked you for your sweet, sweet attention earlier."

"No thanks needed." She turned her head and smiled up at him. "You don't understand how much I enjoyed myself. Seriously, no thanks needed."

"Yeah? Liked it, did you? Liked takin' me apart like that? Enjoyed wrecking my world?" He rubbed the tip of his nose against hers, whiskers tickling her face so she laughed.

"You have no idea."

***

Horse

The sun was barely breaking the horizon when Horse watched Gunny roar up to the house in a scatter of gravel, barely getting his kickstand down before he was off and running to the door. Horse opened it, let the big man push through, and then slammed it shut behind him.

Things had remained quiet until about fifteen minutes ago when three vehicles had staged along the road. Horse had sent out updates every few minutes and gotten back info from Retro as the situation evolved.

"Well met, brother." He greeted Gunny, moving to take up his post at the front window again. "This is Glenna." He indicated towards where she stood stationed at another window. Stretching out a hand, he trailed fingers across the back of her neck. "She's mine." His declaration was met with deep laughter, and he glanced at the man standing in the kitchen.

"Yeah, I kinda got that from the 'all hands' text with an address I'd never seen associated with the club, man. You wouldn't call us to somewhere that you didn't have a stake in the outcome."

Shamu trotted into the room and pulled up short, staring at Gunny with narrowed eyes and all the attitude Horse had come to expect from the dog.

"Hi, Gunny. That's Shammy," Glenna offered without taking her gaze from the drive out front. "He's my boy."

"That's—" Gunny choked out as he dropped to one knee, the hand not holding a pistol outstretched. "Jesus wept. That's a Peruvian Inca

Orchid. It's a super rare breed. Holy shit, he's gorgeous. Lookit him." His fingers touched the dog's muzzle reverently. "Hey, Shammy. How are you, boy?"

Horse rolled his eyes. "He doesn't like people on first meet. And doesn't seem to like me too much these days."

"Yeah, brother, that emotion's not super rare. Sorry to break the news to you." Gunny laughed at his own joke, now running his hand over the dog's neck and back. "You're a gorgeous boy," he semi repeated, and got a short lick to the side of his hand in response, the dog preening under the attention.

"Oh, fuck me running, seriously, Shamu? You like this asshole but not me?" Horse wasn't surprised when the dog lifted his head to look his direction, a clear growl of disapproval rumbling from his chest. "See, he doesn't like me."

"What'd you do to him?" Gunny gave the dog a final pat, stood, and made his way to where Horse was posted up by the windows. "Musta done something. This breed is hella loyal."

"I closed the bedroom door."

"Aw, hell. That'll do it." Gunny lifted his chin to the window and the road beyond. "That drive I came up the only way onto the property?"

"There's an old access road on the back side, but it doesn't connect to anything, just gives out into a pasture where I've got a deep well for summer water." Glenna angled herself towards Horse, slipping an arm around his waist. "Well met, seriously. I've heard a bit about you."

"Lies," the man cried with a grin. "Lies and prevarications, all of it."

"Even the part about you being a good guy? Shoot, color me wrong then."

Horse liked the gentle teasing already passing between them. He wasn't surprised by Gunny's instant adoption of Glenna, but her engaging as she was made him proud. She trusted him, trusted that anyone he brought into her orbit would be someone he believed in. Trust was earned, and he was stoked he'd gotten that from Glenna.

Shamu growled and Horse understood the sentiment. There was movement by the road, and not from the direction his brothers would come. A truck he recognized as the one Moorcock had used the other day rolled slowly towards the end of the driveway and paused, as if testing the water.

His phone chimed and he pulled it out, glancing at the screen the same time as Gunny did his own.

"Blackie's in town. He stumbled onto a group of them causing trouble, so he's dispatching those assholes now. Things are gonna get busy." Horse paused to shove the phone back into his pocket. "Local rundown for Gunny's sake. This guy in the driveway is the business leader, Moorcock. According to Retro, he's got no official club designation, but he precedes the Monster Devils into every town they take over, smoothing the way with whatever dealings they've decided make sense. He had unsubtle threats the day he showed up here but wasn't as unhinged as the property owner, Snyder."

"I don't see Jackson with him," Glenna offered, peering through a small set of binoculars she'd unearthed when the vehicles first showed up. "He's got one of the guys you called 'muscle' driving. And he's on the phone right now." She huffed. "Why don't men talk with their hands like women do? I can't tell if he's agitated or calm. He's just sitting there."

"Some of us do." Gunny cackled at his own joke. "My ole lady Sharon says I smack the walls every time we have a discussion."

"That's because you're fuckin' nuts. Not because you're connected to your emotional side." Horse squeezed Glenna's waist. "Still on the phone, darlin'?"

"Yeah. No, he just hung up." She grew still. "He's checking his pistol. That's bad, isn't it?"

"He likely clocked us watching and is putting on a show." Horse focused on the other vehicles. "There's movement back by the trucks too."

Moorcock's truck started rolling up the driveway as the men waiting beside the road poured out of their vehicles.

His phone chimed but Gunny beat him to the update.

"Blackie's wrapped up and is on his way."

Glenna laughed quietly. She'd turned the binoculars on the group of men who were now trying to scale the wire fence. "You'd think they'd never seen barbed wire before. You don't climb wire, you go through it."

"With any luck, they won't figure it out." Horse pressed a kiss to the top of her head. "Keep watching and call out with updates. I'm going outside to meet Moorcock and see what he's got to say."

"Where do you want me, brother?"

Gunny's question drew Horse up short. He looked at Glenna, conflicted, and she flicked him an annoyed glance he could read like a book.

"With me."

His words were filled with grit and anger, because it went against every instinct inside him. He knew Glenna would have Shamu at her side, and since the idiots from the MDMC had waited until nearly daybreak, she'd see the men coming. Probably. If he and Gunny presented a united force, and if Moorcock had any intel on the club to identify them, it might be enough to move any impending violence down the road until more backup could arrive.

"At your back, brother." Gunny passed Glenna and Shamu, touching her gently on the shoulder before patting the dog. "We've got your back, little sister. Trust."

"Goes both ways," she returned, her gaze back on the men huddled in a group at the first fence, half inside and half still outside.

Horse threw open the kitchen door and stepped onto the stoop, Gunny filling up the space behind him as the door closed. The truck was still rolling slowly up the drive, and Moorcock had his window down, both arms stuck outside.

"His piece won't be put away." Horse knew Gunny didn't need the insight, but nerves were building with every inch the truck crept closer.

"And the driver is carrying too. I see a shoulder holster."

"He's come far enough. Let's go meet him." Horse stepped off the stoop and into the driveway, striding quickly down the drive to keep the truck at a distance from the house. Crunching from behind said Gunny was with him, step for step.

"Ahoy the house," Moorcock called as the truck rolled to a stop. He didn't get out, staying in the stupid-looking position, leaning far out of the window. "I heard a rumor there were more Freed Riders in town. Glad to see my information was correct."

"What do you want?" Horse let the hand with the gun dangle in full view at his side. "If you know who we are, you gotta know this is a bad idea, whatever it is."

"Well, see. I didn't recognize you the other day, but my friends educated me." He gestured towards the outside door handle. "Mind if I join you on terra firma? This is awkward as hell."

"Just tell the man what you wanna say." Gunny placed himself at Horse's shoulder. "No reason to get comfortable. You won't be stayin' long."

"Is that any way to treat a neighbor?" Moorcock tsked as he opened the truck door, climbing out with an exaggerated stretch. "It's been a long night, gentlemen."

"Then get to it, asshole. You and the MDMC aren't welcome here." Horse didn't see a gun on Moorcock, but he remained half behind the open door, and nothing could be certain.

"My *friends*," Moorcock smiled as he said this, "want to offer an olive branch, as it were. They'll keep the ranch they've already bought and paid for, and you leave them alone. In return they'll not bother the pretty widow woman who owns this place. You'll remember from my last visit that Jackson Snyder would rather the terms be slightly different, but my friends can show him the error of his ways."

Horse was already shaking his head negatively. "No can do, ballsac. The MDMC isn't welcome in our territory, and Belle falls smackdab in the middle of said territory. Your *friends* are gonna have to relocate. Quickly, if they don't want to start something they're not ready for."

"I told them this would likely be your response. I've done my research, you know. I knew the Freed Riders support club had a chapter near here, but my advice of restraint was sadly overruled." Moorcock glanced at the driver of the truck. "No matter how I argued, there was a burning desire to stretch the bounds of their existing territory."

"Don't care." Gunny spat the words. "You knew and did that shit anyway, just means you're extra stupid."

"Yes, well, it does impact negotiations, I can see that." Moorcock glanced at the driver again and Horse saw the man was looking down into his lap.

"Stalling," he clipped, and a startled expression flitted across Moorcock's face.

"Agreed." Gunny's arm lifted, pistol pointed at the driver. "Time to vacate the premises, assholes."

"Horse." Glenna's call wasn't fearful but held a tone of urgency. He whipped his head to see her at the kitchen door. "They're past the fences, and there are more of them."

"Retreat?" Gunny's quiet question was low enough Horse didn't think Moorcock heard him.

Then everything changed because Horse heard the rumble of bike exhausts, what sounded like dozens of them. Followed by a single gunshot sounding in the distance.

"Naw, we can pincher these two." He lifted his gun and aimed at the truck, firing at the front wheel. The sound of the tire exploding was eclipsed by the gunshot.

A hole appeared in the door in front of Moorcock and at first, he thought Gunny had shot at the man, then realized the metal bent outward.

"Fucking hell, he's got a cannon in there." Gunny sounded gleeful as he dropped to one knee and took quick aim. The glass shattered to the side of the driver, who slumped over the wheel. "Oops. Might have shaved that one too close."

Horse took aim at the hole in the truck door, meaning to bend the metal the other direction when Glenna screamed, Shamu barking wildly.

He whirled and saw Glenna in the kitchen door, Snyder behind her with arms outstretched.

***

Glenna

The imminent threat of armed men coming at them was nothing like Glenna ever thought she'd experience, but the idea beating in the front of her mind continued to be that they couldn't take her place, not by wiles and cheating, and not by force. *Never. It's mine, belongs to my family.*

It had been a crazy, busy night and morning, but throughout all of it Horse had been a constant comfort. He'd alternately praised her and argued with Gunny, something she'd found amusing. When they'd gone outside to meet with Moorcock, she'd felt a wave of unease, something not sitting right in her gut.

I have to trust him. If I don't, then he'll not trust himself.

Keeping one eye towards the men out by the road, she'd ignored the sounds from the driveway, putting that trust into action as she left Horse to handle the challenge there.

The men by the road had finally figured out how to cross through the fence, and the length of time it took didn't speak to the level of intelligence in the group. *How hard is it to put one foot on the bottom strand and lift the one above?* They were taking their time moving through the front pasture, though, keeping a wary eye on the cattle in the next paddock, and stepping carefully around cow pies in their way.

Night and day between them and Horse. Jesus.

She moved to the door to let Horse and Gunny know the group was on the move, albeit slowly. Shamu turned and barked down the hallway to the bedrooms and Glenna paused a moment, listening hard.

"You're as spooked as I am, buddy." She fondled his ears as she talked to him. "It's okay. Horse won't let it be anything but."

Update delivered, she took a moment to survey the men on the driveway, relaxing minutely when she saw Horse's open pleasure upon hearing motorcycles in the distance.

A sound behind her had her turning, lifting her gun, then she recognized Jackson standing in the doorway. He grappled for her and

Shamu lunged at him, barking, as Glenna screamed. His heavy hand landed on her mouth and lower jaw, wrenching it painfully to the side.

"Shut the fuck up, bitch." His voice was high pitched, sounding terrified. She gagged at his touch. His hands stunk of chemicals, the scent burning her nose and sinuses. "Shut up. Just shut up. You shoulda taken what I offered."

He shoved her into the hallway and Glenna pinwheeled her arms, trying to keep her balance. Shamu yelped sharply, his snarls increasing in volume but farther away; he was no longer beside her. She fell and landed on her hip hard, eyes blurry from the fumes. Shamu crouched a few feet beyond Jackson, who'd drawn his foot back for what was obviously another kick.

Gunfire from outside told her that help wouldn't be coming immediately. She didn't even know if Horse had noticed Jackson's presence.

Means it's up to me.

She rose to her feet and withdrew another couple of feet to the linen closet, opening the door and taking out a broom. The door was forced out of her hands, slamming closed on her fingers. She screamed as she dropped the improvised weapon, the throbbing roaring through her hands as she fought to get away from Jackson.

He pulled his arm across his body to casually backhand her. Glenna tasted blood as her nose exploded in agony. It overrode anything else that came before it, and Glenna forgot about her fingers as she brought her hands to her face. That double serving of pain drove her to her knees.

Searing pain ripped at her scalp and she toppled over backwards, then was dragged the remaining few feet to her bedroom door.

Shamu darted in and out around her, snapping at Jackson's hand and arm. The dog's teeth connected a few times, Jackson shouting angrily with every hard bite.

He swung her into the bedroom, slinging her across the floor so she fetched up against the foot of the bed. Jackson was on her in an instant, before Glenna had regained her bearings. Ripping at her clothing, his hips were already thrusting at nothing but air, like a dog humping something that excited him. He forced her to the ground as he tore at her jeans, one knee on her chest effectively immobilizing her.

Glenna panicked as she realized she'd lost the ability to breathe. His weight was forcing the air out of her lungs, and when his hand landed on her throat and tightened, she saw stars.

Just as blackness threatened, a square of light appeared behind him.

Horse stepped from the darkness, anger making a mask of his face.

Chapter Eighteen
Horse

He watched helplessly as Glenna's movement to go for her gun was aborted. Snyder struck in that moment, and then they were gone out of sight.

"Fuck," he screamed, whirling to drill three holes into the truck door. Moorcock had moved, but Horse adjusted his aim and didn't even wait for the man to fall.

"Go, brother," Gunny called as he fired again as the bikes Horse had heard coming turned into the driveway.

He heard Moorcock from behind him yelling, "Stop, I yield. I give up." Then everything fell silent, even the roar of bikes fading away.

He hit the kitchen doorway at a full run, yanking the screen nearly off its hinges. A quick glance was all he gave the front of the house, because Shamu's barking was a siren call pulling him to the back bedroom.

He slipped as he came around the doorframe into the bedroom, and on one knee he registered that Glenna was quiet on the floor, frighteningly still. Snyder had one hand on her throat, the other lodged between Glenna's jeans-clad thighs. Blood had formed a red curtain covering the lower half of her face.

Shamu was noisily worrying at the man's back, dodging half-hearted kicks from Snyder. The dog fell back as Horse approached, going around to stand over Glenna's head, foamy saliva flinging from his mouth with every deafening bark.

Horse didn't bother announcing himself, because nothing about this was going to be an even fight. The sight of the blood, and how still Glenna lay told him everything he needed to know. Snyder had given up his right to keep breathing air when he laid a hand on Horse's Glenna.

He gripped the man's jaw and back of his head, wrenched viciously, then followed him to the floor with powerful strikes of his fists.

A hand on his arm pulled him from the red haze of fury and he looked around to find Glenna on her knees behind him. Horse dropped Snyder's body to the floor, letting it land in the puddle of blood and flesh he'd left behind, and Horse wrapped her up, angling himself around her as best he could. He glanced down at Snyder's lopsided head and closed his eyes, burying his face against her hair.

She'd seen him at his worst, but instead of pulling away, she'd burrowed closer. Hands bloody with evidence of his fury against her attacker, he soothed them both, cooing into her ear as they rocked slowly back and forth.

He realized that sometime in the past few minutes the shooting outside had stopped.

"Can you stand?" He pulled back, wincing at the swelling already surfacing in her battered face. "We need to check things."

"If you're with me." She gasped and winced when she tried to clutch at his arms. He cupped a hand underneath her elbow to urge her upright. She came slowly, and swayed, then steadied. "I think I can do anything."

"Atta girl," he whispered, his mind flashing back to the moment he'd come into the room. "Snyder's dead, Glenna. He won't touch you again."

"I know. It's okay." She leaned on him, then looped an arm around his waist. "Come on, Shammy. Leave the asshole alone."

With the dog at their heels, they made it outside to find the MDMC was in full rout, dozens of FRMC members having come, with the IRMC riding alongside.

"Brother," Blackie shouted. "You had all the fun, huh?"

"There's probably a few left around here," Horse responded, angling his head to look at his friend. "Plenty for you."

"Then let's get to huntin'. I'll leave this cocker to you and Gunny." Horse realized Blackie had Moorcock's arm in one beefy hand, and he flung the man at Gunny's feet without seeming effort. "Take care of the trash, boys."

"I yield," Moorcock shouted, sounding panicked now, one hand pressed against a bloody hole in his shirt.

"Yeah, that ain't how this shit really works." Gunny placed a foot on the man's back, effortlessly keeping him in place. "Stay still, fucker. Let us get a handle on shit." He cut his gaze to where Horse stood with Glenna in his arms. "You good, brother?"

"Yeah." Staring at Moorcock, he shook his head. "How's he still breathin'?"

"Luck of the devil." Gunny twisted to fully look at Horse. "Brother, are you good? Your woman's bleedin'. That ain't the definition of good in my book."

"I'm okay," Glenna spoke up. "Horse took care of me."

"Little sister, again, I say you actively bleeding is *not* conducive to my brother havin' his shit together. Or any of us, for that matter. I would feel a fuckton better if he'd take you inside. First, because you're bleeding, in case you missed the first dozen times I mentioned it, and second, because I'm about to do some shit I'd really rather you not have to see." Gunny leaned his weight forward and Horse saw Moorcock's eyes bulge at the extra pressure. "None of the assholes here were the dogs we were looking for. Means we got information we need to dig for, and this asshole is the likeliest source I can think of."

Horse looked down to see Glenna had cupped a hand underneath her face. She was looking at Moorcock with a fierce intensity. "He's the reason for all of this. The reason Jackson's dead in my bedroom, the reason for all this violence." She tipped her chin up and looked into Horse's eyes. "I get that I'm making Gunny nervous for some reason, but whatever he needs to do won't be a problem. Moorcock is the problem here. Gunny's the solution."

Gunny shouted a laugh, the sounds of his humor taking a while to trail off. "I like that, little sister. Gonna get it on a shirt or some shit. 'Got a problem? Gunny's the solution!' Have like a bloody splash behind the words. I can see it now." Gunny reached down and hauled Moorcock to his feet. "Seein' as this one is my problem, I'm gonna see if we can come to that solution together." He pulled one fist back, far enough to be a couple zip codes away, and then unloaded on the man, leaving him swinging in his grip. He shook his fist. "Fuckin' shit, he's got a hard head."

"Dammit, Gunny." Horse turned Glenna towards the house as Shamu trotted past them, arrowing towards Gunny and his captive. "Come on, darlin'. Let the man do his work in peace."

She stumbled as they went up the steps and he swept her into his arms. Tension in his gut settled when she nestled against him, her cheek against his chest.

"Today could have gone badly."

"Don't I fuckin' know it." He elbowed the twisted screen door out of the way and pushed into the kitchen. "But right now, you're safe, and I'm here."

"And you're not going anywhere, right?" The expression on her face was one of loss and grief. "Right?"

"No, baby. I'm not going anywhere." He deposited her on his bed. "Let me get that first aid kit you have, and I'll be right here with you."

He backed to the door, gaze on Glenna, and it was his pleasure to watch her expression change to one of hope instead.

***

Glenna

Sitting at the kitchen table, she angled a glance around the room, letting her gaze rest on each man's face in turn. Horse's hand was on her knee and the possessive move hadn't been missed by anyone in the room, making him the recipient of several harmless jabs. Nothing had fazed him, and he'd simply stayed at her side, making sure she was okay.

She was, and had reassured him so, even if the day had been long and terrifying. Watching the men as they stalked towards the house had been frightening but finding Jackson in her home was another level.

She was shocked that she didn't feel any remorse about his death. He'd gone crazy, or something like it. Nor had there been a second's thought of fear of Horse, even though she'd witnessed firsthand his capacity for violence.

Not when he was threatened, though. She'd seen that as he'd given the men outside every chance to choose a different path.

No, what had tipped him over the edge had been the threat to her.

It had been a very real danger too. When Horse came in, Glenna had been on the verge of passing out, and Jackson had been too far gone inside his own twisted head to do anything but follow through on what he'd set out to do.

"I'm a lucky woman," she murmured, leaning close to press a careful kiss to Horse's shoulder.

"Hush, woman. I'm still talkin' here," Blackie called out and she ducked her head. He'd been talking for minutes now, and nothing he said had made sense to her.

"Be still now," the man named Duane said softly. He was cleaning the last of the blood off her face, and now found a couple of other wounds she hadn't noticed until he applied what felt like burning acid to them.

She hissed as he hit another scrape with the antiseptic and Horse's head whipped around, the glare on his face aimed directly at Duane.

"Quit fuckin' hurtin' her, asshole."

Duane made a sound and Glenna tried to smile at him, resorting to biting her lip when the stinging came again. When Horse had introduced Duane, it had been as a close brother, meaning he trusted Duane with his life. The least she could do was let him finish his self-appointed first aid without getting killed.

"Horse, brother," Blackie called, and Glenna turned her attention back to him. "Glad you finally found your peaches, man. Pleased as fuck for you. Guessin' you'll wanna stick tight here, so Skyd and I talked things through. We're gonna repatch the local chapter as FRMC, and I'm puttin' you top of the cock walk there. Members already voted you in, so you don't get to fuckin' bail on me. I'm not losin' you, motherfucker."

Glenna tried to think if they'd had peaches with any of the meals they'd shared and ran through the contents of her pantry in her mind. *If Horse likes peaches, I'll by God give him peaches.*

Horse's tense muscles went rigid, turning him into a statue. After a beat, he took in a breath, then another before thudding a fist against his chest. "My service will always be yours, brother."

"Well then, don't fuck shit up. We knocked a dent into the aims of those ball lickers, but that don't mean they won't be back. I'll be depending on you to keep up with your building connections in, as well as outside of the club, and to keep us all informed on anything dippin' back to shit." Blackie approached him, his gaze dipping to Glenna's face. "Fuck, she's real pretty without that mask'o blood she had goin' on." He reached out one hand to Horse, then pointed to her with the other. "Can I greet your old lady properly, brother?"

"Mind her head," Horse murmured, taking a fragment of fabric from Blackie. He kept his arm around Glenna's shoulder as Blackie approached, and she sat quietly, waiting to take her cues from both men.

Blackie's hands were gentle as he held both of her cheeks, cupping along the edges of her jaw. "Fucker broke your goddamned nose, pretty lady." He bent towards her and placed a tender kiss on her forehead. "Welcome to the family, Glenna. My old lady, Peaches, is gonna be glad this one finally landed on a keeper. When she hears about how fierce you are, she's gonna be even more glad he waited until he found the right one."

"Peaches?" She was looking up at Blackie and the change that came over his expression was telling. *That's love. Lots of love.* "Is that your wife?"

"Got it in one. Not only is she tough as fuckin' nails and prettier than a miracle, she's also smart as hell. Horse, brother." Blackie backed away and rested a hand on Horse's shoulder, shaking him back and forth. "You're in fuckin' trouble, old man. Hell, gonna have to stay on top of your game all the fuckin' time."

"Yeah." Horse's agreement came with a chuckle. "Gonna love every goddamned minute too."

When Blackie turned away, inserting himself into a conversation across the room, she leaned closer to Horse. Pitching her voice low, she asked, "Was I just adopted?"

Duane's laughter was bright and cheery, and he answered for Horse. "Yeah, you were, little sister. You sure as shit were."

"Hey." Gunny cut in, shoving Duane away as he planted himself beside Glenna. "I thought of another T-shirt idea."

"What now, Gunny?" Horse's words were strung out with humor, laughter echoing in every syllable.

"A blue shirt, because blue's supposed to be peaceful or some shit. And on the front, have in quotes 'Karma according to Gunny: The fuck you did not' with some lines and shit streaking out from behind the words. Whatcha think?"

"I think you're a piece of shit." Horse stood, releasing his hold on Glenna to latch onto Gunny. She watched as the two men came together, clenched fists at their hearts, strong arms around each other's shoulders. "And I fuckin' love you for it, brother."

Gunny looked at Glenna over Horse's shoulder. "He's gonna be a handful, little sister. You up for it?"

She beamed at him through the pain, unable to dial back her happiness.

"Fucking right I am."

The room erupted in laughter and the pride on Horse's face made her sit a little straighter, shoulders back. If this was his family, she wanted to be inside the circle of trust.

It's a start.

Chapter Nineteen
Horse

He checked his phone for the hundredth time that morning, pleased to find "all clear" messages received from everyone he'd reached out to about the MDMC menace. Like Blackie had said a week ago, they'd knocked the East Coast club back on their heels and escorted them out of the territory with a band of riders from various clubs. The massive show of force and unity meant it should be a very long time before the Monster Devils tested this area again.

With the danger gone, he'd found himself making up reasons to stay on the ranch. First it had been to ensure the threat was gone, then to be around during Glenna's healing period. She was well on her way back to the same feisty woman he'd first met, the pain subsiding more every day.

Not that Glenna had mentioned him moving on, thank God. He almost didn't want to take the chance of her declining, so it had become easier to simply not ask.

"Less than a month ago." Horse shook his head as it really hit him. "She's been on her own a long time, wonder what the chances are she'd want a troublemaker like me to stick around?"

Things had been intense between and around them for a few days, and he believed they'd built a bond that was unbreakable. But he hadn't yet pulled up the courage to talk to her about the future. If she rejected him because the risk was past, he didn't know if he'd survive it.

"I sure as fuck don't want to leave."

Shamu's weight against his leg made him smile. The dog had gotten over his huff with Horse during the brief war, and days like this when Horse left Glenna sleeping in their bed, the dog made sure he accompanied Horse on his patrols.

"You don't want me to leave either, huh?" Fondling the dog's ears, he looked out over the pastures dotted with serenely grazing cattle. "This is a good life, Shammy. A place I can see myself in ten years, or twenty." The dog settled heavier against him. "Good to know you feel the same, boy. Good to know."

The next morning, Horse was lying in bed beside Glenna, conversation starting points running through his head. His fingers stroked her back, bared to the waist by the sheet. She'd gone to bed last night in a nightgown, but that and his boxers were gracing the floor next to the dresser.

She's fuckin' perfect for me. I'm not ever gettin' past wanting her in every way. In bed, laughing over dinner, or even just arguing about what show to watch on TV—it doesn't matter, as long as I'm here with her.

She stirred, rocking up slightly to shove an arm underneath the pillow. "Horse?" Her voice was husky, shaded with sleep. "You gonna stay, right?"

"You want me to stay, darlin'?" Was she awake? He wasn't sure, but she moved and pressed back towards him, molding her body against his chest. "Want that?"

"Oh, yeah. Nothing more." Glenna sighed softly, then gave a tiny snore.

Heart lighter than it had been in days, Horse chuckled quietly, his hand continuing to stroke the long muscles in her back. She might be sleep talking, but he believed she'd spoken the truth.

When he finally slid out of bed and dressed quietly, he flipped the coffeemaker on in the kitchen, then stepped outside onto the stoop. Shamu went with him, taking care of business quickly before returning to sit next to Horse's feet.

Phone in hand, he looked out at the pastures and paddocks, then up the hill towards the horse stables. They were still empty, and it was time to change that.

Between the feed store and Reggie/Cooter, Horse spent less than fifteen minutes on the phone, but big things were set in motion.

Shoving the phone deep into his pocket, he clucked his tongue and went down the steps, grinning when Shamu kept pace with him.

He walked the first few stalls on either side, double checking that the things he'd ordered were what was needed. Everything was close to ready, and he couldn't contain the grin on his face. Glenna was gonna go nuts when she saw what he'd done. *Least I hope so.*

Pulling the stable's door closed behind him, Horse glanced across at the smaller shed next door. He frowned, surprised his wrecked bike was no longer laying on the concrete pad under the roof's overhang. He opened the door and stopped in shock. A whole bike waited there, heeled over on its kickstand. The black and blue touring motorcycle had a double seat and was shining as if someone had just finished waxing the striking paint job. A red bow was tied to the handlebars, and as he stumbled closer, Horse saw a small card propped on the seat.

He opened the envelope, glancing at the card's front where the word "Surprise" sat centered over a hand-drawn version of the Freed Riders MC logo. Inside was a brief note from Blackie.

"Give any brother shit about this and you'll answer to me. Woman's a keeper, brother. She had the ideas. We just made them happen. Be happy, Horse. That's repayment enough." His voice wavered by the end of the note.

Staring down at the bike, his heart thudded fast, the echo beating hard in his ears.

A new bike, given to him by the club.

"What the fuck?" He walked around the bike, admiring every angle and shiny piece of chrome. Peeking inside one saddlebag, he found the registration and insurance in his name. "Motherfuckers thought of everything." Swinging a leg over the seat, he rocked the bike up onto its wheels where it balanced with ease. "Son of a bitch." It was heavier than his old bike, but the double seat would come in handy when he could talk Glenna into riding with him. "Son of a fucking bitch."

Pulling his phone out, he hit a button and set the device against his ear. It only rang once and Blackie's laughter filled his hearing.

"Finally looked in the barn, huh?"

"How long has this been in here?" He ran a reverent hand over the gas tank, finding only the barest skim of dust. "Motherfucker, what the hell?"

"Three days. And trust, it was hard to get that shit in there while you made a trip to town. We had to fuckin' hustle, but it didn't take long to move it from our new base of operations there in Belle."

"New base of—what the fuck?"

"Oh, I didn't tell you?" Blackie's voice quivered as he tried to control his laughter. "We took over the old Snyder place. It's the FRMC ranch now. Gonna move the clubhouse out there. Seems we got more than a few ranchers in the ranks, and they're certain it'll be a good income stream for the future."

"Jesus fuck, man. If I'm the president up here, shouldn't you have run that shit past me before makin' it a done deal?"

"Wouldn't have mattered, and I had to move fast. Fuckin' Mason was already sending out feelers about it." Blackie's grumble was audible. "Asshole. You and I know he wants our patches, but I'm damned and determined to make it hard on him."

"So the club is invested in cattle now?"

"Good base of operations, like I said." Blackie's tone was pointedly neutral, and Horse laughed. They were on a normal call, not through the secure app, so Horse let it drop. He understood the things Blackie wasn't saying, and couldn't be bothered to find an argument that would hold water.

"And the bike?"

"Glenna's idea, as were the updates in there. She was determined to give you everything you needed there, brother. I get the feelin' she wants to keep you."

Horse glanced around and saw the other changes Blackie mentioned. In one corner of the shed was a mechanic shop setup, and his old bike sat there, up on a jack.

"Jesus, Blackie. I'd say it's too much, but I don't want you to second-guess anything, so I'll just say thanks."

Shamu barked and Horse looked up to see Glenna framed in the open barn door, sunlight making her redonned nightgown transparent.

"Thank you," she mouthed, gesturing behind her towards the ranch.

"I gotta go, brother."

Blackie was laughing as Horse disconnected.

He settled the bike back onto the kickstand, stepped off, and covered the distance between them in huge, ground-eating strides. Pulling her into his arms, he whirled, lifting her so her feet were off the ground, grinning down at her smile while Shamu chased the flare of her nightgown's hem.

"You're fuckin' perfect, Glenna Richeson."

"I think you're pretty nice yourself, Graeme Nass." Hands on his shoulders, she lifted herself to place a kiss against his mouth.

Horse stopped twirling them, holding Glenna close as he took control of the kiss. He poured everything in his heart into the caress, renewing it again and again until they were both breathless.

"Never gettin' rid of me, woman."

"Who said I wanted to?"

Shamu barked as if to emphasize the thought, and Horse captured her laughter with his mouth.

***

Glenna

The next morning, Glenna woke alone, something that had worried her the first few times, but now just made her smile. She stretched and worked her jaw side to side, muscles still aching from what she'd heard Horse referring to as "The War." He'd been surprised she hadn't suffered bad dreams, but she knew every night he'd be there beside her. *Nothing to fear.*

The special emphasis he placed on the name always gave it capital letters in her mind. He wasn't wrong; there were no other words she could find for it. As brutal as the entire day was, when she gave it space in her head, she tried not to think about the men killed, but focused instead on the brotherhood exhibited on Horse's side of things.

To realize he had been able to pick up the phone and call—or text—and have men ride to their defense without question hinted at a relationship she could only equate with family. Her grandmother would have done the same, and so would Penn.

She grimaced.

Cooter, not so much. They were still friends, but only on the surface, anything deeper had been cut out like a tumor. Knowing how she felt about Horse now, after only a short time, the idea that Cooter had been serious about asking her out was laughable. She'd never hold him close to her heart like Horse.

With thoughts of Horse on her mind, she slipped a hand between her legs, healed fingers playing delicately within the wet folds of flesh there. She'd always believed herself a sensual lover and being with Horse seemed to have reawakened that side of her. The simple memory of making love with Horse could have her wet and wanting within seconds, remembering how he thrust deep, the way he had of rolling his hips—*nugh*.

The screen door for the kitchen banged quietly and a few moments later, she heard soft footfalls up the hallway. With a grin, Glenna shoved the covers down the bed and spread her legs wider, one hand still busy playing.

When Horse came through the doorway, he stumbled to a halt with a grunt, fingers grasping the doorframe tightly.

"Close the door." Glenna stretched her neck back, arching with pleasure.

"Yes, ma'am."

From the corner of her eye, she could see him fumbling with something, then heard, "Goddammit, Shamu. No cockblocking today." The door latch clicked, and Horse rushed the bed as the dog scratched at the door, demanding to be let inside.

"Good call, honey," she told him, pushing herself up onto her elbows. Watching him undress was a treat she wasn't willing to miss.

He stripped his shirt over his head, revealing the planes and valleys of his belly. Low, just above the waistband of his jeans, there was the most delicious treasure trail she loved to follow with her tongue. The muscles of his chest bunched as he unfastened the jeans and hooked his thumbs to push them down along with his boxers. Deftly stepping out of his socks, he'd gotten naked in less than a minute, and she held her arms out to him.

"How do you want me?" The question was muffled by his mouth against her breast, teeth grazing the inside curve in a delicious tease.

"Over me. Behind me. Under me. However we want to love." She nuzzled the side of his head, then gripped a handful of hair to lift his face. "But inside me is most important."

"You got it, darlin'." He rolled over her legs and reached to the nightstand, plucking a condom out of the half-closed drawer. Sheathing himself with a hiss, Horse slipped into bed alongside her, pressing his hip to hers as his heavy cock arced across her belly. "You ready?" He dipped the broad fingers of one hand between her legs, groaning when he found how worked up she'd made herself. "Fuckin' hell, woman. Sexy as shit me walkin' in on you like that. Nearly passed out the way all the blood rushed from my head. Thought I'd fall and knock myself for a loop. Death by sudden erection. Hella way to go."

His thumb teased her clit, rolling the tip side to side across the pearl of flesh. Just as she was regaining her breath from that, he speared two fingers inside her, working them as deep as he could. His head dipped to her breast again, latching on with a deep suck. He released with a pop, then skimmed his teeth across the budded nipple.

"So fuckin' sexy, baby."

Glenna's hands were roving with a mind of their own, fingers threading through his hair and scratching at his beard, her flattened palms caressing down every inch of skin she could reach. She arched up against his mouth, then bowed her back to thrust into his touch.

Dimly, she realized she was chanting his name. Each new sensation pulled the sounds from her, and when he drove her up and over the peak with just his fingers, her cries turned more guttural, raw.

Just as she was easing back down from her climax, he rolled so he covered her like a blanket, spread her legs wide, and thrust inside. Bottoming out on a single deep, slow push, Horse paused there, his gaze fixed to her face. She lifted a leg and he caught at her calf, bringing it to his chest as he rocked forward. The circling of his hips rekindled her passion, sending her soaring high enough to see stars, and Glenna found herself clutching at the sheets to anchor herself.

Her other leg came around his waist, and he supported it with ease as he bent over her. The shift in position brought her hips higher, opening her to his every movement, and he slid in deeper than ever before.

"Love this," she whispered. "Love the way you fill me up. Love the way you love me up."

"Oh, darlin'," he groaned softly. "You were made for me. So fuckin' perfect—I can't help myself when I'm around you. Gotta have my hands on you, be in you."

"Fuck me, Horse." She rocked her pelvis up to meet his thrust and the jarring collision pitched her lust higher. "Hard, baby."

One hand fisted against the mattress next to her head, Horse did as she demanded, slamming into her over and over. The sounds of their bodies were punctuation to her cries and his groans, and she reached down between them to pinch her clit.

"Fuckin' hot, woman. Watchin' you take what you need." Sweat beaded on his forehead, wetting his hair, and Glenna saw his face sharpen with extra strain. "Need you to come, Glenna. Get yourself there."

"Almost." She angled her leg out, pushing her heel against the mattress for more leverage. "Gonna come, gonna come." Her voice cracked as the tsunami broke over her, burying her in the sudden uncoiling of the tension, limbs shuddering with the force of it.

"Fucking yes," he grunted and picked up the pace. Three thrusts and his back curved, bringing him down over her, his eyes locked to hers as he stuttered through another couple of thrusts, then buried himself.

"Fucking love you, Glenna."

He collapsed on top of her, breathing as ragged as hers, their sweaty skin slippery. With a wiggle and a twist, he'd slid to the side, removed the condom and disposed of it, then hauled her up beside him, wrapping his arms around her to keep them close.

"I'm so glad I found you."

Sleep was coming, pulling her underneath its comforting blanket, but not before she heard his answer.

"We found each other, darlin'. And I'm glad too."

Chapter Twenty

Horse

Standing in the shed next to the mangled bike, Horse plotted in his head about the best place to begin. He'd sent a picture to Medric, receiving back a **WTF** text, then a series of messages with links to the same junkyards they'd utilized the first time he'd rebuilt the bike. Seeing the old man's investment in him made Horse grin.

In the near distance, a truck's engine growled as it downshifted, turning cautiously into the ranch's driveway. Horse made his way outside fighting a smile, because he knew who it would be and what they were bringing. He got halfway to the house before Glenna came through the kitchen door, Shamu at her heels. She glanced at the truck a dozen times before she came to a stop next to where Horse stood.

He didn't move or offer Reggie anything other than a cool nod when the man climbed out of the truck's cab, shoving his hands into a pair of gloves. Glenna had stiffened when she'd recognized Reggie, and now turned to Horse with a question on her face.

"What's he doing here?" Hurt flashed across her expression, quickly suppressed, and Horse knew the shambles of their long-time friendship still bothered her. "Do you know?"

"I do." He grinned wider at her as a thunk came from the back of the trailer Cooter was pulling. "Why don't you go see." Reaching out, he gave Glenna a tiny shove, then thought better of it and hauled her back by her hand to kiss her soundly. After making sure she was steady on her feet, he planted a hand at the small of her back. "Come on, darlin'. Let's take a look."

Reggie nodded at him as they rounded the side of the trailer, walking up a ramp he'd already lowered. He disappeared inside as a low nickering came from inside and Glenna cocked her head, listening.

The first horse Reggie unloaded backed out slowly, head down as it carefully navigated the ramp. Once its feet were on the ground, the head came up and the horse pranced in place, dancing on its hooves, mane snapping in the wind.

"Oh my God," she said reverently, automatically taking the lead Reggie held out her direction. "Oh my God," she repeated as she stroked a hand up the horse's neck. "This is Golden."

Reggie grunted as he trudged back up the ramp and Glenna led the horse to the side, making way for the next horse to be unloaded. This one was just as excited to see Glenna, head held out to the side as it backed down the ramp, nickering with joy.

"Mildred," Glenna whispered, reaching for this lead rope without prompting. "She's here." Lifting the hand holding the rope, she rubbed the horse's face roughly, the mare leaning into the touch with clear pleasure. "She looks good."

Reggie was almost back with the third horse now, this time turning the animal in the back of the trailer and taking a straightforward path to the ground. "And here's Namby." He paused a few feet away from Glenna. "I've got two more at home, your geldings, if you decide you want them back too." Looking at Horse, he glowered, then sighed. "It's a nice thing he did for you here. Something I should have done long ago."

"Come on up," Horse said softly, not wanting to break the mood with any kind of a response to Reggie. The man was right, he should have fucking done the right thing as soon as possible after Penn died. Horse wasn't arrogant enough to think he was the first person she'd talked to, and it only made sense she'd have discussed it with her closest friend. "Let's go to the stables."

"How?" Glenna gave the leads a tug, positioning a horse on either side of her, her movements effortless. "Why?"

"Because." He reached out a hand and stroked down the sloping shoulder of the horse nearest him. "Seemed the right place for them was right here, and Reggie was a big help in making it happen." He'd let Reggie decide if he wanted to fess up about already having the horses, but Horse didn't need to throw him under the bus.

He slid open the stable door and pointed. "Which horse goes in each?"

The question was moot, because the horses clearly remembered their home, each of them angling towards a stall. It was the work of minutes for Glenna and Reggie to settle them, removing halters and leads and hanging those on hooks Horse had installed on the outside of the stall walls. He'd taken every suggestion Reggie and the feed store owner had offered, so these were flush to the wall, inset so the hooks weren't a danger to the animals.

Glenna started a silent inspection, starting with the hooks and moving inside one of the stalls to review the watering system Horse had installed, the molded plastic corner feed bins, and hanging hay mangers, already stuffed with flakes from bales delivered two days ago. What she couldn't see were the pads in one of the far back stalls, waiting to be installed underneath the bedding, or the beam hooks ready for balls to be hung. He'd gotten a ton of shit done, but a few details were just out of reach in the time available.

She patted the horse she'd called Golden a final time, whispering to it as she buried her face against his cheek. Horse saw her shoulders shuddering and had a brief debate with himself, but she broke away before he could make up his mind, turning back to him with wet cheeks.

"You did this." It wasn't accusatory, just a statement of fact, and he held back his smile as he nodded. "You did this," she repeated, softer, pulling the stall door latched behind her. The horse came to the opening and leaned over, lipping at her hair. "Horse, you did this for me."

"No, baby. I did this for me. Because I want to see you happy. Want to be the one to make you happy. For the rest of our lives, it'll be the biggest pleasure for me to make you happy." Horse held out his hands, arms spread wide, aware and uncaring of their audience standing near the stable door. "Come here, darlin'. Let me love you."

She flew to him, hitting so hard he had to go back a step, steadying them both with a shout of laughter. He lifted and her legs wrapped around him, arms tight around his neck. She peppered his face with kisses, a few of them hitting the mark of his mouth. Not enough of them, so he slipped a hand up the back of her neck, taking a handful of her hair as he took over. Angling their mouths together, he nipped at her bottom lip, sliding his tongue along hers, loving the stuttering gasp drawn from her throat when he did.

I'd do anything to hear that every day. Rest of my life, here in my arms.

A throat clearing behind them had Glenna pulling back, cheeks flaming red as she looked over Horse's shoulder.

"I'm gonna get outta here. Let you get them settled. I've got some feed in the trailer. I'll just leave it by the stoop."

Glenna was wiggling now so Horse let her slide down, slowing her travel when her belly grazed his cock just to hear her gasp again.

"Cooter, I don't know what to say." She crossed to him in long steps and pulled him into a short hug. "Thank you. I didn't know where to even start looking." Reggie held her delicately, tentative in his embrace of the woman he'd claimed to love.

His guilty expression when she pulled back should have given Reggie away, but Glenna didn't recognize it. She kept her hands on the man's arms, and repeated, "Thank you."

"Happy things worked out the way they did." Reggie broke free from her hold and advanced to where Horse stood. Shoving out a hand, Reggie met his eyes and all Horse saw now was deep regret. No more anger, no jealousy, just a sadness over how he'd extended the suffering of his best friend. "You're a good man, Graeme."

Horse gripped his hand and pumped it twice, then used it to drag him into a one-armed clinch. "Call me Horse, man. Thanks for all your help, Reggie."

"It's Cooter," the man choked out, his arm tight around Horse's shoulder before pulling away. "See you guys around."

He turned and fled the building. Horse watched him working at the side of the trailer for a moment, then turned his attention back to Glenna. She was walking through the stables slowly, looking in each of the stalls. When she got to the last two, she looked at Horse. "Supplies to finish things out?"

"Yep. Ran outta time." He spread his hands. "I coulda finished it all, but I spent more time lovin' on you than I'd calculated."

She flashed him a grin, wild and free. "You did this for me." Not a question, but he treated it as such.

"Yeah, but also for me, like I said before."

"I think the same way. There's an us that overweighs the me." Angling her head to the side, she pointed to the empty stalls. "He said he's got my two horses too?"

"Yeah. I didn't know if you'd want them back. When we talked about it earlier, you didn't sound entirely eager."

"It doesn't make sense." She drifted back up the aisle, detouring to the first stall with a horse and taking her time petting it. "I've got three to ride now, which'll take up a lot of my time."

"Doesn't have to make sense." His argument went unanswered.

She traveled from horse to horse, promising treats and rides, as soon as she could organize it. Turning to Horse, she nodded towards the stable entrance where Shamu stood, his ears flicking back and forth. "We'll see how Mr. Possessive takes to having to share more of me. He really likes his ATV rides."

"He can have that with me." Horse slapped his leg and the dog trotted to him, leaning his shoulder heavily against Horse. "I don't ride."

"The hell you don't," Glenna shot back. "No way am I having a boyfriend named Horse who doesn't know how to ride his namesakes."

"That's not where the name came from." This argument didn't earn a response either as Glenna turned back to Golden, brushing his forelock off his face. "Glenna, I can do the ATV and Shammy can ride with me."

"We'll see," she responded finally, turning away from Golden to grab Horse's hand. "Let's go find out what Cooter left us."

The truck and trailer were gone from the driveway when they came out into the sunshine, a small pile of blankets, bags, and buckets next to the kitchen door. Glenna reached back to grab the handle of a wagon he'd noticed inside the stables, dragging it behind them. She stumbled and uttered a soft oof and he turned to see Shammy sitting regally inside the wagon, ready for a ride.

"He's adaptable, see?" Horse was laughing as Glenna turned around, pulling the wagon backwards with both hands. "Boy's gonna do what's necessary to stay with his momma."

"He's being an asshole."

"We could change his name to Gunny, and it'd make more sense."

"Gunny's a good namesake."

"Yeah," Horse agreed, "but Shamu still fits him better. That or moo cow." She laughed softly. "Maybe hairless rat."

Glenna laughed the rest of the way to the house, harder when Horse reached over and took the wagon handle out of her hands. Harder still when he bent to one knee, and she climbed on his back, clinging to him like a monkey as they went the last few yards.

***

Glenna

In bed, snuggled against Horse's back as the sun turned the sky to pinks and blues, Glenna sighed softly as she thought about the changes in her life. Penn dying wasn't something she could have anticipated, and neither was Horse coming into her life at the exact time she was open to something new. If she'd met him a year earlier, things would have ended totally different, involving an ambulance and tow truck, instead of her couch and Cooter.

It hurt to think things might happen for a reason, because what was good about losing Penn? *Nothing at all.* She couldn't argue with herself on that one. But if Penn was still alive, she wouldn't be lying here in bed with a different man she now loved with all her heart.

"Life's a mystery, and sometimes we just gotta take things as they come." That was something her grammy had said more than once. She'd lost her husband early, too, but never found someone she wanted to spend the rest of her days with. Instead, she'd filled her house with Glenna, and then with Glenna and Penn.

"I think you'd like this one too, Grammy." Glenna pressed a kiss to Horse's back, fingers trailing a path from his neck to where his skin disappeared behind the waistband of his boxers. He had freckles dotted here and there, and she dragged a fingertip from one to the other, then wrote the word "love" with a smile.

"You havin' fun back there?" His voice was gruff, raspy with sleep, but also laced through with humor.

"Just thinking about how life changes in a minute, and how much my grandmother would have liked you," Glenna answered honestly, laying her lips on his skin, trying to cover as many freckles as she could before he got tired of her playing and rolled over. She'd made it to ten kisses before he turned in the bed, arms wrapping around her gently as he pulled her close.

"I'm glad to know that." His smile was somber, and Glenna frowned. "Medric is as close to family as I've got, other than Blackie and the boys, and you already know you've got their approval. Medric would fuckin' love you for me. Would be so fuckin' pleased."

"I thought your mother was living?" As she realized there was much they didn't know about the other yet, she asked this tentatively. "If it's a tender topic, we don't have to go there."

"Nah, it isn't a big deal. She never wanted me, then tuned me out as soon as I was old enough to take care of myself. When I left home for good, she gave me a little money, but only because the bartender guilted her into it. I hardly think about her. Only time I've talked to her since was after an issue with the same motherfuckers who fucked around out here."

"You don't miss her?"

"Hard to miss what you never had," he stated matter-of-factly, his lips still curled slightly at the corners. "Now you, however? I'd miss you like

I'd miss my arms and legs. You're part of me, darlin'. Gonna always be this way between us."

Shamu whined in the doorway, waiting until he caught their attention before he turned away. His nails clipped into the kitchen, and she heard him whine again.

"Sun's up," Horse murmured, leaning in to kiss her. "Shammy's ready to hit the outside. He doesn't like to hold his piss much, does he?"

"Nope. That's what happens when Mom spoils you." She laughed and returned the kiss with one of her own before pulling back. Threading her fingers through his beard, she scratched his jaw softly. *Gah, he's so handsome.* "I better get rolling. There're more chores now that we've got horses back on the place."

"Still happy they're here?" He cupped her cheek in one hand, callused thumb trailing across her bottom lip. "Still glad?"

"Fuck yeah," she grunted the words, doing what she believed was a passable imitation of him. "Yes," she continued in her normal voice as he laughed, burying his face against her neck. "I'm ecstatic that they're home."

"I'm fuckin' glad, darlin'. Really glad, even if it's more work." He tightened his arms, then relaxed them, helping her sit on the side of the mattress. "You hit the shower, I'll get coffee rollin', let the mutant moo cow outside."

"I'm gonna tell Gunny you're calling him a cow. A mutant cow," she teased as she made her way to the bathroom. "He'll come back and explain to you how regal that dog really is."

"Regal my ass," Horse muttered, pausing for a moment to sit on his side of the mattress.

His side. She melted a little inside at the thought.

His side, her side, their routines that meshed so well, his mechanics corner. Everything pointed to what she wanted more than anything, but she was also a little terrified he'd balk when she laid out how she felt.

Lots of time for that.

With that thought, she turned on the shower, adjusting the temperature by rote.

An hour later, she was headed to the stables, Shamu at her side. The dog audibly grumbled when she took Golden out of his stall and tied him near the tack room.

Glancing around the stables as she brushed out the horse, she saw all the things Horse had done in preparation. How he'd managed without her knowing was a mystery. Even the deliveries of things had been done during her brief absences from the ranch. All so he could keep it a secret and surprise her.

Like I did with the bike and other stuff. She smiled, flicking an escaping strand of hair out of her face. She'd put it up into a messy bun this morning, planning on turning it into a tamed plait later, but now was later and the bun would be it for the day.

Mounted, she rode the horse out of the stables to find Shamu waiting by the ATVs, his ass stubbornly planted on the seat of the one she normally rode.

"Sorry, boy, it's a horse ride today." She rode past him, angling the horse towards the gate. Golden hadn't lost any of his training, scooting close so she could lever the latch open, then swinging his body tight around the post so she could close it easily. "On the ATV I'd have had to do that from the ground," she told the dog, now pacing the horse while giving them snarky side-eye. "Maybe you should learn to ride up here." She patted the back of the saddle's skirt, keeping a tight hold on the reins. "You can jump this high. I know that for a fact."

Shamu turned to face her, his muzzle lifting in a disgusted snarl.

"Okay, suit yourself." She pressed the horse's sides with her calves, moving smoothly into a loping canter. "Could be riding, but noooooo."

Shamu barked sharply, then danced out ahead of them, his attention already turned on the cattle. Golden's focus was there, too, and Glenna grinned. She'd forgotten how much fun this could be when you had a partner in the work.

Later, she was walking Golden back to the stables, reins in hand as she and Shammy strode along side by side. Horse appeared out of the shed next door, wiping greasy fingers on a rag. He checked his hands before tucking the rag into a back pocket, reaching out stroke the horse's withers.

"Good day?" His question came through smiling lips, and it was clear he already knew the answer.

"The best." She paused, staring at him. "You're a real good man, Graeme Nass."

"Parts of me aren't so nice," he argued softly, fingers twitching the rag out again as he wiped his hands again. "But I'm glad you like me anyway."

"Love you," she corrected, grinning. Shamu barked from inside the stables, and she laughed. "Somebody's ready for me to put up this horse."

"He's a mite jealous of the attention, that's for sure."

"He worked well with Golden today, though. Sometimes I forget how stinkin' smart the doggo is. Smooch me." She pushed to her toes, lifting her face in a demand he immediately met. Their lips touched and lingered, and she steadied herself with one hand on his arm. "Remind me later I still need to thank you." Backing away, she grinned again as Horse touched his mouth with fingertips that left a tiny smear of grease behind. "But you'll have to wash your face, first."

"Dammit," he grumbled as he scrubbed his mouth against the shoulder of his shirt. "Gonna hold you to that, darlin'."

"Gonna let you hold me against anything you want," she returned, turning to go into the stables, adding an extra swing to her hips.

"Daaaammmmmmmnnn," he drawled, and she glanced over her shoulder to find him clearly appreciating the view. "Woman, you are F-I-N-E, fine."

He disappeared behind her as she continued into the dimly lit stables. Thirty minutes later, she was finishing up with the horses, Golden brushed out and back in his stall, then all of them fed. Shamu rested patiently in the sunshine at the front of the building, head stretched out so his jaw lay on his paws. He jumped up as she approached.

She walked into the kitchen, dog at her heels, to find Horse at the stove. He was stirring a pan that was sizzling nicely, the smell of frying meat filling the room.

"Whatcha making?" She pulled off her boots and left them on the tray next to the door, stopping for a moment to appreciate the fact her footwear was no longer alone. Horse's boots and single pair of sneakers were lined up next to hers. "Smells good," she offered over her shoulder.

"Food," he responded, and she turned to see him smiling at her. "Chef Horse needs an assistant."

"Oh, does he?" She went to the sink and washed her hands. "Before the assistant even gets a shower? What needs doing?"

"Chef needs a kiss." He leaned close, lips puckered ridiculously. "Now. Quick, before things get spoiled."

"I see how it is." She rested her shoulder against his side and glided her lips across his, then pulled back for a quick peck, ending with a loud, smiling smack. "How's that? Enough to hold Chef over until I get a chance to clean up?"

"Not sure." Horse angled his neck again and Glenna gave him what he'd asked for, pausing longer as their lips moved together. He lapped at her bottom lip until she opened, turning to face him as his hand came to cup the back of her head. His fingers tangled in the bun, leaving it messier than before. "Okay, that might do it." Now he was the one leaning in for a final smack. "Go clean up, woman. Supper'll be ready in a flash. We're havin' tacos tonight."

"Okay." She rested her weight against him for another moment, reluctant to move away. "I'll go." Her head touched his shoulder and his arm swept around her waist. "In a minute."

"You stay here long as you need to." She heard more than felt the delicate kiss against her hair. "I got you."

He'd been like this since regaining consciousness. It didn't matter what was needed, he was happy to pitch in and help. If it was something he didn't know, he set himself to learning quickly, ensuring he'd become a dab hand at everything around the ranch.

I love that about him. One of the many things.

She pulled away. "Gonna shower, and I'll be right back out."

"Take your time. Tacos are forgiving. You need to soak a bit, it'll be okay." His hand trailed around her waist as she walked away, fingertips keeping contact until the last moment. "That said, I selfishly want to you hurry through it and come back to me."

"I'll do that, then. Can't disappoint my best fella."

Hands full of suds, she scrubbed her scalp in the shower, thinking. He'd made himself at home here. Made the cold house a home again for her. Suddenly, she desperately needed to make sure they were on the same page, so she rushed through the rest of her shower. Roughly toweling her body off, she dressed as quickly as possible, shoving still-damp legs into a pair of loose pants meant for lounging around the house.

Seams in the shirt popped as she yanked it over her head, Glenna uncaring as she flipped her wet hair out from underneath the collar.

He had their plates set on the coffee table, which was where they seemed to eat most meals. She'd finish her food and stay right beside him, cuddling into his side while giving him room to clear his plate before he leaned them both forward to set the empty dishes onto the table. Later, he'd take her into his arms, and they'd talk or watch TV, snuggled as close as possible. Or they'd make out like teenagers hoping to get every last caress in before the porchlight curfew.

Horse seated himself and smiled up at her, handing her a plate and paper towel napkin as soon as she was settled.

"They're messy," he warned as he picked up his own plate.

"That's the only way to eat tacos." She picked up the first rolled tortilla and laughed. "These are more like burritos than tacos. They're ginormous, Horse. How much stuffing did you shove inside?" After taking a bite, she groaned. "Doesn't matter what it looks like. I approve a hundred percent. This is delicious."

"Grease is where it's at with tacos." He reached across and dabbed at her chin with his towel. "You got a little something there."

"Don't care." She gobbled down the first one, aware of his amused attention. "I was hungrier than I thought, and this is so good."

"You forgot to eat lunch again." Horse's brows came together, gaze still locked on her face. "That shit's not good for you. I'll do better reminding you tomorrow."

"Tomorrow—" Her throat tightened, closing off whatever she'd been going to say. Her mind whirled with images of Horse. Coming out of the shed to greet her. Making dinner. Putting his boots next to hers. Curling around her in bed.

"I want to have all the tomorrows with you." The words were choked, but she pushed through it, eyes suddenly watery. "I don't want you to go. To leave. I want you to move in here. With me. And stay."

The plate was gone out of her hands, followed by a clunk from near the coffee table, then Horse's arms were around her, his mouth at her ear with a soft, "Shhhhh." He pulled her into his lap, positioning her across his thighs so she was close to his body.

She leaned against the warm hardness of his chest and wept, still managing to force out the question that was so important. "You won't ever leave?"

"No, darlin'. I'm not leavin'. Not ever. And of course I'm movin' in here with you. Hell, I'm already here, darlin'." He kissed her ear, then nuzzled at the side of her head. "Of course I am. You didn't think you'd get rid of me, did you? I'm a stage-five clinger with you. Me and Shammy, we're tied for first clinger spot where it comes to you."

Glenna laughed through her tears, swiping at her cheeks with the backs of her hands. Then she grasped the sides of Horse's head and turned his face towards hers. Their lips met with a groan from him and a soft cry from her, and the tacos were forgotten on the table as he lifted her, walking quickly towards the bedroom.

***

Shammy

He watched his person and her person walk away, the light resonation of the door latch sounding loud as thunder.

Lifting his head higher, he sniffed the edge of the flat wood they used to hold food and feet.

With a glance towards the sleeping den, he heard the first sounds from his person that told him they'd be in there a while. Maybe forever. Like they'd done yesterday. It had been forever.

He stood and wedged his chest against the flat wood and stretched his neck out so he could easily reach the food holder. His person wasn't here to chide him. It was her loss. Within minutes, each holder was emptied and tongue-swiped clean with an intense focus. No flavor was wasted.

Then he walked to the door of the sleeping den and thudded down, sprawling out across the opening.

And he did what he did best.

He guarded his person. And her person.

And sighed heavily as he accepted his new spot in the pack.

His lip lifted as he snarled silently.

Grudgingly.

Chapter Twenty-One

Horse

He parked the ATV near the back of the sprawling ranch-style house, taking in the number of motorcycles and cages already there.

Horse definitely approved the idea Duane'd had to put in a narrow road and fence-crossing cattle guard between the two ranches, making it infinitely easier to make a direct trip between home and the clubhouse.

Home. That knowledge would never get old.

Walking inside felt very much like entering the Longview clubhouse. FRMC club memorabilia was mounted proudly on the walls, making ownership of the place clear to any visitors. *No mistake there.* There were a dozen men standing around the kitchen, most with IRMC patches on their backs.

That shit changes tonight. He grinned at the knowledge they were moving forward with many things, and this, in his opinion, was the most important.

He strode through the house to the den, which had been turned into a meeting room with the addition of a large table. They'd found one at an auction, scarred from use in a mechanic shop, and perfect for club church.

The plan was to bring Blackie in via video tonight. He was sticking close to home with Peaches entering the last few weeks of her pregnancy. But it was important that the club's international president be present at major changes for any chapter. This night certainly qualified.

"The pool out back needs a little work, but it'll make a nice addition for family parties." Duane looked up and gave Horse a nod as he walked into the room, then eased over to make space in the circle of men chatting before church began. "This whole setup is gonna be the envy of chapters all over. I bet Blackie uses it for big officer meetings, because with all the new chapters, the room in Longview is a little bit small."

"Mother's important, though." One of the IRMC members spoke up, and Horse nodded but left it to Duane to answer. The man was Horse's VP now, after all; it should be in his job description to take the teaching moments.

"It is, and that house in Longview will always be a special place for all members. But just for ease of coordination, this property isn't far and is a good fit for us all." Duane wrapped an arm around the man's shoulders. "Good question, though. Real good. I like that."

"We about ready?" Horse glanced around, seeing the faces he'd expected to find already present. "It'll be an open-door meeting, because every man has to make the jump. This isn't something that we can force down the pipe and hope they're all on board."

"What happens if someone isn't willing to go from small time to the big dogs?" The man next to Duane was frowning. "I'm not part of this chapter, but can they go to another IRMC if they want? That's what Nolan said."

"Fuck yeah," Horse jumped in. "That's why this is an all hands for the chapter, with invites out to anyone else. We don't fuckin' want people who aren't ready. Unhappy members makes for the start of assholes, and don't nobody need that in their charter. Nolan's a good brother. I'm real proud of what he's doing in his IRMC chapter."

"Have you always been so fuckin' smart?" The bellowed voice came from the doorway and Horse groaned as he turned. Gunny was beaming at him as he shrugged off his jacket, leaving him in his club vest.

"Smarter than you," Horse called back, leaving the group of men so he could meet Gunny in the middle of the room. They gripped right thumbs, pulling each other forward so their chests met with a solid smack of leather. "Well met, brother." Gunny's arm was so tight around his shoulders, it was all he could do to not wheeze, but he managed. Just.

"You're smart and fuckin' strong. Proved it. Now, let me the fuck go, asshole." Gunny twisted away, scowling at Horse as he dusted down his front. "No reason to manhandle the merchandise."

"I didn't know you were coming in." He tapped Gunny's shoulder with a closed fist. "I'm glad you're here. You'll stay with me and Glenna." Pulling his phone out, he sent her a quick message, waiting until he got a response of a thumbs-up emoji. "Might as well put the guest room to use."

"There's plenty of room here, if it's a pain in the ass." Gunny swept his arms out expansively. "Likin' this setup you got here. We got a good house in Baker, but this is tight, man. Fuckin' nice."

"Yeah, Blackie did us right." Horse stood next to Gunny and swept the room with his gaze. "I heard one of the guys calling it a destination chapter the other day, and I can see that happening. Folks traveling here with family to stay for vacation, soaking in the brotherhood at the same time."

"You should contact the Rebels and see if Myron can cook you up a booking app or some shit."

"Not a bad idea. I'll run it up the flagpole, see what Blackie says." Horse felt his muscles relaxing. Here, surrounded by men he trusted with his life, the camaraderie was easy, comfortable.

After a few moments of silence, Gunny asked, "Everything still copacetic around here then? Locals cool with the changes?"

"After a little campaigning by Glenna and her friend Reggie. Everything settled out net positive for town folks, and they've seen real good trade from the brothers who are movin' up here. We're funding some of it, but either way, it's income for the shop owners in Belle." He rocked back on his heels. "It's all good, brother."

"Nothing less than I expected." Gunny turned and hooked a thumb over his shoulder. "Gonna get a beer before you call church to order. Want one?"

"Nah, I'm good." He watched Gunny walk away. Checking the clock verified it was time, and he made his way to the president's seat at the middle of the table. He picked up the gavel and chuckled. There'd been no time to gather anything formal, so he had a mechanic's rubber-headed mallet as his business knocker.

"Get where you'll be comfortable," he called out, watching to ensure everyone heard him. "Gonna start as soon as I get Blackie on the horn."

Duane appeared at his elbow, bending to pull the laptop closer. "I got this, Prez. We'll be all set in a couple shakes of a dog's tail."

Silence fell over the crowd, and Horse took one last look around the room before the monitor mounted on the wall came to life. Blackie's face filled the screen, and he cried, "What's up, motherfuckers? Y'all ready to become Riders for real?"

Later that night, Horse was back home, sharing a final beer with Gunny. He'd sat on the edge of the stoop behind the kitchen, while Gunny stood, one foot propped on the edge of the raised platform.

"You'd tell me if you needed me, right?"

"I would," he responded to Gunny's question. "Things are good. I don't think we'll see the MDMC this way any time soon."

"They're still bunkered in about a hundred miles from Baker. Motherfuckers." Gunny lifted his beer and drained it. "Might be me calling you for assistance next time."

Horse finished his own beer then stood, gripping Gunny's shoulder. "And you know I'll answer that call, brother."

"Counting on it."

Back inside the house, they split up where the hallway turned, Gunny headed to the guest room and Horse making his way to the room he shared with Glenna.

It was the work of minutes to strip down to his boxers, and he slipped into bed next to her. She mumbled when he reached out, then burrowed closer as he wrapped his arms around her.

Her cheek found its way to his shoulder, and she sighed deeply, a lock of hair draped over her face.

Horse tucked the hair behind her ear and bent his neck, pressing a gentle kiss to the crown of her head. She mumbled again and her arms and legs gave him a squeeze, bringing a smile to his lips.

This is how every day should end, he thought. Letting his body settle against the mattress, he listened and heard Shamu's soft snores from the dog bed underneath the window. Outside, a cow lowed once, then fell quiet.

He tightened his arms around her and thought about the small box hidden in the nightstand drawer. His desire to see that ring on her finger lit up everything inside him. This was what he'd needed, without knowing it. Someone as good as Glenna loving an old outlaw like him.

Fuckin' love my life.

Grinning, his eyes closed as sleep danced closer, pulling him under to dream about their future together.

***

Blackie

"Myron, brother. What's got you up so late? Mouse not pullin' your ass to bed yet?" Blackie stifled a yawn as he reached for his pants and stepped into them one-handed. A glance at the bed showed Peaches sprawled on her side, sleeping, arms and legs curled into her torso, in the same position she'd been after he'd cleaned her up following their epic lovemaking. Late pregnancy revved her engines, and he was always on call to keep his woman happy. The swollen walls of her stomach moved gently as their child stirred inside.

"I've got information, but Horse didn't pick up." Myron's voice was clipped and brusque, not his normal jovial tone, which got Blackie's full attention.

He pulled the door to the bedroom closed quietly behind him, hitching his yet-unfastened pants on his hips. "We had a big club meeting tonight, lasted a long time. Reckon he's resting quiet next to his new lady. Give it to me, brother. I'll take notes and pass it along."

With the unrest in the area, the fact the Rebel technical wizard was calling meant the message was important.

"It's about Nelms." Myron's voice went rigid with tension, the words falling into the air with an impact like a depth charge. "I've cracked the final section of the code in his notebook finally."

The serial killer masquerading as a bull rider had been the subject of a lingering inquiry. After the asshole had been eliminated, his men and the Rebels had been searching through the information left behind to try and bring closure to families. So far there'd been more than twenty body recoveries, the remains returned to still grief-stricken parents and siblings. It had been a dance of delicate choreography to get just enough information to their law-abiding contacts to stir the waters with a desire to look—but without drawing attention to the fact the killer was done and dusted, covered over by years of wind-driven sand.

"That's good news, My." Blackie propped the phone against his shoulder and used both hands to secure his pants, leaving the belt hanging open. "Means maybe we can finally put an end to this whole shitty thing, yeah?"

"Maybe. Depends on if I'm right about this. I hope so."

"Hit me, brother. Let's do a mind meld or whatever that shit's called." Blackie glanced at the clock and decided it was late enough for coffee. Randi would be up in an hour, and there'd be no sleep for him after. Hands working on automatic, he set the pot to humming, anticipating that moment when the scent of burnt beans would fill the air.

He realized Myron hadn't responded and paused, his focus on the phone now. The man's breathing was quick and labored, sounding pained.

"Myron, what'd you find out?"

"There's a complication. Someone else has been researching the same killings. Of the ones I've identified, half have been found already. It's like they're working on things from the missing persons reports, but they seem to have found a commonality that ties them to Nelms. But, without finding Nelms."

"That's good news, right? Less work for us, less chance of exposure." He shrugged. "I'm not seeing the problem."

"If they found the dead girls with nothing more than public information, and plotted out the pattern from that, there's nothing to keep them from following the ones we've already helped solve. It's not a far jump to think they'd then turn their attention to how those others were resolved. It might be an exposure for the clubs, Blackie." Myron huffed out a heavy sigh. "I don't think I'm over stating the danger either. Whoever this is has to be wicked smart. And they're covering their tracks like we've done. Means they're likely not on the law side of things."

"Is there anything we can do about it right now? Should this be a wait-and-see thing, until we know more?" Blackie stilled his restless feet, realizing he'd been pacing through the kitchen. "I don't see a path forward for us yet. Do you?"

"No, and that's what worries me. I see the pattern, but I don't see the origin."

"Yet." Blackie infused certainty in his voice. "Not yet, My. If I were a betting man—and we both know I am—I'd bet you've been up all night wrestling with this. What you need to do is shut it all down now and take your ass to bed. Sleep with the knowledge you wrecked Nelms' last attempt at control from beyond the grave. You wrecked his ass, man. Proud of that shit." He smiled. "Bet Mason will be proud of it too. But you're going to hit the hay before you make that fuckin' call. Let me have a few hours of this before we bother the man, yeah? I'll hit Horse up in a bit, turn his brain on and let him stew. Let's plan on a conference call tomorrow. Give everyone a chance to noodle on it."

"Yeah, okay. Sleep sounds good." Myron yawned and Blackie grinned wider. "Thanks, Blackie."

"No worries, brother. You're the smartest man I know, but shit at takin' care of yourself. Get to bed."

"Yeah. I'll do that."

Blackie disconnected the call and placed the phone face down on the counter. He propped both hands against the edge, head hanging low as he closed his eyes.

He was still lost in thought when two hands crept around his waist, and a warm weight settled against his back.

"Peaches, darlin'. You were sleepin'."

"And now I'm awake, smelling coffee I can't drink." Her body moved against his, belly thrusting against his ass in a way that made him laugh. "Think we can work in another round before Randi gets up?"

He turned in her arms, wrapping his around her back, pulling her close enough to kiss. Tongues tangling slowly, he registered the flavor of mint and smiled against her lips. "Momma want some lovin'? I'm down for that."

Scooping her into his arms, he made his way back to their bedroom, kicking the door closed behind them.

The sound of Peaches' laughter covered the buzzing of his silenced phone against the kitchen counter.

Fini

THANK YOU FOR READING
Gotta Dig Deep!

ABOUT THE AUTHOR

Raised in the south, *Wall Street Journal* & *USA TODAY* bestselling author MariaLisa learned about the magic of books at an early age. Every summer, she would spend hours in the local library, devouring books of every genre. Self-described as a book-a-holic, she says "I've always loved to read, but then I discovered writing, and found I adored that, too. For reading...if nothing else is available, I've been known to read the back of the cereal box."

More info and extras about her books can be found on **mldemora.com**.

Want sneak peeks into what she's working on, or to chat with other readers about her books? Join the Facebook group! **bit.ly/deMora-FB-group**

deMora's got a spam-free newsletter list she'd love to have you join, too: **bit.ly/mldemora-newsletter**

~~~~~

ADDITIONAL SERIES AND BOOKS

Please note that books in a series frequently feature characters from additional books within that series. If series books are read out of order, readers will twig to spoilers for the other books, so going back to read the skipped titles won't have the same angsty reveals.

Freed Riders MC

Born from characters who simply wouldn't allow their stories to die, this spin-off series includes men and women who will be familiar to the RWMC and NTNT fans.

Gotta Dig Deep, #1
Always My Fate, #2 (coming soon)
Somewhere in Texas, #3 (coming soon)

Rogue Maniacs MC

With a first book set within the collaborative worlds of the Mayhem Makers, these stories will introduce brand new characters and tales.

Downward Dawg, #1 (2023)
Raggedy Dan, #2 (coming soon)
Tinder Heart, #3 (coming soon)

Rebel Wayfarers MC series

A motorcycle club can be a frightening place, filled with hardened men and bad attitudes. Rebel Wayfarers is a club with their own measure of hard and dangerous, led by their national president, Davis Mason. This book series follows members as they move through their lives, filled with anguish and heartache, laughter and love. In the club, each of them find a home and family they thought long lost to them.

Occupy Yourself band series

Stardom doesn't happen overnight. Hell, it doesn't even happen after a decade in the business, as the members of Occupy Yourself have found out. But, with the right talent and the right representation, they might still have a chance to make it big. As long as they can keep their lead singer sober, keep their drummer focused on the music, keep their guitarist out of trouble … well, you get the idea. Come and join us, stand side stage for a close-up view of the backstage happenings in a rock-and-roll band. It's guaranteed to be a show you won't ever forget.

Born Into Trouble, #1
Grace In Motion, #2 (TBD)
What They Say, #3 (TBD)

Neither This, Nor That MC series

Legends are born from moments like these. Folktales spun around a single point in time so perfect, you can almost hear the click resonating through the universe as things align. Meet Twisted, Po'Boy, Retro, and Ragman, good old boys from southern states who have many things in common. First, is a bone-deep love of the biker lifestyle. Second, would be their love of the brotherhood, and knowing that you trust the man at your back. Finally, these men have the love of a good woman. None of these come without a price, and it is our pleasure to journey along with them as they discover the blessings that can be won, and lost along the way.

Rebel Wayfarers crossover stories

Enjoy these stories that tie the different worlds of my MC universe together, bringing Rebel Wayfarers MC and clubs like Neither This Nor That and other series into glorious alignment.

Going Down Easy
No Man's Land
In Search of Solace

Mayhan Bucklers MC series

The Mayhan Bucklers MC has been part of the rolling hills of Northeast Texas for decades. Now, new life is being breathed into this reborn club, a legacy resurrected by grandsons of the founder. The MBMC is set to surpass its original glory, fortified with an honorable purpose: Helping wounded warriors reintegrate back into society, gifting those who've given so much with a safe place to land.

Learning how to navigate life while war still echoes inside you isn't easy, but with solid brothers at your back, anything is possible.

Most Rikki-Tik, #1
Mad Minute, #2
Pucker Factor, #3
Boocoo Dinky Dau, #4

Borderline Freaks MC series

When you can't count on anyone else to save you, there's only one real choice. Borderline Freaks MC is a series of books about the men of the club and their brotherhood — and of course the love they have for their women. Take a trip along with Monk, Blade, Wolf, and Neptune, and feel for yourself the connection these men have for each other.

Service and Sacrifice, #1
More Than Enough, #2
Lack of In-between, #3
See You in Valhalla, #4

Alace Sweets series

Dark romantic thrillers, these books are not light reads. Filled with edge-of-your-seat suspense, these intense stories command the reader's attention as they drive towards their explosive endings. Alace Sweets is a vigilante serial killer, with everything that implies and is sure to trip all your triggers. Be ready.

Alace Sweets, #1
Seeking Worthy Pursuits, #2
Embarrassment of Monsters, #3
All the Broken Rules, #4 (TBD)

With My Whole Heart series

Sweet as pie and twice as delicious, these romantic love stories are a guaranteed happily-ever-after read.

With My Whole Heart, #1
Bet On Us, #2

If You Could Change One Thing:
Tangled Fates Stories

When threads in the tapestry of life are cut short, inexorably changing the future for those you love, would you be willing to tempt fate to set things right?

There Are Limits, #1
Rules Are Rules, #2
The Gray Zone, #3

Additional Books:

Hard Focus
Dirty Bitches MC: Season 3

~~~~~

deMora's Rebel Wayfarers MC and the Neither This Nor That MC series do cross over, along with the Occupy Yourself band books, so readers have a couple of choices. The series can be read independently beginning with RWMC, OYBS, and then NTNT without too many spoilers. There's also a crossover between deMora's RWMC world and Lila Rose's Hawks MC world. Or they can be read intertwined—in chronological order.

Here's the recommended reading order if you want to follow according to timing:

Mica, RWMC #1
A Sweet & Merry Christmas, RWMC #1.5
Slate, RWMC #2
Bear, RWMC #3
Born Into Trouble, OYBS #1
Jase, RWMC #4
Gunny, RWMC #5
Mason, RWMC #6
Hoss, RWMC #7
This Is the Route of Twisted Pain, NTNT #1
Harddrive Holidays, RWMC #7.5
Duck, RWMC #8
Biker Chick Campout, RWMC #8.5
Watcher, RWMC #9
Treading the Traitor's Path: Out Bad, NTNT #2
Living Without, Lila Rose's Hawks MC: Caroline Springs #4
Shelter My Heart, NTNT #3
A Kiss to Keep You, RWMC #9.25
Gun Totin' Annie, RWMC #9.5
Secret Santa, RWMC #9.75
Trapped by Fate on Reckless Roads, NTNT #4
Bones, RWMC #10
Gunny's Pups, RWMC #10.25
Not Even A Mouse, RWMC #10.75
Road Runner's Ride, RWMC #12.5
Never Settle, RWMC #10.5
Fury, RWMC #11
Christmas Doings, RWMC #11.25

Gypsy's Lady, RWMC #11.5
Tarnished Lies and Dead Ends, NTNT #5
Going Down Easy
No Man's Land
In Search of Solace
Tangled Threats on the Nomad Highway, NTNT #6
Cassie, RWMC #12

More information available at **mldemora.com**.

Ingram Content Group UK Ltd.
Milton Keynes UK
UKHW020714200323
418846UK00015B/958